PRAISE FOR THE LADY DARBY MYSTERIES

"[A] history mystery in fine Victorian style! Anna Lee Huber's spirited debut mixes classic country house mystery with a liberal dash of historical romance."

—*New York Times* bestselling author Julia Spencer-Fleming

"Reads like a cross between a gothic novel and a mystery with a decidedly unusual heroine." —*Kirkus Reviews*

"Includes all the ingredients of a romantic suspense novel, starting with a proud and independent heroine . . . Strong and lively characters as well as believable family dynamics, however, elevate this above stock genre fare." —*Publishers Weekly*

"[A] clever heroine with a shocking past and a talent for detection." —National bestselling author Carol K. Carr

"[Huber] designs her heroine as a woman who straddles the line between eighteenth-century behavior and twenty-first-century independence." —New York Journal of Books

"[A] must read . . . One of those rare books that will both shock and please readers." —Fresh Fiction

"Fascinates with its compelling heroine who forges her own way in a society that frowns upon female independence. The crime itself is well planned and executed. The journey to uncover a killer takes many twists and leads to a surprising culprit."

—*RT Book Reviews*

"One of the best historical mysteries that I have read this year."

—Cozy Mystery Book Reviews

A Brush with Shadows

Anna Lee Huber

Berkley Prime Crime
New York

BERKLEY PRIME CRIME
Published by Berkley
An imprint of Penguin Random House LLC
375 Hudson Street, New York, New York 10014

Library of Congress Cataloging-in-Publication Data

Names: Huber, Anna Lee, author.
Title: A brush with shadows / Anna Lee Huber.
Description: First edition. | New York, New York : Berkley Prime Crime, 2018.
Identifiers: LCCN 2017042934| ISBN 9780399587221 (paperback) |
ISBN 9780399587238 (ebook)
Subjects: | BISAC: FICTION / Mystery & Detective / Historical. | FICTION /
Mystery & Detective / Women Sleuths. | GSAFD: Mystery fiction.
Classification: LCC PS3608.U238 B78 2018 | DDC 813/.6—dc23
LC record available at https://lccn.loc.gov/2017042934

First Edition: March 2018

Printed in the United States of America
1 3 5 7 9 10 8 6 4 2

Cover art by Larry Rostant/Bernstein & Andriulli

For my sister, Elizabeth.
I've loved you forever and I'm so proud of you!
Thanks for sharing my tears and laughter, and for bringing out
my silly side, whether it's the Gingerbread Beast, a water
trampoline, or dancing in the aisles of stores. XO

ACKNOWLEDGMENTS

Writing a book is truly a labor of love, one that involves the contributions of so many. This book, in particular, would not have been possible without a great deal of assistance.

Thank you to my editor, Michelle Vega, for her sharp eye and sterling advice, and for loving Lady Darby and crew as much as I do. Thank you to the entire Berkley team for all of your amazing expertise.

Thank you to my agent, Kevan Lyon, for her sage advice and confidence in me as an author.

Thank you to my critique partners Jackie Musser and Stacie Roth Miller for answering my flailing e-mails asking for help, for reading early drafts of chapters, and for talking me down from the rafters.

And I cannot possibly offer enough thanks to my husband and my mother for all they do so that I can write. I know my young daughters are in good hands when they are with their father or their grandmother, and that is invaluable peace of mind. They also keep our household running when the dishes need to be washed, or the floor needs to be swept, or any million other little things. Thank you from the bottom of my heart for all you do and for your unfailing belief in me.

Thank you to my daughters for filling me up with so much love and emotion, and for forgiving my distraction at times when I'm deep in the process of writing a book.

Thank you to all my friends and family, who shower me with their excitement and support.

And thank you to my readers. None of this would be possible without you. You've been clamoring for another Lady Darby, and I hope the longer wait than usual is worth it.

CHAPTER ONE

The devil's boots don't creak.

—SCOTTISH PROVERB

JULY 1831
DARTMOOR, ENGLAND

The first time I laid eyes on Langstone Manor, I could not blame my husband for having stayed away for over fifteen years. I'm sure it didn't help that the weather was far from hospitable. Heavy gray clouds filled the sky, releasing sheets of rain that obscured the horizon, all but concealing my view of the infamous moors rising to the east. But even on a bright, sunlit day, I struggled to imagine the house being more inviting. In truth, it appeared downright foreboding, even without the painful memories that plagued Gage.

Memories I could see weighing on him now. They were written in the tautness of his brow and the deep pools of his eyes as he stared up at the stone manor through our hired carriage's window. Sebastian Gage had conducted dozens of precarious inquiries, had faced down Turkish warriors in the Greek War of Independence, and had most recently been winged by a bullet fired by a temperamental Irish housemaid during our last inquiry only a week before, but this place somehow still troubled him.

Perhaps I shouldn't have been surprised. After all, if I were about to enter my first husband, Sir Anthony Darby's, London town house—that place of so many unhappy remembrances—I wouldn't have been so sanguine. It's never easy to confront the demons of our past. But to see my normally unflappable husband so apprehensive unsettled me.

I reached out to touch Gage's hand where it gripped his leg, hoping to offer him a bit of reassurance. I wanted to do more than that, but with our maid and valet seated across from us, that would have been highly inappropriate. As loyal and trustworthy as Bree and Anderley might be, and privy to more intimacies than most, having assisted us with numerous murderous inquiries, there were still some things that should remain private between husband and wife.

Gage turned his hand over to squeeze my fingers and offered me a fleeting smile before turning back to the view outside his window. I followed suit, curious about this place where he had spent so much of his childhood.

He'd told me little about his time here with his mother while his father had been away at sea, fighting Napoleon and manning the blockade. However, what he had revealed had spoken volumes, and I'd been able to infer even more than he probably realized from the things he hadn't said. Whatever else he felt about this place, it was clear he'd not been happy.

I stared upward at the manor's edifice of coarse stone and tall mullioned windows, their glass dark and oily in the gloom. Two symmetrical wings projected from the main block, their exteriors echoing that of the one before us, but for the long narrow windows which I suspected had once been arrow slits, now fitted with glass. The roof was covered in small slate shingles only a shade lighter than the clouds. The tall chimneys and sprocket eaves with their gabled ends added angles and dimension to the bland façade, but they failed to lighten the overall melancholy feel of the setting in any way.

The manor didn't look much different than I anticipated the granite-shattered outcroppings of the tors would look. I wondered if that had been the builder's intention. If so, he'd succeeded, but at what cost? As beautiful as the landscape of Dartmoor was purported to be, it was also treacherous, and this home had taken on many of the same characteristics.

The garden which had sprung up in the courtyard before the manor also did nothing to help matters. Hedged in by an imposing metal gate and stone walls, thick beds of green plants and a few straggling pale flowers had taken root at the edges of the gravel lane. Trees ringed the edge of the property, their twisted trunks seeming to sprout from the very walls themselves as if they would not be denied access, or allowed to escape. The garden was clearly well kept, its verges rigidly maintained, but some more colorful flowers and a bit of judicious pruning would have done much to lighten the space. But perhaps those plants did not grow in this climate and the dense foliage refused to be stunted.

"Do you think they realize we've arrived?" I asked, beginning to question whether we should send Anderley to knock on the door.

In the failing light, it was impossible to see much of anything beneath the pale stone archway through which I presumed one accessed the main door, but a footman hurried forth from its recess, allaying my uncertainty. However, any question as to whether our arrival had been anticipated was swiftly answered by the widening of the young man's eyes as he scrutinized our trunks strapped to the roof of the carriage.

"Good evening, sir," he murmured upon opening the chaise's door. "Were you expected?"

Gage's mouth tightened in what looked like annoyance, but that I knew to be an emotion far more complicated. "Yes," he announced before stepping down into the loose gravel without offering the servant any further explanation. Taking the umbrella from the startled footman's hand, he reached back to assist me.

I wrapped my shawl tighter around me against the wind, and opened my mouth to remind him it wasn't the servant's fault he'd been caught unprepared. But one look at Gage's face made me fall silent. He already knew this, and his tight-lipped displeasure was not directed at the footman, but at his grandfather, the Viscount Tavistock.

Regardless of our delayed arrival, the viscount should have made his staff aware of the prospect of our coming. After all, he'd been the one to write to Gage, begging him to visit—a move which Gage assured me was entirely out of character for the proud, taciturn man. His urgent missive had originally been sent to London and had to be forwarded on to us in Ireland, where we had just wrapped up our latest murderous inquiry, causing a delay of more than a week. In our rush to reach Langstone Manor, we'd not paused to send a message ahead of us to confirm our plans, knowing it wouldn't have arrived much before we would.

Given that postponement, it was possible that the matter for which we'd been summoned had already been resolved. Or perhaps Lord Tavistock had simply given up on us. Whatever the reason, the household was not prepared for our visit.

Gage hurried us forward, pausing once we'd stepped through the arch into the covered porch, where he turned to address the footman who trailed behind us. "The coachman has driven us all the way from Plymouth, and I've promised him lodging for the night for himself and his horses. Please see to it, as well as our servants and luggage."

The flustered expression on the footman's face would have been comical had I not also felt some empathy for him. He was young and inexperienced, and so could not be blamed for his failure to recognize Gage after his long absence, or perhaps for even being cognizant of his existence. The footman glanced back and forth between us and the carriage, uncertain whether he should insist he announce us or do as Gage had instructed.

Fortunately, an older man came to his rescue. "Timothy, do as he asks," said a slight man standing in the shadows next to the door before shifting his gaze to meet my husband's. "I'll show Mr. Gage inside."

It took a moment for my eyes to adjust to the dim light underneath the porch, but Gage already recognized the speaker.

"Hammett, I'm surprised to see you're still with us."

I stiffened, surprised by the rudeness of my husband's comment, but the other man didn't seem the least insulted if the grin that cracked his thin mouth was any indication.

"Aye. Yer cousins haven't rent me from this mortal coil yet. Nor your grandfather neither."

A flicker of a smile crossed Gage's face.

The elderly man, who I now recognized must be the butler, ushered us out of the damp into a small vestibule. He tilted his head to inspect Gage and then me, dislodging the few stray gray hairs still clinging to the top of his head. "This'll be yer bride, then?" Though he was merely a servant, I felt I had been assessed and judged, and apparently found acceptable, for his creaky voice warmed. "Welcome to Langstone Manor."

"Thank you," I replied.

Then his eyes narrowed on Gage. "You've been gone a long while."

Gage was not fazed nor chagrined by the old retainer's censure. "If I wasn't already conscious of that, the sight of your wrinkled face would certainly remind me. But what are you still doing here? I thought you would have retired to one of the estate's cottages or shuffled off to the seaside long ago."

"And leave his lordship to fend off these leeches alone?" His scraggly brow lowered. "Not that it'll matter much longer."

The remainder of Gage's levity fled at this comment. "How is he?"

"You'll see for yerselves," Hammett replied gruffly, turning at the sound of footsteps.

I followed his gaze toward the gleaming wooden staircase on the opposite side of the long stone entry hall, where a tall woman dressed in a midnight blue gown had paused a few feet from the base of the steps. I could not immediately discern who she was in relation to Gage, but it was evident from the manner in which his eyes hardened and his nostrils flared that she was not someone he was fond of. And the feeling was mutual.

I was accustomed to everyone liking my husband. Those who weren't already won over by his good looks were quickly persuaded by his charm and easy nature. Even his father, who was derisive and sometimes unforgivably hard on him, still cared for him in his own contrary way. However, this woman took few pains to conceal the loathing shimmering in her eyes. Where this naked animosity came from, I didn't know, but it took me aback.

Maintaining a façade of polite composure, Gage stepped forward to greet her, but halted when a dark-haired man came bustling into the hall through a doorway on the left.

"Mother, did you know a carriage has arrived? Do you think it could be . . ." His words faltered as he followed her gaze toward where we stood. His eyes widened.

Given my reputation, it was not the most awkward welcome I'd ever received, but considering the fact that I suspected these people were related to Gage in some way, it was certainly the most disconcerting. Indignation began to build inside me, not on my behalf, but on Gage's.

I was used to people thinking the worst of me. The scandal over my involvement with the work of my first husband, the great anatomist Sir Anthony Darby—specifically my sketching his dissections for an anatomical textbook he was writing—had blackened my name and made me a figure of fear and revulsion in many circles. Few cared to note that my participation had been forced, or that in spite of it, my drawings had been beautiful and flawless. For them it was proof enough of my unnaturalness that as a gentlewoman I had not only survived such a gruesome ordeal, but also gone on to use that reluctantly accrued knowledge to help solve murders and other crimes.

Gage, on the other hand, was a different story. As a gentleman inquiry agent of some renown, he did not suffer the same slights to his character. In fact, the work he undertook as a diversion—for he had no need to earn his living—only enhanced his reputation. Combined with the fact that he was perhaps the most charismatic and attractive young gentleman in all of England, he was practically guaranteed an eager invitation from every hostess in the country. I had feared that our marriage would harm his standing, but thus far our unlikely match had only raised his prominence to almost mythical proportions.

But apparently this partiality did not extend to his late mother's family. Watching the trio eye one another, their expressions ranging from wariness to outright enmity, I now better understood my husband's initial reluctance to come here. Even though it had been quickly overridden, by his own inclination and my admittedly uninformed opinion, it said a great deal about his relationship with the maternal relatives he'd spent much of his childhood with that he wouldn't immediately wish to come to their aid.

The dark-haired man was the first to speak. He took a few hesitant steps toward us before resuming a more assured stride. "Gage, is that you?" His mouth curled into an uncertain grin. "By Jove, it is!" He reached out to shake his hand. "Dashed it's been a long time."

"It's good to see you, Rory," Gage replied. Much of the hostility he'd directed at the woman had faded from his eyes as he greeted the other man, but there was still a guardedness to his demeanor.

"And this must be your wife," Rory guessed. "Grandfather told us you'd wed." His expression couldn't help but hold rabid interest, though he did at least try, rather unsuccessfully, to mask it.

"Yes." Gage gazed down at me with a glint of protective pride. "Kiera, allow me to introduce my cousin, the Honorable Roland Trevelyan."

I offered him my hand, which he clasped respectfully. "I'm pleased to meet you, Mr. Trevelyan."

"Likewise, Mrs. Gage." His pale blue eyes, just a few shades darker than Gage's wintry hue—obviously a Trevelyan trait—softened with regard. "Is this your first time visiting the West Country?"

"Yes," I replied. "Before today, I'm afraid I'd never set foot on English soil farther west than Oxford." I paused to consider. "Unless you count Cumberland. I suppose that's farther west than Oxfordshire."

Rory's expression turned self-deprecating. "I wouldn't know. I'm afraid I never was very good at geography." His eyes flicked to Gage. "Got my knuckles rapped more than a few times for not being able to point out Devonshire on the map."

I smiled at his attempt at levity even as his jest failed to amuse the others. Though I didn't yet know what his relationship with Gage had been like in the past, I couldn't help warming to the man before me. There was something about his lack of pretension and his almost bumbling charm that made him quite agreeable. He wasn't as handsome or alluring as Gage, but in this instance I think such slick assurance would have worked against him, making me question his sincerity.

The click of footsteps crossing the granite floor recalled us to the presence of the other woman in the room, who had observed her son's greetings with cool detachment. Rory glanced over his shoulder. "Mother, come meet Mrs. Gage."

Though past fifty, she was still a remarkably beautiful woman with dark hair sparsely streaked with gray, smooth skin, and flashing dark eyes. I could see now that the lovely gown I'd viewed from a distance was also terribly stylish, and undoubtedly purchased from a London shop. Combined with her rigid posture, elegant coiffure, and what I suspected were artfully applied cosmetics, I began to feel rather unkempt and dowdy in my striped carriage dress of straw, rose, and pale blue. Little as I cared for fashion, I felt grateful my more sophisticated sister had insisted on helping me choose the new gowns for my trousseau before I wed Gage three months prior. Otherwise, I had no doubt the woman before me would have judged me even more harshly than I could see she'd already done.

She lifted her chin to stare down her nose at me as her eyes gleamed with cold calculation. "But it isn't Mrs. Gage, is it? Properly you should be addressed as Lady Darby, should you not?"

It was questioned with quiet civility, but I knew better. So did Gage, though he didn't even flinch as she skillfully slid the dagger of her insult into his side. She was not the first person to point out this ridiculous bit of etiquette to us. Because my first husband had been a baronet, a higher rank than Gage as a mere mister, by courtesy—though not by right—I was allowed to keep Sir Anthony Darby's name and rank. To address me as Mrs. Gage would be considered a snub by many in society, but I was more than eager to shed my first husband's name, regardless of the correct forms of address.

And so I told her. "Actually, I prefer to take my new husband's name." I favored Gage with a loving smile lest she think he had been the one to insist upon this request.

Out of the corner of my eye, I saw Rory's grin broaden.

"I see," the woman replied stonily, though it didn't slip my notice she hadn't actually agreed to my appeal.

"Good evening, Aunt Vanessa," Gage proclaimed, the sharp glint returning to his eyes.

Her perfectly arched eyebrows lifted. "Sebastian."

I didn't like the grating manner in which she pronounced his name, absurdly adding an extra syllable, which she accented. I was quite certain she was doing it that way on purpose.

"Kiera, allow me to present my aunt, the Dowager Baroness Langstone."

So she was not a blood relation, but Gage's uncle's widow, and his late mother's sister-in-law.

"Not that I'm not happy to see you," she said to Gage after nodding to me, her inflection stating that's exactly what she meant, "but what are you doing here?"

I looked up at Gage, wondering how he would take the news that his grandfather had evidently not shared his plans with the other members of the family, but he did not seem surprised. That in and of itself said a great deal.

"Grandfather sent for me," he explained, giving us both the satisfaction of startling Lady Langstone. "We're here to find Alfred."

CHAPTER TWO

G age's aunt and cousin blinked at us in astonishment.
"Or barring that, at least uncover what has happened to him," Gage added. When still neither of them replied, he scowled. "Unless he's no longer missing?"

Rory was the first to react, his demeanor brightening. "Capital! We could use the help, if you ask me. He's been gone over ten days now, and while at first I thought my brother was simply off on some lark, he's begun to worry me."

"Grandfather said he walked out onto the moors one day and disappeared?"

He nodded. "No one's seen hide nor hair of him since." His mouth twisted. "At least, no one who'll admit it."

"Why would they keep something like that to themselves?" I asked, not understanding what he meant.

But before he could answer, Lady Langstone recovered herself. "Then I suppose you'll wish to stay here?"

It seemed an odd response to such a revelation, particularly given the fact that Gage had traveled all this way to help locate her missing son. But perhaps that's exactly why she couldn't address it. Perhaps her hatred was such that she couldn't contemplate the fact that Gage was here to lend his assistance, so she turned to safer topics.

"The emerald chamber, I think," she murmured, frowning at the tapestry hanging on the wall.

"No need to go to the trouble. We'll be more than comfortable staying in Windy Cross Cottage," Gage interjected.

Rory darted an uncertain glance at his mother as she lifted her gaze to meet Gage's.

His brow furrowed upon seeing their reaction. "Are there other tenants?"

Lady Langstone turned her head, studying him with one eye as she drew out her words slowly. "No, but the viscount had the cottage demolished."

None of what had come before had seemed to disturb Gage, but at this pronouncement he winced. "Demolished! When?"

She glanced at her son, as if giving the matter some thought. "Oh, a dozen years ago or so. Not long after your dear mother was laid to rest." She didn't smile, but nonetheless I could tell how much satisfaction she had derived from relaying this bit of news to him.

Why it seemed to affect Gage so profoundly, I didn't know, but I would have liked nothing more than to douse the twinkle in his aunt's eyes.

"Then I suppose the emerald chamber will be satisfactory," Gage replied, not bothering to hide his displeasure any longer.

The dowager baroness nodded assent and turned to the butler, who I'd almost forgotten still hovered in the shadows behind us. "Hammett, please see to it."

"Aye, my lady," he replied as he stepped forward. "Just as soon as I've shown them up to his lordship. Told me to bring them straight up just as soon as they arrived, he did."

Based on the defiant curl in Hammett's lip, I suspected this

statement wasn't strictly true, but whatever his reasons for circum-
venting Lady Langstone, I wasn't about to argue with him. I was
anxious to meet Gage's grandfather and to hear his own thoughts
on his missing heir and what exactly he believed we could do
about it. But I did find it interesting that Gage wasn't the only one
who appeared to be none too fond of the dowager baroness.

Hammett did not wait for her ladyship's agreement, but led us
past her up the elegantly carved staircase and through the corridors to the master bedchamber.

As bleak as the exterior and entry hall had been, I still held
hope that the remainder of the interior would be more welcoming.
After all, my brother-in-law, the Earl of Cromarty's, castle in the
western Highlands appeared somewhat cold and austere from the
outside, despite its lovely setting. The soaring hall was festooned
with the weaponry of his ancestors—hardly an encouraging first
sight for a weary traveler. But once you passed deeper into the
castle's recesses or stepped into the sweeping rooms, you felt the
heart and life of the family living there, the echoes of the centuries of clan members who'd resided within its sheltering walls.

Not so at Langstone Manor. Though the floors were carpeted
in plush rugs and the walls hung with paintings and tapestries—
some of which I would have liked to pause and examine—there
was no light or warmth, quite literally. A chill seemed to have
permanently invaded the corridors despite it being the height of
summer, and the few windows there were contained such dusky
glass that they did little to peel back the shadows. The air was
close and thick with must even though the adornments were spot-
lessly dusted.

As simple as the configuration of the manor appeared from the
outside, the inside proved to be nothing of the sort. Apparently
there had been numerous modifications and additions made to the
house over the years, though for some reason these alterations
hadn't included many more windows than the original structure
boasted. Whether the people residing here had simply wished to

lessen their window tax or they'd been determined to hide something within, I didn't know, but either way the result was a dark labyrinth of corridors and staircases.

I shivered, pressing closer to Gage's side, wondering at his relatives, and ancestors, that they'd been so content to live in such environs. The lavish possessions adorning the space had been placed there in an attempt to alleviate the somber atmosphere, but wouldn't their money have been better spent on widening the windows or reglazing those that already existed?

My thoughts turned to Gage's mother. Had she been eager to escape? Was that one of the reasons she'd been so susceptible to Gage's father's charms? Though I'd never been on the receiving end of his allures, Gage's father was supposed to be an even more legendary charmer than his son. As such, there had never been any doubt why she'd fallen for his golden good looks. But I'd wondered at her eagerness to marry someone below her social standing, a man who at the time had been a lowly mister with no hope of ever gaining a title, a man whom her family had threatened to disown her over. Ultimately they hadn't, though her father had made certain to tie up much of the money she would inherit so that in the event of her untimely death it would go to her children and not her husband, but that had not meant they'd ever been accepting of her choice, merely tolerant. And in the end, her escape had been short-lived. Because of her illness, she'd returned here to live with her son while her husband was away at sea.

I glanced up at Gage, curious whether he was also thinking of his mother. It was impossible to tell whether his furrowed brow was evidence of reminiscences of the past or anticipation of the interview with his grandfather to come.

Hammett's shambling gait finally drew to a stop before a heavy wooden door. He looked back at Gage almost in reproof before lifting his hand to knock. I didn't understand what had been communicated between the two men, but from the manner in which his jaw clenched, it was apparent that Gage had. From within, we heard the sound of coughing, and then a rough voice called out for us to enter.

"Master Gage has arrived, m'lord, and his wife," Hammett announced as he opened the door, and then stepped back to allow us through.

I'm not sure exactly what I'd expected to find, but it was not the wizened old man leaning back against a mound of pillows in a massive four-poster bed. Gage had described his grandfather as a proud man, a man to whom rules and propriety were very important. So for him to greet us in such a manner meant one thing. He was incapable of receiving us any other way.

I flicked a glance up at Gage's stiff features, knowing he must be concerned by the discovery that his grandfather was quite ill. The old man had made no mention of his health in his letter. But then, a man like him wouldn't.

Gage guided me a few steps closer, affording me a better view of the man who'd quite possibly had more influence on my husband's upbringing than his own father. It was difficult to know how much of his appearance had been ravaged by illness and how much was part of his normal aspect. Whatever the case, in marked contrast to his renownedly beautiful daughter and handsome grandson, I doubted the viscount had ever been classified as appealing in all his life. In truth, Gage looked nothing like him. The only feature he might have inherited from his grandfather was his height, though Lord Tavistock's stature was taken quite to the extreme. Even reclining in bed, he was close to six and a half feet tall, and whipcord lean.

It was good to see that despite his sickness, his will remained intact. He glared across the room at us with sharp silver eyes, the crystalline color made all the more arresting by being paired with the silver hair slicked back from his forehead. His rather prominent brow ridge and long, thin nose put me in mind of nothing so much as a greyhound or a whippet. And when he spoke, biting off his words in a hoarse growl, it did nothing to dispel the notion.

"Well, you took your time in coming, now, didn't you?"

With all of the tension radiating from Gage, I'd expected him to scowl or snap back, but instead the old man's surliness seemed to relieve Gage. A fond smile even curled the corners of his lips.

"Good evening to you as well, Grandfather."

"Yes, yes," the old man replied impatiently. "What took you so long?"

Gage pressed a hand to my back to move us toward the side of the bed, refusing to be hurried. "Considering the fact that we've come all the way from Ireland, and that Father had to forward your message on to me, I would argue we made admirable haste."

I didn't miss the way his grandfather's mouth tightened at the mention of Lord Gage. "Suspect your father took his time about sending it." His eyes flicked over me before narrowing on Gage in consideration. "Ireland, hmm?" Then he shook his head as if changing his mind. "I don't want to know. But now that you're here, perhaps someone can make heads or tails of this business."

Gage's eyebrows arched. "Maybe. But first I'm going to present my wife."

The viscount's gaze bored into mine as my husband performed the introductions. I suspected he was trying to intimidate me, but any effect his frosty glower might have had was rather diminished by the fact that he was also trying to stave off a coughing fit. I wasn't sure what, if anything, he thought of me, but I couldn't help but smile at the crotchety picture he seemed determined to make. "It's a pleasure to meet you," I murmured, offering him my hand.

It appeared for a moment the viscount might snub me. Then he slowly lifted his hand to clasp mine, allowing me to feel how his tissue-thin skin stretched over his bones even through my gloves.

"Now that that's done, you can leave us," he declared with finality as he turned back to his grandson. "We have family matters to discuss."

This was a response I was accustomed to. Most people believed a gentlewoman had no place in a delicate inquiry, be it murder or something more benign. Even with my scandalous reputation, they often balked at my involvement, and I'd expected Lord Tavistock to be no different. As such, since it was his family, I was prepared to follow Gage's lead, but I'd not expected such an impassioned response.

"Yes, and *she* is family now." He wrapped an arm around my waist, anchoring me to his side. "She also happens to be a skilled investigator in her own right. If you wish to find out what happened to Alfred as quickly as possible, it would behoove you to enlist her help as well."

My cheeks warmed upon hearing his praise, and I straightened my spine farther, hoping to help prove his point.

His grandfather's eyes flashed with irritation.

"I'll tell her everything you say anyway," he pointed out. "Allowing her to stay simply saves us time."

The viscount's mouth remained clamped in a thin line for several moments longer, but upon seeing that his grandson was not about to relent, he grumbled his concession. "Like I told you in my letter, your cousin Alfred is missing. He walked out of the back garden gate onto the moors eleven days ago and vanished."

"And no one saw which direction he was headed?" Gage glanced distractedly behind him, before crossing the room to move two ladder-back chairs positioned against the wall closer to the bed.

"No. At least, none who'll admit it."

Whether his words were an unconscious echo of his grandson Rory's or not, I found it interesting that they both suspected someone of withholding information. I wondered if they were referring to the same person.

"And I suppose you've already searched the moors and the surrounding villages and countryside?" Gage asked.

The wooden chairs creaked as we settled into them, a fitting accompaniment to the wind and rain buffeting the windowpanes. I reached up to remove my straw crape bonnet and then tugged my fingers from my traveling gloves, a move I regretted, for my hands cramped with cold. A blazing fire crackled in the hearth on the opposite wall, but its heat did not reach far into the room. As sumptuous as the furnishings and fabrics were, they could not patch the drafty windows or shrink the size of the chamber. Nor could the scents of bay rum and lavender fully mask the sour stench of illness.

"Of course," Lord Tavistock said. "There was no trace of him."

"That or it hasn't been found yet," Gage replied gravely.

His grandfather nodded, his silver eyes darkened by some troubling thought.

I glanced between the men, trying to understand what they knew that I didn't.

Noticing my confusion, Gage attempted to explain. "Much of Dartmoor is extremely isolated. It's all too easy to become lost and disoriented. Especially if the weather shifts, which it is notorious for doing. It can be bright and sunny one instant, and then suddenly the sky clouds over and pours rain or snow, or a fog rolls in so thick you can't see your hands in front of your face. There are more tales than one can count about people becoming lost out on the moors and never being seen again." He glanced at his grandfather. "And anyone who lives near the moor can name at least half a dozen people they've personally known who've suffered a similar fate. Though most of the time it's discovered later that they stumbled into a bog or froze to death."

My eyes widened. "So is that what you suspect happened?" I asked, not wishing such a fate on anyone. Though I was curious how *we* were supposed to be able to help if that was the case. Surely the neighboring farmers and miners who worked on or near Dartmoor would be of much greater assistance than Gage or I ever could.

Gage studied his grandfather, who sat frowning down at the

deep green blanket draped across his lap. "Did the weather shift that day?"

"No, but you know as well as I do that the weather on the high moors can change even when it doesn't here," he replied, still never lifting his gaze.

"But that's not what you think happened?" Gage guessed, seeing the same obstinate light in his eyes that I did.

He lifted his liver-spotted hand to smother a cough, before retorting, "Did they tell you their balderdash theories?" He nodded toward the door. "That it's all a bit of japery. That Alfred has taken himself off on some exploit and not seen fit to inform us."

I shared a look with Gage, finding it interesting that, on the contrary, Rory had seemed to refute just such a possibility. Had he changed his mind?

"Has Alfred gone away without telling anyone before?" Gage asked.

"Not for more than a day or two," the viscount argued.

"So it wouldn't be *entirely* out of character?"

His grandfather scowled. "For a day or two," he reiterated sharply. "And one of his ne'er-do-well friends always knew where he could be found."

Gage's lip curled into a sneer. "I see he hasn't changed, then."

At first the viscount looked as if he wanted to argue, but then realized he couldn't. "No."

Gage looked away. "Well, if he's still anything like he was at school, I wouldn't be surprised to hear some wronged husband or father shot him and sunk his body in a bog."

"He is engaged to be married," his grandfather countered between rasping coughs, as if this made a difference. "Or, at least, nearly so."

"I'll be sure to offer her my condolences."

Before receiving his grandfather's letter, Gage had spoken of his cousin only in passing, and after he'd relayed only the bare essentials because I'd pestered him for them. All I knew about Alfred was that he was two years older and, as his grandfather's heir, claimed Lord Langstone as his courtesy title. Gage's silence on the matter had seemed indicative of his concern, but now that assumption proved wrong. For it was becoming apparent that, whatever else was true about Alfred, Gage felt a great deal of animosity toward him.

Animosity that did not surprise his grandfather, who merely frowned at this last comment. "He will settle down after he marries. Most men do. Besides, Lady Juliana will be a viscountess, and a rather wealthy and influential one at that. That should be compensation enough for any trifling indiscretions."

Spoken like a lord who had no concept what it was like to be a lady who has given all her power, all her wealth, all her independence to a man who doesn't deserve it.

It was Gage's turn to glower. "The Duke of Bedford's daughter?"

"Yes. It's a fitting match."

"It's a disastrous match! Lady Juliana is much too soft-spoken and gentle for the likes of Alfred. He'll run roughshod over her."

The viscount's voice grew more strident even as he struggled to get his words out. "She'll be deferential. As a wife should be."

"That's not how I remember Grandmother. Or my own mother, for that matter."

The viscount thumped his fist against the counterpane with more force than his cough-choked voice could manage. "Do not speak of your grandmother that way."

"And my mother?" Gage countered, almost rising from his seat. "But we already know she wasn't deferential enough or I wouldn't be here."

"Gentlemen," I interrupted before either of them could say something they would regret. "Please. This argument about Lady Juliana is of no consequence if we cannot find Lord Langstone." I glanced between the two men, who continued to bristle at one another. I waited for the viscount to catch his breath, concerned by the rattle in his chest. He sank deeper into the pillows propped behind him, tiring from exertion. Nonetheless, we couldn't leave our conversation as it was.

I urged Gage to pour him a glass of water from the ewer on the nightstand. "Now, Lord Tavistock, you seem to be certain that your heir is not absent of his own will. And you don't believe he was a victim of the natural hazards of the moor. So what *do* you think happened to him?"

The viscount accepted the glass from Gage's hand and gingerly sipped from it. I frowned. As strong as the bark of his cough had been, I'd expected him to gulp down the water. But the pain that crossed his features every time he swallowed told me this ailment was far more serious, affecting his tonsils and throat. If he had this much trouble ingesting water, how much food was he able to eat?

He met my gaze over the rim of his glass, and something in my features must have communicated what I'd deduced. Gage was forever teasing me that I was terrible at hiding my thoughts, and though I'd improved over the past months during our inquiries, I'd not taken care to guard my impressions from his grandfather. In the future, I decided it would be best if I did, for he scowled at me in annoyance. Breathing more heavily than before, he sank back into his pillows, passing Gage the glass, of which he'd only drunk a quarter of the contents.

The skin across Gage's face stretched taut, having likely been reminded of his mother's own battle with a similar illness. He'd once described to me her racking coughs, and his fear when she'd struggled to catch her breath.

"Why are Gage and I here?" I murmured, rephrasing my query in more succinct terms.

He continued to frown, clamping his mouth shut as if refusing to speak. He almost seemed angry that I'd asked him such a thing, that I was making him put it into words.

In truth, I already knew the answer. I had known it from the moment Gage had read his letter and explained how little communication he'd had with his grandfather in the past fifteen years. The last time my husband had set foot in Langstone Manor, he'd been here to bury his mother in the family plot at the churchyard nearby. Something had happened then. Something worse than the circumstances surrounding his mother's death and the subsequent discovery that she'd been murdered. Something he'd yet to tell me, yet to explain. Until I better understood, I wasn't about to spare Lord Tavistock's sensibilities by saying the words he didn't wish to utter.

But Gage was not of the same mind. "You think he's met with foul play," he surmised sharply, perhaps impatient for this interview to be over.

The viscount's features seemed to sink in on themselves, becoming even gaunter. "That is my worry."

"So the angry husband or father of a woman Alfred has trifled with *isn't* outside the realm of possibility?" Gage charged.

His grandfather's mouth pursed, but he stopped trying to deny it.

"Why do you suspect Lord Langstone has met with violence?" I persisted. "Do you have any proof?"

"Why do you think I asked *you* here?" he remarked stiffly.

I glanced at Gage, whose mouth was twisted in frustration. However, there was something in his eyes, something in the way he scoured his grandfather's features that made me think he wasn't completely attending to the conversation.

"Yes, but you must realize we need a reason to trust your assertion," I explained, feeling like I was addressing one of my nieces or nephews, not an octogenarian. "How else are we to know where to begin?"

"I know that boy. He's my heir. I would know if he's in trouble, and I tell you, he is." He raised his eyebrows imperiously in challenge.

I nodded, stifling a sigh. I wasn't one to doubt the power of intuition. It had aided me more times than I could count. But surely Lord Tavistock understood we needed more information to go on than that.

I began to gather my things to rise, thinking perhaps it was time to bring this interview to an end. His lordship was fatigued. Just in the past quarter of an hour the hollows around his eyes had deepened. But then he surprised me.

"Sebastian is right," he murmured, frowning at his legs. "Alfred has always had a . . . thirst for drink and women. If he'd taken the carriage or his horse into the village or off to a friend's home and been gone for a night, maybe two, I would not be surprised. But eleven days?" He shook his head. "No. And certainly not walking on foot."

I sat back, pondering what he'd just told us. "Why don't you think he met with an accident—"

"Because he knew those moors! Knew them like his own face."

"Yes, but Grandfather, men who've known Dartmoor far better than we ever could have still met their deaths out there," Gage contended.

"Do you think I don't know that?" he snapped. "I tell you, your cousin didn't fall into a bog or any such a thing. At least, not of his own folly."

"But if he were drunk—"

"He wasn't! Not when he left here."

But I could tell he wasn't so sure of that, and Gage's skepticism was patently clear.

Whatever the real reason for Lord Tavistock's certainty, it was apparent we were not going to coax it from him this evening. Not when he began coughing again, nearly doubling over from the effort.

Gage stood up, alarm tightening his features as he tried to assist his grandfather. Once he'd helped the old man rest back against his pillows, the viscount shooed him away. He shut his eyes as his chest rapidly rose and fell.

I pressed a reassuring hand to my husband's arm. "Should we call for someone?" I asked his grandfather.

"No."

I wanted to press, but it would do no good. He was not at death's door, but if this illness persisted, at his age, it could not be far off.

CHAPTER THREE

I was not surprised to find Hammett waiting for us in the corridor. Gage closed the door softly behind us so as not to wake his grandfather, who seemed to have already fallen into a shallow slumber, before turning to address the servant.

"Be honest with me. How ill is he?"

"The doctor says he'll be lucky if he sees the harvest. But you know yer grandfather. Stubborn as stone. Never was one to let another have his way. Though, I'm not sure, but I suspect the Lord's will is stronger than his."

"What is he suffering from?" I asked curiously. "Bronchial ailments are usually a winter complaint."

The butler shrugged. "I couldn't tell ye, m'lady. But whatever 'tis, it's plagued him since before the spring thaw. 'Twas not but a tiny cough then." His eyes fastened on the door as if to see past it. "Not so tiny anymore."

Gage frowned. "Why didn't anyone write me sooner?"

Hammett looked up at him, a tight line of censure running

between his brows. "Didn't know ye cared to be told." He turned away, striding down the corridor. "I'll show ye to yer rooms."

Though to most my husband's face would appear a mask of indifference, I could see the pain radiating across his features. I reached out to link my arm through his, lending him what comfort he would take as we followed Hammett down the hall.

The chambers we'd been assigned seemed to be at the opposite end of the house from his lordship's. Whether this had been intentional on Lady Langstone's part, I didn't know, but I couldn't fault our accommodations. As was customary for most married couples among the aristocracy, we were given two adjoining bedchambers, and like the viscount's, they were both spacious and drafty. However, the furnishings and fabrics were shiny, plush, and crisp. Gage's aunt might not have been the most pleasant person, but she certainly knew how to run a household.

Because of its positioning at the corner of the manor, my chamber also boasted two large windows, affording the room more light than I'd yet to see elsewhere. I was standing next to one of these windows, trying to see past the rain-splattered panes to the mist-shrouded moors beyond, when Gage entered through the connecting door.

His eyes scoured the room before lifting to meet mine. "I see your luggage hasn't arrived either."

I glanced toward the dainty dressing table fashioned of cherrywood where Bree would have customarily already laid out my brush and comb, as well as other grooming items. Crossing to the wardrobe, I opened the doors graced with the carved image of a rowan tree to find the space inside empty.

"You're right. Could your aunt have changed her mind about which bedchambers we were to be assigned?" For there was no doubt after seeing the emerald green silk wallpaper adorning the walls that this was the emerald chamber of which she'd spoken.

"It's doubtful," he replied, nodding to the fire crackling in my hearth. Not even the most frivolous of noblemen wasted money on lighting fires in unused guest chambers. He reached out to pull the cord that would summon a servant from belowstairs.

"I take it Anderley wasn't waiting in your chamber."

He shook his head, sinking down into the ivory cushions of the rosewood fainting couch positioned near the hearth.

I moved across the Aubusson rug to join him, a thought having occurred to me. "You don't think this is Anderley's way of expressing his displeasure at being here, do you?"

I'd only recently learned that Gage's valet had an impish and somewhat childish inclination to play small pranks when he was irritated or determined to have his way. Or, in the case of my missing gray serge painting dress, when his aesthetic sensibilities had been offended.

"No. Anderley is undeniably underhanded at times, but his actions are always considered and far more subtle. Causing our luggage to go missing now would serve no purpose other than to aggravate us. We've already arrived. There's no turning back." He draped his arm around my shoulders and sighed. "Undoubtedly the servants were misinformed."

"Well, if our trunks don't arrive soon, I suppose we'll have to dine in our traveling clothes, and your aunt will simply have to screw up her nose and accept it."

Gage ran his fingers absently through the loose hairs that had fallen from their pins to tickle the back of my neck. "Yes. Aunt Vanessa is rather haughty."

Trying to ignore the way my skin tingled at his touch, I peered up at him through my lashes, cautiously broaching a subject that had puzzled me. "I couldn't help but notice there was no love lost between the two of you."

His face creased into a humorless smile. "Yes, well, now you can understand why I've avoided her and my cousins' presence whenever possible when they're in London. She never did approve of my playing with her sons, let alone sharing their tutor."

"Because of your father?"

He nodded. "I didn't mind so much for my sake, but she treated my mother like she was a pariah unworthy to dine at the same table with her." His eyes narrowed. "Which was ridiculous. Regardless of who she'd married, Mother was still a viscount's daughter. But Aunt Vanessa could never let her forget how far she'd sunk to wed a mere Royal Navy captain."

"And your grandfather allowed her to treat his daughter that way?" I asked, aghast.

"Oh, she behaved icily correct whenever he was present, though I always felt he must have known about it. It wasn't so terrible when my uncle was alive. He made her keep a civil tongue in her head. But after he passed . . ." He shook his head. "She was as mean as a viper."

I pressed a hand to his chest, wishing I could heal the hurt his aunt had so callously caused. "I'm sorry."

He shrugged as if it didn't matter, but I could tell it did. How much more so had it troubled him as a young boy?

"It must infuriate her to know that my father now holds a title. All those years of slighting us and now the cause of her condescension ranks alongside her, *and* has the ear of the king."

"Yes, I imagine that must eat at her. Especially now that she will never be the viscountess. Does she act as your grandfather's hostess, then? Is that why she still lives here instead of London or the dower house?" I paused to consider. "*Is* there a dower house?"

"Yes. We passed it along the lane, though you could not see much of it beyond the hedgerows." Gage rested his ankle over his other knee, leaning deeper back into the cushions. "She does act as hostess in what little entertaining my grandfather does. But I'm certain she stays here more to keep an eye on her sons' interests than anything."

It was my turn to frown. "What do you mean? Alfred is your father's rightful heir. Your grandfather can hardly disown him."

"Yes, but not all of his property is entailed. A significant portion of Grandfather's wealth derives from the stakes in the tin and silver mines he owns. He's free to bequeath those to anyone he pleases."

I arched my eyebrows. "Including you."

The corners of his lips curled into a cynical smile. "Yes."

"No wonder she wasn't happy to see you. She's obviously worried your grandfather sent for you for other reasons than locating Alfred. Though, I can't understand why she would be more concerned with whatever you might or might not inherit than the fact that her son has disappeared." I tapped my fingers against the cushions beneath me. "Unless she has no reason to worry about where he is."

"I had precisely the same notion, my perceptive wife. If Alfred got himself into some sort of trouble, his mother might have convinced him it was best to lay low for a time and let the matter blow over rather than risk Grandfather's wrath."

"What sort of trouble?"

His mouth twisted. "The usual. Gambling. Fisticuffs. Damaged property. A maid or respectable female he's seduced and gotten in the family way."

I blinked. "Your cousin is capable of all those things?"

"Oh, yes. He's a recurring offender." He sighed, sinking his head back against the couch. "And if it proves to be true my dear aunt is hiding him, then by now she's realized she made a grave miscalculation. I can't imagine she ever anticipated Grandfather would summon me here to find him."

I studied the intricate medallion surrounding the chandelier hanging from the ceiling, considering everything he'd told me. "Do you think your grandfather suspects?" I glanced to the side to see Gage blinking open bleary eyes to gaze up at me. I smiled in apology for disturbing him. If he felt anything like I did, I imagine he'd been seconds from falling asleep.

It seemed we'd been moving nonstop for over a fortnight, bouncing from one inquiry to another, racing from the Lake District of Cumberland to Ireland and now on to Dartmoor. Setting off for Ireland from our honeymoon had only made the journeys and investigations that followed all the more jarring. That day alone, we'd docked in Plymouth just before midday and promptly climbed into a hired chaise to travel on to Dartmoor with the rainy weather at our heels. When it caught up with us outside of Tavistock, the gateway to the moors, I'd suggested we find a room in one of the town's inns for the night and venture on to Langstone Manor in the morning, but Gage had insisted we press on.

I hadn't argued, though fatigue dragged at my bones. But now that I'd met this loving family of his, I began to question his haste, for I could think of nothing we could do to locate his cousin on a night like this. Morning would have been soon enough to begin our search. If, in fact, there was even a search to be conducted.

"Do I think he suspects Aunt Vanessa knows where Alfred is?" Gage asked as if to refocus his own drifting thoughts as much as to clarify.

"Yes. Do you think that's why your grandfather had trouble answering our questions? Is he calling their bluff, so to speak?"

Gage's brow furrowed in consideration, and then he shook his head. "No. I don't think my grandfather would have caused such a fuss, dragging us all the way from Ireland, if that's all this is."

"Yes, but he didn't know we were in Ireland," I pointed out. "He sent his letter to London, expecting you to be there, or somewhere thereabouts." I bit my lip, debating whether to mention the other inkling that had occurred to me.

Gage lifted his head, sensing I was withholding something. "What? What else are you deliberating over in that astounding little brain of yours?"

I hesitated a moment longer, uncertain he would wish to hear it. "Has it occurred to you that your grandfather might have been grateful for the ruse such a feigned disappearance afforded him?" I proposed gently. "You said yourself he's very proud. And now he's ill and probably knows he's not much longer for this earth. It's been fifteen years since he's even set eyes on you. Maybe he wanted to see you again, but he was afraid that if he wrote and asked you to come for his sake, well, that you might refuse."

Gage's pale blue eyes fastened on the embroidered ivory bed skirt, as if trying to imagine such a scenario and finding it bewildering. Just the fact that he was so staggered by such a suggestion made my heart ache for him. Despite the difficulties our hasty voyage had caused us, part of me wished it was true. That his grandfather truly had been desperate enough to lie to bring us here, if only to make Gage feel as if he was wanted by at least one person in his family.

I watched as he struggled to form a response. But before he could reply, a peremptory rap on the door preceded Bree's entrance. My maid bustled inside carrying my valise, followed by a footman hefting my trunk over his shoulder.

"My apologies, m'lady," Bree proclaimed breathlessly, before directing the pale-headed footman. "Over there." She resumed eye contact with me and then darted a suspicious glare over her shoulder. "*Somebody* told the lads to deliver yer trunks to the attics instead o' bringin' 'em to the rooms."

"Thank you, Bree. We were beginning to wonder." Regretfully abandoning the comfort of the couch and Gage's solid presence at my side, I forced myself to rise to my feet as the footman turned to leave, averting his eyes. "I'm sure it was all an honest mistake."

A bizarre one, but an honest one nonetheless.

Bree harrumphed as the footman passed her, plainly not agreeing with me.

"I trust Anderley has also located Mr. Gage's trunk and is awaiting him next door?"

"Aye, m'lady."

I nodded at Gage, who was trying rather unsuccessfully to hide a grin at Bree's ruffled outrage as he departed through the connecting door.

She plopped my valise on the pristine ivory counterpane beside my discarded gloves and bonnet, and opened it to begin pulling out the items I would require.

"Something simple this evening, I think," I told her, beginning to unfasten my own pelisse.

"The Prussian blue gown with gold trim?" she suggested promptly, as if she'd already been considering the matter. "It almost matches yer eyes."

"Yes, that should do."

I was slightly taken aback by her harried movements and sharp responses. This wasn't the first time we'd found ourselves in a strained situation among unfamiliar society and staff, and Bree usually responded with unruffled amusement at the foibles of others. So seeing her in such an agitated state was somewhat of a novelty, and spoke volumes as to the conditions belowstairs.

I watched as she crossed back and forth between the bed and the dressing table, laying out my possessions with her usual precision, all the while wearing a scowl that made her eyes flash with fire. "That bad?" I murmured when she swiveled to approach my trunk of clothes.

She paused to glance up at me, and seeing the sympathetic smile curling my lips, exhaled shakily. "My apologies, m'lady." She shook her head. "This bungle wi' the trunks just has me flustered."

"Are you sure that's all?" I asked as I settled onto the padded bench before the dressing table, not bothering to hide my skepticism.

When she didn't respond, and merely continued to rifle through the contents of the trunk, I decided she might need a little encouraging.

"How is the staff? Do you think this . . ." I searched for a diplomatic word ". . . *confusion* with the trunks is uncommon?"

She scoffed, rising to her feet and allowing the skirts of my gown to unfold. Her eyes scoured the delicate fabric.

"Bree," I said, waiting for her to look up at me. "Truly, I would like to know. The state of this household might give me and Mr. Gage some helpful indications as to what is really going on."

A self-deprecating smile quirked the corners of her lips. "You know me, m'lady. I'll no' spare my opinions." She lifted the wrinkled gown. "But if I'm to have ye respectably dressed in time for dinner, I'll need to press this immediately."

I shrugged. "I don't mind the wrinkles. Lady Langstone will simply have to suffer the sight of them. It's not our fault the viscount's staff lost our luggage."

Bree's face tightened, and I remembered then that I wasn't the only one who would be judged lacking if I turned up in the dining room with my appearance being anything but impeccable despite the day's difficulties.

"I see." I tilted my head. "It seems the servants take after their mistress."

Bree didn't respond, but it was obvious I'd guessed right.

I nodded to the gown. "Go on, then." I swiveled to stare into the mirror, pushing a hand through my tangled deep chestnut brown tresses. "And send a maid up with some water so I can bathe away this dust."

Draping the gown over her arm, she moved toward the door, but before she could open it, someone rapped softly. I watched in the mirror as Bree opened it to let in a young, mousy-haired maid. The girl bobbed an awkward curtsy, sloshing the water in the ewer she carried. I should have known my ever-efficient lady's maid had already requested bathing water.

The maid's eyes dipped to the gown Bree carried as she set the ewer beside the washbasin. "Mr. Anderley told me her ladyship would be needin' a gown pressed. And that I'm to 'take extra care not to damage it.'" The way she spoke Gage's valet's name and quoted him so precisely made it clear she was already smitten.

Bree and I were accustomed to this reaction to the tall, dark, and handsome servant. The black eye he currently sported, courtesy of a scuffle during our last inquiry, only made him look roguish and all the more attractive to the female staff. I could see Bree suppressing a roll of her eyes as she passed the dress over. "Please, see that you don't." There was no need for further warning. Not when Anderley's approbation was at stake.

The girl bobbed another curtsy and then exited the room carrying the gown before her like it was the Crown Jewels.

I waited until the door shut before speaking. "Now, out with it," I ordered Bree, lifting the ewer to pour the warm water into the bowl. "Gossip at will."

She didn't need to be told twice. "They're no' but a lot o' puffed-up Sassenachs. Said they couldna understand what I was sayin', even though I ken they could. And then tried to blame the missin' trunks on *me*."

Though it was true Bree had an accent, it was not nearly as thick as many Scots', and perfectly intelligible even to someone who had not spent a great deal of time in Scotland. She had originally been employed in my father's and subsequently my brother's households at my childhood home in the Borders region of England and Scotland. The staff there was a mixture of both nationalities, and almost indistinguishable from each other. Anyone from that area recognized the Borders were almost a country unto themselves, identifying less with the people in London or Edinburgh and more with their neighbors, whichever side of the arbitrary boundary they happened to fall on.

Given that fact, it was no wonder Bree found the viscount's staff's condescension infuriating. But I was afraid she was going to find this to be quite typical of English servants, who at times could be even more pretentious than their aristocratic employers. I hoped she would be able to make the adjustment. I'd already lost one maid who could not handle the challenges and rigors of being parted from her family and her Highland home.

"Did Anderley defend you?" I asked, blotting my face with a towel. I had long been curious how my and Gage's personal servants behaved with one another outside of our presence. They seemed to fare well enough with each other, though I wouldn't have called them friends.

She bent over the trunk again, extracting the rest of my dresses and stomping across the room to lay them across the bed in a pile until they could be properly hung. "He's no more impressed by the lot o' 'em than I am. Though bein' an Englishman, he can comport himself wi' that icy disdain o' his and no one says a thing edgewise."

I grimaced in commiseration. Some things were no different belowstairs than above. I was sorry to hear they were being so condescending not only for her sake, but for that of the investigation.

"Are they *all* so patronizing?"

"No, no' *all*." Having located my slippers and undergarments for the evening, she moved behind me and took over the task of unbuttoning my traveling gown. Her nimble fingers moved quickly down my spine. "Mainly the upper servants. The lowers maids and footmen wouldna dare do more than titter." She sighed. "And I suspect some o' 'em are even sympathetic."

I glanced over my shoulder. "What of Mr. Hammett?" Having witnessed the surly banter he'd traded with Gage, which masked a long-held fondness, I had a difficult time imagining him harassing my maid.

"The butler? Nay, he's a correct one, like our Jeffers. Wasna puttin' up wi' the others' nonsense once he found oot aboot the trunks. You'd still be waitin' for 'em if it wasna for him."

Bree whisked my dress over my head and draped it over the fainting couch before beginning on the fastenings of my corset. I waited until I could see her face in the mirror before continuing.

"Well, I need you to cozen those who'll speak to you and find out what you can about the family, particularly the missing grandson, Alfred, and his mother, the Dowager Lady Langstone. Enlist Anderley to help you, if Gage isn't doing so already."

Bree's eyes flicked up to meet mine, sharp with intellect. "You suspect her o' bein' involved?"

"Possibly," I admitted. "Her reaction to our arrival and to her son having gone missing was peculiar to say the least. Definitely not what I would have expected, given the circumstances."

Bree nodded. "Consider it done."

I pivoted as she pulled my arms from the garment, looking at her directly. "Given her employer's haughtiness, I suspect her ladyship's maid is one of your worst offenders. But if there's any way you can convince her to trust you, that might prove beneficial."

Bree's face screwed up in confirmation, and then smoothed into a taut smile. "Well, they do say those who are prickliest have often had the most thorns stuck in 'em." A twinkle lit her brown eyes. "I 'spose I'll just have to employ some o' that charm my Irish gran taught me."

Relieved to see some of her good humor had returned, I tugged at an errant curl resting along my neck. "Now, what do you propose we do with this mess?"

Bree studied my head and shook her own resignedly. "Oh, m'lady, how you manage to muddle yer hair so I'll never ken."

CHAPTER FOUR

Despite our best efforts, Gage and I still descended the stairs a quarter of an hour later than the designated hour we'd been given for dinner. I thought our haste had been admirable, but Lady Langstone seemed to be of a different opinion, even though it was her staff's fault our trunks had been taken to the attics.

"How good of you to finally join us," she drawled, her eyes sharp with derision. Lifting her chin, she turned with a swirl of maroon silk and led us from the hall down a corridor to the left. That she'd been lying in wait for us at the base of the stairs instead of the drawing room said much about her impatience. "I can't promise anything will be warm at this point."

I arched my eyebrows, hoping none of the servants had heard her make such an assertion. A well-run household knew how to keep its dishes warm and when to time their final preparation. The incident with the trunks aside, I had seen no indication that the staff wasn't anything but exemplary. Given the fact that Hammett, as butler, would be presiding over the dinner service, I had no doubt everything would run smoothly.

This held true to my expectations when we settled into our chairs before a gleaming table service, and bowls of lightly steaming creamy white chicken soup were set before us. The light from the chandelier overhead glistened off the silverware and reflected in the mirror over the fireplace and off the ornate gold frames of the paintings adorning the walls. However, contrary to being pleased, Lady Langstone seemed only more irritated by this sign of the staff's efficiency. I found it baffling that she would rather be proven right in her vindictiveness than be presented as a good hostess. After all, an efficient household was as much a credit to her as to the staff.

I did my best to ignore her sour expression, turning to address Rory, our only other dinner companion. "So Gage tells me he was schooled with you and your brother." I cast a mischievous smile at my husband. "Tell me, what was he like as a boy?" I urged, as curious to know the answer as I was to see how Rory would respond.

"Well, in the classroom he was quite studious and earnest." He flashed his cousin a grin. "To tell the truth, he was always more clever than my brother or me."

"Only because he had to be, dear," Lady Langstone interjected between spoonfuls of soup.

Rory's cadence faltered hearing this casually delivered insult, but otherwise he ignored it. "And I suppose he was just as resolute outside of it. Always doggedly determined to be the best at everything." He gave a bark of sudden laughter. "Alfred used to say . . ."

But he broke off upon seeing Gage's face, which had turned stony. A slight flush crested Rory's cheeks and his brow furrowed as he seemed to reconsider his words. "He used to say, well . . ." He cleared his throat. "It doesn't really matter what Alfred said. Never did like to come in second, and the way he'd snarl at you made you wish you'd let him win. It ruined the fun more often than not." His eyes dipped to his bowl, seeing something the rest of us couldn't, so he missed the black look his mother cast his way, perhaps for being disloyal to his brother.

I glanced at Gage, wondering what he thought of his cousin's admission and found that the forbidding expression had faded from his eyes to be replaced with quiet consideration.

"I seem to remember you boys fighting a great deal," Lady Langstone said as her soup was whisked away and replaced by filleted sole simmered in butter and lemon juice. Though she spoke as if she cared very little about the matter, her lips pursed.

Gage and Rory exchanged a look rife with unspoken things. Things neither of them seemed eager to reminisce over.

"I suspect most boys do," Rory remarked before taking a long drink of his wine.

"Too true," I said, hoping to relieve some of the tension. "My brother and cousins were constantly pounding each other for some perceived slight one moment and then happily engaged in some bit of sport the next. Our nanny always said that so long as they didn't actually maim each other, it was best to let them have it out, and it would all be over quicker."

I looked up to find my husband watching me with a small smile. I'd never been one to chatter, so I guessed my efforts to distract had been obvious. At least to him.

Regrettably, the effort was all but wasted, for Lady Langstone seemed determined to pursue the topic and her grudge.

"Well, for members of civilized families I suppose it's not cause for alarm," she sniffed. "But I'm afraid the matter is quite different when some of the parties involved have the blood of ruffians and smugglers running through their veins."

It was evident she was talking about Gage, for his father's maternal relatives were rather notorious for their activities along the Cornish coast. This was also a point she'd evidently made numerous times before, for Gage stifled a sigh before rather aggressively attacking a bite of fish.

His head lifted in surprise when Rory spoke up in his defense. "Well, I don't know about blood, other than the fact that we were all guilty of spilling a bit of it." He tipped his cup toward Gage. "But I'm certain you gave your mother much less grief than we gave ours."

I imagined that was true. Gage had a fiercely protective streak. One I'd long suspected had developed from watching his mother's battle with illness while his father was so far away for much of the year. Now that I realized she'd also been contending with the slights of some of her own family, Gage's behavior made all the more sense. He would not have wanted her to suffer on account of his poor behavior, too.

His aunt pushed away her plate with a small shove, as if she'd suddenly lost her appetite. "Except the incident with the Brays' ceremonial dagger."

Her sharp gaze flicked to me and then to Gage, who returned it with a pointed glare of his own. I didn't know what she was referring to. My husband had never shared anything about a dagger with me, and I wasn't about to ask him to elaborate now. But the incident she had referred to clearly troubled Rory. He shifted anxiously as he observed their silent standoff, before signaling to the footman to refill his glass.

Though I'd never been one to overindulge, I found myself following suit. I drained my first glass of wine and requested more. If I was to make it through this dinner with all its barbed commentary, I wasn't sure I wanted my wits completely intact. In any case, my head already ached. Whether it was because Bree had put a little too much force into braiding my hair into a coronet or a result of the long days of travel, it seemed unlikely that drink could make it worse.

I pressed a hand to my temple and broached the subject that was most pressing to us all, and yet the one no one seemed to wish to address. In doing so, I knew I might be overstepping myself, for I'd planned to let Gage take the lead of this investigation, whatever form it took. But witnessing the antagonistic behavior of his aunt, I thought it might be better if I were the one to force the issue.

"You must be beside yourself with worry, Lady Langstone." I arched my eyebrows, struggling to mask my sarcasm. "Concerned for your son's whereabouts and whether he's injured himself or fallen into trouble."

Her posture turned rigid, her eyes bright like two pieces of hard jet, but she did not speak.

"Lord Tavistock seems all but certain Alfred is not absent of his own volition. Not for so many days. But Rory, you indicated you assumed otherwise," I prompted.

"Initially, yes." He frowned. "But now I'm less certain."

"Why did you believe he was off on some lark?" I questioned, harking back to the comment he'd made in the entry hall after learning why Gage and I were here.

"Because it's not uncommon for him to do so. For a day or two or three," he qualified, tapping his fingers against the base of his glass. His eyes narrowed in deliberation. "In London, he often disappears for a few days, returning home whenever he's had his fill of whatever vice he's been pursuing."

His mother made a sound of protest, but he cut her off wearily.

"There's no point in hiding it, Mother. I know you're as aware of the truth as I am. And it will come as no surprise to Gage." His eyes lifted to meet mine. "I suspect his wife wouldn't care for us to dance delicately around the situation either. She seems to be eminently logical and levelheaded."

I nodded my thanks, grateful he hadn't touted the unsavory events in my past as evidence I was unlikely to be shocked by the fact that some gentlemen drank to excess, gambled, or visited the demimonde. What was there to be taken aback by about a man bedding someone other than his wife when I had seen the internal anatomy of a human being laid open on a table for me to sketch?

"But this isn't London," I murmured, finishing his thought for him.

"No, it isn't. And so there are fewer . . . opportunities for him to indulge himself. He might hie off to his chum Glanville's home at Kilworthy Park, or visit one of his other friends in the vicinity. Barring that, I know he's visited the local pubs a time or two, looking for willing company among the barmaids. But he's never away for more than a night or two at that."

"Mr. Glanville called a few days ago," Lady Langstone chimed in to say. A frown still pleated her brow. "He's been very helpful with the search. He wanted us to know he'd spoken to all of their friends and no one has seen or heard from Alfred."

Given her earlier behavior, I couldn't help but be skeptical of her willingness to supply such information. Was Mr. Glanville in collusion with her and she wished us to leave him alone? Or was she concerned with our discovering the full extent of Alfred's proclivities? Regardless, I felt a visit to Kilworthy Park was in order. One glance at Gage's curious expression told me he harbored a similar intention.

"What of Plymouth?" he asked, spearing a parsnip. "Did Alfred ever venture there?"

"I couldn't tell you." Rory's mouth twisted. "My brother wasn't exactly forthcoming about his pursuits. Glanville, or perhaps the coachman, would be able to tell you better than I can."

I glanced at Lady Langstone, wondering how she would react to her son's suggestion that we question Alfred's friend, but she feigned absorption in her food.

Gage's eyes strayed toward the heavy rose damask drapes that had been pulled across the windows, shielding our view of the darkness falling over the garden and the sharp pings of cold rain that continued to be flung by the wind against the glass. It was not a night to be out, especially on the exposed expanses of the high moors.

"What do *you* think happened to him?" His gaze swiveled to spear first his aunt and then his cousin, giving them no quarter. "Where do you think Alfred is?"

Lady Langstone paled and for the first time I could see that she was not as sangfroid about the matter as she appeared. I studied her, wondering if perhaps I had judged her a bit too harshly. After all, her son *was* missing, and if she *wasn't* somehow involved, she must be racked with worry indeed, no matter how she strove to hide it.

However, she was not the first to speak. Instead, her younger son straightened in his chair, narrowing his eyes at the centerpiece of white roses. "It simply doesn't seem possible he fell into a bog or wandered out to a part of the moors we have yet to search." His gaze lifted to his mother before meeting Gage's. "But he was ill during the days before he disappeared. Not like Grandfather's ailment. Laid low by some stomach complaint worse than normal crapulence." He paused, his mouth pressing tight. "I wonder . . ." He hesitated, beginning again. "I *worry* he was not really well enough to be out of bed. What if he fell sicker or became delusional?"

Lady Langstone's fingers tightened around the fork she grasped in her hand, turning her knuckles white. She didn't even seem conscious that she was doing so, until she caught me watching her. Then she inhaled, forcing her shoulders to relax, and carefully set her utensil aside, resting her hands in her lap before speaking. "It's possible. Though, I do not like to think that is what happened."

Gage's manner softened in answer to her distress. "What *do* you hope happened?"

She swallowed, her words emerging haltingly. "That he took himself off to Plymouth or a friend's home farther afield than Kilworthy Park and couldn't be bothered to inform any of us."

"Without a horse or carriage?"

"Yes, well, the walk to Peter Tavy or even Merrivale isn't so very far. And there are a number of smaller farms bordering the moor. Perhaps he borrowed a horse from one of them."

None of us pointed out how improbable her suggestion was. In any case, I suspected she already knew. If Alfred had borrowed a horse, surely the farmer or hostler would have spoken up when they discovered the viscount was searching for his grandson. That is, *if* he'd borrowed one. From what I'd learned of Gage's cousin, he scarcely seemed the type to travel any distance on a borrowed nag when he could easily do so in greater comfort and style.

Which led us back to one glaring point. If Alfred hadn't gone into hiding of his own volition—with or without his mother's help—then something unpleasant had probably befallen him.

We finished our meal on that somber note and retired to our chambers. I was largely quiet as Bree helped me undress and ready myself for bed. My things had all been put away and the room tidied while I ate dinner. Knowing my maid must be as tired, if not more so, than I, I sent her off to find her own bed.

My thoughts kept returning to the moors, to their silent but relentless presence beyond the garden wall. There was something preternatural about them, something ancient. I could not forget they were there. Their existence seemed to always be lurking somewhere in the background of my mind as a sort of hum of anticipation.

I lifted aside the gold damask drapes to peer out into the rain-soaked darkness, knowing I would not be able to see anything, and yet not able to resist. Perhaps it was the very fact that I had not been able to truly glimpse them yet that made the moors seem so fascinating to me. The weather and then nightfall had maddeningly kept them cloaked. I only hoped tomorrow would be different, for my sake and for Alfred's.

When my husband entered the room a few moments later through the connecting door, he found me still peering out at what little I could see of the manor's back terrace and gardens. I'd been expecting him, for we'd yet to spend a night apart in the three months of our marriage, despite it being unfashionable to share a bedchamber. Instead, Gage used his assigned room merely to dress with the assistance of his valet, affording me and Bree some privacy as she helped me with my ablutions. I hoped it would always be this way.

I glanced up as the door clicked shut and allowed the heavy drapes to fall back into place.

"Curious about the moors?" he guessed, knowing me all too well. He smiled tiredly, pausing at the foot of the bed. "I'm sorry our arrival couldn't have been under more auspicious circumstances."

I knew he was speaking about more than the weather. I waved the matter aside. "You look as if you could fall asleep on your feet," I murmured, reaching up to caress his jaw. Tilting my head, I studied his pale blue eyes. "But your mind won't let you."

His arms wrapped around my waist, pulling me against him. "Perceptive, as always." His grin turned humorless. "Though I suppose it doesn't require a great deal of acuity to deduce there is much weighing on my mind."

I rested my head against his chest, pressing my hand to the warm skin over his heart revealed by the part in the collar of his burgundy silk dressing gown. "Do you wish to discuss it or will that only make it more difficult to sleep?"

A long exhale shuddered through him as he rested his chin on my head. "Oh, that I *could* ignore it."

I inhaled the spicy scent of his cologne and the natural musk of his skin, feeling my body soften further to mold against his as my blood thickened. "I could . . . attempt to distract you." I gazed up at him through my lashes, fighting the blush cresting my cheeks.

Although I'd been a widow when he and I wed, relations between myself and Gage had been a complete revelation. And while I had grown bolder and more comfortable with the physical side of our marriage, I was still by far the shyer of the two of us, and the least likely to initiate intimacy. Though I was more than happy to partake.

Gage's eyes darkened and his lips curled into a smile that could only be termed wolfish. "Could you?" he drawled, lowering his head to capture my lips.

But before they could touch, he drew back, staring over my shoulder at something.

I turned my head, trying to follow his gaze. "What is it?"

A pleat formed between his eyes. "Just one moment."

He crossed the room toward the corner where a tall bureau stood. Then he leaned down to press his shoulder against it, slowly sliding the heavy oak desk across the floor to the right.

I stared at him in bafflement. "What are you doing?"

He paused to catch his breath and then with a grunt continued his labor, sliding the piece of furniture over about two more feet. "There," he proclaimed, standing tall again as he rested his hands on his hips in satisfaction. "That should do it."

"Do what?"

He nodded at the bureau, or rather the wall behind where it now stood. "Block the entrance to one of the secret passages."

CHAPTER FIVE

"What?!" I gasped, striding across the room to stand next to him.

Gage pointed toward the edge of the wood paneling that spanned the wall from floor to ceiling on either side of the fireplace. I hadn't noticed it earlier—then, of course, I hadn't been looking—but there was definitely a narrow groove running up the wall that was not evident on the other side. About a foot to the left hung a long woven tapestry of medieval knights and maidens, which I assumed was meant to mask any further evidence of the mechanism.

"I apologize. I should have mentioned it sooner. In all honesty, it slipped my mind," he explained.

"How many secret passages are there?" I asked, still somewhat shocked by such a discovery.

"Three. Four if you count the priest's hole in the back parlor."

He spoke so nonchalantly, as if all of this was common. I'd heard of castles and manor houses that boasted secret passages, but I'd yet to knowingly stay in one. And rather than intrigue me, it somehow made this foreboding, unwelcoming place seem all the more cold and heartless. To think someone could have snuck in and out of our chamber without our knowledge made me feel angry and violated.

My spine stiffened, and I crossed my arms over my chest. "Do you think your aunt assigned us this chamber because of it?"

"I can't help but think that was part of her consideration." He frowned in deliberation. "But surely she must have known I would be aware of them. My cousins are."

I turned to scour the chamber for signs that anyone else had been in the room other than Bree, but I had no idea what to look for. Upon being shown into the chamber before dinner, I hadn't really given the space much consideration, having been distracted by other things. And if changes had been made even prior to that, we would never have known.

"Perhaps she didn't realize you were aware of them, or she anticipated you'd forgotten." I scowled at the couch where earlier we'd reclined discussing matters. "Or she'd hoped you would trust them not to intrude." I turned back to the wall behind the bureau, searching it for any signs of holes or other crevices.

Gage draped an arm around my shoulders as if sensing my unease. "The walls are too thick for them to eavesdrop," he assured me. "And the tapestry muffles what sound that does filter through."

I glanced up at him, curious how he was so certain of such a thing, but seeing the tightening at the corner of his eyes, I decided not to ask. Instead, I leaned closer, absorbing his warmth. A draft coming from somewhere on this side of the chamber—the secret door?—had crept over my toes and up under my night rail.

Feeling me shiver, my husband urged me up into the bed and under the thick covers. He leaned back against the pillows plumped in front of the headboard, and I rested my head on his shoulder. He'd not removed his dressing gown, so I knew he had something to say before we indulged in any sort of distraction.

The clock ticked away on the mantel while he contemplated whatever it was he wished to discuss. My eyes began to droop—his heat and solid presence lulling me into slumber—when finally he spoke.

"You can ask me."

I blinked open my eyes to look up at him.

He dropped his gaze from the point he had been staring at on the opposite wall. "You don't have to dance around asking the questions I can see forming in your eyes. I know I haven't proven to be the most forthcoming individual, especially about my past, and I can't promise I will always give you a straightforward answer, but that doesn't mean you shouldn't try." He swallowed. "I . . . I want you to try. Otherwise, I'm not certain I will ever bring myself to speak of it."

I sat taller to look at him, surprised by this change in him. Given the fact that I'd practically had to drag information out of him at knifepoint in the past, it was a welcome one. I well understood secrecy, for I had never been one to share a great deal of myself. I also had my fair share of skeletons I would rather remain in the closet. But Gage had transformed reticence into an art form.

"How do you know the walls are too thick?" I asked softly, sensing something fragile behind his eyes.

His Adam's apple bobbed up and down as he swallowed again. "Because my father met with Aunt Vanessa here."

His revelation of the secret passage had been shock enough, but this pronouncement rendered me completely mute. Fortunately, he didn't seem to need further coaxing in order to continue.

"I followed him here once, through the passage. My father had come home to us for one of his leaves, and he'd been acting strangely ever since his arrival. Mother hadn't seemed to notice, but then, she was particularly ill that spring." One side of his mouth curled upward in chagrin. "I'd been trying to avoid him whenever I could because he tended to try to pack in an entire six months' worth of paternal scolding and correction into his short visits." His eyes narrowed in remembrance. "But unlike other visits, evasion hadn't proved difficult *or* earned me extra reprimands."

"Because he was slipping away as well," I surmised.

He nodded. "I needed to know why. To understand what was more important than staying by my mother's side or even lecturing me."

Though Gage strove to conceal it, I could hear the hurt, lonely boy he had once been struggling behind his words. These were events he had never come to terms with. Memories he had never fully confronted. And they affected his relationship with his father even to this day. It also further explained his abhorrence of his aunt.

I reached down to touch his opposite hand where it rested in his lap, rubbing my thumb up and down over the back of it. "Were he and your aunt . . . were they . . . ?" I broke off, not knowing how to finish the question.

"No. Not that time, at least." He stared down at our hands. "I could hear their raised voices, but not what they were saying. And I had to dart into a cobwebbed alcove to avoid being seen by my father when he left through the passage."

"So you didn't confront him about it?" I already knew the answer, but I asked anyway.

"No. Not then. Not ever." His brow lowered into a fierce scowl. "I'm not sure I trust my father to give me an honest answer. If he even deigned to give me an answer at all."

Having firsthand knowledge of Lord Gage's high-handed, disdainful demeanor, I suspected he was right. "Did your mother know?"

"I don't know. I hope not."

I studied the intricately embroidered pattern on the counterpane as Gage lifted his fingers to thread them through mine. "What of your aunt?" I voiced in hesitation.

He lifted his eyes to meet my gaze.

"Have you ever asked her?"

He arched a single eyebrow. "Asked her what? If my father proved unfaithful to my mother, the woman who degraded herself by marrying him?"

"That's no worse than your aunt degrading herself by becoming his lover after she mercilessly mocked and derided your mother for *years*." I paused. "But I see your point. If whatever happened between them wasn't an affaire de coeur, then by questioning her about it, you've all but admitted your father is the knave she's accused him of being."

Having labeled the relationship what it could have been, another thought occurred to me. "Is it distasteful to sleep here? Would you rather we slept in the bed in your chamber?"

"My room is even colder than this one because the fireplace is not drawing correctly." He tightened the arm draped around me from behind, snuggling me closer to his side. "No. I shall be fine. Particularly with you here to help banish unpleasant imaginings."

I smiled coyly. "I'm so pleased I can be useful."

He reached up to coil a loose tendril of hair brushing my cheek around his finger. "You are ever so much more than useful," he murmured with a roguish twinkle in his eye. But then his expression turned more serious. "I'm glad you're here with me, Kiera. This would have been much more difficult on my own." He gazed up at the bed hangings above us. "I'm not sure I would have even had the nerve to come."

I lifted a hand to his chin, forcing him to look at me. "Well, I am. Having seen you with your grandfather, there's no doubt in my mind that you would have accepted his summons, no matter how much you dreaded it."

They must have been the words he'd needed to hear, for his brow smoothed and his shoulders relaxed. Until that moment, I hadn't realized the prospect that he might have ignored his grandfather's letter had been bothering him. Evidently the discovery that the viscount was ill rattled him more than he wished to admit.

He turned his body to press more fully against me and lowered his mouth to my neck. "Now, weren't you saying something about distracting me?"

I sighed and set about being as diverting as possible. Though, to be honest, I wasn't sure whether I was the diversion or the diverted. Either way, I had no complaint.

Despite the long journey and our tiring nocturnal efforts, I woke early the next morning. The pale light of dawn had just begun to filter through the curtains, casting a shadowy glow over the room almost like the gloaming in the Highlands. It was that hour when the light seemed almost tangible, a hazy wash of color over the darkness. I lay in bed staring up at the bed curtains, which we had never closed, still trying to shake off the bonds of slumber.

However, far from relaxed, I felt unsettled. I didn't have to struggle to recall why. It was because of the dream I'd had sometime during the night. The vision of someone standing at the foot of the bed. They hadn't moved or spoken, merely hovered over us while we slept before vanishing into the gloom.

It didn't take much insight to guess where this worrying apparition had originated. I turned my head to look at the wall where the bureau Gage had moved still blocked the entrance to the secret passage. I breathed a little deeper at the evidence that the heavy piece of furniture had not been disturbed, but a shiver still worked through my frame at the memory of that figure watching us while we were unaware.

Another shiver ran through me and I realized it wasn't entirely my distressing nightmare that caused me to tremble. The room was also bitter cold. The fire in the grate had long since died, and no servant had yet entered to coax it back to life. Then a gust of air brushed over my skin, rustling the bed curtains and the drapes over one of the windows.

I stiffened, shaking with renewed force from both the chill and the realization that a window was open. A window that had been shut the night before.

I burrowed deeper under the covers, pressing close to my husband's side. "Gage," I whispered.

He hummed sleepily and lifted his hand to cup my hip to pull me back against him, mistaking my intent.

"Gage!"

The second time the frantic tone of my voice must have penetrated through the fog of sleep, for he lifted his head off the pillow and cracked open one eye to look at me.

"The window is open," I hissed.

He glanced in the direction I indicated with my nodding head, clearly not understanding why this alarmed me. Just as he opened his mouth to question me, I saw comprehension dawn. His eyes widened and he pushed upright, allowing the covers to slide off his bare shoulders down to his waist. He turned to look at the bureau and the secret entrance as I had before tentatively rising from the bed.

Snatching up his dressing gown, he covered himself and cinched the belt at the waist before he approached the window. He cursed, lifting his foot as he stepped into a puddle of undoubtedly frigid water. The drapes fluttered inward and he grasped them, yanking them aside. As suspected, the casement window stood open to the chill air, both panes having swung outward, though one gaped wider than the other.

Clutching the covers up over my chest, I sat up to watch as he leaned forward to peer out. I found it odd that the casements swung outward when normally they swung inward, but it was not the first time I'd encountered such an anomaly. In any case, they should have made it harder for an intruder to enter, but someone had opened those windows, and it hadn't been me or Gage.

My heart kicked in my chest at the prospect that my dream had been real. That someone *had* stood over us in our sleep.

Gage lifted his head and then looked left and right along the side of the house, before grasping both casements to swing them shut. But prior to latching them, he paused to examine both frames.

He lifted his finger to fiddle with something, then closed the windows and locked them tightly.

"What did you discover?" I asked.

He crossed to the other window to check its lock, all but ignoring my query.

"Gage?"

When he was satisfied, he hurried back to the bed and under the warm covers. I squeaked as his cold feet and hands brushed against me.

"Well?" I prodded impatiently.

"I should have checked the locks last night," he replied with a frown. "You can be sure I'll do so from now on."

"Yes, but what did you find outside the window?"

His gaze met mine, debating how much to reveal. I arched an eyebrow in scolding, letting him know he'd best not attempt to fob me off.

He grinned sheepishly. "The light was not strong enough to tell for sure, but there appeared to be footsteps in the mud below the window."

I stiffened. "But how did they climb up? And how did they open the casements?"

"As for the climbing, I'm not certain. There's nothing attached to the outside of the building to assist them. Possibly a rope secured to the roof." He sighed and raked a hand back through his golden locks, sending them into even more disarray. "As for opening the windows, it appears they used an old rope trick. There's a hook attached to the outside of the frame. One that shouldn't be there. They must have tied a quick-release knot like the type used to secure a horse's reins. Looped it around the hook and left both ends dangling. Then after they pulled the window open, all they had to do was tug the other end to release the rope."

"Removing any proof of how they did it. But who would do such a thing? Surely such an effort would require premeditation?"

"Yes. The rope must have already been secured to the hook before we retired."

I clutched the covers tighter to my chest. Had they tried entering our chamber through the secret passage but found it blocked? Had they suspected Gage would do so and the rope was merely a backup plan? "I don't understand. Why would they go to such lengths to enter our chamber in the middle of the night? What was the purpose?"

Gage lifted one arm, placing his hand behind his head as he reclined back. He seemed far less concerned about the matter than I believed he should be. "I don't know why. There's certainly nothing remarkable to be found unless they wished to steal your jewels." He narrowed his eyes at the window. "I'm not even sure someone *did* enter."

"What do you mean?"

"I find it hard to believe we wouldn't have heard them clambering in through the window with naught but the aid of a rope. There is water on the floor, but the drapes are merely damp, so I suspect they waited until after the storm had passed to open the casements. Even so, I still think we would have woken if someone had attempted to enter our chamber through the window. But perhaps that wasn't the point."

I bit my lip, apprehending what he meant. If their only goal had been to unnerve us, then they'd succeeded, at least for my part. But, of course, I hadn't told my husband about my vision in the middle of the night. Perhaps if he was aware I'd either dreamt of or woken up to find someone hovering over us, he wouldn't be so blasé about the matter. It was on the tip of my tongue to tell him when a faint knock on the door presaged the entrance of the young maid who had ironed my gown the night before.

She blushed at the sight of us together in my bed looking back at her. "I . . . I'm to tend the fires," she stammered, lifting her bucket of implements.

I nodded and sank back under the covers next to my husband and closed my eyes. Saying anything to her would only embarrass her further. So we lay quietly listening to the soft scrape and shush of her efforts as she rebuilt the fire in the hearth. Under normal circumstances, we would have still been asleep and never even marked her presence.

I would have liked to fall back asleep, but my mind was too alert. And so, it seemed, was Gage's, for the moment the maid slipped out the door, he threw the covers off him.

"I need to speak to Rory."

"Why?" I watched as he rolled out of bed to approach the crackling fire.

"Because I've just remembered that Alfred used that very method to climb into our tutor's chamber and leave insects and other nasty surprises for him."

This pronouncement made me sit up, pulling my knees to my chest. I gingerly lifted the covers to search underneath. "You think your missing cousin climbed into our window?" I asked, not having considered the possibility that Alfred might have been our nighttime visitor.

He lifted his eyebrows significantly. "That or someone wants us to think it was him."

I looked underneath his pillows and then mine. "Who else knew about his trick? I assume his brother must have been aware."

"Oh, yes. As well as several members of the staff. Though, truth be told, it's hardly a secret maneuver. Kiera?"

I glanced up to find him watching me with a gently reproving smile.

"I hardly think he climbed up here to put a snake in our bed."

I lowered the blanket I'd been searching beneath. "Yes, of course." But just in case, I decided it would be best if I rose for the day as well.

Contemplating the matter, I donned my own sapphire dressing gown and crossed the room to perch on the edge of one of the rosewood armchairs with needlepoint upholstery positioned before the hearth. "It's doubtful that whoever wished to disturb us came from elsewhere. The stormy weather alone would have discouraged anyone from being out and about."

"And no one outside of Langstone Manor even knows we're here."

"So they must be from the manor." I frowned. "We've speculated your aunt might be helping your cousin to hide. Do you think she could have gotten a message to him?"

Gage stared into the fire, his brow furrowed in consideration. "Not unless he's very close by. Perhaps even somewhere on the manor grounds."

"*Are* there places he could hide for such a length of time and not be discovered?"

"I can think of a few. Although such a feat would require the assistance of at least one of the servants. I can't imagine my aunt fetching and carrying food and other unmentionables, even for her own son."

"If Alfred *is* hiding nearby, do you think Rory knows? Do you think he suspects? After all, your grandfather isn't in any shape to search the grounds, so Rory would be the only one he truly needed to avoid."

"And Hammett," he replied, sinking into the other chair. "I have a difficult time imagining my grandfather's majordomo being duped in such a manner. I suspect he's already searched the manor and its grounds. Extensively."

A smile crept over my lips. "He doesn't trust Alfred?"

Gage snorted. "Not unless his opinion has drastically changed in the last fifteen years." His mouth tightened as if he'd just realized it very well could have. Fifteen years was a long time. "But as far as whether Rory would help to shield him, I'm not certain. Though I think it's evident neither he nor my aunt are sharing all they know."

"You sensed that as well, hmm?"

"I would have to be the most obtuse person in all of England not to."

I tilted my head, ever curious about his family. "Tell me about Rory. He seems fairly kind and amiable."

"He does, doesn't he?" His brow was puzzled.

"I take it that wasn't always the case?"

"He was never as malicious as Alfred." One corner of his lip curled derisively. "Though, that's not saying much." He exhaled. "No, I suppose looking back, Rory doubtless followed his older brother's lead so that he wouldn't turn on him. After all, if Alfred was focused on me, then he couldn't tease his slower, smaller brother. But either time or Alfred's absence seems to have given Rory courage and perspective."

"He did seem to feel genuine remorse for whatever memories he'd dredged up during dinner yesterday evening," I offered.

Gage nodded distractedly.

"But based on everything I'm hearing, I don't think I like Alfred much." I scowled. "He sounds like an utter blackguard. One I'd like to give a piece of my mind as well as a sound thrashing."

Some of the warmth and light that had faded from my husband's eyes returned at this pronouncement, and I was happy to see it, even if it was somewhat at my expense. "I would like to see that."

I lifted my chin. "I bet you would."

He reached for my hand across the distance between our chairs and I gave it to him. The frisson of attraction and reassurance I always felt at his touch raced along my skin. "Then let's hope you have the chance." He squeezed my fingers before releasing them as he stood. "For now, I have a letter to write to a contact in Plymouth. I would like to know whether Alfred has recently made an appearance in that fair city." His countenance darkened again. "I suppose I should also write my father and ask him to make some discreet inquiries about my cousin there."

"Do you honestly think he traveled all the way to London without leaving word of his intentions, without taking his valet or his possessions?"

"No. But it's worth verifying." His eyes shone with vindictive delight. "Besides, all it costs me is a few moments to pen a letter. *I* won't be the one searching the city on what is almost certainly a wild-goose chase."

I couldn't help but laugh. After everything we'd gone through during our last inquiry—an investigation we'd undertaken at Lord Gage's behest—it seemed only fair we should return the favor in some small measure.

"After that I believe we should have a chat with Hammett and Rory." He whirled toward the door connecting his assigned bedchamber with mine, speaking over his shoulder. "And then, dear wife, I think it's time you caught your first glimpse of the moors."

CHAPTER SIX

"You're welcome to search yourselves," Hammett said when we tracked him down in the butler's pantry a short time later. "But I assure ye, I combed the house and grounds myself soon as the Dowager Langstone sounded the alarm."

"It was Lady Langstone who first suggested Alfred was missing and might be in distress?" Gage asked, sharing a look with me.

He nodded, continuing to polish a piece of silverware. "Said he was 'sposed to join her for tea, and when he didn't appear, she discovered he hadn't been seen for two days. Not since one o' the gardeners spied him walkin' out on the moor."

"Did the gardener see which direction he was headed?"

"Couldn't tell. Not for sure. But he supposed he might be walkin' up toward White Tor."

Gage leaned casually against the door frame, crossing one ankle over the other. Contrary to his indifferent appearance, I knew this meant he was ruminating over some idea. "Did Alfred often go for walks on the moor?"

This question made Hammett slow his ministrations, his brow

furrowing. "Not as a rule, no. But recently I'd heard tell o' him going for a stroll a time or two. More often he'd take his horse."

"Do you know the reason for this change in his behavior?"

He shook his head, seeming puzzled. "Truth to tell, I hadn't even contemplated it before now. Wouldn't think twice about hearing the viscount, or you, or even Master Roland amblin' o'er the moors. But Lord Langstone? He wasn't one for constitutionals or quiet reflection. And what else could he be doin' out on those moors?"

That was a leading question if ever I'd heard one. What *had* Alfred been doing on his treks over the moor? And did it have anything to do with his disappearance?

Gage glanced back into the dining room as if to be certain we were still alone. "How were relations between the viscount and Alfred?"

Hammett peered at Gage over a pair of spectacles perched on his nose. "You know how they always were. Never saw eye to eye." He turned back to examine the utensil in his hand, then set it aside and reached for another. "Well, not much changes in this old manor."

"Had there been any particularly nasty arguments in the weeks before Alfred disappeared? Any more altercations than usual?"

"Not that I'm aware of. Why?" He spared him another glance. "You'll not be thinkin' your grandfather has anything to do with this, now will ye?"

"No," my husband replied distractedly. "I'm just trying to understand what my cousin's state of mind was before he disappeared."

"A dangerous thing, to be sure."

The majordomo looked up at me and winked. It was such an unexpected bit of levity from the crusty old man, and so swiftly done before he turned back to his task, that I questioned whether it had actually happened.

Gage straightened from his slouch. "Thank you, Hammett. Do you know where we might find my cousin Rory?"

He bobbed his head to the left. "Master Roland is usually in the viscount's study at this time o' the morning. A scapegrace your cousin Langstone might be, but at least that one understands some-one 'll have to be capable of taking o'er the reins o' the viscount's estates," he added with approval. "I expect he hopes his brother 'll keep him and their mother about if he proves himself to be useful."

An unwelcome thought occurred to me as Gage took my arm and led me out of the dining room and down a corridor to the right. I was glad he knew where he was going, for I was certain I would have become lost. Even in the light of a new day, the halls and chambers were dark and shadowy, requiring the glow of sconces and lamps to peel back the gloom.

"Gage," I began cautiously.

"Hmmm?"

I hesitated, hearing the preoccupation in his voice. "Who in-herits the viscountcy after Alfred if he dies?" I already knew the answer, but it somehow seemed gentler to lead Gage into it.

It turned out I had no need for delicacy, for the look in his eyes when they met mine told me he'd already harbored a similar notion.

"I'm sure you already know that until Alfred marries and con-ceives a son, it falls to his younger brother. So unless Alfred has a secret wife stashed in a cottage somewhere, Rory would become my grandfather's heir."

"Then I suppose you've considered—"

"That Rory is behind Alfred's disappearance?" he finished for me in a tense voice. "Yes. Though I don't like to think it."

Sensing his turmoil, I tried to lessen the pain such speculation caused by asking after the rest of his family. "How many children did your grandfather have? Do you have any other cousins?"

"Only three who survived infancy—my mother; her brother, Alfred and Rory's father; and my aunt, Matilda. Aunt Matilda and her husband and two children—Edmund and Hester—have always split their time between London and a cottage a short dis-tance from here. Though, Hester has since wed and lives with her husband and children, of course."

"And Edmund? Is he married?"

"Not the last I knew."

His voice was taciturn. There was no loving inflection when reflecting on his relatives, only a reserved recitation of facts, and that saddened me.

I'd always known I was fortunate in my family. In my parents, my brother and sister, and even my grandparents, aunts, uncles, and cousins. I recalled all of them with mostly love and affection. Long ago, I'd realized that Gage had not been so lucky, but I hadn't recognized how intolerably so.

Except for his mother, whom he still adored fifteen years after her death, I couldn't name a single member of his family he held in esteem. Even his father, Lord Gage, was a thorn in his side. And a thorn in mine, if the truth be told. After watching them together, I believed there was some fondness between Gage and his grandfather, though if pressed I suspected they would demur.

"Then I would hazard a guess that they would be at their cottage nearby," I said. Given the fact that most of the nobility and gentry preferred to escape the heat and stench of London during summer, it wasn't a detail that was difficult to construe.

"Likely," he replied.

And yet they weren't here assisting with the efforts to locate their lost relative. None of Gage's family had even mentioned them, nor did my husband seem eager to visit them. I didn't know how to view this level of disinterest. It seemed a bit heartless to me, but then my numerous aunts, uncles, and cousins would have been swarming all over the hills had I gone missing. They would have descended on the location like vengeful angels, teasing and annoying each other and stepping on each other's toes, but also nurturing, defending, and bolstering those who needed it.

As if sensing some of my confusion, my husband squeezed my arm where it linked with his. "I do usually see Aunt Matilda and her children in London several times a year. By no means do we avoid each other. At least, not like Aunt Vanessa and Alfred when they come to town."

I was bursting with more questions about his family, but I didn't want to press too hard too quickly and risk him falling stubbornly silent as he had so often done in the past, regardless of his assurances that he wouldn't. But before I could tactfully voice another query, we found ourselves outside the study. He gave a peremptory knock and pushed the ajar door further open.

Rory looked up at us over a document clasped in his hands and grinned. "Good morning. I hope you both slept well." He sat back in the chair he occupied behind the sturdy oak desk positioned before a small stone hearth. The surface overflowed with papers, all arranged and organized into stacks.

"Good morning," Gage replied, his eyes flitting over the paperwork. "Hammett suggested we would find you here. That you've been helping Grandfather with the estate management."

Rory dropped his gaze to the paper still clutched in his hand before setting it aside. "Yes, well, we caught him trying to descend the stairs when we all know he's in no condition to exert himself in such a manner. I volunteered to handle all the trivial matters and bring those papers that required his attention to him. At least until he's well enough to venture forth again."

Someone had to do it.

The words weren't spoken, but they gleamed in his eyes, hanging in the air between us nonetheless. Gage was not so willing to ignore them.

"Shouldn't Alfred be doing this?" It wasn't voiced as an accusation, but more of a concerned query.

"Probably," Rory admitted with a sigh. He turned to look out the window, narrowing his eyes. "But you know Alfred. He never was one to interrupt his fun."

They shared a look of silent apprehension, undoubtedly wondering what was going to happen when Alfred inherited the title.

Rory pushed up from his chair with determined cheer. "But I'm certain you're not here to discuss the flooding in the south pasture or the masonry crumbling over the fireplace in the billiard room. Did you wish me to show you where Alfred was last seen?"

I was surprised when Gage did not reply. He appeared to be distracted by something on the wall opposite the window, and it took me a moment to realize why. There were three portraits spanning the length of the wall, but it was toward the one of the woman on the left that Gage took several steps.

It was his mother.

I'd never seen an image of Emma Trevelyan Gage, yet I felt certain the blond beauty smiling mischievously down at us from the wall was she. There were the pale winter blue eyes and the softly tousled curls my husband had inherited. But if I had held any doubts, the longing and tenderness that flashed in his eyes would have confirmed it. An answering twinge pricked in my chest, a yearning for my own mother who had passed when I was only eight years old. I supposed no matter how old you were, or how long ago your mother had passed, you never stopped wanting her.

The portrait had been completed by a painter of some skill, though his brushwork was unfamiliar to me. However, I would have chosen a different color palette to capture her complexion. One more similar to the woman rendered at a slightly older age in the portrait hanging next to her. I quickly deduced this one was a wedding portrait of her mother—Gage's grandmother. She also boasted the same blue eyes, but a pointier chin and a more somber demeanor. On her other side hung a young man who could only be her son—Rory's father and Gage's uncle. His looks were a match to the current viscount, though softened in some way, either by nature or by the artist's fancy. I supposed the man could be a depiction of Lord Tavistock as his younger self, but given the fact this portrait was hanging beside the other two deceased members of his immediate family, I decided it must be his son.

"When did Grandfather have her portrait moved here?" Gage asked quietly.

Rory moved forward to stand beside us. "I don't recall exactly. It's hung there for years now." He turned to study his cousin's profile. "I keep forgetting you haven't been here in fifteen years."

Gage lowered his gaze to meet his, but Rory had already looked away, staring up at the portrait again.

"Have you visited St. Peter's Churchyard yet?"

Had I not been watching him so closely, I'm not sure I would have seen the swift tightening of my husband's jaw and brow.

"No," he murmured, seeming to gather himself before turning to his cousin once again. "Did you say you can show us where Alfred was last seen?"

If Rory considered this abrupt change of topic odd, he didn't indicate so by word or expression, but merely gestured toward the door. "Let me just change my shoes." His eyes dipped to my dainty slippers. "And you might wish to as well."

A quarter of an hour later, appropriately shod and attired for the rough, boggy ground of the moors, we stepped out onto the back terrace. The garden at the rear of the manor was not any more impressive than that at the front, and largely echoed its presentation. Neat and tidy, constrained by the walls, and for the most part colorless, except for a profusion of purple flowering butterfly bushes near the west corner. Though now that I could see a glimpse of what was beyond the stone boundaries, I better understood why more time had not been spent cultivating a more pleasing aspect. For what could compete with the view that unfolded once one followed the path through the faded wooden gate and out onto the commons?

Heather-covered moorland stretched toward the cloud-speckled cerulean blue horizon, rolling and rising, unbroken by anything but a small brook that trickled northward. I could see now that Langstone Manor sat on a sort of peninsula of pastures and straggling forest that pushed out into the high moors, so that the house was nearly surrounded by heath. From this vantage, I could see no fewer than four of the tors Dartmoor was so well-known for towering in the distance. These hills topped by their craggy granite outcroppings, each one uniquely shaped, their faces etched and weathered by time, silently stood watch over the bleak landscape surrounding them.

I nearly gasped at the windswept scenery laid before me. There was such a stark beauty to it, a sort of wild desolation, that I felt my breath catch. In many ways it reminded me of the Scottish Highlands, and yet it had a mysterious quality all its own. This was a land that was still untamed and unpredictable when so many stretches of Britain were not, and in that knowledge lay the treachery of its splendor.

"Yes, it does rather have that effect on one, doesn't it?" Gage murmured, standing close beside me.

I tore my gaze away from the moors to look up at him. The gleam in his eyes was almost as poignant as when he'd been staring up at his mother's portrait.

Until that moment, I hadn't known what this place meant to him. He never spoke of it, and I hadn't dared to raise its specter. Not until we received that letter from his grandfather. And even then, when I questioned him, trying to learn about the childhood home we were racing hundreds of miles to reach, not once had he made me suspect he felt anything but aversion for this place. To discover now that had all been an illusion left me reeling.

This place obviously stirred something inside him—something warm and lasting—and yet he had not shared it with me. How much more of my husband did I not fathom? How much more did he keep hidden deep within him, somewhere I could not see to reach?

He blinked against the sudden glint of the sun breaking through the clouds and turned to meet my gaze. Something of my thoughts must have shown on my face, for his expression grew shuttered. I could almost physically feel the door he had opened between us last night being shut, not with a bang, but with a gentle nudge.

"That's the direction the gardener said he assumed Alfred was headed." Rory pointed to the north, over the warbling brook toward a squat tor in the distance. "He'd crossed the beck and might have been peeling off toward the Langstone."

A frown formed between Gage's eyes as he planted his hands on his hips to survey the landscape. "Was he certain the man was Alfred?"

It was some distance to the brook. Far enough that you would not be able to see a person's face clearly, though you could observe their clothing and mannerisms.

"I suspect so, as Alfred had passed him striding through the garden." Rory glanced back toward the manor through the weather-beaten boards. "The gardener found a piece of paper on the ground and supposed he might have dropped it. That's why he stepped through the gate to call after him. But Alfred either didn't hear him or didn't wish to be delayed, for he never turned back."

"A paper?"

"Yes. Torn from one of the Plymouth newspapers. I've no idea why."

"Did the gardener keep it?" he asked.

Rory's head reared back slightly. "I'm not sure. I hadn't considered it. You'll have to ask him."

Gage nodded, taking several strides in the direction Alfred had gone. "Let's follow in his footsteps, shall we? I need to become reacquainted with the lay of the land, so to speak."

The narrow path was scarcely more than a track worn down amid the vegetation. It was plainly little used, and as such, rough going. Rocks and pebbles littered the ground between the tufts of gorse and heather in some places, while in others the plants hid boggy depths which grasped at our boots, trying to steal them from our feet.

As we approached the brook, my husband turned back to warn me. "Be careful here, Kiera. There are loose quarrying stones from an old tin workings flung about."

I followed his advice, shadowing his footsteps as best as I could. We forged the brook with the aid of a few strategically placed stepping-stones, and turned our steps northwest, trailing another branch of the same brook. The land there became easier to traverse, gentler on the soles of my feet, though muddier.

I was glad I'd chosen to wear my short reddish fawn redingote and matching walking dress, for the hem was certain to be crusted with dirt and grass by the time we returned to the manor. If only women could respectably wear pantaloons and riding boots. Though I was sure Gage had selected the color on purpose, his walnut brown breeches still appeared neat and tidy despite the muck splattering his tall boots.

"I know this might sound odd," Gage said, falling into step beside his cousin. "But since you've been handling Grandfather's paperwork, have you noticed anything alarming? Anything that would explain Alfred's disappearance? A large bill or an angry letter . . ."

Rory shook his head. "I apprehend what you're suggesting, but the answer is no. I'm afraid not." He tilted his head in thought. "Unless Hammett circumvented me and delivered it straight to Grandfather."

"Has he done so before?"

"Once or twice." His voice turned wry. "I suppose when it's something sensitive he doesn't believe I should see." He turned to look at Gage. "I know he delivered a letter from your father. I saw it on Grandfather's nightstand."

I could hear the frown in my husband's voice. "When was this?"

"About a week ago."

And yet the viscount had not mentioned it.

But Gage plainly didn't want that to be evident to his cousin, for he nodded. "Ah, yes. What of a will?" he added, switching topics. "I assume he has one. Is it stored in his study or in the possession of his solicitor?"

Rory's mouth twitched. "What do you think?"

"With the solicitor." Gage grinned. "He always was precise."

"And well aware of my mother's machinations."

Gage glanced at him in surprise.

Rory arched his eyebrows. "Don't pretend you're not aware that my mother is constantly scheming to see that Alfred and I inherit all of Grandfather's property. She's done so all our lives."

"I'm just surprised to hear you admit it."

"Yes, well, I no longer have any illusions about my mother. Or my brother, for that matter." He sighed heavily. "They are who they are." His eyes flicked to me and then to Gage. "Just as I have no illusions that I must be a suspect in Alfred's disappearance."

"Why do you say that?" Gage replied, his tone neither confirming nor denying it.

"Because if something should happen to Alfred, I'll become Grandfather's heir."

Gage studied his cousin's features, seeming to try to see into his head.

I decided that while his cousin was being so straightforward, we might as well ask the question we were all thinking. "*Do* you have anything to do with Alfred's disappearance?"

My husband scowled at me.

But Rory only smiled. "No, Mrs. Gage, I don't."

Perhaps it was the fact that he'd listened to my request that he should use my new married name and not my courtesy title that influenced my perception and not genuine intuition, but I felt almost certain he was being honest.

Gage must have agreed, for he ventured to ask another question. One that was perhaps more fraught. "Would it surprise you to learn that your brother wasn't in distress? That he might have decided to go into hiding of his own volition." He paused. "And that your mother might have helped him."

Rory didn't even blink before answering. "That wouldn't surprise me in the least."

CHAPTER SEVEN

I'm not sure who was more shocked by his blunt answer—myself or Gage. Regardless, we both stumbled to a stop.

"Do you think that's what happened?" Gage pressed, finding his words first. "Do you think your mother was either persuaded to help Alfred or pushed him to hide herself because some . . . situation arose where she deemed it necessary?"

"I trust you mean because he's done something that would have infuriated Grandfather, not that he's killed a man or some such thing?" Rory remarked.

"Yes."

He shook his head in bafflement. "I don't know. I doubt they would have qualms about doing just such a thing. But Alfred hasn't angered Grandfather. At least, no more than usual. There's been no reports of misdeeds or irate visitors." He glanced between us. "If he's done something for which he needs to hide, I'm not aware of it."

Gage began slowly pacing forward again, considering his cousin's words.

"Perhaps he doesn't know about it yet," I suggested, falling in step beside Rory.

"It's possible," Rory admitted, though his eyes remained trained on Gage's perplexed profile. "Does this mean you don't think Alfred is really missing?"

"We don't know what to think," he replied honestly. "We're merely attempting to explore every possibility, and everything I know of Alfred tells me he's capable of such a ruse."

Rory nodded.

"*And* someone utilized the same rope-and-knot trick on our bedchamber window that Alfred used to terrorize our tutors."

And possibly stood over us, watching while we slept. Though I hadn't yet mentioned that to Gage, for surely it must have been naught but an eerie dream.

Rory's eyebrows shot skyward. "You think it was my brother?"

"Maybe," Gage replied, watching him as closely as I was. "Or someone else familiar with it."

It was Rory's turn to stumble to a stop as he realized what Gage was implying. "Me?" He gave a harsh bark of laughter. "Why on earth would I do that?"

"I don't know."

Rory frowned at the tightness in Gage's voice. "I did no such thing. I have no reason to." His brow furrowed angrily. "Unless you think me a thief."

Why this statement caused Gage to recoil as if he'd been punched in the stomach, I didn't know, but an entire conversation passed between the two men without either of them saying a word.

"No," Gage finally answered aloud, turning away. "But I had to ask."

There was a new stiltedness in their demeanors as we pressed onward uphill across the moor. The ground here was spongy with peat, and I was beginning to make out the shapes of large rocks nestled among it on the ridge before us. Several sheep from a larger herd milled about the stones, grazing on the tall grasses.

Though I was curious about whatever secret lay behind their silent altercation, I was not sorry for the hush that fell so I could reflect on my surroundings. I was a portrait artist, so landscapes had never been my specialty, but I could well see that Dartmoor was rich fodder for painters of that type. Especially on a day like today when the heath was speckled with vibrant colors—pink heather, yellow gorse, and the amber-tipped grass waving in the wind—and the canvas of the sky was dotted with puffy clouds for contrast. The sun shone bright, almost making me wish I'd left off my cloak, but the clear, cool air brushing my cheeks made me glad for it. Just being there among it all, my artist's muse awakened and stretched. My mood lifted with each step I took deeper into the expanse of the moor and away from that oppressive house.

Unfortunately, Gage did not seem to share my contentment.

"To be honest, I was surprised to hear that Alfred was even staying here at Langstone Manor." His voice was subtly laced with challenge. "I presumed he'd still be in London, pursuing all the pleasures it has to offer, and steering clear of Grandfather's watchful eye."

I was relieved when Rory didn't take up the gauntlet Gage's barbed comment had thrown down, but instead answered with something close to weariness.

"Yes, well, I suspect he's only here for the summer."

"He doesn't usually leave town like the rest of society," Gage replied more tamely.

His cousin kicked at the grass before his feet. "I also think it has something to do with the fact that he'd heard you would be returning to London, with your fascinating new bride in tow." He flicked a glance at me. "He never could stand to be outshone. And you seem to do it at every turn."

Gage didn't attempt to respond to this, and I wasn't sure if it was because he agreed or he was stunned by Rory's answer. Perhaps a little of both.

We'd been prepared for the interest our marriage would draw

among London society. After all, Gage was the handsome and charming golden boy while I was a scandalous outcast. Our union had caused no small amount of shocked and perplexed speculation. We'd been subjected to a degree of unwanted attention and conjecture in Edinburgh during the three months of our engagement and marriage when we'd lived there, but we'd known it was but a taste of what was to come in London. I was not looking forward to such scrutiny.

As we drew closer, I could see that the rocks before us were large indeed. And what seemed to be a random pattern began to take on a definite shape. These had quite obviously been moved here.

The first stone we encountered also happened to be the biggest. The menhir would have stood about nine feet tall had it not fallen out of its socket into the soft peat. It was the end point of what appeared to be a row of smaller stones. A short distance away, the other large stones—most of which had also fallen—formed a stone circle, a rather forlorn formation among the vast emptiness of the moor.

Gage paused next to the menhir, propping one foot on it. "This is the Langstone." Removing his hat, he let the wind riffle through his hair and narrowed his eyes against the sun to survey the rest of the site. "Hence the name of the manor." His arm swept from left to right. "And this area is called Langstone Moor. It stretches up toward Cocks Hill and over to the River Walkham and the bogs and marshes of Greena Ball. A bit to the southeast you can see the granite outcroppings of Great Mis Tor." His arm continued its arc, gesturing to the landscape south of the manor. "That hill further in the distance is Roos Tor." His hand moved past the manor to point toward a mound a quarter of a mile or so to the west. "And then, of course, this is White Tor."

To the north and east, I could see a few farms and pastures, but from northwest around to the south stretched only the expanse of the bleak moor and its enigmatic tors. "What lies beyond?" I asked, wondering what existed past my line of sight.

"A few miles to the south, there are a few towns and settlements. Princetown and its infamous prison are about five miles away as the crow flies. But that way . . ." He gestured toward the brow of Cocks Hill. "You could walk for days without encountering another soul. And if you became lost . . ." There was no need for him to finish that statement.

Despite the warm sun beating down on my back, I shivered at the thought. I now better understood what Gage and his grandfather had meant when they said that men had become disoriented and vanished, never to be seen again. Even in sunny weather, I could imagine the difficulty. But if rain, or snow, or fog hampered your visibility, it would be impossible to know where you were or in what direction you were headed.

Rory's mind seemed to have followed the same track, for his voice when he spoke was somber. "If, for whatever reason, Alfred set off in that direction, I'm not sure we'll ever find him."

We all fell silent, I supposed contemplating the sobering and terrifying possibility.

Then Gage inhaled and straightened. "Well, first we need to figure out just where he was going. Just because the gardener saw him headed in this direction doesn't mean he didn't change course or double back." He turned to his cousin. "What was Alfred doing before he set off on his walk? Who was he with?"

Rory's gaze had strayed to the southwest in the direction of Great Mis Tor, and his thoughts seemed to have followed, for it took him a moment to respond. "Oh, um, I don't know. I remember passing him in the hall on my way to review some correspondence with Grandfather a short time before he must have set out. I asked if he was feeling better, but he didn't reply, just continued walking. He seemed . . . distracted."

"Had he spoken with Grandfather?"

He shook his head. "Not for several days, if I recall correctly. Not since his stomach complaint had begun."

"And how did he seem after that interview?"

"Well, he left the manor, and took his horse and rode off hell-bent for somewhere, if that's any indication. But that wasn't uncommon."

So there could have been an altercation of some kind, one that perhaps Rory wasn't privy to. But if that was the case, if that was the catalyst, then why hadn't Alfred disappeared that night? Had he needed to make arrangements? Had his stomach ailment prevented him from following through?

Or had something unexpected truly befallen him, and all of this speculation was for naught?

I glanced at Gage, curious how he wanted to proceed.

"Before we do anything further, I want to climb White Tor and get a better view of the land surrounding the manor. I suspect you'll appreciate it, too, Kiera."

I eagerly agreed and we set off toward the west. But before we'd even taken a dozen steps, there was a loud snap and I stumbled, almost tumbling into the peat. Gage's arm shot out to clasp my elbow, keeping me upright.

"Are you well?" he asked, his voice tight with concern.

"Yes," I replied uncertainly as I recovered myself. "I . . . I think it was my boot."

We bent to examine my right foot and found the lace had broken. Too neatly, to my mind.

"I don't think it can be fixed," Gage said, examining the cord. He began to pull at the longer lower part of the lace. "But I think I can tie this part around your ankle to keep the boot on your foot. It won't be the most comfortable fastening, but it should allow you to walk back to the manor rather than be carried."

I sighed. "Do it."

I could sense Gage's frustration as he wound the cord twice around my ankle and knotted it with a hard tug.

"How is that?" he asked, rising to his feet again.

I tested my foot, moving forward gingerly. The boot slipped as I walked, the leather gaping, but there was nothing else to be done. I dropped my skirts back into place. "It will have to do."

My husband moved to my side to take my arm. "Then I suppose White Tor will have to wait . . ."

Pressing a hand to his bicep, I cut him off. "There's no reason you and Rory shouldn't continue. I can see the manor from here. I can make my way back alone."

Gage's expression brightened in eagerness, but still he hesitated, out of concern for me. "Are you certain?"

"Yes," I assured him, and then set off by myself before he could argue. "Now go on."

"We won't be long," he called after me.

I waved my hand in acknowledgment and continued my shuffling steps back toward Langstone Manor. I could already feel my spirits, which had been lifted by the walk on the moor and the sunshine, lower again. It was partly disappointment at my not being able to climb the tor, and partly the dread of returning to that dreary house.

Irritation also pricked me, for I had a dawning suspicion that someone at the manor was determined to cause us difficulties and discomfort. First the trunks, then the open window, and now my bootlace. I supposed the trunks and bootlace could simply be coincidences, but combined with the window, I had a difficult time believing that.

Bree was nothing if not careful and efficient. She would have known I intended to use my walking boots while I was here, and she would have inspected them as she polished them this morning. In any case, I had seen the crisply severed edges of the lace. Only one strand of the cord seemed at all stretched. It had not frayed over time, but appeared to have all but snapped in one fell swoop. Such things did not happen. Not often, anyway.

By the time I reached the manor and found my way through

the labyrinth of corridors to my bedchamber, I was in something of a rage. So rather than ring for Bree, I marched into Gage's connecting chamber and tugged the bellpull there. It was only a matter of minutes before Anderley answered the summons.

"Back so soon, sir. I thought you'd be . . ." The valet's voice trailed away in surprise at the sight of me glaring at him instead of his employer.

"Mr. Anderley, I want you to tell me the truth this instant. Are you up to no good?"

I didn't care what Gage's assurances were; I wanted to hear straight from his valet's mouth that he wasn't playing pranks again. Gage might trust him with his life, and likely for good reason. After all, I'd witnessed their cool coordination when a situation grew serious or potentially dangerous. But that didn't mean *I* believed Anderley always behaved with our best interests in mind.

"I . . . I don't know what you mean, my lady."

He seemed genuinely confused; however, I also knew him to be quite a good actor when the situation called for it.

"Are you playing pranks because you're unhappy to be here?"

His eyes widened. "No, my lady. Of course not."

"There's no 'of course' about it."

His mouth opened and then closed, and then he voiced a question of his own. "Are you talking about the trunks?"

"As well as our window being opened during the middle of the night. And now my bootlace snapping." I gestured down to my foot hidden beneath my skirts.

"I've had nothing to do with any of that," he replied adamantly. "Mr. Gage mentioned the window, but he alleged his cousin might be responsible." He tilted his head. "I take it he's not."

I narrowed my eyes, scrutinizing his expression, trying to tell whether he was being truthful. "He says not, and I'm fairly certain he's being honest."

Anderley nodded, gazing back at me uncertainly. He didn't

rush to add further assurances, which swayed me. In my experience, liars often provided too many details.

I crossed my arms over my chest. "Well, given your past actions, you can't blame me for suspecting you."

His shoulders lowered a fraction, sensing my mistrust was waning. "I suppose it serves me right. Miss McEvoy warned me this would happen one day if I did not stop my mischief." His nose scrunched up as if he didn't like admitting Bree had been correct.

I lowered my arms, crossing toward the escritoire where Gage's traveling desk still sat open from when he'd penned his letters this morning. "Yes, well, perhaps it was precipitous of me to assume there's one person behind all of these things," I admitted, wondering if I had been somewhat rash now that my temper had cooled. "Maybe the misplaced trunks and my bootlace snapping *were* both accidents." I frowned, still unhappy with that explanation. "But there's something decidedly odd about it all."

"Yes, well, maybe not so odd."

Suspicion gleamed in the valet's dark eyes.

"You know something." He didn't reply, but I could tell I was right. "You believe you know who is behind all this." When he still didn't answer, I arched a single eyebrow, letting him know I was not going to be fobbed off. He was well aware I was no ordinary society wife, and that my and Gage's marriage was not of the traditional sort.

His scowl darkened. "Lord Langstone's valet, a rather repugnant toad named Cooper."

"You sound as if you are acquainted."

He gave a single sharp nod. "We've been forced to endure each other's company more than we'd like. Though, truth be told, once is one time too many."

"From what I've learned of his employer, I can only imagine, but what in particular makes Mr. Cooper so objectionable?"

"He can't abide the fact that Mr. Gage is considered more attractive and fashionable than his employer, that Mr. Gage's attendance is courted above Lord Langstone among members of society in London." His lips creased into a humorous smile. "Perhaps you don't realize, but a good valet prides himself on his employer's appearance and presentation. If he is not turned out to perfection, then it's a reflection on us. And while we have no control over our employer's charm, or wit, or ability to act like a gentleman, we still take credit for it nonetheless."

I was not familiar with all the particulars of the life of a valet, but having already realized that my appearance was either a credit or discredit to my maid's abilities, none of this came as a surprise. If Mr. Cooper was intent on comparing his abilities to others, it must have been doubly insulting that Gage's company should be preferred over his employer's, given the fact that Lord Langstone was higher in rank and would presumably inherit a greater fortune.

"And this is why you think he's determined to make our stay uncomfortable?"

"What other means does he have to retaliate?"

As a valet, not many.

The idea that Alfred's valet might be responsible for all of this both relieved and aggravated me. In one sense, I was reassured to hear all of it might only be the work of an aggrieved servant. But that same suggestion also made me angry and affronted that he would carry out such petty actions.

It also raised some interesting questions.

"Do you think Mr. Cooper knows anything about his employer's disappearance?" I asked, curious to hear his opinion. I'd presumed since Alfred had left his clothing and his valet behind that he was not involved, but perhaps I'd been too hasty.

Anderley clasped his hands behind his back. "My impression is that he does not, simply because Cooper has never been any good at hiding his thoughts. He seems far too frustrated and out of humor to be parcel to any scheme. I would have expected him to be more twitchy." He cleared his throat, rocking back on his heels. "But just to be sure, I've asked Miss McEvoy to do what she can to convince him to share what he knows with her. I would attempt the matter myself, only I'm certain Cooper would rather don a sackcloth than confide in me."

My lips quirked at the notion.

"As for the damage to your bootlaces, I'll help Miss McEvoy keep a closer eye on your garments, as I've been doing with Mr. Gage's. I didn't think Cooper would sink so low as to tamper with a lady's attire, otherwise I would have said something before."

"Thank you," I replied and then hesitated, another thought having occurred to me. In truth, I'd been lucky my bootlace had snapped where it did. Had I been further out on the moor or descending a staircase, the situation might not have turned out so well. Such a realization made me uneasy, especially when coupled with my troubling dream and the open window. "You don't think he's . . . capable of violence, do you?" I asked as casually as possible.

I appreciated the way Anderley paused to consider my question.

"Not directly. He might slash the dresses in your wardrobe, but he would never have the stomach to assault another person."

I nodded, wishing I felt more comforted by his answer.

Anderley seemed to sense this, for he offered me a reassuring smile. "Allow me to handle him, my lady." His eyes hardened. "And if it turns out he's not the one causing trouble, I'll find that culprit, too."

CHAPTER EIGHT

As expected, Bree was indignant when she saw the damage to my boot. Though she didn't need to tell me, for I already knew, she swore up and down she'd inspected my boots that very morning and there had been nothing wrong with them. In fact, I suspected she was even angrier about the incident than I had been. I assured her I didn't blame her, but her face was still red with outrage when she stomped out to see to the stains at the bottom of my walking dress.

I located my sketchbook and settled onto the fainting couch with my stocking feet tucked up beneath my cornflower blue gown. Despite Anderley's assurances that he would get to the bottom of all this nonsense, I couldn't help feeling a bit out of sorts. Which I supposed was the culprit's exact intention. Part of me questioned whether I was making connections and assigning culpability where there were none. But another part of me—the part that perked up when I sensed something was not as it seemed—told me I was right to be suspicious. And I'd learned long ago not to ignore my intuition, or the consequences could be dire.

In any case, sketching always seemed to settle me when I was tired or strained. Unlike painting, which absorbed all of my attention and made me nearly oblivious to the world around me, sketching merely distracted me from the present while still allowing my brain to percolate on what it wished in the background. I paused with my charcoal poised over the paper, intending to draw the moor, but then I realized a drawing in black and white could never do it justice. A proper rendering of the moor would require paint and a large canvas. And while I would have dearly loved to unpack my supplies and escape into my art, I hadn't the time for such a luxury. Not to mention the fact that Gage needed me here with him, not disappearing into my head. So instead I set about capturing the likenesses of the people who populated Langstone Manor, hoping maybe something my artist's eye had noted might shed light on the investigation.

I began with Lord Tavistock, before moving on to Lady Langstone and Rory. Then, almost without realizing it, I began to draw Emma Trevelyan Gage. My sketch was hazy at best, having only the portrait in Tavistock's study to model it off of, but it seemed somewhat fitting, seeing as my understanding of Gage's mother was also hazy.

I couldn't help but be drawn to the puzzle of who Emma had really been. After all, she had arguably been the single most important person in Gage's life, and yet, I knew so little about her. I knew she'd defied her family to marry the man she loved, even though he was beneath her in rank. I knew she'd brought her son back here to live rather than remain in Plymouth alone, presumably because of the illness that plagued her for most of Gage's life. I knew she'd been murdered by her maid, Annie—poisoned to keep her ill and in need of Annie's care, until one day the poison became too much for her body. But that was all.

Gage shared his memories of her so rarely. He seemed to keep them locked away inside him, somewhere I couldn't reach. After meeting several members of the Trevelyan family, I could better understand his intense loyalty to her, but I didn't really have any better sense of who she was than I had before.

Who was this woman who had chosen to return to a place she must have been desperate to escape rather than tough it out in Plymouth? Had she been so ill she feared for her safety? Had she believed raising her son at Langstone would provide him with better opportunities, that it would prepare him for a future beyond what Gage's father had at that time been able to provide? If so, I couldn't fault her logic. After all, had Gage not shared his cousins' tutors, had his grandfather not insisted he attend Cambridge, he would not be the man he was today.

It was difficult to imagine Gage without his veneer of gentlemanly polish. Even without the benefit of the education Lord Tavistock had been able to supply, I had no doubt Gage would have acquired knowledge somehow. He was far too intelligent not to. And his mother would have instructed him in at least the basics of correct behavior. But he would not have been the smoothly refined, elegantly charming man he was today, nor the darling of society. He would have been like his father, feigning an ease with the world he lived in, but knowing he was never truly of it.

I frowned down at the woman I'd sketched. And that was part of the trouble, wasn't it. Perhaps Emma hadn't known she and her son would face such harassment and belittling when they arrived at Langstone, but once she discovered the treatment Gage faced, had she questioned her decision? Had she wondered if this was the best place for him? Why had she stayed?

Upon his return, Gage found me reclined on the fainting couch still grappling with these conundrums. I blinked up at him, wondering how long he'd been standing over my shoulder without my realizing it. I opened my mouth to speak, but then noted the somewhat haggard look in his eyes. Glancing down at the sketch of his mother his gaze was riveted on, I apprehended why.

"I'm sorry," I murmured, closing my sketchbook. My cheeks flushed with guilt, feeling somehow I had trod where I shouldn't.

"Perhaps I shouldn't have . . ." I fumbled for the right words, not wishing to upset him more.

But before I could find them, he gently rested a hand on my shoulder. "No. It just . . . caught me off guard, that's all. I don't mind if you sketch my mother. Though that portrait artist painted her nose wrong. It was more like my grandfather's, but not quite so long."

I set my sketchbook aside and rose to my feet. Smelling the scent of Gage's cologne and the starch applied to his cravats, I noted that he'd already changed into fresh clothes. His hair was also slightly damp, curling about his forehead and the base of his neck.

Pressing a hand to the navy superfine fabric of his coat, I leaned up to press a kiss to his lips. I sensed this was not the time to ask him about his mother, about their past. The look in his eyes had been too raw. So I returned to more pressing matters. "Discover anything else of interest?"

He shook his head. "Not particularly. Everything seemed just as I remembered it."

I waited to see if he would mention anything about Anderley or the bootlace, but his mind seemed consumed by other things. In any case, I had not expected his valet to tattle about our conversation. That would be up to me whether I chose to do so. Anderley might have his faults, but he had never tried to interfere between me and Gage. At least, not since his employer's interest in me had become fixed.

"I'm going to have a word with Grandfather," Gage said, his thoughts still distracted. "Would you like to accompany me?"

"Of course."

Hammett had explained earlier that one of the best times to visit the viscount was after his midmorning nap. By that point the congestion from overnight would have had time to clear and the morning dose of medicine to take effect. Combined with the extra rest and the sun shining through what windows there were, it usually rendered him in the best mood.

Regrettably, today that wisdom did not hold true.

As we entered his chamber, he was barking at a servant I suspected was his valet, sending the man scampering from the room. His eyes lifted as he passed me by, seeming to communicate he wished us luck in dealing with his irascible employer.

Lord Tavistock reclined back into his mound of pillows, smothering a cough. "Well," he rasped upon catching sight of us. "Have you found my grandson yet?"

"I think you know the answer to that," Gage replied calmly as he approached the bed. "After all, we're investigators, not wonder-workers." He paused, studying his grandfather's gaunt face. "How are you?"

"I'm old," he snapped, waving his grandson's concern aside. "Tell me what you've learned."

But Gage wasn't willing to be ordered about. Instead, he took his time settling into his chair next to the bed. "When did you last speak with Alfred? How long before he disappeared?"

The viscount's scowl deepened. "What concern is that of yours?"

"It may have some bearing on the investigation."

"How?"

Gage didn't sigh aloud, but I could tell he was suppressing his exasperation. "Grandfather, you asked me here to find Alfred. If you wish me to do so, you need to trust my methods." His brow furrowed in annoyance. "And you cannot expect me to report on my progress twice a day."

Lord Tavistock's face contorted as if he'd bitten into something rancid and he was about to spit it out. It was evident he wasn't accustomed to being defied, but given his circumstances he was in no position to make demands. He flicked a glance at me and then begrudgingly relented. "I spoke with him three days before he vanished. Among other things, we spoke about his neglect to take any interest in the estate. *Which* he promised to remedy."

Gage was not willing to be diverted so easily. "What other things?"

His grandfather's expression remained thunderous despite the cough that rattled up from his throat. "My health, the state of the roads, his engagement. I can't recall every last thing!"

"Did you argue?"

His silver eyes turned piercing. "You think he snuck away. That he chose to leave. But I *told* you I know that's not what happened. I *know* it."

"Yes, but how do you know it?" Gage persisted. "Simple intuition could be telling you something is wrong, I'll grant. But I doubt it's being specific enough as to tell you that natural causes are not to blame."

His grandfather turned away, his mouth clamped in a stubborn line.

"Do you have any enemies we should know about? Did Alfred?"

"No more than usual," he muttered.

Gage's hands fisted in aggravation, and I sympathized. For a man who'd gone to such lengths to bring us here to find his heir, his grandfather was remarkably unforthcoming. Which only made me wonder if I had been correct in my initial suspicions. Did he already know where Alfred was and had used his grandson's hiding as an excuse to draw Gage here? If that was the case, if reconciliation was the goal, he wasn't doing a very good job of it.

"You haven't received a ransom note, have you?" Gage asked. "Do you suspect he's been kidnapped?"

The viscount turned back at this bit of guesswork. "No, I haven't. That would make this entire matter a bit easier, wouldn't it? At least knowing what happened to him." His voice tightened with strain at the end, and I wasn't certain his suppressing a cough was entirely to blame. He seemed genuinely troubled.

However, Gage did not hear it as such. His eyes flashed in anger. "I heard you tore down Windy Cross Cottage."

His grandfather stiffened. "It wasn't being used anymore. You made it clear you had no need of it." He shrugged in feigned indifference. "And after a time it simply became an eyesore."

"Yes, it always was one, wasn't it?" Gage snarled before rising to his feet and striding from the room.

I offered the viscount a tight smile of commiseration before following my husband. It was evident to me there was a world of suppressed emotion behind much of what Lord Tavistock had said. Emotion my husband could not sense while repressing his own hurt. But although I didn't know all the details that had led to Gage refusing to set foot here for fifteen years, I was strongly of the belief that the fault did not lie with my husband. As such, any further efforts toward reconciliation needed to begin with Lord Tavistock. After all, Gage had already set aside past hurts to come to his grandfather's aid. Whether the stubborn old viscount was capable of doing what needed to be done remained to be seen. But if we found Alfred before Lord Tavistock could put his pride aside long enough to make things right, I didn't think Gage would ever give him another chance.

I frowned. I couldn't let that happen. Not when I sensed Gage needed this.

If his grandfather didn't act soon, I might be forced to meddle.

By the time I caught up with Gage, he'd already turned the corner toward the stairs that would lead him to the more public rooms of the house. I grabbed his arm before he reached them.

"Sebastian, wait," I murmured, using his given name as I did when we were alone. I hoped it might gain his attention since his other name had not.

He whirled about to face me, anger and resentment still flashing in his eyes. And beneath those were the ever-present pain and confusion I suspected he'd been carrying nearly all his life.

I pressed a hand to his chest, wishing there was something I could do for him. Some way to ease all the old hurts that had resurfaced. For him, being here was like prodding an old wound, one that had never fully healed.

"I suppose you think I'm being too hard on him," he snapped.

I shook my head, answering calmly. "No. But . . ." I hesitated to say more. "I do think you need to be a bit more patient with him."

"Patient?! Alfred has been missing for twelve days. How long does he want him to remain so?"

I arched my eyebrows in gentle chastisement, for we both knew that was not what I was referring to. "He has things he wants to say to you. You just need to give him a little more time to get there. You said it yourself, he's stubborn and proud. It's not easy for him to admit weakness or failure."

He exhaled heavily as if laboring under a great weight and turned to stare at the dull suit of armor situated in the corner where the corridor made an abrupt turn. "I suspect you're right. He just . . ." His hands fisted at his sides. "He makes me so furious."

I grimaced in understanding. "If it's any consolation, I think you infuriate him as well."

"Good," he retorted, but then as he considered what I'd said, he gave a low chuckle. "Oh, what a pair we make," he sighed.

My smile turned more genuine. "Yes. The two of you together make lovely company."

He chuckled deeper, pulling me into his side.

Seeing his good humor restored, I ventured to ask the question that was nagging at me. "What is Windy Cross Cottage?"

He glanced down at me.

"It's been mentioned twice, and given your reaction just now it's obvious how much it means to you."

His embrace slackened, but he didn't release me. "That's where my mother and I lived."

"Not here at the manor?"

His gaze hardened again. "We weren't fit to reside in the manor. They were determined to never let her forget what her choice in a husband meant." He shook his head when I would have offered him consolation. "But it turned out for the best anyway.

Then my mother didn't have to contend with Aunt Vanessa's constant slights or hear my cousins mock me. All told, I was up at the manor, for my lessons and such, far more often than she was."

I couldn't help but feel a stab of empathy for Emma Gage. How lonely that must have been. To have your husband far away at sea for nearly fifty weeks out of a year and then be separated from the rest of your family because they were ashamed of you. However, I also couldn't repress the irritation that had been simmering inside of me at the continued evidence of her failure to shield her son. From everything I'd heard thus far, he was the one who had protected her at every turn—keeping all the hurtful things inflicted on him to himself rather than upset her. They'd moved here when Gage was but three years old. What mother allows a child so young to carry such a burden? I knew she'd been ill off and on, but I had a difficult time believing she was not aware of what was happening.

Yet another piece to the puzzle that was Emma Trevelyan Gage.

I repressed a sigh. Perhaps I was being too hard on her. Perhaps my own dormant motherly instincts had been roused by my delayed courses a few weeks before and had made me too sensitive to the subject. Though I wasn't expecting now—at least, I didn't think so—it was only a matter of time before I was.

In any case, there was no doubt Gage's mother had loved him. And I wasn't about to share my conflicting reflections about her with her son. Gage adored his mother, and if he wasn't resentful of her behavior, I wasn't going to make him so. The rest of his family had already proven to be less than loving. Giving him doubts about the one person who had truly loved him would be horribly cruel. If only the rest of his family, including his father, had loved him so well, there would have been no need for either of them to protect each other.

Hearing the sound of someone stirring at the end of the corridor to our left, Gage tucked my arm through his and led me down the stairs.

"So how do you propose we spend our afternoon?" I inquired, hoping to steer our conversation toward lighter topics, especially given the fact that we might encounter Lady Langstone or Rory at any moment.

"I think a visit to Alfred's friend at Kilworthy Park is in order."

Recalling his aunt's comments on Mr. Glanville at dinner the evening before, I had to agree.

"I've already checked with Hammett and discovered it's only five miles distant. And in any case, I would welcome the chance to gather my thoughts."

I nodded, hearing his unspoken feelings as loudly as if he'd voiced them, for they echoed my own. Apparently, I wasn't the only one feeling confined by the stone walls surrounding us. Any opportunity to step away for even a short time was a welcome one.

CHAPTER NINE

Kilworthy Park sat nestled in a wooded valley to the west of Langstone Manor. The lands themselves would have been quite impressive if not for the obvious neglect. Gates hung off their hinges, a window in the gatehouse was shattered, and the lane was overgrown. Even the rambling Georgian monstrosity of a manor seemed to be falling apart—quite literally, if the pile of masonry near the base of the south tower was anything to judge by. Mr. Glanville was obviously in dun territory, and dangerously so if his house was crumbling around him.

I didn't know what to anticipate from such a man, and told Gage so.

He'd been quiet most of the trip, mulling over everything we'd learned. But as we rolled by the derelict gatehouse, he leaned forward to gaze out the window at the property. "Mr. Glanville is the very definition of a wastrel. I've had the dubious pleasure of his company on occasion, and while he's relatively unobjectionable, he's also perfectly useless. And content to be so."

We heard the thwack of a branch hitting Tavistock's carriage and then a rather colorful curse from the coachman above.

"What does he do with himself?"

"Drink, gamble, and visit dubious establishments." Gage tilted his head toward me. "As I said, nothing useful. I think his only goal is to spend his father's money. Which he seems to be doing at remarkable speed," he added as we rounded the unkempt lane in front of the manor.

"Who was his father?"

"Sir Francis Glanville. He was knighted for some service to the Crown, served as a Member of Parliament, and was attributed as a highly successful investor in the East India Company, among other things. From what I recall, he actually disowned his son for his profligate ways, but then relented just before he died."

I stared up at the gargoyles projecting from the roofline. "Perhaps he had no one else to leave the money to," I murmured softly, uncertain I would like to live in such a building even if it were in better repair.

"Whatever the reason, I'm afraid that's not really our concern. However, the fact that this building has upwards of thirty or more rooms, any of which Alfred could be hiding in, is."

We were shown into a massive drawing room with mismatched floor rugs and high ceilings smudged with soot. The fire in the hearth cast little heat, even when I was standing directly in front of it, and I wrapped my arms tighter about me, grateful I'd retained my sapphire blue redingote instead of passing it to the butler with my hat and gloves. Between the dented wood and saggy cushions on the furniture, and the fading wallpaper and chipped plaster along the fireplace, it was clear the interior of Kilworthy Park had fared no better than the exterior. The air smelled sour and not altogether pleasant, and I found myself eager to finish this errand and be gone.

When Mr. Glanville charged into the room, I was more than grateful for the distraction from our surroundings.

"Gage," he boomed, reaching for my husband's hand. "It's good to see you, old chum." Glanville was broad shouldered and tall, nearly as tall as my husband. But what must have been an impressive physique at one time had since softened with indulgence. Most of his clothes stretched taut over his frame, straining at the seams, save for his coat, which hung from his shoulders. It was evident that garment had once belonged to someone else—a man whose figure must have been massive in order for his coat to dwarf the man before me. I guessed Glanville was only about five years older than Gage and his cousins, but he looked much older.

"And this must be your mysterious wife," he proclaimed, turning to me to bow in greeting. "Please, please, have a seat. What brings you to my neck of the woods?" he quipped, jauntily using the Americanism as we all settled into our chairs.

"We're here about my cousin, Lord Langstone," Gage replied.

This pronouncement sent all the humor fleeing from our host's face. "Yes, I'd forgotten you and Alfy were related," he muttered almost under his breath before raising his voice once again. "Well, whatever trouble he's gotten himself into, I'm afraid I've nothing to do with it. Not this time, anyway."

For a moment, this vehement response made Gage fumble for his words. "What makes you think he's in trouble?"

He sat forward, gesturing broadly. "Because the Dowager Lady Langstone came charging in here making all sorts of accusations. As if I had him locked up in my attics. And I'll tell you what I told her. *I don't know* where Langstone is. Haven't seen the fellow in over a month." He sank back with a sigh of exasperation. "If ye ask me, he probably hared off to London without telling her."

Gage and I shared a look, wondering why his aunt had been so quick to imply that Glanville had come to her and not the other way around. Except that a lady racing off to confront one of her son's profligate friends was not exactly becoming behavior.

"Could he be staying with one of his other friends in the area?"

Gage asked, testing to see how much of what Lady Langstone had said was true and how much was fiction.

"How should I know?" he snapped. Some of the irritation began to drain from his face as he glanced between us, clearly having realized something. "Wait. You're inquiry agents. So if you're here, then . . . Is Alfy actually missing?"

"It appears so."

Glanville scraped a hand through his thinning hair, making some of the strands stand on end. "Well, dash it all. I thought he was just dodging his mother."

Gage leaned forward, bracing his elbows on his knees. "Why would he need to do that?"

"Because . . ." Our host paused, considering us before he continued. "Because she could be a right harpy when she had a mind to be. Always haranguing him for one thing or another."

Considering who we were, I supposed he'd decided he didn't care what we reported back to Lady Langstone, or if his words got his friend into trouble.

"Was there anything in particular she harangued him about more than anything else?" Gage asked, struggling to mask his disapproval at the man's rude comments. He might not like his aunt, but she was still a lady.

"Marriage, for one. Wanted him to settle down. Put his neck in the parson's mousetrap."

"I'm told he was about to become engaged."

Glanville gave a bark of laughter. "To Lady Juliana? Not if he could help it."

"What do you mean?" I asked in surprise.

"They were pressuring him to marry her, but he was having none of it. Not that he objected to *her*, precisely. Or the dowry she would bring with her. But he wasn't interested in being leg shackled to anyone."

Gage didn't appear to be shocked by this pronouncement. "Were they threatening to cut him off if he didn't comply?"

"I don't know about that. But I doubt he would spread that about were it true." He winked at me where I perched in the most comfortable spot I could find on the far edge of one of the settees. "Doesn't exactly ingratiate yourself to the publicans or the ladies."

Gage's brow furrowed in annoyance. "You said you hadn't seen him in over a month. Was that normal?"

Glanville sat back, rubbing his jaw. "That's the thing. When he was down from London, I usually saw him a couple of times a week. Not that we kept a schedule or anything. But he would kick over the traces and come see me, or I'd find him acting corky at one of the local taverns and join in."

"But not recently?"

He shook his head. "And the last few times I did see him, he acted strangely. I would have said he was simply having a fit of the blue devils, but there seemed to be more to it than that."

"You say he was in low spirits?"

He grimaced. "Yes. Sort of. Maybe," he vacillated. "To tell you the truth, I don't really know what to call it. I only know he wasn't his usual self."

"And what was usual?"

I could hear the same frustration in Gage's voice that was growing in me. Though Glanville was sharing plenty of information with us, most of it was unspecific. This seemed to be his nature and not a deliberate attempt to stymie us, which only made his blather all the more irritating.

Glanville's eyes flicked toward me. "You know. On the cut. Friendly with the muslin. Happy to stand huff."

I nearly rolled my eyes at his ridiculous overuse of cant. Evidently, he assumed it was some sort of code I wouldn't be able to decipher.

Gage's tone was droll when he responded in kind. "So because he wasn't jug bitten, and consequently unwilling to frank you and pay your way, that meant he was behaving oddly?"

"Exactly," he exclaimed, missing Gage's use of sarcasm. He

frowned. "The barmaids were always keen on Alfy. I couldn't understand why he was suddenly turning them away."

"Maybe he was weary of it all."

"Maybe," Glanville conceded, though his expression communicated he considered such a notion to be cracked.

Gage opened his mouth to say more, but then closed it again as a young maid entered the room, stumbling under the weight of a tray. The dishes rattled as she set the salver down on the chipped surface of the table before her employer. Her relieved sigh was audible as she straightened and bobbed a quick curtsy before escaping the way she'd come.

Glanville sat forward and reached for the decanter of amber liquid, pouring a liberal splash into his glass. "Help yourselves," he declared, pushing the tray across the table toward me.

I might have been offended by his terrible manners if I hadn't already been anticipating them after listening to his absurd mode of speech. Had he been born to a lower class or even at the disadvantage of being an American, his behavior would not necessarily have incensed me. But I was quite certain Mr. Glanville had been raised properly, with every opportunity a gentleman is afforded. His uncouth comments and complete disregard of etiquette were nothing more than evidence of a rude, selfish man.

As such, I didn't bother to hide my scowl. Not that it deterred him in the least.

Gage accepted a glass of brandy as well, perhaps wishing for some fortification to help him through the rest of this conversation. For a moment, I considered pouring myself some of the libation, but then decided my disregarding the rules of decorum would only sanction Glanville's boorishness. However, after taking one sip of the weak, tepid tea, I wished I'd followed my first inclination. Rather than choke it down, I set it aside, not bothering to hide my distaste.

This only made Glanville grin. "Now you know why I prefer the brandy."

Before I could snap back a retort, Gage lowered his glass and redirected the interview to the reason for our visit. I bit my tongue, knowing the sooner we got the information we came for, the sooner we could leave.

"In the past, had you and Langstone ever traveled to Plymouth?"

We'd already spoken to Tavistock's coachman about this very topic, but I was curious how Glanville would answer.

"Together? No. But I've seen him there, at the theater and the pubs along Union Street." Glanville gestured with his glass, sloshing the liquid inside. "Is that where you think he's gone?"

"We're looking into it, but I have my doubts."

Glanville nodded as if he agreed and drained his glass before reaching for the decanter to refill it.

Gage studied him intently. "So you truly have no idea where Langstone is or what might have happened to him?"

Lowering the glass bottle with a clatter, our host glanced up at him almost in surprise. "Haven't the foggiest." When Gage continued to scrutinize his demeanor, a glower creased his features. "Listen here, if you're trying to imply I'm hiding him here somewhere, in my attics or wherever, you're welcome to have a look. Search the entire house for all I care." He sat back, lifting his glass to take another swallow. "You won't be wasting *my* time."

My husband glanced at me and I shook my head, having a difficult time believing Glanville would be a loyal enough friend to conceal the fact that Alfred was here, let alone allow him to stay under his roof for an extended amount of time in the first place.

"What if you had to speculate?" Gage pressed. "Is there someplace he might have gone we haven't thought of?"

Glanville shook his head, his mouth set mulishly.

"How about enemies? Do you know of anyone who might wish him harm? A wronged lover or her male relatives? Another drinking companion? A . . . a tenant of Langstone?"

Glanville's brow lifted. "This might be nothing, but has Lord Tavistock mentioned the Swing letters he received?"

Gage stiffened. "Alfred told you Lord Tavistock received some Swing letters?" His voice was sharp with shock.

Our host nodded. "We talked about it mostly in jest, for a handful of the landowners in the area got them, including me. Though I've no idea why. Couldn't afford one of those new threshing machines even if I wanted one." His lips curled, trying to make light of the matter even now, though it failed to amuse me or Gage.

"Swing letters?" I asked, hoping one of the men would explain what they were talking about.

"There's been widespread rioting among the agricultural workers in the south and east of England since last autumn," Gage turned to say. "Thus far it's only included the destruction of threshing machines and the burning of wheelhouses and hayricks—things of that nature. My father has been keeping me apprised of the situation in case it should escalate into anything more serious."

Into something that should require his investigative skills. I could read between the lines.

"Yes, but why? Don't the threshing machines make their jobs easier?"

"For the laborers whose jobs the machines don't displace, yes. But farmers and landowners now require less men to bring in the harvest, and have lowered the wages of those whom they do still employ. The workers have been banding together, and in some cases sending these Swing letters to the farmers, magistrates, and others who they think are responsible for their problems. They threaten to take action if their demands aren't met."

"Namely raising wages and getting rid of their threshing machines?" I asked.

"Precisely." He glanced at Glanville, who had been listening quietly while nursing his latest glass of brandy. "Though I hadn't realized there was any rioting occurring so far west."

"For those with land to be planted, there's been some unrest." He gestured with the hand holding his glass, splashing liquid onto the floor. "Not like we've heard of to the east. But some." ·

"Has there been much destruction?"

He shrugged. "A burning or two."

I sat forward away from the cushions, wondering if the sour stench I smelled clinging to the settee was spilled liquor. "Is that the only action they threaten to take? Setting fire to the machines and such?"

"From what I understand, the threats are quite vague." Gage's tone trailed away in bemusement as we watched Glanville try and fail to rise from his chair twice.

When finally he gained his feet, he crossed to the writing desk positioned in front of one of the windows and rummaged around in the drawer. Having located what he was looking for, he grunted in satisfaction and returned to thrust something under Gage's nose. "Here."

I leaned forward to see they were letters of some kind. Gage read the first one aloud.

Sir, This is to acquaint you that if your threshing machines are not destroyed by you directly we shall commence our labors. Signed on behalf of the whole, Swing.

His mouth twisted wryly. "Fairly straightforward." He passed me the first letter while he unfolded the second.

Sir, Your name is down amongst the Black Hearts in the Black Book and this is to advise you and the like of you . . .

He broke off, and I glanced up from my perusal of the first note. Clearing his throat, he started to read again.

This is to advise you and the like of you to make your wills.

His eyes flicked up toward me as he continued.

Ye have been the Blackguard Enemies of the People on all occasions. Ye have not yet done as ye ought. Swing.

"That sounds like they're threatening more than the destruction of property," I said.

"I would say so."

He spoke lightly as he passed the second letter to me, but I could see that his eyes were troubled.

"And you said Alfred claimed the ones they received at Langstone Manor were similar?" he asked Glanville.

"I assume so. We didn't discuss the specifics."

Our host's words had begun to slur, and I realized it was time to bring our interview to a close. But first I had one more question.

"Who is Swing?"

"That would be Captain Swing, a sort of mythical mouthpiece for the rioters," Gage explained. "It refers to the swinging stick of the flail used in hand threshing."

"So it's not a real person?"

He grimaced. "No. And Father says all the letters he's seen have exhibited different handwriting, so there's no reason to think any one person has taken on that personification. The rioters seem to use it at will."

Which meant tracking down the specific man who had sent these letters and the letters to Lord Tavistock would not be so simple. *If*, in fact, the same person had even sent them.

"May we keep these?" Gage asked Glanville, who slouched lower in his chair.

He waved them away. "Take 'em. Oh, and if ye do find Alfy..." He grinned as we rose to our feet. "Let him know he owes me fifty quid."

CHAPTER TEN

"Well, that was an enlightening conversation," I remarked as we jolted down the uneven lane.

"Which part? The part where we discovered Aunt Vanessa lied, or the part where we learned my grandfather is not sharing everything he knows?"

I reached over to touch Gage's hand where it rested on his leg, drawing his gaze away from the window. I heard the frustration in his voice, felt it tightening his muscles.

At the sight of my empathetic smile, he exhaled, sinking his head back against the squabs. "I'm not sure why I expected them to be forthcoming. People always have something to hide. Even family." He gave a dry chuckle, revising his statement. "*Especially* family." His eyes slid toward the view outside the window again. "I guess I hoped that given the stakes, they would be more forthright with us." His mouth screwed up in disgust. "Unlike my father."

Lord Gage had much to answer for, particularly when it came to his deception and dishonesty during our last inquiry. But now was not the time to rehash that. There would be plenty of time during our journey on to London after this matter with Alfred was resolved.

"I suppose I can understand why your aunt wasn't truthful with us," I said, beginning with the person whose lies Gage found easiest to stomach. "Given what I know about her, she would hardly want it known she lost her cool composure and rushed off to confront a known profligate in his own home. Somehow I suspect she would deny she ever screamed like a harpy."

Gage's lips quirked, as if he might enjoy witnessing such a sight. "True. She rarely ever lost her temper that I can recall. The icy slices of her tongue were usually more than effective."

I jostled into his shoulder as the carriage wheel thudded into a particularly nasty rut and then turned out of the drive onto the road. "I suppose this explains the odd manner in which she hastened to tell us Glanville had called on her without our even asking. She wanted to discourage us from visiting him because she didn't want us to know the truth."

His leg bounced restlessly beneath our joined hands. "Given the fact that Aunt Vanessa rushed off to confront Glanville, and Hammett's assurance that he searched every part of the manor's property, I think we have to conclude that my aunt is not helping Alfred hide."

He sounded less than pleased to concede such a thing. I supposed because it was the simplest solution. And one that would do his aunt and Alfred no credit.

"I agree," I replied. "That doesn't mean Alfred isn't hiding somewhere, but I don't think Lady Langstone is involved if he is. I also think Glanville was being honest when he said he had no idea where his friend was. I don't think he would have bothered to fib for him if he had."

Gage nodded. "He would've had to make some sort of effort to retrieve Alfred from the moors, and I can't see that happening. You'll recall, no one at any of the farms along the roads bordering that part of the moor reported anything suspicious. I have just as hard a time imagining none of them saw Glanville's carriage rumble by as I do believing one of those people would lie about loaning my cousin a horse, as Aunt Vanessa suggested."

I released his hand and shifted in my seat so that I could see him better. "So if he's not with Glanville or being hidden by his mother, then where is he?" I nibbled my lip in deliberation. "Could he be with another friend?"

Gage tapped his fingers against his leg. "I don't know. But . . . I think we have to consider the possibility that he actually met with some sort of harm."

"Because of the Swing letters?"

"Among other things." His expression grew grim. "The truth is, I find it increasingly difficult to believe Alfred would disappear on his own in such a manner, and for *such* a long time. Without his clothes, or his valet, or his horse. From what I know of my cousin, he would *never* have the patience to hide for so long. Not merely to avoid my grandfather's wrath."

Even though the things he said about his cousin were less than complimentary, genuine apprehension crept into his voice. He might not like the man, but he plainly still cared about him.

I rubbed a hand over his arm in comfort. "Maybe Alfred has changed?"

"Maybe," he replied, though his tone of voice said that was doubtful.

Having never met Alfred, I had to defer to Gage's knowledge of him. But I was also aware that sometimes those who were closest to us also held the greatest bias.

"Glanville claimed Alfred started acting oddly a month before he disappeared. Drinking less, ignoring women, refusing to pay his friend's way, avoiding him. Do you think he might have begun to reconcile himself to an engagement with Lady Juliana?"

Gage scoffed. "I think it more probable he was already suffering from a stomach complaint."

I gazed at him in gentle chastisement. "You're not being very impartial."

He scowled as if he wanted to argue that point, but then sighed. "You're right. I'm not." He raked a hand back through his golden hair, thinking over the matter. "It's possible. It's also possible Grandfather simply cut off his funds. Though, such a thing has never stopped Alfred from buying on credit in the past, and I can't imagine it would now either."

"Has anyone spoken to Lady Juliana? Perhaps she knows something."

"We can ask, but I doubt it."

"Then perhaps we shall have to pay her a visit as well."

He pressed a hand to the breast of his coat, underneath which he'd stowed the letters Glanville had given us in his inner pocket. "I would like to ask her father if he's received any of these Swing letters, either at Endsleigh House or any of his other properties."

"Why do you think the viscount failed to mention them to us? If they're worded anything like Glanville's letters, wouldn't the sender have been an obvious suspect?" I tilted my head, mulling over the possibilities. "Could he have forgotten?"

It was clear Gage didn't like the suggestion his grandfather might have forgotten such an important thing. "I don't know. Given his certainty that someone caused Alfred harm, I would have expected him to eagerly show us any such letters." His eyes narrowed as a thought occurred to him. "Unless he doesn't know about them."

"Rory," I murmured, following his line of thinking.

"He said he's been handling much of the estate business, as well as Grandfather's correspondence. At least, the missives Hammett doesn't confiscate first. And I doubt he would trouble himself over a few nondescript letters."

"Perhaps Rory decided, given the viscount's health, it would be best not to trouble him over them."

Gage tilted his head in acknowledgment. "It's probably what I would have done."

I plucked at a piece of lint clinging to my cornflower blue skirt. "But . . . then why didn't he tell *us* about them?"

"That's a very good question." He turned to look out the window into the slanting rays of the late afternoon sun. "One I think we should ask him."

"To be honest, I hadn't connected them to Alfred's disappearance," Rory told us when we cornered him in the viscount's study a short time later. He must have been able to read the skepticism in both of our faces, for he hastened to explain. "They just seemed so . . . ridiculous. I set them aside and never gave them a second thought."

"Did you read them?" Gage asked incredulously.

His brow furrowed in mild affront. "Of course. But their grammar was so horrendous, and the threats . . . well, I thought them naught but toothless yammering."

I arched my eyebrows at this excuse. So a man needed to use correct grammar in order for his threats to be taken seriously? Could Rory not hear how foolish he sounded?

"Here." He bent over, rummaging in one of the lowest drawers in the desk. Finding what he was looking for, he thrust the folded papers toward Gage. "Read them yourself."

I leaned closer to see over his shoulder, discovering two of the letters read almost exactly like the first one Glanville had shown us. The third grew harsher in tone, but unlike Glanville's second letter, it made no reference to causing bodily harm. It merely declared that the destruction of the threshing machines would be coming, as would a list of their further demands.

Gage shuffled back through the pages. "These are all the letters you received?"

"Yes. The last one arrived about three weeks ago. But no one has damaged any of the estate's property *or* made any further demands." Rory raised his hands in bewilderment.

"Have you shown Grandfather any of these?"

He shook his head. "I didn't think he needed to be bothered by them. You know how he is. They would only make him livid."

The cousins shared a look of mutual understanding.

"What of Alfred? I assume he was aware of them?" I asked. Glanville had said as much.

"Yes, I showed him two of them," Rory replied. "He thought them a colossal joke."

"Could he have decided to do something about them?"

Rory's gaze was rife with scorn. "I suppose it's possible."

I looked up at Gage. "Maybe he confronted someone over them and the matter turned ugly?" I shrugged, not really knowing if that was a likely scenario or not.

"Perhaps someone from one of the farms bordering the moor to the north?" He narrowed his eyes on the tall stone hearth beyond Rory, considering the matter. "That would explain why he was seen walking in that direction. And why no one in that area has admitted to seeing him. If someone caused him bodily harm, or intended to cover for someone who had, they wouldn't speak up." He huffed an exasperated breath. "It's as good an explanation for his setting off across the moor as any I can think of."

Had I not been looking at Rory, I might not have seen the loathing that flickered briefly over his face. His gaze lifted from where he stared down at the desk and caught me watching him. A beat passed before he spoke, and it was that tiny hesitation that made me wonder if what he told us next he'd intended to keep to himself.

"As to that, I've been thinking. I believe I may have an alternative explanation." He tapped the edge of the desk. "I think he might have been paying a visit to Lorna Galloway. Her cottage doesn't lie directly on that path, but it's not a terribly roundabout way to go. Especially if the moor was swampy that day and he wanted to avoid some of the more spongy heath that lies to the east."

"Who is Lorna Galloway?"

Here he hesitated again, as if he wasn't certain how to describe her. "She's a local woman who lives out on the moor. A by-blow of Lord Sherracombe's. He set her mother and her up in a cottage along the River Walkham. A rather isolated place. People rarely venture out that far. The mother died several years ago, but her daughter still lives there."

"Alone?" Gage asked in disapproval.

Rory nodded. "I've heard Sherracombe has offered to find her a better situation, but she refuses to leave."

I sympathized with this Miss Galloway. As the illegitimate daughter of a nobleman, the term "better situation" was rather misleading. The best she could hope for was either a position as a teacher at a girls' boarding school or an arranged marriage to a man who was willing to overlook her low birth in favor of the connection to her father. At least by remaining out on the moor, she was somewhat the master of her own fate. The cottage might be owned by her father, but she was free to do as she pleased. Though her life could not be easy, and must be quite lonely at times.

"I guess she prefers her solitude," Rory added with a shrug, dismissing her decision as something akin to a whim.

"But why would Alfred visit her?" Gage tilted his head. "Unless you're implying she's taken after her mother."

"Well, do you honestly expect any different? Living out there on her own, no husband, no guardian."

The sins of the mother . . .

It was generally expected that the child of a parent with loose morals must necessarily follow in their footsteps, but Rory's words left a bitter taste in my mouth nonetheless. In truth, his callous opinion made me worried for Miss Galloway. Whether she entertained men of her own accord or not, the fact that men assumed she would placed her in a dangerous position, particularly residing in such an isolated place. I only hoped her father had made it clear she was under his protection. That would at least give her some shelter from blackguards, even though their scruples would be held in check by their desire not to cross his lordship rather than qualms about overpowering a woman.

Similar considerations flitted through my husband's mind, for his mouth pursed in distaste, and I loved him all the more for it.

"I hope Alfred isn't . . . taking advantage of the situation," he remarked with disapproval.

Rory huffed. "I should say it's much more likely the other way around." He leaned forward, giving Gage a significant look. "She's a genuine eye-biter, if ever I've met one."

Gage scowled. "You don't mean . . ."

"I do," he stated with conviction.

When my husband's scowl only deepened, my curiosity rose.

"What's an eye-biter?" I asked.

"An eye-biter is . . ." Gage paused to consider his words, almost as if he didn't want to say them. "Well, she's a witch who enchants men with her eyes."

The base of my spine tingled. "A witch?"

He looked uncertainly at his cousin. "Yes."

The use of that word always alarmed me, for I'd been tarred with the same brush by those who saw my enforced involvement with my late husband's anatomy work as proof that I was unnatural. They'd made up all sorts of appalling rumors to support this belief, even going so far as to accuse me of being a siren, a murderer, and a cannibal. So I was always wary when the term was bandied about without any further proof whatsoever of its veracity.

That being said, I did have Scottish blood flowing through my veins. As such, I wasn't quick to dismiss the existence of superstitious things. After all, I'd encountered my fair share of strange phenomena I couldn't easily explain—second sight, ghostly apparitions, unsettling curses. However, the intensely logical side of myself found it difficult to wholeheartedly accept any of it as truth. There was always room for doubt.

Gage, on the other hand, had rarely wavered in his belief that such occurrences had a rational explanation. Perhaps one we simply could not yet deduce or understand. Which was why I found it so intriguing that he didn't immediately contradict his cousin's assertion about Lorna Galloway. Though his reply was not without a hint of skepticism.

"And you think she's . . . bewitched Alfred?"

At this Rory seemed to soften his disdain, for he shrugged. "I know he's visited her several times in the past few months." He leaned forward in his chair. "And Mother claims he's been drinking some sort of tincture Miss Galloway gave him."

"I assume you're suggesting this tincture is connected to his stomach complaint," I asked when Gage didn't speak up, but instead silently studied his cousin.

"Can you tell me that's not suspicious?" Rory challenged.

"I would say it's interesting, but until we know what was in that tincture and when exactly he started ingesting it, I wouldn't care to speculate."

Rory's eyes hardened and I could tell he wanted to make an angry retort, but he merely jerked his head in confirmation.

In truth, I did find the fact that Alfred was taking some sort of remedy from Lorna Galloway highly suggestive, but not necessarily for the reasons Rory did. Had Alfred sought out Miss Galloway specifically for the tonic, and if so, why? Had he been suffering from his stomach complaint much longer than we realized? Or was some sort of other illness plaguing him?

"Did Alfred keep the tincture in his chamber?" Gage asked.

Rory shrugged. "I assume."

"Then we'll have to search his rooms for it. I suppose a visit to this Miss Galloway is also in order." He slid forward in his chair, preparing to rise. "*After* we speak with those in the village and surrounding farms about these Swing letters."

A soft creak issued from the direction of the doorway, but when I glanced behind me, no one entered. I turned back around to find both men watching me. "I thought I heard something."

"It's an old house," Rory replied, as if that were explanation enough. But he cleared his throat as Gage pushed to his feet. "You might want to speak to Grandfather before you go to the village."

"To tell him about the Swing letters? I intend to."

"Well, yes, and . . ." He grimaced. "I'll let him explain. Just . . . don't go anywhere without speaking to him first."

Gage and I shared a look of mutual exasperation. What else had they been keeping from us?

CHAPTER ELEVEN

"What do you mean most of the villagers don't know Alfred's missing?" Gage's voice snapped with restrained ferocity. A ferocity I couldn't blame him for. I also felt it itching along my skin.

Lord Tavistock scowled up at his grandson from his bed. Even though the evening light filtering through the windows should have been kinder to his appearance, he looked worse than he had that morning. Dark circles ringed his eyes as he struggled to remain upright even with the support of his mound of pillows. But the stubborn man wouldn't recline further. He was determined to face us on as equal a footing as he could manage.

"Discretion was called for." His throat rattled with congestion. "The situation is delicate. I couldn't have the Duke of Bedford finding out before I knew what had happened. Otherwise he might withdraw his permission for Alfred to court his daughter. And if the worst should come to pass, forbid Rory from paying court in the future. So I instructed the men to be circumspect in their search."

"Yes, and I'm sure that approach yielded adequate results," Gage sneered, turning to pace up and down the length of the bed.

"I'm sure their search was thorough. Probably saved us a lot of unnecessary trouble by not having every commoner from here to Yelverton knocking on the door to offer up one made-up story after another in exchange for a reward."

Gage paused in his pacing and joined me to glare down at his grandfather in disapproving disbelief. Did he wish to find his grandson or not?

Had one of my loved ones gone missing, I would have scoured the earth for them, left no stone unturned to find them, especially if their safety were in question. But Lord Tavistock continued to give conflicting information. One moment he was certain something bad had befallen Alfred—even going so far as to suggest it had been foul play—and the next he was telling us not to ask questions in the village. Not yet.

If I was frustrated by his fickle, contradictory behavior, Gage must have been beyond exasperated.

"Are you expecting him to just come strolling up the lane?" he demanded.

"No! I expect *you* to find him." His grandfather stabbed a finger up at him. "Without a lot of fuss." He pressed a handkerchief to his mouth, trying to stifle the cough that rattled up from his chest.

The hoarse sound of it alarmed me. When I flicked a glance at Gage standing next to him, his face seemed to close in on itself, wiping away all trace of emotion.

"That's why you asked me here to investigate, isn't it?" he asked once his grandfather's coughing subsided. "Your chief concern was discretion. And by asking me, a family member, to handle the matter, you believed you would get it."

He spoke with indifference, as if the truth didn't greatly concern him, but I could sense the roiling sentiments beneath the surface. I knew how much such a realization must cut him.

His grandfather didn't know him as well as I did, so he could not know the pain he caused. Or perhaps he did and didn't care. Either way, his only response was a cold stare.

To break the standoff, I stepped closer to the foot of the bed. "So I take it no one has spoken to Lady Juliana about the matter?"

Lord Tavistock turned to me in annoyance. "No."

I considered the viscount. His body appeared to be shriveling before our very eyes, sinking into the mattress. And yet his eyes gleamed like two silver daggers, resolved to exert his will, whatever the cost.

"*Would* Lady Juliana know anything about all of this?" After everything we'd learned, I found it difficult to believe Alfred had shared more than pleasantries with her.

"How should I know that?" Lord Tavistock replied defensively, perhaps unwittingly providing an answer to my question.

"Somehow I don't think Alfred was as keen to marry Lady Juliana as you've led us to believe."

He lifted his chin, attempting to stare down his nose at me. "The boy will do as he's told."

Gage's mouth quirked derisively, telling me that was doubtful. "Is that what you and Alfred argued over? Was he refusing to marry the Duke of Bedford's daughter?"

His fists clenched where they rested over the counterpane as he bit out his next words. "He had some misguided notions I had to correct him over." Then suddenly the tension in his body released and his face paled as he sank deeper into the pillows. "I don't wish to talk about this anymore." He closed his eyes. "It has no bearing on the matter at hand anyway." He blinked open his eyes to look at Gage for a brief second before shutting them again. "Just find Alfred."

I wasn't so certain his impending engagement to Lady Juliana was unrelated to what had happened to Alfred, and I could tell Lord Tavistock wasn't either, but it was pointless to pursue the matter now. Not when he could barely open his eyes. Our conversation had fatigued his already exhausted body. He needed to rest.

Gage followed me from the room, but when I would have turned left to return to our chambers, he grabbed hold of my hand and pulled me to the right instead.

"Where are we going?" I gasped as we hurried around several corners.

"To search Alfred's room."

"Are we racing someone?"

He slowed his steps. "My apologies." His voice was stilted with residual anger. Seeing his grandfather in such a weakened state palpably upset him, but it was easier to be irate. Less complicated.

"I'm as eager as you are to find out if any of the tincture Rory mentioned is in Alfred's chamber, but shouldn't we be dressing for dinner?"

"I can't stomach the idea of eating dinner with Aunt Vanessa and Rory just now. We'll have trays sent up. Do you mind?" he asked almost as an afterthought.

"Of course not." As if dining alone with my husband was any hardship. After all of our travel and this day's rushing about, I would have quite happily secluded myself in my chamber with naught but Gage for company for an entire week. But given our current investigation, I would take what I could get.

In truth, much of the urgency of our quest had drained from the situation. Alfred had already been missing for nearly a fortnight, so any trail he *had* left behind had already grown cold. Combined with the fact that his family, many of the key players in this melodrama, were being less than forthcoming about all they knew, it was impossible not to notice that our inquiry was hopelessly stagnant. One night away from our hosts could not harm our progress any more than their deception was already doing.

We veered down a corridor heavily cloaked in shadows and stumbled to a stop. Even the sconces in this part of the manor were not lit.

Gage backed up a step. "Stay here." Retracing our path, he picked up two candlesticks sitting on one of the tables. Then he reached up to light their wicks from the flickering flame of the last wall sconce left burning. Returning to me, he passed me one of the candles and took my hand to guide me down the passage.

The air here seemed cooler than in the other part of the manor. Perhaps because it felt uninhabited, almost forgotten. And yet Alfred's bedchamber was here.

Unless Gage was wrong. Maybe his cousin had switched rooms in the years since Gage last visited.

I opened my mouth to question him when something fluttered in the corner of my eye. Something pale and gossamer. My heart climbed into my throat and my steps faltered.

"What is it?" Gage asked as I forced myself to look behind me. There was nothing there.

"What?" he reiterated.

"Nothing. I . . . I just thought I saw something, but I . . . must have imagined it," I replied haltingly. But even as I spoke the words I felt a chill across the back of my neck. It trailed downward, as if someone had stroked a finger along my spine.

"It's probably just the ghosts."

"Ghosts," I squeaked.

"Be calm," he chided gently, pulling me forward. "I was joking." I swallowed. "Oh."

We halted before a door and he frowned. "My cousins used to try to tell me the manor was haunted. They swore a gray lady and a man named Stephen roamed the corridors. Stephen? Really?" he scoffed. "You'd think they could have been more subtle."

Given the fact that Gage's father's name was Stephen, and since he had been away at war fighting on a Royal Navy vessel so they never knew from one day to the next where he was, I thought it particularly cruel. "They claimed it was your father?"

"They never went so far as to do that. But they implied it." His brow furrowed. "Though Rory told me once he supposed it was actually the spirit of the Stephen who has a grave marker at a crossroads on the moor near White Tor."

Before I could ask why that Stephen was buried there, Gage pushed open the door to the bedchamber. The scents of sweat, cologne, and traces of smoke wafted toward us, confirming that this room was indeed still inhabited. But one step deeper into the chamber also told us that in Alfred's absence it had not gone undisturbed.

In the gloom, I might have mistaken the mess for simple untidiness, except that it seemed apparent someone had been searching for something, and recently. Drawers hung open, their contents rifled. The doors of the wardrobe gaped, the clothes hanging inside having received similar treatment. No self-respecting valet would have left his employer's garments in such disarray, and from what Anderley had told me, I gleaned that Alfred's valet was even more fastidious than most.

I turned to ask what Gage made of the matter, and was surprised to see that he'd expected this. His eyes registered no shock, only weary acceptance.

"How did you know we would find Alfred's room like this?"

He leaned down to pick up a book that had fallen to the floor. "Because I fear our presence has set something in motion rather than bringing it to an end."

"What do you mean?"

He shook his head resignedly. "I'm not sure how to explain it, except . . ." His gaze lifted to meet mine. "No one was looking very hard for Alfred before our arrival. Not even Grandfather. Not truly."

"And yet he urgently sent for you," I murmured, trying to follow his line of thought.

"Yes, he sent for me, and then proceeded to hamper our search with half-truths and omissions. He told us he's concerned Alfred may have met with foul play, but he doesn't want us to ask too many questions. It doesn't add up."

I hesitated to ask the question that needed to be asked, knowing it would cause pain, but it had to be addressed. "Do you think your grandfather's illness might have . . . compromised his faculties in some way?"

He set the book carefully on the nightstand and lit another candle as he considered my query. "I don't know," he reluctantly admitted. "It's possible. He certainly wouldn't want to admit it if that were true." His jaw hardened. "On the other hand, he seems perfectly capable of refuting or dodging *only* the questions he doesn't wish to answer."

"True," I murmured, crossing to the dressing table, where a few bottles were arranged on a silver tray. Either the person who had been here before us had taken greater care not to disturb their placement, or whatever they'd been looking for would not be found in liquid form. I glanced cursorily through the labels, finding nothing out of the ordinary—cologne, pomade, ointment.

Gage opened and closed drawers behind me while I sifted through the contents of the dressing table, finding nothing of interest. Leaving my candle on the table, I moved on to the wardrobe and flicked through the array of clothing, checking the pockets of the coats. I was about halfway through my search when I paused to wonder if there was any way to tell whether there were garments missing. Alfred's valet would know. But would he tell us?

"I assume this is the tincture Rory mentioned," Gage said.

I joined him on the opposite side of the bed, taking the bottle he cradled from his hands. It was nearly empty and filled with a muddy brown liquid. I tilted it closer to the light of his candle, trying to analyze its contents.

"There's also this." His hand reached into the top drawer of the second nightstand and extracted a bundle of plants, roots and all, tied together with a white string. Now wilted and withered, some of the once-green stems sported tiny flowers while others supported a bristling seed head.

"What is it?"

"Herb bennet. It grows in the hedgerows all throughout Dartmoor." He brushed his finger over one of the dead heads. "And these little burs stick to everything. Including little boys' clothes."

I smiled at the image of a young Gage traipsing home covered in burs, but my amusement quickly fled. "Why did Alfred have some of it tucked inside his bedside drawer?"

"That I don't know."

Scrutinizing the dried stalks, I wondered if there was a book on plant and herb lore in Langstone's library.

He replaced the sad bouquet in the drawer while I retained hold of the bottle.

"What did you think of what Rory said about Lorna?" I asked as he sat on the edge of the bed to open the lower drawer.

He paused for a second before reaching in to sort through the jumbled contents. "I assume you mean that bit about her being a witch." He lifted out a sheet of foolscap and then tossed it back in after a brief glance. "Well, there are many definitions of a witch—a wisewoman; a healer, or hedge witch, as the locals would say."

I crossed my arms over my chest. "You know very well which definition your cousin was implying."

He sighed and glanced up at me, closing the drawer. "I do. And you know me well enough to know I think it's a lot of nonsense. I'm not sure why Rory is spouting such claptrap. I would have thought him more sensible than that." He raked a hand through his hair as he stood. "Whatever the case, if Miss Galloway gave Alfred this tincture, then she's a hedge witch. And Rory plainly mistrusts her."

"I agree. Which makes me wonder why he didn't mention her or her tincture sooner. And why didn't your aunt?" Setting the bottle next to my candle, I resumed my search of the shadowy confines of the wardrobe while Gage moved on to the escritoire.

"As I said, half-truths and omissions," he groused. "Ones that seem pointless." He shuffled through the papers and detritus littering the top of the desk, not bothering to take care with their contents.

When the rustling stopped, I looked over to see him holding what appeared to be a newspaper. "Have you found something?"

When he didn't respond, I moved closer to see what had captured his interest. It was an edition of *Woolmer's Exeter and Plymouth Gazette* dated July second. He flipped the newspaper over to what should have been the front page, running his thumb down the torn left edge.

"I suspect *this* is where that article Alfred dropped came from," he said.

I had to agree. "Have you spoken to the gardener about it?"

"No, but I'll ask Hammett to arrange an interview tomorrow morning." He folded what remained of the newspaper and tucked it under his arm. His eyes strayed toward the nightstand. "Then, if the fine weather holds, I think it would be best to pay Miss Galloway a visit." He frowned. "I suppose we'll have to ask Rory to show us the way."

I only hoped he was better at hiding his disdain for her than I presumed or Miss Galloway must certainly be aware of it. If that awareness tainted her perception of us, then any of our attempts to gain information from her might prove futile. I'd been on the receiving end of such contempt many times, and it always made me less than willing to cooperate.

"Do you think he's the person who searched this room?"

"Perhaps. If so, it's hard to know what exactly he was looking for. After all, we found the tincture and this newspaper." He scowled at something in the shadows near the hearth.

Picking up his candle, he crossed the room and knelt next to the corner of the rug. Rather than lying flat, it had rolled up under itself, as if something had caught on it. *Or* someone had lifted it and not replaced it correctly.

"Hold this." He passed me the candle and paper and pulled the corner of the rug back to see beneath it.

At first nothing seemed amiss. Nothing was stashed beneath

the rug, and the smooth wooden floorboards appeared straight and even. But when Gage stepped forward, there was an audible creak. He stomped his foot, locating the exact board that was making the sound, and then knelt to pry at the cracks. I leaned closer, holding the light up for him to see.

Once Gage found the right grip, the board easily lifted away from the floor to reveal a cavity beneath. He reached for the candle and shone the light down into the hole, finding it empty of all but dirt and dust. Even so, for good measure, he cautiously prodded the opening for anything that might have been left behind.

"Well, it appears whoever searched this room before us found what they were looking for," he declared, sitting back on his legs. He sighed in exasperation. "And I haven't the foggiest idea what it was." He dropped the board back into place with a thud and then rose to roll the rug back over it.

"If not Rory, who do you think it could be?" I asked. "Lady Langstone? Alfred's valet, Cooper?"

He shook his head, staring at the rug. "I don't know. But it's clearly something they didn't want someone else to find. Whether that means it has something to do with Alfred's disappearance, I don't know. Not yet."

I knew that tone of voice and that set of his jaw. Stubborn resolve practically exuded from his pores.

"But we're going to find Alfred by whatever means necessary. Even if my grandfather doesn't approve." His expression turned troubled. "Whether I like him or not, as his cousin, I owe Alfred that much."

I didn't contradict him, though my opinion was precisely the opposite. He didn't owe his blackguard cousin anything. Not after the way Alfred had treated him.

But because Gage was a good man, an honorable one, I understood why he needed to try.

"You think something bad has befallen him, don't you?" I

murmured, able to read between the lines. "You're worried he's been injured . . . or worse." I reached for his hand, taking it between my own.

He spoke quietly. "It seems more likely now than it did before." He swallowed. "And dead or alive, he deserves to be found."

He didn't mention anything about bringing him justice, but if the worst should have happened, if Alfred had met with violence, that desire would swiftly follow.

CHAPTER TWELVE

Cresting a windswept rise, we pulled our horses to a stop to gaze out over the landscape. From our vantage at Langstone Manor, and even walking northwest toward the Langstone, I'd not realized how varied the terrain was. Instead of one gradual, continuous rise, the moor undulated in dips and waves, sinking into valleys carved by the rivers and streams that flowed through it before climbing again. Below us the River Walkham ambled its way gently southward. But across its banks soared Great Mis Tor, its craggy slopes speckled with rocks and its summit topped by impressive towering stacks of granite.

A smoky haze had settled over the moor overnight, one that the brighter rays of the sun hadn't yet burned its way through. But in spite of the mist, the air boasted a crisp, clear quality I'd experienced few other places. One that had a sharp, almost acrid undertone, and made the mouth pucker, but not unpleasantly.

Turning my eyes to the south, I glimpsed the stony peaks of Roos Tor and Great Staple Tor. Behind us to the east lay the manor and the village of Peter Tavy beyond. To the north stretched the desolation of Langstone Moor, its gorse and heather broken only by the occasional stone, and what appeared to be the remains of an old settlement.

I should have been overawed by the site—and I was—but I also felt uneasy, skittish. I'd dreamt again of a man watching us while we slept—a shadow looming over the end of our bed. But when I woke, there was no one there. Although, unlike the night before, the window had not been open.

I wasn't sure what to make of it. Was it a dream, an image conjured by my imagination? Perhaps influenced by our inquiry and the secrets that seemed to hide around every corner of Langstone Manor.

Or was someone haunting us, entering our chamber by another means? Gage had blocked the entrance to the secret passage, but what if there was another? Or what if the intruder had simply entered through one of our bedchamber doors? If so, how was it possible that I was awake enough to be conscious of his presence and yet unable to rouse myself to confront him?

I repressed a shiver at the disturbing prospect.

Sensing my apprehension, my horse danced to the side and tossed her head. I took a firmer grip on her reins and my tumbling nerves, and brought her back around while I forced calm, steady breaths through my lungs.

Gage cast me a curious glance, and I offered him as reassuring a smile as I could muster. In any case, it must be obvious to him that something was amiss. He knew well my skill with horses, and if a spirited gelding was unable to throw me, then I was certainly capable of handling this docile mare. Rory, however, was not familiar enough with my proficiencies to know better, and I'd done nothing to dispel that notion as he and Gage discussed horseflesh during our ride.

"What's gotten into you, Eyebright?" Rory chided, reaching over to grip her bridle.

The pretty bay mare whickered in protest and then sank her

head in shame. I felt guilty for letting her take the blame, but it was better that I not explain my anxieties to Rory.

Now that the horse was settled, he gave me a gentle smile and lifted his hand to point to a spot across the river. "That's Lorna Galloway's cottage."

Nestled among the bell heather and bilberry on the lower slopes of Great Mis Tor, not far from where the river curved to the east, perched a small stone cottage. *Cottage* being a somewhat ubiquitous term, ironically encompassing everything from humble one-room dwellings to lavish country residences boasting upward of twenty rooms. I hadn't known precisely what to expect. But this home definitely fell closer to the modest end of the category.

I found it difficult to picture Lord Sherracombe riding his horse all the way out here to visit his mistress. I wasn't sure if such an arrangement spoke more to his character or his mistress's. Whatever the case, I hoped she'd loved the moor, just as I hoped her daughter did, because they certainly lived in the depths of it.

I couldn't help being curious about this woman who'd been raised in such relative isolation, with naught but her mother and occasionally her father for company. Dartmoor was hauntingly lovely, but also wild and unforgiving. Such an environment must have imprinted on her soul somehow. Perhaps that was why Rory was so certain she was a witch.

I nudged my horse forward, trailing Rory down the hill toward the river. Our steeds carefully picked their way through the rocks along the banks of the river upstream until Rory found a place for us to cross. Along this upper valley, the river was by no means wide, but it was riddled with slick rocks. One wrong step by man or beast could result in broken limbs or a deadly head injury.

"There's a stone slab bridge further upstream." Rory nodded toward the north. "But it's too narrow for the horses."

But not too narrow for Alfred to have used. It further explained why Rory had suggested he might have headed northeast away from the manor and then across to the east before turning south.

Rory guided us to a spot where the river was shallow enough I could see the pebbled bottom. Thirty feet or so further up the stream, the water cascaded musically over a stretch riddled with rocks, slowing the flow of water. This ended in what amounted to a crisp little pool where small trout darted to and fro. The location of Miss Galloway's cottage had been chosen with care. The cascade would provide clean drinking water, and the pool offered an abundance of fish.

Once across, we followed a narrow trail along the river's edge, which utilized a natural indentation in the rising slope of Great Mis Tor so the climb was not so steep. The path then leveled off and led away to the north and the stone cabin.

Glancing about me, I couldn't see another habitation or living soul, merely rocks, heath, and sky. If one climbed to the top of the tor, I imagined you could see for miles around on a clear day. But at this lower point you might have believed yourself the only person in the world.

It was beautiful, and its solitude called to my artistic nature, making me want to hole myself up here in this desolate spot and paint until I was too exhausted to stand. And then wake up and paint some more. I'd rarely had time to indulge myself in such a manner in months. I could already feel my fingertips tingling with the desire to grip my specially weighted brushes.

The idea of living such an isolated existence also chilled me. Not so long ago, I'd considered just such a life. Worn down and disillusioned by all that had befallen me after the scandal over my involvement in my late husband's anatomy work, I'd thought to seclude myself in a cottage much like this. My sister and brother would have both been happy for me to continue shuffling between their households, but I'd begun to feel the weight of being such a burden to them. Withdrawal had seemed like it might be a better option. Had Gage not suddenly entered my world and made me long for more, convincing me to risk my life and my heart even after all I'd been through, I might very well have ended up just like Miss Galloway.

Except I wouldn't have been completely alone. I knew my family. They might have let me live in my little cottage, but they would never have stayed away. I would have had frequent visitors. But according to Rory, Miss Galloway had no one but an absent father.

"Miss Galloway lives here all alone?" I asked Rory again, feeling a sort of trepidation at the prospect of seeing the other side to the coin I'd flipped.

Rory glanced over his shoulder, allowing me and Gage to ride our horses up alongside his before he answered. "Yes. Gossip in the village says she let the charwoman go who used to come out to her cottage to cook and clean several times a week. The same woman whom Sherracombe had hired to do so for her mother since he moved her out here." His voice was tight with a disapproval I didn't understand, for this action had no bearing on him. Unless he alleged the charwoman's dismissal was to keep her from prying into Miss Galloway's witchy activities.

As we drew closer to the stone cottage, I could see that it was indeed small, likely boasting only two or three rooms. A curtain in one of the windows twitched, and a few moments later a young woman emerged onto the small stone porch extending from the house in the direction of the river. She moved toward the corner closest to us, crossing her arms over her chest as she watched us approach. Her stance didn't appear the least inviting.

Neither did her face as we drew near enough to see it, though it was lovely. Large, heavily lashed eyes narrowed at us, and her pale pink lips puckered in antipathy. I could hardly blame her, especially when I glanced at Rory and saw the thinly veiled contempt gleaming in his eyes. Had I been able to reach him and also do so subtly, I would have elbowed him in the ribs.

Rory might distrust her, but thus far she'd done nothing to earn our disdain. We were the ones trespassing on her favor, so to speak. Unless the sight of her unbound hair was what had so riled him. Her long blond locks fell past her waist, tied back from her face with a ribbon like a young girl might have worn. As a rule, women did not wear their hair down among polite society, but then again, she probably hadn't been expecting company. However, the rest of her appearance was faultless, even somewhat modest, given her high-necked, lace-trimmed rose-patterned dress and kid boots.

In any case, Gage seemed unruffled by her appearance, giving her one of his most charming smiles. "Pardon us for the intrusion," he demurred, breaking the rules of protocol to speak to her before his cousin could properly introduce us, undoubtedly out of fear of what rude remark Rory might open with. "We don't wish to impose upon your time." He nodded to Rory. "But my cousin said you might be able to help us."

"How is that?" she retorted, not softening in the least under Gage's attention.

Ignoring the hostility in her gaze, he dismounted so that he could speak with her at her level. Or a little below her level, as the height of the porch put her above anyone standing below. "I'm Sebastian Gage, and this is my wife."

She flicked a glance at me as I also dismounted, quickly dismissing me.

"We're looking for my cousin, Lord Langstone. His grandfather is concerned because he's been missing for nearly a fortnight. The last anyone saw of him, he walked out onto the moor and never returned."

Miss Galloway tilted her head. "And what is that to me?" It was spoken as almost a challenge. She must have known what people presumed about her. She would have to be soft in the head not to. But it was obvious she resented those assumptions.

"We thought you might have seen something." Gage hesitated. "Are you acquainted with Lord Langstone?"

Miss Galloway arched a single eyebrow, clearly aware we knew the answer to this question. I almost smiled at her refusal to be taken in by Gage's charm and careful handling.

"I'm sure Mr. Trevelyan has already informed you of that fact."

She shot Rory a venomous look where he still remained on horseback.

"Is he here?" Rory replied bluntly.

I could see that Miss Galloway wanted to deliver him a scathing set down, but she settled for a sharp-worded "No" instead.

Rory narrowed his eyes in suspicion.

"When was the last time you saw him?" Gage interjected before Rory could speak again. "Could he have passed this way?"

She exhaled in frustration. "I already told the men who were out searching for Lord Langstone during the days immediately after he apparently went missing that I'd not seen him in over a week. I'm sorry he's missing, but I can't help you." She spread her hands. "I don't know where he is."

"Did he ever say that he planned to go away, or mention any friends he intended to see?"

She shook her head, her patience growing thin.

"Was he acting strangely in any way that last time you saw him?" Gage hastened to ask before she cut him off.

This question made her brow furrow, though I couldn't be sure why. Truth be told, I was having difficulty interpreting her mannerisms. She was guarded and irritated by our presence, but had she also adopted her angry, rigid behavior to mask the fact she was lying?

Before she could form a reply, Rory spoke again, making me wish we'd left him behind and found our way here on our own.

"Why did you dismiss old Mrs. Dunning?"

I assumed he meant the charwoman he'd mentioned earlier. A matter which, as far as I could tell, had no bearing on Alfred's disappearance.

Any softening that Gage had painstakingly achieved with Miss Galloway was lost as her spine stiffened. "I don't believe that's any of your business."

"What are you doing in that cottage that you didn't want her to see?"

She gave a mocking laugh. "What do you *think* I'm doing? Brining cats? Filleting fenny snake?" she quipped, borrowing from Shakespeare's *Macbeth*. "Poisoning entrails?"

But this last taunt struck too close to Rory's suspicions, and he pounced on it like a cat with a string. "Are you making poisons? Is *that* why you sent Mrs. Dunning away?"

Miss Galloway scowled. "Why should I pay someone else to do something I can do for myself?"

"If Lord Sherracombe is willing to compensate her, why would you want to do the work yourself?" Rory sneered.

I could sense the frustration simmering within her that she would never be able to make such a man understand, so I quietly answered for her.

"Because life is fickle."

She lowered her gaze to meet mine for the first time since we'd been introduced.

"Because Lord Sherracombe might not have the decency or the foresight to leave her anything in his will, and his heir might not wish to continue to support her."

Something flickered behind her eyes, a sort of understanding, as she recognized I was far more familiar with her situation than she would have ever guessed.

When Sir Anthony had died, he'd left me little more than a pittance. The rest had gone to his cousin—a man who had never liked me, and absolutely despised me after learning of my part in Sir Anthony's work. Had my sister and her husband not welcomed me into their home, I would have had nowhere to go, and barely enough money to live respectably, albeit humbly for a handful of years. After that my only choice would have been to remarry or find some form of employment in the few positions open to impecunious gentlewomen. That is, *if* I could convince a man or an employer to overlook my lack of fortune and scandalous past. I shuddered to think what would have become of me if not for my family.

Men like Rory and even Gage had never had to worry about such eventualities. Even as a second son, Rory could rely on Lord Tavistock to bequeath him a significant enough portion that he would never need worry about survival. His brother might eject him from Langstone Manor when he inherited, but he would have enough funds to live elsewhere without difficulty. Just as Gage had known since a young age that he would always inherit the portion Lord Tavistock bestowed on him as the future child of his mother in Emma and Lord Gage's wedding contract. This had enabled Gage to live his life without being under his father's thumb, and had made our marriage possible. Otherwise, I was certain Lord Gage would have cut him off without a farthing for daring to defy him and wed me.

As such, even though Miss Galloway's life had been very different from my own, I still felt an affinity for her. Her intelligence and spunk only made me predisposed to like her more, as well as her refusal to cow to either Rory's badgering or Gage's charm. Such delight in her actions was counter to our aims, but I enjoyed it all the same.

Miss Galloway's green eyes gleamed at me, as if she recognized the pleasure I was taking in her defiance.

"I comprehend your predicament, Miss Galloway," Gage replied politely. "But it really is most urgent that we find Lord Langstone. Is there truly no assistance you can give us?"

"I suggest you search her cottage," Rory declared. "I wouldn't be surprised to find she's hiding him. That or you'll find evidence of his belongings. Perhaps when her poison didn't work on him she killed him by a more direct method."

Miss Galloway's glower returned, though this time it was also tinged with a perplexity I shared. Why was Rory so antagonistic? His remarks went above and beyond mere condescension. And why was he suddenly so certain she had played some part in Alfred's disappearance? The location of her cottage, isolated out here among the moors, was convenient to the last place Alfred was seen, but one could hardly cast blame based on the placement of a person's dwelling.

"*You* are not entering my cottage," Miss Galloway retorted to Rory and then nodded at Gage. "And neither is he." Her eyes then fell to me. "But I'll allow Lady Darby to search if she wishes."

So she was aware of who I was. Gage had introduced me as his wife. He'd made no mention of the title from my first husband I retained out of courtesy. Who had told her about me? Alfred? The villagers?

I stepped forward, willing to put our curiosity to rest, and hopeful she would more readily answer our questions without Rory glaring sullenly down at her from the horse he'd never dismounted. But Gage reached out a hand to halt me. I looked up into his pale blue eyes, able to read his concern. Though he had the courtesy not to say the words aloud, I knew he was asking me whether following Miss Galloway inside was a wise thing to do.

I arched my eyebrows, uncertain what exactly he assumed would befall me inside. Did he think Miss Galloway would attack me? Or was he more worried about her casting a spell?

"I'll be fine," I assured him in a low voice.

Miss Galloway stood by her door, ushering me inside. Although I didn't share Gage's trepidation, I still paused ever so slightly at the threshold. Yes, I felt a kinship with this woman, but I didn't truly know her. What if I was wrong to believe she didn't wish me ill? After all, I'd been fooled in the past.

I met her gaze, and the steady, watchful regard she returned helped me take the final step inside. If she were intent on harming me, wouldn't she have given me a reassuring smile in order to coax me into her domain?

Even so, my heart kicked in my chest as she slammed the door shut behind us.

CHAPTER THIRTEEN

After all of Rory's allusions to witches, I'm not sure what I had expected to find, but it wasn't the cozy room into which she ushered me. The cottage was indeed tiny, but every space had been used with such clever economy that it didn't feel confining. The front half of the main room was set up as a kitchen, including a table and benches, a cupboard, and an iron rack from which pots hung. Various herbs hung from another part of the ceiling, being dried before they were stored in the jars that lined several shelves below them.

A large stone hearth dominated the center of the room, dividing the kitchen from a small sitting area with two well-worn chairs. Thick woolen blankets draped over the backs of each, while a round table set between them boasted a stack of five or six books. Below it rested a basket of mending on a threadbare but well-cared-for rug covering the slate floor.

My eyes were first drawn to the chairs and then the door at the far side of the room. It was impossible to tell whether both chairs had been used recently, for they both sported permanent indentations in the fabric. But if Alfred was hiding here, he was likely through that door.

"You can take a look," Miss Galloway told me, following my gaze. "But I assure you, there's no one there."

I wanted to believe her, but I also knew I needed to at least peek inside. Crossing the small space, I opened the door and quickly scanned the contents of the room. They were few, naught but a bed covered in a faded quilt, a dresser, a rug, and a few dresses hung on hooks. Though I felt silly and somewhat embarrassed doing so, I lifted aside the quilt and peered under the bed. There was nothing but a few boxes, just as I'd expected.

Still, as unobtrusively as possible, I sniffed the bedding and the air, trying to detect if a man's scent lingered here—his cologne, his musk, anything that was unlikely to belong to Miss Galloway. But the sheets smelled of lavender, and the flowers sitting in a vase on the dresser concealed most of the other odors.

Returning to the main room, I noted that the drying herbs also perfumed the air, overpowering even the scents of any recent cooking. It was obvious this had not been done with intention, but if Alfred had been here it would be a happy coincidence.

Miss Galloway stood next to the table, patiently watching me as I took all of this in.

"I apologize," I told her as my skin tingled with embarrassment. "But Lord Langstone has been missing for so long. His family is growing a bit frantic." I hoped that was explanation enough for our prying.

Her eyes dipped to the wood of the table as she trailed her fingers over the grain. "I was under the impression they were not so caring."

I studied her downturned face, wondering just how well she knew Alfred. How much had he shared with her?

"But I suppose a missing heir does constitute a problem," she added, lifting her eyes to meet mine again.

"Yes, well, I've learned sometimes those who care the most

also exhibit the gruffest demeanors. They simply don't know how to express it." Despite my animosity toward him, I hated to think that Alfred believed none of his family cared for him. And then I thought of Gage, of the family's callous, brusque treatment of him, and sighed. "And sometimes things are exactly how they appear."

Miss Galloway tilted her head, sensing there was more to my statement than I admitted, but she did not press.

Before she could change her mind, I nodded toward the plants hanging from the ceiling. "This is quite an impressive collection of herbs. Do you grow them yourself?"

"Many of them. I have a small plot on the eastern side of the house. The others I gather from the moor and the riverbeds."

"We found a brown tincture in one of the drawers in Alfred's chamber. Did you prepare it for him?"

I tried to word my question in as conversational a manner as I could, which seemed to amuse Miss Galloway, for her lips quirked upward at the corners. Her shoulders relaxed and her brow smoothed of its last pleats. Apparently she had decided to trust I meant her no harm.

"I did. It was a receipt I learned from my mother. I mix a batch every few weeks, for I always have villagers asking for it."

"What is it used for?"

"Stomach ailments."

My eyes widened, though this somehow shouldn't have surprised me.

"It contains things like chamomile, catmint, aniseed, fennel seed, dill weed, and a few other ingredients. Nothing particularly unusual." She crossed the room and reached into one of her cabinets and extracted a bottle similar to the one we'd found in Alfred's room. "This is from the same batch if you wish to test it."

I took it from her, opening the lid to smell the contents. "Was this the first time he'd purchased a bottle from you?"

"Yes. Though . . ." She hesitated and I arched my eyebrows in question.

Her lips compressed in an awkward grin. "It wasn't the first remedy he'd purchased from me." She cleared her throat, dropping her gaze. "Though, the first was done more in jest than actual need."

I frowned in confusion, examining her averted eyes and the pink tinge of her cheeks, until comprehension dawned. "You mean . . . ?"

She cleared her throat again. "Yes. He purported to have . . . masculine difficulties."

It was my turn to blush. "Is that how you met?"

"Yes. I discerned immediately he was doing it as some sort of jape. He wasn't the first man to think such a ruse would be amusing and cause me no end of discomfort."

I scowled, annoyed on her behalf.

"But he was the first to return and apologize."

My surprise must have been evident, for she actually laughed.

"I take it you haven't heard very complimentary things about him. Perhaps justifiably, I might add."

"Well, he was quite cruel to my husband growing up, and he's done nothing in the years since to make me believe he's any different. So you'll have to excuse me if I'm not inclined to think good things about him."

Her smile turned wry. "I well believe it. And if it's any consolation, I wanted to slap his smug face the first time I met him, as I'm sure you wish you could."

"Oh, I'd like to do a bit more than that."

Her grin widened.

I inhaled. "But I shall restrain myself." I grimaced. "If I ever get the chance."

Her smile vanished as she nodded, acknowledging the fact that he was still lost. And for the first time genuine concern crossed her features.

"So you became friends?" I guessed, slipping the tincture she'd given me into the pocket of my dark charcoal gray riding ensemble.

"Of sorts." Her gaze strayed toward the window where a beam of sunlight had broken through the mist. "Actually, I found him to be quite amiable, once he stopped behaving like such a wretch. I shall be sad if I hear something unfortunate has happened to him."

There was something in her voice, something fraught and apprehensive. She opened her mouth as if to say more, but then restrained herself, casting me a humorless smile. I wasn't quite sure what to make of her reaction, but I suspected she was being honest about one thing. She *had* grown to like Alfred. But as merely a friend, or something more?

"I know you don't know me," I began hesitantly. "But . . . if you know something . . . if you need someone to confide in, I will do my best to keep what you tell me in confidence."

Her eyes widened, making me certain I'd guessed correctly. There was something she was not saying. But was it about her personal relationship with Alfred or something to do with his disappearance? She seemed to consider my offer, but ultimately only nodded.

Then her gaze fell to my chest, and I realized she was staring at my amethyst pendant. I reached up to finger it, curious at her interest.

"Someone who loved you gave that to you," Miss Galloway murmured with quiet certainty.

"Yes, my mother. Just before she died." She'd claimed it would protect me, and being only eight years old I'd believed her. Now I wore it as much as a way of keeping her near as for security.

Her gaze lifted to bore into mine. "Keep it close. Don't take it off."

I blinked, startled by her pronouncement. "Why?"

Her eyes clouded with trouble. "There is a darkness that hovers over that house. A shadow that seems to touch every life that falls within its reach."

A chill swept through me as I continued to try to make sense of what she was saying.

"I can't explain it. But I sense it. And I can tell you that Lord Langstone is not the first person from Langstone Manor to go missing."

"What do you mean?"

She shook her head, unwilling to say anything more about it. "Just wear your pendant. And keep that tincture. You might have need of it."

She turned toward the door, dismissing me, and I glanced up to see a drying bouquet hanging over the entry—one just like the flowers we'd found in Alfred's chamber.

"That's why you gave Lord Langstone the herb bennet," I guessed, before she could open the door.

She pressed her hand flat to the wood, turning her head to speak over her shoulder. "Yes, it's for protection. Among other things." She exhaled heavily. "But apparently it didn't work."

Before I could ask her anything further, she pulled open the door and stepped to the side to allow me to pass. I accepted her dismissal this time without demurral. Gage and Rory, who had finally dismounted, stood by the horses, staring up at us quizzically. Before I could join them, Miss Galloway stopped me with a hesitant touch to my arm.

"If . . . if you should like to come again . . ." She glanced at the men. "Just you. You would be welcome." Her voice was timid, as if she was uncertain how I would accept such a proposition and wary of giving it because of that. I couldn't help but wonder how many times she'd made similar overtures of friendship over the years and had them rebuffed. "You could bring your sketchbook. I can show you some beautiful settings."

So she definitely knew my past, for we'd made no mention of my talent as an artist. And yet, she still wanted to befriend me.

I smiled, having no trouble making it genuine. "I would like that."

Her eyes brightened and she nodded, leaving it at that.

Gage arched his eyebrows in question as I approached, but he said nothing as he turned to help me remount. In sharp contrast, Rory was practically bursting to ask me what had happened. I ignored him, lifting an arm in farewell to Miss Galloway as we turned our horses and rode back down the path in the direction of the manor.

As much as I liked Miss Galloway, she was still a puzzle. Rory had led me to believe her mother had come from a lowly birth, but Miss Galloway's manner of speech said otherwise. She was intelligent, articulate, and poised. Isolated out here on the moors in that small cottage, she could only have learned such comportment and enunciation from her mother. She must have come from a family that was gentry, if not nobility. Which meant her family had almost certainly disowned her. But who were they?

Before I could contemplate the matter further, questions and accusations burst from Rory's lips. "You were in there quite a long time. Could you tell if Alfred had been there? Was she brewing more potions?"

I cast him a quelling look. "No, there was no sign of Alfred. And she wasn't *brewing* anything. Her cottage appears perfectly common, perfectly normal. She has an impressive array of herbs, but that's to be expected considering she makes medicinal cures for the villagers."

I elected not to mention the bottle of tincture thumping against my leg in my pocket. I wasn't sure I wanted Rory to know I had it. As for the rest, I decided it was best to keep what I'd learned to myself until Gage and I were alone.

"Well, then if Miss Galloway is not hiding him or conscious of his whereabouts, I suppose we shall have to try elsewhere," Gage declared, spurring his horse forward to lead us down the track leading to the river.

"Surely you don't believe her?" Rory protested. "The woman is as skilled a liar as they come."

I scowled over my shoulder at him as I urged my mare to follow Gage's. "Why are you so determined to distrust her? I was under the impression you were barely acquainted with her."

I didn't have a chance to view Rory's reaction, as my concentration was needed to maintain my seat as the path steeply dropped down to the stream. In any case, Rory didn't try to answer, but seemed to be ruminating on something unpleasant when I glanced back at him again just before we forded the river at the same calm pool. It wasn't until our horses had climbed the slope out of the valley and back onto the higher part of the moor that he drew up alongside us.

"I wasn't going to say anything, but perhaps it's best if I do."

Still, he hesitated. His eyes almost looked stricken, and my stomach tightened in dread, somehow knowing I wouldn't like what he was about to say.

"I distrust Miss Galloway because . . . because we always suspected her mother was the person who sold Annie the poison she used on Gage's mother."

My gaze flew to my husband. I felt sick with shock, but I was more concerned with how he would take this revelation. He sat stonily in his saddle, his hands gripping his reins as he struggled to keep his feelings in check. It was evident that Rory's admission was as new to him as it was to me. He'd known his mother's maid, Annie, had poisoned her, but I'm not sure he'd ever contemplated *where* Annie had gotten the poison.

"You said 'suspected,'" I said when it became obvious Gage was not capable of making a reply. Not at the moment. My heart squeezed at his distress. "So you have no proof it was Miss Galloway's mother?"

"No. But there simply wasn't anyone else." Rory shrugged. "Not unless Annie traveled far afield to obtain it."

Which was possible, but not very likely. And all but impossible to discover now—fifteen years later. Not to mention the fact there was no way of knowing if Miss Galloway's mother had known what Annie intended to use the poison for.

With Annie having been hanged long ago for her crime, and Miss Galloway's mother dead, there was really no point in stirring it all up again. But Rory's warning was duly noted. Just because I'd felt empathy for Miss Galloway didn't mean I could trust her. I pressed a hand to the fabric concealing the bottle of tincture she'd given me, curious whether its contents would match those inside the bottle we'd found in Alfred's room.

Upon our return to Langstone, Gage set off to visit his grand-father. He invited me to join him, but I demurred, figuring the two of them needed to spend some time alone. Maybe Lord Tavistock would feel more comfortable delving into private matters without me hovering in the background.

Rather than remain in our chamber where Bree was puttering around, I elected to explore the manor. I could have dismissed my maid, but it was already difficult enough for her to complete her tasks in a strange house without my impeding her just so I could be alone. Besides, I'd been eager to poke my nose into some of the other rooms and corridors ever since our arrival. The unsettling sensations I'd experienced outside Alfred's chamber had damp-ened my enthusiasm somewhat, but I was still determined to dis-cover what I could.

So armed with a candle and a tinderbox tucked in my pocket, just in case a stray wind—or mischievous ghost—blew it out, I set off down a corridor I'd yet to traverse. My progress was slow, as I took my time to examine some of the treasures—or lack thereof—gracing the walls. I was surprised to find valuable and exquisite paintings by Vermeer and Titian interspersed with other poorly executed works of art. Had the worthless pictures all represented the same style, I would have attributed them to a family member, but it was clear most of them had been created by different people.

I couldn't decide whether that meant Lord Tavistock and his ancestors had been clueless about art, or they hoped to flummox any would-be thieves.

I nearly gasped at the sight of a Rembrandt hanging haphazardly above a mahogany side table with a bust in one corner. This masterpiece should be hung with more care, taking pride of place high on the wall of the dining room or drawing room, not tucked next to a stand filled with spears that could topple over and tear the canvas. The only thing reassuring about the random placement of these artworks was that the corridors were so dark, at least sunlight certainly couldn't damage them.

I found dusty bedchambers with their contents covered in white sheets, and private sitting rooms with their writing desks still stocked with stationery. I even stumbled into an old garderobe with its hole carefully covered by a plank of wood. Down a flight of stairs at the back of the house, I stumbled into a billiard room with its balls racked, ready to be played. It appeared less abandoned than many of the chambers, making me suspect it had seen more recent use.

Retracing my steps, I turned right down the next corridor, hoping to locate the library, and found myself at the end of a long passage that overlooked some shadowy chamber below. I realized, with a start, that this was the portrait gallery. Peeking over the railing spanning one length of the corridor, I could see down into what I presumed to be some sort of great hall or ballroom.

Turning back toward the portraits, I inched my way down the gallery, examining each one. Before my eyes, the Trevelyan features regressed through the centuries. A large portion of the males seemed to have inherited the same striking silver eyes Lord Tavistock possessed. Though I pondered if maybe the artists had exaggerated the intensity of their sheen in several of the pictures.

One painting in particular drew my attention, for it boasted three people as its subjects. The man held pride of place, glowering down at me with his silver eyes, while a rather dowdy woman hovered behind him. Then almost in the background stood another woman, her face averted as if she were looking over her shoulder. She appeared as if she weren't supposed to be in the portrait at all, as if she'd accidentally meandered into the background, but, of course, the artist would have had to have added her with intention. But why had he painted her thusly?

I recalled what Miss Galloway had said about Alfred not being the first person to have gone missing from Langstone Manor, and I couldn't help but wonder if this woman was the other vanishing resident. Lifting my candle higher, I studied all of the portraits with renewed interest, curious which of these people might also have disappeared. Had they ever been found, or was this the last trace of their existence?

I shivered in a stray draft. My sense of foreboding and the flickering light of the candle combined to eerily magnify the emotions captured in the faces of Gage's ancestors, making them all the more intense. So that the jaded Georgian gentleman in his curled wig seemed to roll his eyes; the laughter of a simpering debutante in a golden gown with large hoops almost tinkled aloud from behind her fan; and the fiercely scowling Roundhead all but leapt out at me. His glaring visage made me startle and nearly drop my candle.

Or perhaps it was the sharp realization that I was not alone.

CHAPTER FOURTEEN

I spun around to see the Dowager Lady Langstone step out of the shadows at the other end of the gallery. How long she'd been watching me, I didn't know, but I felt a pulse of irritation at her for behaving so. She could have announced herself.

She wore a gown of chartreuse silk—another dress that was elegantly fashionable and all but put my simple forest green gown with bows at the shoulders to shame. Her thick hair was arranged in ringlets on either side of her head and topped with a thin gold diadem. I couldn't help but admire her cool beauty, though it made me wonder why she'd not remarried. Though I couldn't say much for her personality, her attractiveness and impeccable breeding should have attracted a second husband. In my experience, most gentlemen never looked past the exterior and the basic niceties. I assumed she'd not wished to enter into matrimony again, but why? Was she all consumed with her sons' inheritances, or was there another reason?

Her dark eyes gleamed at me in the candlelight like hard gems. "Admiring our artwork?"

I scrutinized her features, trying to tell whether she was slyly implying she'd been observing me for even longer than I suspected. But I already knew if I asked her outright she would deny it. Instead I turned back to the portraits on the wall. "Some more than others," I replied indifferently.

She stepped up beside me, gazing up at the fine lines etched into the face of a woman attired in an Elizabethan ruff. It was one of the oldest paintings in the collection. Possibly the wife of the first Baron Langstone, long before Viscount Tavistock was added to their titles.

"They say she was mistress to the king. Another lady-in-waiting plucked from the queen's service. And that's why her husband was granted the title and these lands."

She could only have been talking about Henry VIII, for no other king would have been the right age, though she spoke as if she were gossiping about the current monarch.

"How many titles do you think have been won thusly? By a woman on her back." Her piercing gaze turned to meet mine before returning to the portrait.

I suspected she'd just insulted me, and that I was supposed to respond with righteous indignation. Contrarily, a bubble of amusement rose inside me. After all the dreadful names I'd been called, all the gruesome acts I'd been unjustly accused of, being charged with seducing Sebastian Gage, the golden lothario, into marriage was almost laughable. It certainly wasn't worth getting ruffled by. Not when it was what Lady Langstone clearly wanted.

I smothered a giggle and strolled on to the next portrait, trusting she would follow. "I understand Lord Tavistock is hopeful of an engagement between Lord Langstone and Lady Juliana Maristow."

"Yes." She paused for so long after that single statement that I thought she was going to refuse to elaborate. Whether she'd been weighing her words, or my silence had prodded her into saying more, I wasn't certain, but it seemed far more likely to be the former. "It is a good match."

"Was Alfred pleased by it?"

Her chin arched a degree higher as she replied almost in challenge. "Why would he not be?"

I turned to look at her, finding her answer interesting. Lady Langstone seemed to me a very deliberate person, and though she could be startled into giving a reaction or response that hadn't been first carefully considered, I didn't think this had been one of those instances. If she had believed her son was pleased by the engagement, would she not have said so? Did that mean she knew better? That Alfred had not liked it. Had she joined Lord Tavistock in pressuring him to accept the match regardless?

As if aware of the topic of my contemplation, she switched to another topic. "I trust your rooms have been satisfactory."

"Our rooms are lovely. Though . . ." I hesitated, uncertain whether to mention the pranks to Lady Langstone. In the end, I decided I was more curious what her reaction would be than worried she would dismiss my concerns as silly. "I believe some of your staff might be intent on making mischief."

"The missing trunks?" she surmised without removing her gaze from the portrait of a mother and her five children we were standing before. She sighed. "It is *so* hard to find good staff in this area. Especially since the manor presses into the heart of Dartmoor. It's always been this way," she added as we sauntered down to the next painting. "Maids coming and going. And the ones that do stay often aren't of the best quality. As Mrs. Gage found out."

I blinked at the portrait before me, shocked she'd referred to the maid who poisoned Gage's mother in such a conversational manner. However, I refused to give her the satisfaction of seeing she'd disconcerted me.

But Lady Langstone wasn't finished.

She sighed again, rather affectedly. "I told her to get rid of that maid. There were plenty of other girls from the villages nearby she could have employed. But she wouldn't listen. And look where it got her."

"Buried cold in the ground?" I couldn't help but retort, made furious by her casually cruel remarks.

She flinched, but then recovered. "Well, yes."

I silently fumed, trying to keep my temper under control, and almost missed what Lady Langstone said next.

"She brought that maid with her from Plymouth, you know. She wasn't a local girl."

I turned to her quizzically. "Annie wasn't Mrs. Gage's maid before she married?"

"No," she scoffed. "She couldn't afford the woman her father employed for her. Her husband hadn't yet attained his riches." She spoke with distaste, as if Lord Gage had been a privateer, pillaging and looting, not the captain of a Royal Navy vessel who'd captured a number of large ships for the Crown as war prizes.

Ignoring the tone of her voice, I tried to focus on the content of her words. "So life in Plymouth was rather less grand than here at Langstone, especially in the early years of her marriage."

She wrinkled her nose. "I suspect it was downright squalid."

Coming from her, such a description could imply any number of conditions, so I did not concern myself with the details. A Royal Navy captain might not boast of impressive accommodations, but he also wouldn't live in ramshackle lodging. However, it was plain Gage's mother had come down in the world. Greatly.

"When she returned here with young Sebastian and that maid in tow, she claimed it was her illness that convinced her to make the move, but I didn't believe it." She sniffed. "It was evident to me she was simply tired of her life in that tiny house by the sea, doing much of the work she was accustomed to the servants managing. That's the real reason she showed up here without warning. She wanted to come home, but she couldn't. Not really. So she claimed she was only here for a visit, just until her health improved, until her husband came back from the sea."

I didn't want to give her story any credence, especially not when it was delivered in such a self-righteous tone. But there were elements of it that struck me as being perhaps more accurate than what I'd always assumed given the little information Gage had relayed to me.

"Wasn't she ill?" I asked, turning to face her directly.

She brushed this aside with a flick of her wrist. "No more than a convenient cough when it suited her. She didn't truly become ill until a year or two later. And then . . . I suppose you know the rest."

About the poisoning. About how her maid, Annie, had feared she would be replaced and so began dosing her mistress with poison from time to time to prolong her illness.

It was heartless the way Lady Langstone spoke of it as if it were merely a trifling matter. It made me angry, and determined that she wouldn't escape this conversation unscathed.

"We visited Lord Glanville yesterday."

Had I not been watching for it, I might not have detected the way her eyes flinched.

"Did you," she replied with an admirable amount of nonchalance. "Then I assume he confirmed the information I already relayed to you." Her eyebrows arched in accusation.

"Yes . . . and no." I furrowed my brow as if she had confused me. "Why did you tell us Lord Glanville visited you when it was *you* who went to *him*?" I elected not to mention the flurried state Glanville had described her being in.

"Did he tell you that?" she asked with cool reserve. She shook her head as if in bemusement. "The man is a drunk, and likely can't recall one day from the next."

"Are you saying you didn't visit him?"

Her smile tightened to something akin to pity. "I'm saying the man can't be trusted."

Once again, she hadn't really answered my question, and her implication that I was to be pitied for my naïveté was grating. "Does that mean you think he's involved in Alfred's disappearance?"

"No," she huffed. "It means you shouldn't believe everything you hear." She started to turn away, but paused to offer me one last bit of advice. "Lady Darby, if I were you, I would spend less time worrying about the veracity of Lord Glanville's memory and more time concerned with the violent man you married."

I blinked in astonishment.

"Ask him about the dagger," she said, and then swept from the room before I could recover from my state of shock to demand she explain.

I didn't believe for even one second that Gage was a violent man. I'd known violent men. I'd seen the way they operated. I'd survived a marriage with one. Yes, it had only been three months since Gage and I wed, but never during that time or the eight months before had he displayed any sign of those characteristics. Not to mention the fact that two of his closest friends were also my brother-in-law and an old family friend. I had no doubt Philip and Michael would have warned me if Gage exhibited any forceful tendencies.

That being said, Lady Langstone evidently wanted me to find out about something. She'd mentioned a dagger, and I could only assume it was the Bray ceremonial dagger referred to at dinner two evenings prior. I'd perceived then how the mention of it affected Gage, but I hadn't yet asked him about it. I supposed now was as good a time as any.

Unfortunately, when I returned to our chambers, Gage was nowhere to be seen. And by the time I heard him return to the connecting room, I was already dressing for dinner. I was curious where he'd been all afternoon, and told him so when he joined me to escort me down to the dining room.

"Hammett arranged for me to speak with several members of the staff, including the gardener who last saw Alfred." He glanced at me in puzzlement. "Did a servant not relay my message asking you to join me if you were available?"

I shook my head.

He frowned. "An oversight, I suppose."

But I could tell neither of us really believed that.

"In any case, the gardener no longer had the newspaper clipping Alfred dropped." Frustration tightened his voice. "Said no one told him it could be important, so he burned it as kindling. He seemed genuinely distressed when I asked for it, so I don't think there was any malice intended."

"Did he read it?"

"He couldn't. He's only literate enough to recognize his own name and a few place names and such. But he said he noticed the words *Langstone*, *Tavistock*, and *Gunnislake*, which is a small village southwest of Tavistock. Beyond that, he couldn't make anything else out."

"That's not much to go on."

"No, it's not. But perhaps my grandfather will have some idea what the article was about." He exhaled wearily. "Barring that, I suppose I could search for an intact copy of the edition of *Woolmer's Gazette* we found in Alfred's chamber."

I lifted the skirts of my claret red evening gown with black braid as we descended the stairs, lowering my voice so as not to be heard by anyone hovering in the entry hall below. "That might require an awful lot of effort to discover something we're not even certain has anything to do with your cousin's disappearance."

He grimaced. "That's why I'm hoping Grandfather can enlighten me instead."

I wanted to ask him about his visit with his grandfather earlier that day, but we were nearly to the bottom of the staircase and would soon be joining Lady Langstone and Rory. In that little time, I knew I wouldn't receive a satisfactory answer. Not to mention the fact that I wished a few moments to prepare myself before seeing Gage's aunt again. I'd wanted to plead a headache, except I'd known it simply wouldn't do for either of us to miss two dinners in a row. My suspicion that Lady Langstone would view my absence as some sort of triumph also steeled my resolve.

That being said, I did not dally over dinner. There were only so many of Lady Langstone's venomous looks and sly cutting remarks I could endure, especially when Rory did little to help direct the conversation elsewhere. I might have felt annoyed with him, except that he seemed so apologetic when I did manage to pull his attention away from whatever preoccupied him. Clearly something was bothering him, and I hoped he would take the opportunity to confide in Gage when I slipped away, claiming fatigue.

In any case, I had something much more interesting to devote my evening to.

Lifting the skirts of my dress, I hurried back to my bedchamber. I was pleased to see Bree had found the items I'd requested. After tugging on the bellpull to summon her, I hurried over to the dressing table to examine the platter, clear glasses, and sieve.

I pulled the key out from where I'd secured it inside my corset and leaned over to unlock the bottom right drawer. Inside sat my jewelry case, as well as the two bottles of Miss Galloway's tincture. I set the bottles on the table and rose to fetch some sheets of foolscap to jot down my notes when Bree arrived.

She'd merely arched her eyebrows earlier when I relayed the list of items I needed her to procure for me, accustomed to my odd requests. But now she studied the arrangement on the dressing table with mild alarm.

"Dinna tell me that's poison in those bottles," she chided.

I glanced down at them and back at her. "Most likely not." Then I narrowed my eyes, curious what she might have heard belowstairs, and from whom. "Why did you suspect poison?"

She scoffed and pushed away from the door. "Because why else would ye be intent on examinin' their contents? Yer no' tryin' to duplicate a recipe." Her mouth quirked wryly. "You an' Mr. Gage *do* investigate murders, m'lady. That means poison."

I smiled at her logic and allowed myself to be spun around.

Her fingers deftly began working their way down the buttons. "I hope ye werena plannin' to strain potions in this dress. One splash and the silk would be ruined."

"Of course not," I lied. "I was just getting everything prepared."

Her quiet harrumph told me she didn't believe me for a second. "What's supposed to be in those bottles? Something Lord Langstone drank?"

"A tincture for a stomach ailment. At least, that's what Miss Galloway claims. We found the nearly empty bottle in Lord Langstone's chamber. Miss Galloway gave me the full bottle this morning and claimed it was from the same batch."

"And you want to compare their contents to find oot if she's tellin' the truth?"

"Exactly."

With little warning, Bree whisked my gown up over my head. "Who's this Miss Galloway?"

"She's the illegitimate daughter of Lord Sherracombe. Lives out on the moor in the same cottage she grew up in with her now-deceased mother." I swiveled so I could see Bree's image in the looking glass as she began loosening the strings of my corset. "Actually, Mr. Trevelyan tried to convince us she's a witch."

It turned out I hadn't needed to see my maid's reflection to observe her reaction, for she tugged so sharply on the corset strings I nearly lost my balance.

"My apologies, m'lady."

"If anything, I would say she's more of an herbalist," I continued. "Or simply a hedge witch, as Gage says they're called on Dartmoor." I turned to glower over my shoulder at her. "Now, tell me why the suggestion that she's a witch so startled you."

"'Tis nothing. Only . . ."

I arched my eyebrows, waiting impatiently for her to explain.

"The other servants have been tellin' me some o' the local folklore."

"I imagine there are quite a few colorful tales connected with Dartmoor." The land was too isolated and atmospheric not to be the subject of myth, especially when one considered the high number of deaths connected to its natural hazards. Combine all that, and the moors must be rife with legends.

She nodded, removing my corset. "Aye. Pixies bent on mischief, vanishin' cottages, beasts protectin' treasures, even a lady who turns into a black dog every midnight and runs alongside a coach made from her husband's bones."

I sat on the bench and leaned over to remove my shoes and stockings. "Is she the witch you're so concerned about?"

"Nay," Bree assured me as she returned with my nightdress. "Least no' 'til she removes every blade o' grass from her castle. 'Tis only then she can be at rest. Or free to cause more mischief."

I looked up at her, trying to tell if she was serious or pitching the gammon. She seemed to be in earnest, but that still didn't explain her reaction. I cast her a long-suffering look as she lifted my night rail to drop it over my head, refusing to raise my arms until she acknowledged it.

"But they did tell me another tale that was aboot a witch," she hastened to add. "Named Vixana."

I let the folds of the nightdress settle around me and swiveled to allow Bree to remove the pins from my hair while she related the tale. "She lived in a cave at the foot o' a tor to the south, no' far from here, and she hated people. Despised 'em. Though no one could remember why. Anyway, she spent her days perched on top o' her tor, waitin' to cause harm to any who passed. Near her tor lies a bog, and when travelers would try to take the track past her home, she would summon a thick mist to disorient 'em, so that they would stumble into the bog, ne'er to be seen again. Because of it, locals took another trail, which led through the roughest part o' the moor, miles oot o' their way, just to avoid goin' past Vixana's home."

Bree picked up a hairbrush, running it soothingly through my hair before she began to plait it. "This went on for many years. No one kens how long. Until a young moorman who'd been given special powers because o' a favor he performed for the pixies decided to investigate Vixana's tor. When Vixana saw him walkin' along the track toward her, she summoned the mist as she always did. But because o' the gift o' clear sight that the pixies had given him, the moorman was able to stay to the path and cross the bog unharmed. When Vixana saw this, she screamed in frustration and began to weave another spell. But the moorman heard her shriek, and realized he was in danger. So he slipped on a ring that would make him invisible—his other gift from the pixies. Vixana was baffled when she could no longer see the man she wanted to direct her spell at, so she moved closer to the edge o' the rocks, leanin' over to search for him. But while she was distracted, the moorman crept aroond to the other side o' the tor, climbed the rocks, and snuck up behind her to push her o'er the edge to her doom. Vixana no longer lives there, but the tor is still named after her."

I studied Bree in the mirror as she tied the ribbon to secure my braid. "That's a very affecting story, but . . . what does that have to do with Miss Galloway?"

Bree shrugged. "Probably nothin'. But one o' the servants muttered something aboot Vixana's descendants still bein' aboot before Mr. Hammett could shush her. Just be careful." Her eyes met mine steadily in the mirror. "I ken ye like to believe the best o' ladies who've been wronged, an' goodness kens I think that's admirable. But . . . they're no' *all* innocent. Sometimes where there's smoke, there *is* fire. And sometimes when there's blather, the rumors are true."

I considered her words as she turned to gather my clothes and straighten the room. She was right. After hearing Rory's speculations about Miss Galloway's mother's involvement with Annie, I'd already decided I needed to proceed with caution. Hearing Bree—someone I trusted almost implicitly—say the same thing only drove the matter home.

That being said, I knew listening to folktales wasn't the only thing Bree had been doing with her time belowstairs. "Have you made any progress with Lady Langstone's maid?"

Bree sighed and shook her head. "She's a prickly one. No' easily charmed. But I'm workin' on her."

"Anderley told me he asked you to try to cozen Cooper, Alfred's valet."

"Aye. Noo, he's more promisin'. Just wants someone to listen to his complaints, and I can do that." Her nose wrinkled. "Even if he *does* whine more than my three-year-old nephew."

I chuckled and she smiled.

"Leave the dishes on the dressin' table when yer done. I'll take care o' 'em in the mornin'." She glanced between me and the bottles, as if debating whether to issue another warning like a little mother hen. "Mr. Gage will be up soon?"

My brow furrowed in irritation. "I imagine so."

Wisely sensing she'd pushed me far enough, she bobbed a curtsy. "Good night, m'lady."

"Good night," I replied, waiting until the door was firmly shut before spinning around to begin my analysis of the tinctures.

CHAPTER FIFTEEN

I was perched on the bench, dabbing my pinky fingers into each of the two tinctures and touching them to my tongue to try to decipher any difference in taste, when Gage entered the room through the connecting door to his chamber.

"What the devil are you doing?!"

I startled as he strode closer to stand over me. His eyes flicked furiously over the contents of the dressing table.

"Testing the tinctures."

"Are you mad?" he demanded, reaching for the ewer of water and a clean glass. "It could be poisoned. Wait." He halted abruptly in pouring the water, making it slosh onto the floor. *"Tinctures?"* He emphasized the plural.

"Yes," I replied calmly. "Miss Galloway gave me a bottle of tincture she claimed was prepared from the same batch as the bottle we found in Alfred's room so that I could compare them."

"And you decided to *drink* them?" He thrust the glass of water into my hands.

"No! I was merely tasting them. And I already have a glass of water. How do you think I've been cleansing my palate?"

"Kiera, they could be poisoned!" He pushed the glass toward my lips. "Drink that."

I scowled, but obliged, restraining myself from pointing out that drinking the water would force more of the tincture down into my stomach. "I highly doubt it," I said when his hand moved away. "Besides, even if they were, drinking nearly an entire bottle didn't kill Alfred. So there's little chance a few small tastes is going to harm me."

"Maybe not. But it might harm . . ." He stopped himself before he said the words, his eyes dipping to my abdomen and then back to my face.

My face flushed with warmth at the implication and I couldn't stop myself from pressing a hand to my flat stomach. I wasn't yet expecting. Or, at least, I didn't think I was. It was too early to tell if any of our most recent efforts had yielded results. But there was the possibility. And I hadn't even considered the effect my examination of the tinctures might have on him or her.

That thought made me go cold. Possibly days into motherhood and I might already be doing an abominable job. Considering all the uncertainties I'd been wrestling with recently, this was not a welcome revelation.

I set the glass of water carefully on the table, trying to calm my suddenly swirling stomach. Courtesy of my anxieties or the tinctures?

"Well, I haven't noted anything suspicious that might lead me to believe these contain poison." I spoke evenly, trying to use reason to allay my own concerns as much as Gage's. "I compared their appearance, their texture, their scent, and . . . and even their taste. In addition to the gin the ingredients are dissolved in, I was able to distinguish all the herbs Miss Galloway mentioned, as well as a few more. As far as I can tell, there is nothing to cause alarm."

Gage rested a hand on my shoulder in comfort, sensing my

distress despite my attempt to hide it. Following my gaze, he read over the list of suspected ingredients I'd noted on the paper before me. "What did Miss Galloway say the tincture was used for?" His voice was still edged with tension, but kinder than it had been moments before.

"Stomach ailments."

His eyes dipped to my face, not missing the irony of dosing such a substance with poison. "Did she know why Alfred needed it?"

"No. At least, she didn't share the specifics. Though she did mention she sells this particular treatment to the villagers. Says she makes a new batch every few weeks."

He cupped my elbow, helping me to my feet, and guided me toward the bed. I perched on the edge while he moved about the room, checking the locks on the windows.

"What else did Miss Galloway have to say?" He glanced back at me over his shoulder. "You were in her cottage longer than I expected."

"Preparing to storm the castle, were you?" I quipped, trying to lighten the mood.

"Actually, yes."

His reply made my tentative smile vanish.

"And Rory didn't help matters. Toward the end, I practically had to restrain him."

"He truly believes she means us harm?"

"He does."

The last set of drapes closed with a snap, but when he failed to join me on the bed, I looked up from where I'd been worrying my hands in my lap to find him studying me.

"But what do you think?"

I paused to sort through my impressions of her before I spoke, waiting on Gage to sit by my side. The silk of his dressing gown brushed against the cotton of my nightdress.

"I rather liked her. She's not responsible for the hand she's been dealt, and yet, I think she's made the best of it she can."

"She could have let her father arrange a marriage for her."

"And be made to feel grateful her entire life that her husband condescended to take her as his wife?" I shook my head.

"They don't all turn out that way," he reminded me quietly.

"And some of them end up quite worse." I stared up at him through my lashes, reminding him how I felt about arranged marriages. After all, my first marriage had been arranged, and had turned out to be the worst mistake of my life. "Regardless, you cannot blame her for wanting to retain control of her own fate." I propped my foot up against the mattress, clasping my hands around my bent knee as I considered my observations of Miss Galloway. "She's intelligent and capable. She doesn't seem to tolerate nonsense, and yet she's not without empathy, even for the likes of Alfred."

Gage laid back, turning to his side to face me, and propped his head on his hand. "What do you mean?"

I reclined beside him, staring up at the bed curtains. "From the little she said, I could tell she was better acquainted with him than I'd expected. I think they were friends, of a sort. If not something more." I turned my head to look at my husband. "He seemed to confide in her."

His pale blue eyes glistened with interest. "About?"

"His life here at Langstone. His perception that no one truly cared for him."

Gage's eyebrows shot skyward briefly before furrowing in a frown. "If so, it's his own fault."

Amusement curled my lips. "Oh, she was well aware of that. And I've no doubt she pointed that out to him."

His eyes trailed over my features as he mulled over what I'd said. "You think there might have been something between them?"

I shrugged. "Stranger matches have been made."

His face softened at my obvious reference to our own union, and he reached out to roll me onto my side closer to him. His fingers lifted to toy with the end of my braid. It was only a matter of time before he removed the ribbon and destroyed all of Bree's efforts to keep my hair tame. "If that's true, do you think she would have helped him? Either to hide or escape, if the situation merited it?"

I chewed on my lip in contemplation, not failing to note how Gage's eyes became riveted to my mouth. "If the motive was solely to escape your grandfather's wrath, then no. But . . . if the reason was good enough, perhaps if he was in danger, then yes." It was my turn to scrutinize him. "What are you thinking?"

He frowned. "Nothing as of yet. I'm just . . . curious."

I raised my eyebrows, hoping he intended to elaborate.

"Do you remember the bouquet we found in Alfred's room?"

"The herb bennet? Miss Galloway claimed it's for protection."

"She admitted to giving it to him?"

"Yes."

"Interesting," he murmured as his gaze drifted to my right ear. When he didn't explain, I prodded him. "Why? Is it not true?"

"No. She's right. It's traditionally used for protection. What I find interesting is that it's often used for a specific *type* of protection." He settled in closer, as if imparting a secret. "Herb bennet has religious associations, namely that it can ward off the devil and evil spirits, in particular the venom of any beast. This is because St. Benedict, for whom the plant is named, was once given a cup of poisoned wine. But when the saint blessed it, the glass shattered and a demon emerged, exposing the giver's evil intentions."

My eyes widened. "How did you find this out?"

"I had a few extra minutes to spare this afternoon, so I looked it up in the library."

I pressed a hand to the warm skin revealed by the gap in his dressing gown. "Well, then, if that's true, it would hardly make sense for Miss Galloway to have given Alfred a plant to protect him from poison if she intended to dose him herself."

Gage nodded, gripping my hand to quell my excitement. "But that also means she may have suspected he was being poisoned by someone else."

I subsided deeper into the bedding, recalling something else she'd told me. "She might be concerned for us as well."

"What do you mean?"

"Before I left, she . . . she told me not to remove my mother's pendant." I reached up to feel its solid weight hidden beneath my nightdress. "And she told me to keep the bottle of tincture because I might have need of it."

His eyes flashed. "Was she *trying* to frighten you?"

"No, I don't think so. She seemed genuinely concerned. The same as she looked when we discussed Alfred." I hesitated, suspecting he wasn't going to like what I had to say next even more. "She warned me there's a shadow over this house. And suggested Alfred isn't the first person to disappear from Langstone Manor."

But contrary to my expectations, Gage didn't even recoil from the possibility. In fact, he looked pensive.

"You're not surprised," I remarked in astonishment.

"There are . . . rumors. I heard them when I was young. About some ancestor before my grandfather's time. Someone who went walking on the moors and never returned."

"So you don't know if it's true?"

He shook his head.

Had Lorna merely been repeating popular lore, or did she know something? Something maybe Alfred uncovered?

"Would your grandfather?" I asked, pressing the tips of my fingers against his skin to recall his attention.

"Maybe." He grimaced. "But will he share it?"

"Perhaps I should press Miss Galloway for more information."

His eyes searched mine, understanding what I was really asking. He exhaled, as if answering against his better judgment, and touched his forehead to mine. "Yes, perhaps you should."

I moved my head back so that I could see him better, surprised he hadn't objected to my suggestion I revisit Miss Galloway. "Truly?"

His lips tightened in irritation. "I feel like I should be insulted.

I know I'm protective of you, but I've never stopped you from taking reasonable actions, especially in the pursuit of an investigation."

I wanted to argue that statement, for we seemed to have differing opinions on what constituted "reasonable actions" in the past, but I overlooked it in favor of a more interesting point. "I thought you'd be less inclined to trust Miss Galloway's intentions given the accusations Rory leveled against her mother."

"Yes, well, we have no way of knowing whether that is true or not, and as you already pointed out, it's not fair to fault her for the sins of her mother. Heaven knows, I don't want to be saddled with my father's," he muttered almost under his breath.

I brushed a stray golden curl back from his forehead, empathizing with that sentiment.

"To be perfectly honest, I'm not sure we should give any credence to Rory's claims." His jaw hardened. "He never displayed an ounce of loyalty toward my mother in the past. Not even at her funeral. It seems a tad too convenient that he should claim to now."

Not knowing what had occurred at his mother's funeral, I couldn't respond with any confidence, but I felt I should try. "Yes, but you said yourself he seems to have changed in the fifteen years since you last saw him."

"But enough for him to become outraged at an accused woman's daughter on my mother's behalf?" The ribbon in my hair gave way as he tugged on the end. "That's too far."

"You think he dislikes her for a different reason?"

"I don't know." He lifted the white ribbon, gazing at it without really seeing it, and then tossed it aside. "But I trust your intuition more, and if you think she's not out to harm you or Alfred, then I think we should ask for her help. If she'll give it."

"She's invited me to visit again. Offered to show me some places I can sketch." I bit my lip. "But perhaps tomorrow is too soon. She's canny. If I show up on her doorstep so quickly she might be too suspicious to talk."

Gage's fingers combed through my hair, unplaiting my braid, though from the faraway look in his eyes I knew his mind was elsewhere. While he was distracted, I leaned closer, inhaling deeply.

"So you spent all of your afternoon interviewing the staff and in the library?" I murmured as I smoothed my hand over the silk of his dressing gown's lapel.

His eyes met mine briefly before sliding away again. "Mostly. Tomorrow won't work for you to call on Miss Galloway again anyway. I have other plans for us."

"Oh?" I replied, baffled by his decision to omit the fact that he'd been working with wood. The faint smell of sawdust still clung to his skin beneath the cleaner scents of his soap and his spicy cologne. I knew his grandfather had been the one to teach him such a hobby, while at the same time admonishing him to keep quiet about it, for gentlemen simply didn't work with their hands. It was only natural that he should be drawn to the wood-working shed where he'd first learned, so why the secrecy?

"I want to visit the farmers and tenants bordering the moor to the north of White Tor. I can't help but think that if Alfred walked away from the manor, it must have been in that direction. Perhaps some skilled questioning will yield more details than the men Grandfather sent were able to gather."

"You're going to go against your grandfather's wishes?" I asked in surprise.

"Not entirely. I don't intend to ask them directly about Alfred, or to let it slip that he's missing." His voice firmed with resolve. "But I'm not going to stay away when those people are the likeliest to hold the key to my cousin's location."

"I suppose you know many of them." If so, that would make our surreptitious interrogations that much easier.

"If they're the same landowners as fifteen years ago, yes. And land in this part of the country doesn't change hands often, so I suspect so. The Seftons, the Porlocks, the Brays."

The last name he listed sent a jolt through me, though I never moved. I'd hoped for an opening to ask Gage about the dagger, and I hardly believed he'd given me one. But still I hesitated. He would not welcome the query, and it would likely cause him discomfort. There was also the chance I would hear something I wouldn't like. But still, the question needed to be asked.

"Sebastian," I murmured, knowing my use of his given name as I did only when we were in private would draw his attention away from wherever his thoughts had gone.

He stilled his fingers and shifted his gaze to meet mine. Could he hear the uncertainty in my voice?

"What happened with the Brays' ceremonial dagger?"

His eyes searched mine, perhaps trying to ascertain how much I already knew. For a moment, he seemed about to feign ignorance, but then one corner of his mouth quirked upward sardonically.

"I wondered when you would raise that specter. I knew it was too much to hope you'd missed Aunt Vanessa's mention of it."

I refrained from telling him that she'd made certain of it that afternoon in the portrait gallery. Nothing would be gained from relaying her hurtful accusations.

He sighed heavily, rolling onto his back to stare up at the bed curtains. "Thaddeus Bray was a boy my cousins and I played with on occasion, oftentimes at their farm northwest of White Tor. Thad's father was a sort of squire, so Grandfather, and Aunt Vanessa, deemed his son fit enough to befriend us."

I shifted closer to his side, allowing him to work his way around to revealing the most pertinent details. I knew from experience that it was easier to share disquieting things once you'd placed them in context, as if somehow that softened the sting.

"The Brays weren't wealthy. Not like we were. But they did have a few priceless possessions that had been passed down through their family for many generations. One of those items was a ceremonial dagger. Mr. Bray kept it in a glass-fronted cabinet behind his desk."

His frame grew tenser with every word, and his eyes gleamed with anger. I couldn't stop myself from resting my hand on his abdomen where his chest rose and fell rapidly with each irate breath, but I didn't offer him any further comfort, knowing he didn't want it. At least not until he'd finished his story.

"One day after we'd been at the Brays' home, the dagger went missing. I knew who'd taken it. He was always taking things that weren't his simply because he wanted them. But I kept my mouth shut, knowing no good would come of my making an accusation. So you can imagine my surprise when Alfred instead accused me of stealing it. He even claimed to know where I'd hidden it. And lo and behold, that's exactly where we found it."

Outrage raced through my veins. I opened my mouth to express my indignation on his behalf, but something in his eyes arrested me. This time it wasn't anger, but shame.

"I was so furious!"

"Rightly so," I assured him.

"I couldn't believe Alfred had done something so underhanded. And that Grandfather and Aunt Vanessa were going to believe him, and report it to my mother. Rory knew the truth. I could see it in his eyes. But he would never stand up for me." The remembered anguish he'd felt as a boy resonated through his body. "I tried to tell them the truth, but they wouldn't listen. And Alfred stood there so smugly, his eyes filled with laughter. I felt so helpless. I always had so little control over what was happening, and I didn't want to be powerless anymore. So I . . . I grabbed the dagger and I . . . I stabbed at Alfred."

I stiffened in shock and Gage's gaze lowered to meet mine for the first time since he'd begun his story. His face twisted with self-loathing.

"Nicked him in the arm. It was barely a scratch, but when I saw the blood, I was horrified. I dropped the dagger and ran."

"Oh, Sebastian," I crooned, lifting my hand to touch his face.

He grimaced. "Funnily enough, that's exactly what my mother

said when she found me hiding in the old stable at the edge of our cottage's garden."

"What did she do?"

"Dried my tears and took me home. She had no need to scold me. She knew her disappointment in me was punishment enough. Particularly when I practically had to carry her back to bed because she was so weak from her illness."

I frowned. "How old were you?"

"Eleven."

No wonder he'd lashed out. Not only had his cousin played an unconscionably cruel trick, but he was almost alone in carrying the burden of his mother's illness. His father had been away at sea, so it fell to him to care for and shield his mother with only the help of the maid who, it later would be discovered, was also poisoning her mistress. Something Gage blamed himself for. He believed he should have realized what was happening, that he should have been able to stop it.

Had there ever been a time when he wasn't responsible for himself and everyone else around him? When someone had shielded him rather than the other way around?

"That's when my father almost had me enlisted in the Royal Navy."

This was not a shock, for he'd mentioned it before, but it still made me sick to my stomach to think of him placed in such danger when he was so young. Particularly with the war against Napoleon raging. "What stopped him?"

"Mother. She fought him tooth and nail to keep me with her. Said my banishment from Langstone Manor and my lessons for a month were punishment enough. And Father relented. I think because Mother asked him for so little. How could he deny her?"

I nodded, but I was really pondering why his mother could fight so hard on that point, but not fight to protect him from her family's barbs. Perhaps such a reflection was unfair, for she couldn't be with him all the time, particularly in her illness. But all the same, I couldn't help feeling a bit vexed that Emma Trevelyan Gage had not sheltered her son more. What would I have done if I were in her shoes?

It was a legitimate question, for given my scandalous past and my current unorthodox involvement in my husband's inquiries, my children were certain to face some scorn. When that happened, how would I respond? Would my children bring such slights to my attention or, like Gage, would they try to shield me? I didn't know the answers, but I would have liked to think I would protect them any way possible.

If they would let me.

I studied my husband's face, wondering if that was the problem. Maybe Gage hadn't let his mother protect him. I quickly discarded the notion. When he was an older boy, that was possible, but at some point when he was young, he'd learned he couldn't rely on others to defend him.

Maybe in some ways I should be grateful for that, for it had made his enduring the gossip attached to me easier. But sometimes I worried he too easily fell back on old habits, sheltering me when he shouldn't.

I leaned over to kiss the honorable man I'd married, pouring all of my regret that he'd had to endure so much pain, and gratitude that he'd chosen me for his wife, into my caress. When I lifted my mouth to stare into his eyes, my chest tightened at the vulnerability reflected there. Gage so rarely showed weakness. Even in our private interactions he was usually so confident and self-assured. To see him expose his pain and insecurities in such a raw way made me want to wrap him up in my arms and never let him go.

Instead I settled for soothing as many of his hurts as I could with my love. Perhaps if I kissed every square inch of him, if I whispered enough words of love into his skin as I held him as close to me as humanly possible, it would be a start.

CHAPTER SIXTEEN

True to Gage's intentions, we spent much of the next day visiting the farmsteads and homes that bordered the moor around White Tor. Gage was at his most charming, setting even the guarded and cantankerous men at ease. It helped that many of them knew him and seemed to respect him, having followed some of his more daring exploits in the newspapers. Even Thaddeus Bray, who had inherited his father's property when he passed, appeared pleased to see him. At the very least, I sensed no rancor from that affair with their family's ceremonial dagger long ago.

The same could not be said of Alfred.

Though Gage was as discreet as his grandfather could wish, approaching the matter of his cousin in as indirect a manner as possible, we had no trouble finding out the information we truly sought and much more. From the beginning, it was evident that Alfred was not well liked. Either these residents didn't care whether their uncomplimentary comments got back to Alfred or they trusted me and Gage to keep their words to ourselves, for they were brutally honest. In truth, I wondered if perhaps they hoped Gage would report some of their disgruntlement back to Lord Tavistock.

The complaints were much the same. Alfred was snide and reckless, uncaring of who or what got in the way of his own pleasure. Just as Gage had feared, there was no end of angry fathers, brothers, and husbands who claimed his cousin had trifled with their female relations in some way. Much of the time it appeared to be mere flirtation, but there were a few more troubling incidents. One farmer claimed Alfred had gotten his daughter in the family way but had refused to admit it. Apparently the allegation had been believable enough, or Lord Tavistock was merely kind, for he had given the girl a handsome enough dowry to attract a decent husband willing to accept her illegitimate child.

Regardless, no one admitted to having seen Alfred in almost a month, and as voluble as they'd been on his sins, I doubted they were withholding anything. No one confessed to witnessing anything out of the ordinary either. Which meant that, while the information we'd uncovered might be important, the day's efforts proved useless in getting us any closer to finding Alfred. There was always the possibility that one of these wronged men—or women—had decided to take the matter of Alfred's appalling behavior into their own hands, but that seemed rather far-fetched.

By the time we'd finished our last interview, the warmth of the afternoon had begun to wane and a stiff breeze picked up over the moor. I was weary from the hours of riding and maintaining interest in the others' conversations, even when it had nothing to do with our inquiry. Contrarily, Gage appeared invigorated, sitting tall on his horse as we ambled down an old bridle path deeper into the moor. Today he had been in his element, giving me a glimpse of the type of lord he would be when he inherited his father's title and estate.

The soft evening light washed over the heath around us, revealing swaths of gorse and milkwort flowers, and prickly bracken intruding on some of the drier slopes. Before us to the east, we were treated to a sweeping view of some of the tors, their craggy formations stark against the azure sky. Skylarks and meadow pipits circled overhead before soaring back toward the woodlands behind us. To the west, tucked into the shadowy folds of a valley, nestled the slate rooftops of two villages. The southern hamlet boasted a stolid gray church tower, and I wondered if it might mark the churchyard where Gage's mother was buried.

I scowled in irritation as another gust of wind blew the wayward strands of my hair about my face. If not for the blustery breezes, the weather would have been perfect. I struggled futilely to tuck my straggling hairs back under my jaunty riding hat, nearly missing the sight of a jagged stone pillar positioned near the intersection of our bridle path and another narrower track. It appeared too small to be another standing stone. Reining my mare to a stop, I glanced at Gage in question.

"This is Stephen's Grave," he said.

Recalling how he'd told me Rory claimed this Stephen's ghost haunted the manor, I surveyed the moss-studded grave marker with more interest. "I sense there's a story behind this." Given the fact that historically suicides had been buried at crossroads, it wasn't a great leap of logic to conclude such a thing.

Gage rested his hands on the pommel of his saddle and turned his head to gaze off over the ridge to the south where the roof of Langstone Manor was just visible above a line of trees. "The legend says that a man named John Stephen, who lived in one of the villages nearby, fell in love with a local girl. However, her parents didn't approve of the match and so she was forced to break his heart." He gestured to the empty, windswept heath around us. "She met him out on this bleak part of the moor to tell him she no longer wished to see him, and he gave her an apple as a parting gift. But the apple was poisoned. And after she fell victim, he also ate of the same apple, in hopes that their bodies would lay side by side for eternity."

"Given the fact that this is called Stephen's Grave, I'm guessing his wish did not come true."

His lips curled humorlessly. "They buried Stephen here at the crossroads, as was the custom for suicides. But the girl was interred in the village churchyard, albeit at the north end since no one could be certain she hadn't also taken her life in a fit of despair, though most agreed she must have been murdered." His eyes narrowed on the lopsided stone, which seemed to be sinking into the fescue beneath it. "His ghost is said to haunt this area on dark nights, searching for his missing love."

"I suppose such a belief isn't surprising considering one of the reasons suicides were buried at crossroads was because it was supposed to confuse their spirits." I glanced toward Langstone. "But why did Rory suggest his ghost was haunting the manor?" I studied Gage's bronzed features. "Was he simply being cruel given your father's name is Stephen?"

"Probably."

But I could tell there was more. I waited patiently for him to continue, watching the darting flight of a rook overhead. When Gage's eyes finally shifted to meet mine, it was evident he didn't like what he had to reveal next.

"There are also ludicrous rumors that a relative of mine is connected to the affair. Alice, my grandfather's older sister. Some say she was the girl Stephen loved and murdered."

My eyes widened in surprise.

He shook his head. "But although Alice did die a young woman, there is no proof she had anything to do with this Stephen. The one time I asked my mother about it, she told me Alice had died from an illness." His gaze turned distant. "She wouldn't say more, and I assumed that was because of her own precarious state of health."

What he didn't say, but I could hear in his voice, was that he wondered now if he'd been wrong. If his mother had refused to share anything more about Alice because she didn't want him to know the truth.

"Have you ever asked your grandfather about her?"

"No. It seemed cruel somehow."

"Do you think Rory did?"

A sharp gust of wind whipped over the moor, almost knocking his hat from his head. He reached up to secure it and then spurred his horse forward, forcing me to follow suit.

"If he did, I can't imagine my grandfather answered him," he replied, eyeing the fast-moving clouds with misgiving. "The weather is shifting. Let's not dawdle. There will be heavy mist on these moors before nightfall."

True to Gage's prediction, thick mist engulfed the manor before we even sat down to dinner. It was rather disconcerting to peer out the windows and discover that the blustery day had suddenly given way to an almost preternatural calm. It wasn't that I hadn't believed Gage and his grandfather when they tried to explain how capricious the weather on Dartmoor could be, but I *had* questioned whether they'd exaggerated.

It was no wonder so many people had become lost and disoriented over the centuries. How many bodies lay as yet undiscovered in the vast nothingness of the moors or sunken in her bogs? I could well imagine how the legend of Vixana the witch and others like it had sprung up. In a less rational age, it must have seemed as good an explanation as any for the rapid shifts in weather.

Somewhat surprisingly, the Dowager Lady Langstone sent her regrets, claiming a megrim kept her from joining us for dinner. Pleading a headache had been used by women for centuries as a polite way to excuse oneself from an engagement, so I didn't worry she was actually suffering a poor turn in her health. She'd seemed a woman of remarkable fortitude, and I decided it was far more likely she simply didn't wish to dine with us that night. Apparently we weren't the only ones who found the present company trying, though for distinctly different reasons.

In her absence, Gage and I enjoyed a rather companionable meal with Rory. His sulky resentment from the day before had subsided, and he returned to the amiable, easygoing nature he'd displayed during the first days of our arrival. I was tempted to ask him how much more, if anything, he knew about Stephen's Grave, but I didn't want to risk lowering the mood. After days of tense, morose exchanges, we were all in need of a bit of lighthearted conversation.

Seeing the good it did Gage to reminisce with his cousin about happier times, I wasn't sorry I'd elected not to press for more information. His shoulders relaxed and his eyes lost that hard edge they'd so often exhibited since our arrival. He even threw his head back and laughed several times as they recounted some of their bouts of innocent mischief. Rory took care not to bring up any incident that might recall the ill-treatment Gage had received, and I was grateful. It was a relief to hear that not all of Gage's childhood had been unhappy.

As we left the dining room, Hammett approached Gage to give him some correspondence that had been delivered earlier. Gage turned each letter over, examining the outsides before breaking the seal on the second one while we all still stood in the entry hall. He quickly scanned the page and then sighed. I could almost see the weight he'd shrugged off during dinner settle back onto his shoulders.

"Alfred is not in Plymouth," he relayed to Rory and me. He slid the first letter out from beneath the other and frowned, but refrained from opening it. "Please excuse me. I must see to this at once."

"Of course," I replied, having already recognized the handwriting on the second note as his father's. He was also the only person I knew who could put that conflicted look in Gage's eyes.

I watched him stride away, wishing the timing of the arrival of his father's letter could have been better. Even from far away, Lord Gage was still able to disrupt his son's good humor.

"I hesitate to do so now," Rory murmured, recalling my attention. "But I have some matters I really should attend to myself." He grimaced in apology. "Though I suppose if they wait another hour, it won't make much of a difference."

"So you can entertain me? No, no. Go on," I assured him. "I shall find something to occupy myself."

"Are you certain?"

"Yes." I smiled when he still hesitated and waved him away. "Now shoo."

He laughed. "Far be it from me to disobey a lady's orders. Thank you."

I nodded, watching him hurry away. I'd assumed those matters had to do with the business of the estate, but perhaps I should have politely inquired. Would he have been honest? Would I have been able to tell?

Shaking my head at my rampant suspicion, I turned to survey the chilly entry hall, wondering what I should do with myself. Perhaps I should take the opportunity to finally locate the library. I was sure Hammett could point me in the right direction.

As if beckoned by my contemplations, the butler materialized in a doorway behind me. "M'lady?"

I swiveled to face him.

"If you're not otherwise engaged . . ."

I almost arched my eyebrows at that comment, for obviously he'd been listening and was aware I was not.

"Perhaps you'd be willin' to sit with his lordship for a time. His illness is troublin' him this evening. 'Tis the damp. It gets into his lungs."

The same complaint Gage's mother had suffered from. Was it something that ran in the family? Or was it merely this dismal, drafty old house?

"T'would give his valet a chance to eat some dinner and gather any supplies he needs for the night," Hammett added in his creaky voice when I didn't immediately respond.

"Of course, I would be happy to." I turned to go and then paused. "Though, you might need to remind me how to get there." I'd mastered the path from our bedchamber to Lord Tavistock's, but not from the entry hall.

His eyes twinkled with suppressed humor. "I'll show ye the way, m'lady."

I followed him up the staircase, finding myself curious about this longtime retainer. He was plainly more than a majordomo. In fact, I would venture to say he was almost a friend to the viscount, though I was certain both men would have balked at such a designation. Hammett also seemed to have eyes and ears all over the house. I suspected little went on that he didn't know about.

"You've been a servant here a long time," I ventured to say, hoping he would pick up the conversational gauntlet.

"Yes, m'lady. Almost my entire life. Started as the stable boy when his lordship was not much more than a boy himself."

That was quite a precipitous rise from stable boy, one of the lowest-ranking male servants, to majordomo, even if it had been done over several decades. The family must have sponsored his education in some way.

As if he could hear my thoughts, he confirmed this. "His lordship's father took an interest in me. Had me instructed and given a bit o' polish."

It also explained his more common accent, which I'd attributed to his being a Devonshire man.

"Did you know the viscount's sister Alice, then?"

Hammett's head swiveled to glance over his shoulder at me, not missing the obvious connotation of such a question. "Aye. But only in passing. I helped with her mount a time or two."

"Gage showed me Stephen's Grave today," I offered by way of explanation.

"And told ye the legend, and the Trevelyan family's possible connection to it," he deduced. "Aye, well, 'tis only natural then you'd be curious about his lordship's sister after that." He paused, turning to face me. "But leave those questions for another night. I'm sure his lordship will tell ye the tale if ye ask, but it's bound to upset him. So save them for a time when maybe he's not so weak."

His words were gentle, but firm—his priority being his employer's health and well-being. I couldn't fault him for that, so I nodded in agreement.

He led me around the corner even though I was now familiar with our surroundings, and came to a stop outside Lord Tavistock's bedchamber door. "I'll have some tea sent up. Is there anything else I can get ye?"

"My sketchbook and charcoals." If the viscount was able to rest, I would need something to occupy my time. "If you send my maid Bree for them, she'll know where to find them."

He bowed in understanding and then opened the door to beckon the valet forward. I switched places with the short, somber man, settling into the chair he'd positioned near the bedside. A blazing fire crackled in the hearth, but as before it did almost nothing to alleviate the chill trapped within these cold stone walls or to drive out the damp seeping in through the windows.

The light flickered over Lord Tavistock's features, making the hollows of his cheeks and the knife-blade thinness of his nose all the more pronounced. The extremes of light and shadow almost made him appear as a caricature of himself. Listening to his rasping breaths, each one an agonizing rattle, there was no doubt that his illness was worse than he let on. Whether this was because he didn't wish to acknowledge it or he didn't want others to write him off so soon, I couldn't say, but I suspected it was a bit of both.

Hammett returned with the tea, my sketchbook, and a warm shawl. I wasn't sure if he or Bree had thought to send the garment, but regardless, I was grateful to them. I settled the woolen wrap around my shoulders and wrapped my hands around my cup of the hot brew. Once my fingers no longer felt like ice, I kicked off my slippers and tucked my feet up under my skirts before picking up my sketchbook.

I sat that way for some time, comfortably ensconced in my chair, drawing from memory a few of the farmers we'd encountered that day, with nothing but the ticking of the clock on the mantel for company. Then I ventured to sketch what my fingers were truly itching to—Lord Tavistock. He would've hated to be captured in such a feeble position as he lay in now, so instead I drew him as I imagined he was before this illness had forced him to take to his bed.

I didn't immediately notice when the viscount woke, but it couldn't have been long. Not when I'd been flicking my gaze up to study his features while I sketched. When I caught sight of his silver eyes staring back at me, I set my book aside and rose to my feet.

"Would you like some water?"

"Yes," he croaked.

Perching on the bed, I helped him to drink, trying not to react to the evident pain it caused him to swallow. When he finished, he waved me away, lifting the counterpane to smother a wet cough that rattled up from his chest.

"A bit of warm tea might help," I coaxed, lifting my pot. "My nursemaid used to tell us it was the best thing for us when either my siblings or I were ill. Especially if a cough was rasping our throat."

He shook his head stubbornly. "Were you drawing me?"

"Yes." There was no point in lying. He knew the answer. But I also wasn't going to explain myself. I could draw who I very well pleased.

His brow furrowed in what appeared to be displeasure, but he didn't castigate me as I'd expected. Instead, he lifted his hand and asked politely, "May I see it?"

I considered refusing, but that seemed petty. The least I could do was remain civil. So I passed him my sketchbook.

I tried not to watch him as he studied the drawing of himself and then began perusing the rest of the book. Part of it was filled with depictions of the people who populated Langstone Manor and the area around it, while the rest were sketches from our time in Ireland. Preliminary illustrations of the Irish people I hoped to paint for an exhibit in London—my first since my marriage to Sir Anthony at twenty-one. However, it was impossible not to sneak glances at him even though his expression revealed little. If anything, he struggled to look disinterested.

So instead I crossed to the windows and lifted aside the drapes to stare out at the swirling haze of darkness. I didn't want to care what Gage's grandfather thought of me or my artistic abilities, and yet my rib cage tightened as I awaited his judgment. Breathing deeply, I told myself it didn't matter, but the truth was I wanted someone in Gage's family to approve of me.

His father certainly didn't. I'd essentially had to blackmail him just to convince him to attend our wedding for Gage's sake. Lady Langstone plainly objected to our association, and while Rory seemed to like me, I was never quite certain of him. He'd proven more difficult to read than perhaps any of them.

But perhaps most troubling was the fact that the more I learned about his mother, the less certain I became she would've accepted me either. I'd comforted myself with the impression that she would've been pleased by our match—a balm against Lord Gage's malice—but now I wasn't so sure. If she'd brought him back here to be educated as a gentleman, to live among such society, then perhaps a scandalous outcast like myself wouldn't have been her choice in a bride for her only son.

It was useless to speculate. After all, had Emma lived, Gage would not be the man he was today. Our paths probably never would've crossed. But that didn't stop me from contemplating it.

Lord Tavistock cleared his throat, recalling my attention, and I turned to see him closing the sketchbook. "You have talent."

"Thank you," I replied, recognizing it for the great compliment it was coming from the cantankerous viscount.

"Lord Gage said you were a woman of rare ability," he said, handing me back my book.

I was so stunned by this comment that I almost missed the seat of my chair. "He did?" I stammered, making an awkward recovery to prevent myself from sliding to the floor.

"He says he has it on good authority that the Duchess of Bowmont is eager to have you paint her portrait."

This was news to me, though who knew what sort of correspondence we'd missed after setting off for our latest inquiry in Ireland. However, I was confounded by Lord Gage's willingness to pay me a compliment.

Or was it truly praise? I found it far easier to imagine him describing me as a "woman of rare ability" with a sardonic edge of irony rather than genuine admiration. But why had he written to Lord Tavistock about me at all?

"You seem perplexed." His sharp eyes didn't miss anything, even when his eyelids drooped with fatigue.

"Yes, I suppose I am," I replied, deciding I didn't owe Lord Gage my silence or my loyalty. Not when he'd always treated me so dreadfully.

A spark of humor lit the viscount's eyes. "I take it you and Stephen Gage are not as close as he would have me believe."

I arched my eyebrows. "Not unless you think I find condescension and disdain endearing."

He chuckled.

"From all I've observed, Lord Gage can barely stand me. And I merely tolerate him for Sebastian's sake."

He folded his arms over his stomach. "Well, don't let it bother you too much. Stephen Gage has always been overly concerned with social status. Though I suppose one can hardly blame him when his ancestors were so quick to throw it away. He married a viscount's daughter, so I suspect he wasn't willing to tolerate anything less than the daughter of an earl for Sebastian."

I wasn't sure whether Lord Gage had written to boast about the alliance he hoped to secure for his son or Lord Tavistock simply knew him that well, but the viscount's inkling was correct. Gage's failure to obey his father's wishes and wed the debutante he'd chosen for him had been the main source of contention over our improbable match.

"If I know anything, sooner or later Gage's father will come to terms with your marriage and work his way around to trying to charm you. He simply can't abide the idea of a female who isn't enamored of him."

That was not the impression I'd been given. He seemed quite content with my animosity.

His throat rattled as he spoke again. "But let's forget him. I'm not really concerned with his opinion. Only mine."

He began to cough and gestured toward the water glass. I sat on the edge of the bed next to him, waiting for his rasping breaths to settle, and then helped him to drink again. But when I would have risen to return to my chair, he stopped me by touching my arm.

"I want you to paint a portrait of Sebastian. One I can have hung in the gallery with all the others." He sank back deeper in his pillows, his face twisting with a pain he tried to repress. "I should have had it done years ago, but . . ."

But Gage had never returned after his mother's funeral.

He sighed and shook his head. "So many mistakes."

"It's not too late to remedy some of them."

"Maybe."

But I wasn't going to let it go so easily. "There is no maybe about it."

He looked up at me, perhaps surprised by my adamant tone.

"The right words go a long way to healing hurts, even when they are late in coming." I studied his wizened features. "Just don't wait too long."

I thought he might argue with me or take offense at my stating the blunt truth. That he wasn't long for this world. Not unless he drastically improved. Instead, his eyes twinkled with the same repressed amusement I'd seen earlier.

"You remind me of my Edith. She would have liked you."

The words were spoken so tenderly I felt a catch in my throat.

As if sensing we were both in danger of turning maudlin, he cleared his throat. "So will you paint Gage's portrait for me or not? I may not be here to see it, but I'll have my solicitor add to my will that the painting should be hung in the gallery beside his mother's when it's moved back to its customary place." His brow furrowed. "They should be hung together."

I nodded. "Yes. I would be happy to."

He patted my hand where it rested beside him on the bed. "Good, good." Then he closed his eyes, seeming more at peace than before. "I think I'll rest now."

I took that as my cue to move back to my chair. Picking up my sketchbook, I opened it to a fresh page. But when the viscount's valet returned to relieve me half an hour later, I'd still not put charcoal to paper.

CHAPTER SEVENTEEN

A shriek pierced the air and I jumped, almost spilling tea on the lilac apron covering my white jaconet morning dress. I set my cup in the saucer with a clatter and glanced across the table at Gage. He'd lowered the newspaper he'd been scanning with a sharp rustle and now cast it aside to rise to his feet. Leaving the breakfast room, we followed the sound of raised voices to the entry hall where the Dowager Lady Langstone stood at the base of the stairs shouting.

"Where did you get this?" she demanded, pointing at something one of the men before her held. "Where did you get this?"

Hammett stood between them, trying to calm her ladyship while the two men seemed to almost cower under her vehement questioning. I recognized one of them from the day before as a farmer Gage had spoken to. He owned a small farmstead north of White Tor. The second man was unfamiliar to me, though from the manner of his rough dress I surmised he was likely employed as a laborer.

Whatever the case, he clutched in his hands the source of Lady

Langstone's distress. As we drew closer, I realized it was a cloth of some sort—a deep blue superfine fabric with gold buttons. It must be a coat. A gentleman's frock coat. I stiffened. And it was stained with something dark.

I glanced up at Lady Langstone's wild eyes. Her reaction left little doubt she'd recognized it.

"Mr. Porlock, what brings you to Langstone on such a murky morning?" Gage said, stepping into the fray.

"Mr. Gage, sir," the farmer gasped, turning to him to explain. His eyes kept darting toward Lady Langstone as if she might pounce on him. "I came as quick as I could. Ye said ye wished to be notified of anything odd or suspicious right away."

"Yes?"

He nodded over his shoulder at the man holding the coat. "Plym here showed up at the farm late yesterday afternoon with *that*, but with the weather turned, I decided it best to wait 'til mornin' to make the trek here."

Gage stepped forward to take the fabric from Plym's hands, swiveling so we could all examine it better. "Where did you find it?"

"'Tween Cocks Hill an' Lynch Tor, a bit off the bridle path what leads between," the laborer answered hastily. "'Twas my hound who found it. Snagged on some heather near a boggy bit."

My stomach dipped.

Gage lifted the cloth toward Lady Langstone, who seemed unable to move except for clenching and unclenching her hands. It was as if she both wanted and didn't want to touch it, to verify it was, in fact, her son's.

"It's Alfred's?" he asked her gently, acknowledging what we could already see was true.

She blinked and then nodded.

Gage lifted his gaze to Rory in question where he stood behind his mother on the stairs, having come clattering down moments before. His expression somewhat dazed, he also nodded.

My husband caught my eye for a brief but significant moment

as he turned back to Mr. Porlock and Plym. "Thank you for bringing this to our attention."

The farmer's face was white with apprehension. "Does this mean . . . ? Is Lord Langstone . . . ?" He clearly didn't want to say the words, not with the dowager present.

"Lord Langstone is missing," Gage replied succinctly. "There was some cause for confusion, so we couldn't be certain that was the case. Which is why we elected to proceed with such delicacy." He frowned. "But it appears now we can no longer deny that fact."

Nor could his grandfather insist we keep the matter quiet.

The men accepted this explanation without further question and allowed Hammett to escort them out while Gage led the rest of us into the drawing room. Shoving aside the objects on the top of a round table near the corner, he spread the coat out across the wood. I moved to his side as he leaned over to examine it. Something had caused a tear in the seam at the shoulder either before or after it was removed from Alfred's torso, and one of the ornate buttons was missing, leaving behind a loose string. But it was the stain splashed across the fabric I found most disturbing, for it was plainly neither mud nor bog water.

"Kiera, tell me your opinion," Gage declared as he flipped the coat over to inspect the back. "Do you think this is blood?"

Trying to ignore Rory and Lady Langstone, I gingerly lifted the fabric to study the stains. The deep blue obscured some of the substance's true color, but hints of dark red showed on the most heavily saturated parts. When I pressed my finger into a swath that was still damp, it came away coated in carmine red. Lady Langstone turned away as I lifted my finger to my nose and sniffed it. The distinctive metallic odor assailed me, as well as the musty stench of marsh water and rotting vegetation.

"Yes. Though . . . I can't say with any certainty that this blood is from Lord Langstone. It could be another person's. Or an animal's. But given the fact that it's staining his frock coat . . ." I didn't need to finish that sentence, for why would someone else's blood be coating Alfred's garment? And in such large quantities.

Gage's eyes were solemn as he passed me his handkerchief. "Given the size of the stains, do you think whatever caused this was survivable?"

I wiped my fingers, but continued to clutch the handkerchief to cover the red still tinting my skin. "I don't think there's enough evidence here to argue for certain. After all, head wounds bleed like the devil. But I still find the quantity to be worrying." Whatever Alfred's injury had been, it hadn't been minor.

Having heard enough, Lady Langstone strode from the room. We all turned to watch her go and I thought Rory might follow her, but he remained fixed to his spot, waiting to hear what we said next.

In any case, without her present, it was easier to speak frankly.

"Perhaps if we could discover where the injury occurred, we might have a better idea of how severe Lord Langstone was hurt." I sighed. "Though after a fortnight, the rain and mist must have washed away most of that evidence."

"I'll speak to Mr. Porlock and Plym again," Gage replied. "Perhaps they can lead us to the spot where Plym found the coat."

"What the blazes was he doing all the way out beyond Cocks Hill?" Rory finally interjected. "There's nothing there."

Gage evidently wondered the same thing. "Maybe that wasn't his final destination," he suggested. "Maybe wherever he was headed was beyond that."

Rory shook his head in frustration. "That still doesn't make sense. There's nothing out there but old tin-mining remnants."

Gage didn't say the words, but I knew he was contemplating the same thing I was. Alfred might not have gone there of his own volition. It was just as possible someone had taken him there, either still alive or already dead.

But there was also another possibility.

"If he sustained a head injury of some sort, he could've become disoriented and lost his way," I ventured to say. "If so, who knows where or how far he wandered."

"He could be miles from here," Gage added, picking up my train of thought. "Further north toward Lydford or even east toward Postbridge."

"Or lying dead out in the middle of the high moor," Rory stated bluntly.

Gage's brow furrowed. "Yes."

Rory's eyes dropped to the floor, staring bleakly at something we couldn't see. When he lifted them again, his jaw was set, as if he'd made some momentous decision. "Are you going to see Porlock this morning?"

"Yes. After I tell Grandfather."

He nodded and swiveled to go, speaking over his shoulder. "I'm coming with you to search. Give me a quarter of an hour to prepare. I'll have Hammett pack us some supplies."

Before Gage could respond, he was gone.

"That was quite a reversal," I remarked.

While Rory had seemed baffled by his brother's continued absence, he hadn't appeared all that concerned. At least, not enough to take the initiative to do any investigating or searching himself. Though he'd said he'd begun to worry something bad had happened to Alfred, I'd gotten the sense that part of him still clung to the belief that Alfred was merely off on some lark.

"Yes, well, *this* changes everything," Gage replied, gazing down at the bloodstained coat.

Because now we had proof that something unpleasant had befallen Alfred. Something that had prevented him from returning home.

Or had it?

"I suppose so," I said, unable to shake the feeling we were still missing something.

He must have heard the uncertainty in my voice. "What is it?"

I scowled, unsure how to explain what was bothering me. "It's just . . . why did Plym only find Alfred's frock coat? Why would it have become separated from the rest of Alfred and his effects?"

"Maybe he dropped it. Or maybe an animal carried it away from wherever he is. There are voles and foxes and such about."

I shrugged, conceding his point. But I still wasn't satisfied. "Did the men your grandfather sent to search not look out near Cocks Hill?"

"I'm sure they did. At least, to a certain point. But the moor is massive, Kiera. There's no way they could have covered every square foot." When still I didn't perk up, he frowned. "You're not trying to suggest he faked his death or some such thing? Because while I can imagine Alfred hiding for a time, this is simply taking things too far. Even for him."

"I'm sure you're right," I relented, deciding I was being silly. After all, Gage knew his family and Dartmoor far better than I did. If he saw nothing peculiar, then there probably wasn't anything.

"Perhaps we'll discover more after we search the place where Plym found the coat," he suggested. "After all, it doesn't sound like he made a very wide search, wanting to hurry home before the weather worsened."

I nodded, wanting him to forget I'd expressed any doubt. "Did you want me to come with you to inform your grandfather?"

His expression grew troubled. "Thank you, but I think it might be best if I do it alone."

I pressed a hand to Gage's arm in comfort. "I'll make ready, then."

But instead of going straight to my chamber when we separated at the top of the stairs, I turned my steps toward Lady Langstone's rooms. I'd stumbled upon them two days before while exploring and found them again with relative ease. I knew I risked receiving a scathing set down, but I felt it only right that someone should check on her. After all, she'd just been confronted with her missing son's bloody coat. I could imagine all the terrible scenarios filtering through her mind.

When I reached the door to her sitting room, I found it ajar. Giving it a peremptory rap, I pushed it open to peer inside. A startled curse met my ears and I swung my gaze around to find Lady Langstone kneeling before the hearth, clutching her hand.

"My lady," I gasped, hastening toward her.

She recoiled at the sight of me, stumbling to her feet. "What are you doing here?" she demanded. "How dare you enter my chamber without my permission." She sucked in a pained breath.

"Your door was open. Please, my lady. You've injured yourself. Let me take a look."

"It's just a minor burn," she retorted, continuing to back away.

"Minor or not, you should have it seen to." I held out my hand, demanding she show me her palm.

She glared back at me, but I did not budge, letting her know I was not going to yield on this. Reluctantly, she lowered her hand toward me.

Until her maid appeared in the doorway. "My lady?" she murmured uncertainly, her eyes darting between us.

Lady Langstone snatched her hand back. "Webley, there you are. I appear to have burned my hand. We have some ointment for that, don't we?"

She arched her chin in triumph, and it was all I could do to keep from rolling my eyes. As if I cared whether I was the person to attend to her wound. So long as *someone* saw to it, that was all that mattered.

"Of course, my lady," Mrs. Webley replied, moving swiftly toward the connecting door that must lead into her ladyship's bedchamber. "Right this way."

Lady Langstone hesitated a second, her gaze flicking toward the fireplace behind me. It returned to meet mine squarely. "You can show yourself out." She didn't add the word *now*, but it was implied.

I moved slowly toward the door, catching the glance she darted over her shoulder before disappearing into the next room. Once she was out of sight, I retraced my steps to the hearth, squatting to see what had so concerned her she'd risked injuring herself.

In the midst of the blaze lay the ashes of a stack of papers, their entirety almost consumed. Grabbing the fireplace poker, I stabbed at the documents, trying to save any small bit of them I could. Except for one singed corner, they were all past redemption, crumbling to dust before my eyes. Hazarding my own flesh, I reached out to snag it, and waved it in the air to extinguish the flame licking at it. I dropped it to the floor and stomped on it for good measure. Worrying I'd made too much noise, I snatched it up and slipped from the room.

Once I'd rounded the corner, I paused to examine the tiny remnant in the light of the wall sconce.

It was the beginning of a letter. Naught but a greeting and a few words. *My dearest Vanessa, I am mo . . .* The rest was burned away.

However, it was not as useless as it seemed, for I recognized the handwriting. I'd seen it many times before, and the same as now, the sight was never pleasant. But why had Lord Gage been writing to her? And why was he calling her "my dearest Vanessa"?

For that matter, why had the dowager burned them? What about them had made her rush back to her chamber to destroy them after seeing her missing son's torn and bloody coat?

I supposed these letters could have been from two decades ago when Gage witnessed them carrying on some sort of affair. But then why the urgency to rid herself of them now?

I frowned, unhappy with this latest development, for it would hurt Gage deeply. Why did his father's involvement always seem to harm him? Even when Lord Gage wasn't present, he still managed to find a way to wound his son.

Not this time. Not if I could prevent it.

Glancing around me to be certain no one was watching, I

tucked the singed paper into my pocket. I would find a way to figure out what those burned letters meant without telling Gage. Maybe they had nothing to do with Alfred's disappearance. Maybe Gage never need know his father might have been carrying on with his viperous aunt for all these years.

Maybe was a fickle word.

CHAPTER EIGHTEEN

The village of Peter Tavy straggled out along a gently wooded valley running along the western edge of the moor in a long, thin line. Having come from Plymouth to the south, we'd not passed through it on our way to Langstone Manor. So although I'd seen its rooftops from our vantage at Stephen's Grave several days prior, I'd not actually visited the village proper. The granite buildings with thatch or slate roofs clustered around a single meandering road over which the tall buttressed tower of the medieval St. Peter's Church loomed at the north end. A short distance to the west flowed the River Tavy, for which the village had been named, though the buildings had been built at some distance. Instead they sat nearer to a spring and the banks of a brook which flowed east toward Langstone, passing over several lovely little waterfalls.

It was a charming setting, thick with summer green and bright, blooming flowers that teemed with butterflies, but I scarcely paid it any heed. Exhaustion plagued me from days already spent in the saddle. I'd hoped the pleasant aspect of the lush coombe would revive me after so much time out on the bleak high moor, but the warm sun and burbling brook we followed into the village only made me drowsy. If not for my sore body, I might have actually fallen asleep to the mare's gently rocking gait.

For two days we'd searched the most desolate stretches of Dartmoor for any sign of Alfred. From the boggy cotton grass of Cocks Hill, we'd swept north and south as far into the interior as we could manage, with the assistance of several members of the staff and even a few neighboring farmers, but all was fruitless. We found nothing to suggest Alfred had ever passed that way, not even the missing gold button from his coat. It truly did seem as if he'd vanished. Fearing the worst, the men even prodded the mossy bogs, but to no avail. If he'd stumbled into one of those morasses, I wasn't certain the moor would ever give him up.

It didn't help that I continued to dream of the shadowy man watching over us while we slept. Given the fact we now suspected Alfred could be dead, that presence had taken on a new, more menacing edge. If only I could see the figure's face. Maybe then I could uncover what the dream meant, and lay some of my wilder imaginings to rest.

The discovery of his grandson's torn and bloody coat had understandably upset Lord Tavistock, but at least it had convinced him of the need to end the secrecy. We'd finally been able to reveal to the landowners and laborers we'd spoken to only days before exactly what we'd been hinting at, and most had willingly agreed to help with the search despite their aversion to Alfred. I couldn't help but note their relations to Rory, who circumstances seemed to indicate would be the next Viscount Tavistock. Although their exchanges with him were somewhat stilted, they seemed to accord him an amiable deference.

I also noticed after so many hours together that Rory envied Gage's easy interaction with the other men, and the genuine esteem they seemed to hold for my husband. Most people reacted to

Gage thusly, so I rarely paid any heed. But Rory was evidently not accustomed to seeing his cousin in such a light. Though he readily allowed Gage to lead the search, directing the others on where to look and hearing their reports, as the hours wore on his expression grew sourer when he looked at my husband. Perhaps Rory had changed for the better, but there were still traces of the seeds of resentment his mother had sown in him earlier in life.

As such, I wasn't surprised when Rory decided to remain behind when we ventured to the village. We hoped to discover what we could about the villagers' dealings with Alfred, as well as learn about any unrest that might be festering. We had no way of knowing who had sent Lord Tavistock those Swing letters, or if they'd come from Peter Tavy, but we intended to at least find out how sympathetic the villagers were to the cause.

As such, we elected to divide and conquer. After stabling our horses, I left Gage at the Peter Tavy Inn, where he planned to confer with those in the bar, a room I wouldn't even be allowed to enter as a woman. Instead, I retraced our route through town on foot toward the church and its rectory, thinking the rector or his wife might have information they would be willing to share. When no one answered my knock at the door, I decided to continue on into the village.

But first, unable to resist, I pressed up to the stone wall to peer past the shield of thick trees into the old churchyard. I'd thought Gage might wish to stop there, to visit his mother's grave, but he'd kept his face pointed resolutely forward, as if he could ignore the graveyard's existence. I'd tried to ask him about it, but whenever I drew breath to speak, he suddenly had words of his own to impart. Eventually, I'd stopped trying, for it was obvious he knew what I wanted to know, and just as obvious he did not want to discuss it.

The trees overshadowing the churchyard blocked much of the sun's direct light, giving the space an atmosphere of somber reverence even on such a warm day. Scattered among the vegetation stood crooked rows of crosses and weathered gravestones, their bases sinking and twisting in the soft, mossy soil. And somewhere in that jumble of graves lay Emma Trevelyan Gage, the stone marker over her shaded resting place as cold as her grave. Even though I imagined it to be far more grand than the average gravestone, finding it would take more time than I could spare.

"Can I help you?"

I whirled about, pressing a hand to my chest. I flushed in embarrassment that I'd been so startled by the sound of the woman's voice who stood behind me. She was not much older than I was, and her puzzled frown didn't appear particularly welcoming. Her gaze flicked up and down the epaulet front of my smart plum riding ensemble while she bounced a young dark-haired girl on her hip.

"My apologies," I replied. "My mind was elsewhere. Yes, you could." I adopted my most concerned expression, hoping to disarm her. "I hoped I might speak with the rector, but he appears to be gone."

"Yes, my father was called away. He won't be back for several more hours." She paused before begrudgingly adding, "Is there something I can do for you?"

"Perhaps. I've come for information, really. My husband and I are here on behalf of Lord Tavistock to find out if anyone might know anything about the whereabouts of Lord Langstone." This pronouncement caused a swift change in the woman's impatient countenance. Her eyes hardened and her mouth tightened into a disapproving moue. But still I pressed on. "He's been missing for over a fortnight, and we have reason to believe he may have come to some harm."

"Likely no more than he deserved," she snapped. "If justice was served, you'd find him in hell."

I stared wide-eyed at her, uncertain how to respond to such an acrimonious statement. That her hatred of Alfred was real, there was no doubt. And I could only surmise such ferocious animosity came from personal experience.

My eyes flicked to the little girl again, wondering if she might have a bit of the look of the Dowager Lady Langstone in her. As if in confirmation, the woman's scowl deepened and she clutched the girl tighter. Had her expression been pleasanter, I realized the woman would have been quite pretty, if a bit jaded. I could well imagine her catching Alfred's eye.

"You're Sebastian Gage's wife, aren't you?" she demanded. "We heard he was up at the manor, though not all of us believed it. When he swore he'd never return, none of us blamed him." Her mouth twisted bitterly. "But I suppose now we know why. Blood is blood, even when half of it is rotten."

Several of her assertions stunned me. Namely the fact that the entire village seemed to be aware that Gage had sworn never to return to Langstone Manor. I could only assume they also knew why, even though I, his wife, did not. But I didn't have time to contemplate that further. Not when this woman glared at me as if I were somehow responsible for Alfred as well.

"Yes, I'm Mr. Gage's wife," I murmured softly, hoping by remaining composed I might also calm her. "And you are?"

Her brow furrowed as if she was considering not answering. "Philinda Warne." She nodded down the lane from which I'd come. "My husband owns the inn."

I suspected this last was added to make sure I knew she was wed and that the little girl I'd scrutinized, who watched me curiously, was legitimate. But just because the child had been born in wedlock didn't mean she'd been conceived thusly. If Alfred had trifled with Mrs. Warne and refused to rectify the situation, her marriage to another man who would accept her, either knowingly or unknowingly in her expectant state, would be a natural next step. This little girl would not have been the first healthy, purportedly eight-month-old baby born in England.

"We've heard Lord Langstone was something of a scoundrel

when it came to women. Do you think any of the women he's wronged or their relatives might have gone so far as to physically harm him, deservedly or not?" I added, echoing her words.

She considered my question, intelligence as well as vengeance glinting in her eyes. "If they did, I'll not help you find out who. I'll only silently applaud them for giving him his just deserts."

I thought it more likely she would be the one clapping loudest. Regardless, the only information she was going to provide me was that Alfred had, indeed, had enemies in this village, and some of them had been angry enough to take action against him if the occasion arose. Had one of them found him wandering the moor alone that day and seized the opportunity?

I thanked Mrs. Warne and took my leave of her, feeling her eyes bore into my back as I returned to the road and resumed my stroll toward the heart of the hamlet. There along the stone bridge that straddled the trickling brook congregated the villagers, old and young alike. The older women sat in chairs in the shade of the oak trees overhanging the water to knit and gossip while the littlest children played at their feet. Splashes of water and the shouts and laughter of older children echoed up from the banks of the stream. A few young girls were put to work carrying pitchers of water up from the brook and down the road to the houses where their mothers worked to hang sheets on a line. Most of the males old enough to wield a thresher would be out working in the fields or their shops, but a pair of stooped elderly men sat along the opposite verge of the road, nattering at each other in the sun. I assumed the rest of their aged number were enjoying some ale at the inn on such a warm day, and hopefully conversing with Gage.

Unfortunately, I didn't have the opportunity to observe this altogether common yet thoroughly fascinating picture of rural life for long. The first woman who saw me striding up the road in my fine clothing, the train of my riding habit draped over my arm, turned to her companions and pointed. Soon everyone had paused in their activities to watch me. All but one small child who continued to poke at something in the dirt and the children playing in the brook, whose cries seemed all the louder in the silence that had descended.

Instinctively, I wanted to check my steps, but I forced myself to keep moving forward and paste a pleasant smile on my lips. Perhaps I should have rejected Gage's suggestion that we separate. He would have felt no qualms about approaching these women and charming them into sharing all they knew. I squared my shoulders, determined to do my best.

I gravitated toward the woman seated near the center of the line of chairs, the woman to whom the others seemed to defer, each darting glances in her direction as I neared. Her gray hair was tightly restrained and her clothing crisply pressed, and I surmised she would be someone who valued plain speaking.

"Good morning," I greeted them. "Such a lovely day."

"And a hot one," the matriarch replied.

I nodded, seeing I'd guessed correctly. But before I could explain my reason for being there, another woman spoke up in a softly melodic voice, though it creaked at the edges with age.

"Would ye like a cool drink, m'lady?" Her eyes were so sweetly earnest beneath her crystal white hair I could hardly say no.

"Yes, thank you."

She called out to one of the young girls clutching a pitcher of water, her steps having been arrested by the sight of me. Apparently, dawdling to hear what I had to say was worth risking a scolding from her mother. The child hurried forward, holding the pitcher out to me as if I were some sort of royalty. I flushed, flustered by such treatment, and smiled as I expressed my gratitude.

Perhaps another lady would have sent one of the women to find her a cup to drink from, but these villagers reminded me of the people of Elwick—the tiny Border village where I'd grown up. It seemed silly to send them scrambling when I could drink the cool, crisp water from the pitcher as any less grand person would do. Maybe this meant I'd failed some test of gentility, but I was content with that.

I must have done well enough, for the sweet-faced woman nodded in approval. The girl practically beamed under my praise, and when I returned the pitcher to her she cradled it close as she stepped back.

"Yer from the manor? From Langstone?" the stern woman prodded, growing impatient.

"I . . . yes."

"She be the one what married Master Gage," one of the women leaned forward to whisper, and the others nodded and clucked in approval.

"I've got eyes, now, don't I?" the matriarch snapped. "None o' those other Trevelyans 've been sharp enough to get themselves a wife. Shoulda known Emma's boy would be the first."

"And Master Gage is so nice to look at," the woman with the melodic voice cooed.

I was forced to fight back a bubble of amusement at the avid look in her eyes. Did Gage know he had so many admirers among the village women?

"I don't think herself is here to talk about her husband's fine figure, Pasca." The matriarch narrowed her eyes at me against the glare of the sun. "What trouble has young Langstone gotten himself into now? The men 've been sayin' he lost himself out on the moor."

I wasn't sure why I was surprised she knew. After all, gossip traveled faster than even the mail coach, whether it was high society or a small country village.

"Yes, Lord Langstone has been missing for more than a fortnight. He was last seen walking out onto the moor, and his torn and bloody coat was found two days ago near Cocks Hill."

Several of the women gasped, leaning toward each other to whisper in speculation. The girl with the pitcher blinked at me with wide eyes, and one of the little ones looked up, as if sensing the tension, and began to cry. His grandmother scooped him up, shushing him absently as she waited to hear what I would say next. Only the matriarch seemed unconcerned.

"Have any of you heard or seen anything? Anything that might explain where he's gone or what has happened to him?"

I looked to each of them in turn, but they said nothing, just slid their eyes toward the stern woman to whom they deferred. All but Pasca, whose brow furrowed as if she was contemplating something unpleasant. When none of them spoke, I decided to try a different tack.

"Mrs. Warne suggested Lord Langstone had many enemies."

The matriarch scoffed. "That girl makes her own trouble," she muttered before lifting her chin in confirmation. "Aye, 'tis true his lordship hasn't exactly inspired our trust. He's trifled with one too many o' our girls. But only those who were saucy bits o' muslin askin' for it."

My eyebrows arched at such a harsh pronouncement. It wasn't the first time I'd heard such an assertion, and unfortunately it wouldn't be the last. Sadly, it was more often the women who paid for men's lasciviousness, in more ways than one.

She turned to look down the road in the direction I'd come. "I suspect he has a few sideslips, but word is his grandfather always makes certain them and their mothers are looked after." She shook her head, glancing at the others. "But none o' our lot would be muttonheaded enough to harm Tavistock's heir. 'Specially not the rector."

I could tell that none of the other ladies would naysay her pronouncement, even if they happened to disagree with her. None of them except perhaps Pasca, who was eyeing me with speculation. So it was to her I voiced my next question.

"What about Lord Tavistock? Has anyone taken issue with him? I heard there was some discontent over his adoption of the new horse-powered threshing machines."

"Now *that* would be a question for our menfolk," the matriarch declared with a hard glint in her eye, as if she knew what I was doing and was not going to allow it.

Realizing I wasn't going to receive any satisfactory answers, not with this stern woman present, I thanked them and turned to stroll back toward the inn. I'd initially intended to continue on through the village, speaking to people individually, but I could see more than one person watching from the front of their homes and businesses. The chances that any of them would break rank and tell me what I wanted to know were slim.

I'd traveled about two dozen steps when a voice called out behind me. I swiveled to see Pasca hobbling toward me carrying the pitcher.

"M'lady," she gasped. "Please, ye must be parched in this heat. Take another drink afore ye be on yer way." Her eyes flared wide, coaxing me to cooperate.

"Oh, yes, thank you."

The other women watched us suspiciously as I accepted the pitcher and drank more of the cool water.

"I like ye, m'lady," she announced. "I can tell ye be one o' the good ones, despite all that nonsense the servants at the manor be spreadin' about ye. An' so I'm goin' to warn ye. Drink again," she ordered, as apparently I'd stared at her too long without sipping. "There be rumors surroundin' Langstone Manor. Ones that've been whispered since I was but a girl in braids. Whispers o' dark secrets that reach out and touch every life that passes through its halls."

The cold water turned to ice, settling like a lump in my stomach. This wasn't the first time someone had cautioned me about the manor. "What secrets?"

She shook her head. "I don't know 'em all. But I do know that family be cursed. That a terrible fate befalls any member who dares defy their kin."

I searched her face, trying to understand. "Like Emma?"

"She defied 'em. And she suffered a terrible fate."

The manner in which she replied, with a shrug and an unemotional recitation of facts, was chilling. But Gage's mother was only one person.

"Who else has fallen victim to this curse?"

She took the pitcher back from me. "Two others that I know of. Now maybe three."

Her direct gaze made it clear what she believed had happened to Alfred. But before I could ask her why she believed this, or how he'd defied his family, she murmured a parting warning to "take care," and turned to shuffle back to the other women.

I wanted to stop her, to force her to tell me the rest, but instead I forced myself to look away. She'd already risked the others' censure by telling me that much; I wouldn't cause her further trouble. But whether it had been the cool water or her unsettling pronouncement, I no longer lamented the heat of the sun. I welcomed it. For I suspected it was all that kept the ice in my stomach from spreading through my veins.

I returned to the inn to find Gage standing at the edge of the carriage yard, staring out toward where the River Tavy flowed. From this vantage, we couldn't see it, but the sound of its rushing water echoed off the trees. From the vexed look in his eyes, I gathered his discussion with the local men had gone no better than mine had with the women.

By unspoken agreement, we remounted our horses and set off toward Langstone Manor, waiting until we reached the edge of the village before speaking.

"I could get no answers to my questions about the Swing letters or who might have disputes with Grandfather's acquisition of the new machines. But their very silence makes me suspect there is someone they wish to cover for."

"I encountered more or less the same response." I glanced up at a curlew as it flew overhead issuing its distinctive cry. "Do you have any idea who those disgruntled parties could be?"

"Some of the other landowners had names to suggest, having also received letters. Mostly the laborers who've been the most vocal about the cuts to their wages. The other farmers felt they could hardly blame them for that." He frowned. "But despite the threats, no one has encountered any violence or loss of property. One farmer over past Brentor had his hayrick burned, and there was talk of a gathering of dissenters in Launceston, but that's all anyone could tell me." He sighed. "It seems rather impulsive to skip over destroying threshing machines and move straight to possible assault or murder."

"I agree. That does make little sense." I tilted my head. "Unless the purpose of those letters was to obscure their real intent."

"Killing Alfred?" Gage asked in surprise. He shook his head. "No. Had the letters only been sent to my grandfather, perhaps. But to send them to all the landowners in the surrounding countryside? That's a great deal of effort, all of which might have gone wasted had Glanville not mentioned the letters to us."

I nodded in acceptance. "I met a Mrs. Philinda Warne."

Gage looked up in interest. "The rector's daughter? She's the only Philinda I remember."

I nodded, relaying what she'd told me, as well as the village matriarch's comments on the subject. When I finished, he didn't appear very shocked.

"Well, Philinda always was a bit . . ." He seemed to struggle to find a polite word. "Eager. But that doesn't mean she was asking for what happened to her," he quickly added. "Alfred was far more worldly-wise than her. Than most of those girls. He knew better than to trifle with them."

We fell silent, picking our way through a narrow part of the trail. When it widened again, I drew up beside Gage once more, venturing to introduce the subject I truly wanted to discuss.

"I had an interesting exchange with a woman named Pasca."

Gage perked up, recognizing the name. "Is she still alive?" He shook his head, a fond smile creasing his lips. "She must be almost ninety."

"She doesn't look it."

"Yes, well, she never has looked her age. But I know she's older than Grandfather by several years. What did she have to say?"

My lips quirked in remembrance. "She commented on your good looks."

Gage threw his head back and laughed. "Saucy old girl."

I hesitated, knowing what I had to say next would dim that amusement. "And she warned me to be careful."

His head swung around so fast I worried he might have hurt himself.

"She told me there are dark rumors surrounding Langstone Manor and your family. That a terrible fate befalls those of you who defy your kin."

His expression closed off and he looked away. "Nonsense."

"She . . . she even went so far as to suggest your mother and now Alfred were victims of the curse," I pressed, trying to stop him from retreating behind the walls he so often threw up around himself. I'd believed we were moving beyond that, but apparently not.

"It's nothing but nonsense," he restated firmly.

"Are you certain? Because she said there were two more Trevelyans who suffered a similar fate. Do you know—"

"There is no curse," he barked, cutting me off.

However, the very fact that he was angry told me there must be something to it.

He inhaled a deep breath so that when he next spoke, his voice was level again. "As I said, it's all a lot of nonsense the villagers dreamed up. Superstitious drivel to explain what they don't understand."

I studied his profile, confused why he refused to discuss this. Perhaps there wasn't a curse, but some more human agent could be at work. We knew Annie had steadily poisoned Emma, but what or who had given her the idea to do so? If there was a pattern of tragic deaths in his family, then shouldn't they be examined and compared with Alfred's disappearance?

"Is your grandfather's sister Alice supposed to be one of them?" I ventured to ask.

But Gage only sighed wearily. "Kiera, let it go."

"Why? Obviously this is important, or you wouldn't be refusing to even discuss it."

"I'm not refusing to discuss it. There's simply nothing *to* discuss. As I said, it's nonsense." He'd adopted his I'm-being-perfectly-reasonable-and-you're-not tone of voice, the one that was certain to make me lose my temper.

"I see," I bit out. "Then I suppose I'll have to speak to your grandfather." I spurred my horse forward, but his hand shot out to snag my reins.

"Do *not* disturb my grandfather with this. He's ill enough. I won't have you making him worse."

I wanted to refuse, but behind his frosty stare I glimpsed genuine apprehension for his grandfather. I'd witnessed myself his steady decline. Would unhappy reminiscences precipitate that further? I'd thought him sturdier than that, but I supposed if the memories were particularly troubling, it was possible. So I gave a sharp nod of acquiescence. For now.

But that didn't mean I was giving up. For in spite of what Gage said, there was something to this talk of a curse. Something disturbing enough to rattle him. And if he wouldn't explain it to me, then I would just have to find my answers elsewhere.

I pulled my horse's reins from his grasp, and spurred my mare on ahead of him, uncaring whether he followed.

CHAPTER NINETEEN

I inhaled a deep breath of bracing air and boosted myself up on top of one of the exposed pieces of granite to survey the moor laid out before me. Gage had said the view on top of White Tor was a lovely one, and he was right. My lips twisted in remembered aggravation. If only he'd seen fit to tell me what his plans were for today, he might have enjoyed the sight with me.

We'd mostly avoided each other since our quarrel the day before. I'd even retired early to our chamber in order to avoid speaking with him, though I'd still been awake when he entered my bedchamber and climbed into bed. My heart had softened when, after a moment's hesitation, he'd rolled over to curl his long, warm body against my back and wrapped his arm around my middle to pull me close. I had felt his fretting, his uncertainty, and unable to endure it, I turned to face him. But before I could speak, the ache in his eyes had arrested my words. So instead I'd kissed him.

The fervency with which he kissed me back had surprised me. There was an urgency to it different than he'd ever displayed before, and I had been helpless to resist it. I think in that moment if he could have consumed me and made me permanently part of him, he would have. Whether it was painful memories or fear of the future, I didn't know, but I knew without hesitation he had been trying to communicate with his hands, his mouth, and his body what he couldn't find the words to say. So I'd responded in kind. Words could wait until morning.

Except morning had come, and when I reached over to touch him, all I'd found was the cold depression where he'd lain.

With the light of a new day, and a good night's rest, I realized I'd been rather insensitive to Gage. After all, who wants to hear talk that their mother was killed as some part of a curse, let alone seriously consider it? I prided myself on my intuition, my perception, yet I'd ignored the signs of Gage's distress. I well knew he closed off his emotions when he was upset or threatened. I should have raised the subject more delicately, and allowed him to retreat for a short time to mull it over before addressing it again. Then I might have been able to coax the information out of him.

At least then I wouldn't have been seated on this cold rock by myself. I closed my eyes and tilted my face up to the sun as it broke through the clouds, welcoming the warmth of its rays up on this blustery tor.

When after I'd prepared myself for the day Gage had still not returned to our chamber, I'd gone searching for him. I'd thought I might find him with his grandfather, but instead I stumbled into the end of an argument between Lord Tavistock and Rory. Neither man could tell me where my husband was, and I'd quickly taken myself off, deciding I didn't need to be in the middle of their altercation no matter how curious I was what had caused the charge in the air between them. Hammett also protested ignorance of Gage's location, though his stilted response made me suspect he had a guess, but one he was unwilling to share.

Thus thwarted, I'd abandoned my quest and decided to go for a walk. If nothing else, it would help me clear my head and sort my thoughts. The day was a fine one, and I figured if I remained close to the manor I wouldn't risk becoming lost even if the weather began to shift.

Since I'd yet to climb White Tor, I set off in that direction first. From my vantage at its top, I could see the western edge of the moor stretched out before me across to Great Mis Tor and up to Cocks Hill and the expanse of nothingness beyond.

I still couldn't puzzle out what Alfred had been doing out here that day he vanished. Could he have been meeting someone? But if so, wouldn't he have chosen a recognizable marker? Perhaps the Langstone? But then why had he continued on beyond it out into the moor where his coat was found? Surely if he were just out for a stroll, he would have taken a different route.

Maybe he'd needed space to think, as I was doing perched up on this tor. Somehow being above it all made my thoughts clearer. I'd learned that fact when I was but a girl. It was why I'd so often retreated to the attics at Blakelaw House, my childhood home. Why I'd turned the loft in the library at my brother-in-law's Highland castle into my own personal sanctuary during the months after Sir Anthony's death and the ensuing scandal that had erupted.

But perhaps Alfred thought better while moving. Perhaps in his distraction, he'd tripped and fallen, striking his head somehow, and become muddled. But then why couldn't we find his body? Had a bog truly swallowed him whole, leaving no trace?

"Oh, good morning."

I blinked up at the sandy-haired man who had rounded the shattered granite stack I was seated on. I'd been so absorbed in my own reflections that I'd failed to note his approach.

"Good morning," I replied, tilting my head in recognition. "It's . . . Mr. Bray, isn't it?"

He nodded. "It seems we've had the same idea this fine morning, Mrs. Gage." He gestured toward me. "Do you mind if I join you?"

"Not at all." I smiled in invitation and slid over to make room for him next to me.

"Where is your husband?" he asked, settling beside me. "Out making more inquiries?"

"Yes," I lied, not wanting to admit I had no idea where he was. "He's concerned for his cousin."

"Understandable. He is family, after all."

I found it interesting he should phrase it as such, narrowing in on the aspect of it being more of a duty rather than a matter of familial affection. But then I remembered he'd grown up with them. They'd run across the moor together, likely climbing this very tor. And, of course, there was that other matter with the dagger. In the interaction I'd observed between them, Mr. Bray hadn't seemed to harbor any ill will toward Gage, but I wasn't about to dredge up the affair.

I studied the amiable man out of the corner of my eye. Mr. Bray might be an invaluable resource of information about the Trevelyans without my having to ask the Trevelyans themselves.

"My husband says you used to play together as boys."

"Oh, aye." His lips curled upward in a broad grin, revealing deep dimples. "He and I more than Langstone and Rory. Those two were a might too high in the instep for the likes of us at times. But that was fine by us. It was usually more fun without them."

"I've heard that same refrain quite often about Langstone. It seems he liked to lord it over everyone."

"Comes from his mother. From what I remember of his father, he would never have tolerated such behavior had he lived to see it."

"But his grandfather hasn't stopped it."

"I think he's tried." He sighed. "But Langstone just refuses to listen. Always has."

"Do you think that's what got him into this trouble? Whatever this trouble might be," I added in exasperation.

Mr. Bray's eyes were sympathetic. "I don't know. It's possible. Maybe he pulled his high-handed routine with someone he shouldn't have. Maybe they drew his cork for it. Or maybe he made empty promises to the wrong person." He fell silent, his brow furrowing. "Or maybe he took something that wasn't his."

I straightened in surprise.

"I don't mean to imply he's a thief," he hastened to explain. "At least, of anything more than a woman's virtue. But . . . he's taken things before."

I hesitated to say the words, but the question had to be asked. "You mean the dagger?"

He gazed solemnly out at the moor where cloud shadows raced across the billowing heather. "We knew all along that Langstone had been the one to take it, and Gage was merely the scapegoat." His eyes lifted to meet mine, dulled by cynicism. "You'll recall I knew them. I knew how Langstone was." He turned away. "And I had some inkling of what it was like for Gage in that house." His scowl deepened. "But how does one tell Lord Tavistock you know he's lying, that his heir is lying?"

"You think Lord Tavistock knew the truth?"

The look he cast my way was rife with skepticism. "If not, he was willfully allowing himself to be fooled."

I hadn't considered the possibility that the viscount had been aware of Alfred's cruel trick, but Mr. Bray was right. Gage's grandfather seemed to have deliberately turned a blind eye to some of his heir's actions. I'd witnessed as much since our arrival. And yet he was so hard on Gage. I wondered if Gage had noticed this contradiction.

I grimaced. But of course he had. How could he not?

I felt a pulse of empathy for Gage, and another stab of fury at his rotten family.

"One of the old women in the village mentioned a family . . . well, I guess you would call it a curse," I said, deciding it was time to change the subject.

"That those who rebel within the family will suffer a terrible fate?" He nodded. "I've heard it before. It's the reason why, in addition to his notorious reputation, it's never made any sense to me that all the local girls should be so eager to fall prey to Langstone's charms."

I could answer that. It was the thrill of the forbidden, the lure of danger. It gave Alfred, who was already reputed to be attractive, an even more heightened allure by turning his rakehell persona into one of possibly tragic destiny. I suspected we could blame Shakespeare for that.

He shook his head. "After all, I know they've all heard the legend of Stephen's Grave."

"That the woman he fell in love with was Alice Trevelyan, Lord Tavistock's sister?" I asked in confusion.

"Aye. And the reason he killed her and then himself was the curse. It made him do it, for she'd dared to defy her parents' wishes by agreeing to run away with him. And then he couldn't live with what he'd done."

I stared wide-eyed, shocked to have my vague suspicions confirmed with so little prodding. "And Gage's mother?" I murmured weakly.

He winced, as if he'd forgotten whom he was speaking to. "Her, too. Though in her case, it certainly took its time enacting itself."

True. Gage had been eighteen when his mother died, nineteen years after she'd married Stephen Gage and rebelled against her family. But perhaps death by slow poisoning was far more terrible than a quick demise.

I frowned. Poison. Was that what connected them all? Even Alfred?

Miss Galloway had given him a tincture for a stomach complaint, as well as a bundle of herb bennet for protection, particularly against poison. Rory had reported that Alfred had suffered from some sort of ailment in the days before he vanished. Had he been poisoned and finally succumbed? But if so, once again, where was he?

I stared across the moor toward Great Mis Tor rising in the distance. From this vantage, I couldn't see Miss Galloway's cottage, for it was hidden behind another rise that concealed the lower slopes of that tor. However, I believed I could make my way safely there. It was not so far, even on foot, and I'd been there before.

Taking my leave of Mr. Bray, I set off across the moor, following the track Gage and Rory had speculated Alfred might have taken when they'd believed he might have gone to visit Miss Galloway the day he disappeared. It wasn't so difficult to follow, for their description had been good, and soon I was at her door.

There was no sign of life as I approached, no twitch of the curtains like the last time we'd called. And when I rapped on the door three times, there was no answer. I tested the handle and the door easily opened.

"Miss Galloway," I called, peering inside. "Miss Galloway."

The cottage appeared much as it had before, though the fire was banked. She must have gone out to run an errand, perhaps visiting a village or gathering more herbs. I glanced in every direction from the porch to see if I could spot her, and even peered around the corner into the garden, but she was nowhere to be found.

Hesitant to venture into her home uninvited, I paused on the threshold. In the tumult of the last few days, hunting for Alfred, I wasn't certain if anyone had informed her about the bloody coat. I'd meant to come sooner, but then it had slipped my mind. I didn't want to leave without letting her know, so I stepped inside. Leaving the door open, I tentatively began to search through the drawers in the cabinet by the door for a piece of paper and a pencil so I could leave a note.

I located the sheets of foolscap in the second drawer, but as I pushed them aside to see if a pencil lay underneath, something gold caught my eye. It was a shiny button with ornate swirls. One, I realized with a start, that I'd seen before. It was the missing button from Alfred's coat. But what was it doing here?

I tried to tell myself there was a perfectly rational explanation for its presence at the bottom of Miss Galloway's drawer, and for the fact she hadn't brought it to our attention. He could have dropped it during a visit prior to his going missing. Or she could have found it on the moor and not realized who it belonged to. But those explanations didn't sit quite right.

I stared at the button, uncertain what to do. Should I take it with me, or leave it here and hope she mentioned it during our next meeting? In the end, I elected to put it back, as sort of a test. After all, the button wasn't evidence of wrongdoing. But if she remained silent about it, even after I mentioned it on my next visit, then that would tell me more than direct confrontation.

I jotted down a short message, along with a promise to call again soon, and left it on the table. But just when I'd turned to go, a soft thud came from the direction of the bedroom.

I slowly straightened, feeling the skin along the back of my neck prickle as if a stray draft had blown across it. "Miss Galloway, is that you?"

I inched forward in the heavy silence that followed my query, eyeing the gap below the closed door. "Is anyone there?"

I paused with my hand hovering over the knob. Should I grab something to defend myself with? I'd left my reticule and the percussion pistol tucked inside back at the manor. But then, if it was only Miss Galloway in distress, I would feel foolish for scaring her.

My breath fluttered in my chest as I turned the handle and thrust open the door.

I gasped as an orange tabby cat leapt off the bed and streaked past me. Pressing a hand over my pounding heart, I laughed.

I knew full well what mischief-makers felines could be. I'd left my own cat, a gray tabby I'd dubbed Earl Grey, under the care of my sister's children in Edinburgh. There were times when I missed his companionship, but it had been for the best that I'd left him behind. Earl Grey would have despised the boat trip to Ireland and the journey here. And I could only imagine the look the dowager would have given me if I'd arrived at Langstone with a cat on my lap. Although further contemplation almost made me wish I'd done so.

The orange tabby leapt up on the chair nearest the hearth,

circled once, and curled into a ball to go to sleep. I smiled. Obviously he was comfortable here.

My smile faded. I didn't remember seeing him during my last visit. Maybe he'd been outside, lolling under the garden flowers in the sunshine.

I glanced into the bedchamber, but there was nothing there. Nothing that hadn't been before, anyway. However, I couldn't quite shake the feeling I wasn't alone. Something seemed to fill the space behind me with an almost audible silence.

I closed the bedroom door and crossed back through the cottage, allowing my gaze to trail over the contents. It was all as clean as it had been before. No cup unwashed by the basin. No embroidery set to the side with the needle poised for its next stitch. No shawl draped over a chair. I wished I were familiar enough with Miss Galloway to know whether she was always this fastidious.

Feeling I'd outstayed my welcome, and vaguely guilty for prying despite my discovery of the button, I left the cottage. I closed the door firmly behind me and stood at the corner of the porch to survey the small vale in which the home was set. All was peaceful, with nothing but the wind and the trickling water of the River Walkham in the distance to break the silence. I looked up the slope at the mammoth granite outcroppings at the peak of Great Mis Tor and decided now was as good a time as any to climb it. I imagined the views from its heights were even more impressive than those of White Tor.

By the time I reached the top, I was panting from the exertion. But it was well worth it. My suspicions had been correct. Not only were the granite formations massive, spilling over each other like towering stacks of crumpets, but the panorama was breathtaking. Now I understood why Miss Galloway, and her mother before her, were willing to live on the lower slopes of this isolated spot. To be able to have such a vantage point almost on your doorstep was ample compensation.

I slowly circled the outcroppings, examining the fall of light over the landscape below, and enjoying the view across the moor from different angles. So when I paused to gaze out toward the north over Greena Ball and the bleak desolation of Cocks Hill, at first I was shocked to find I wasn't alone. From this distance, I couldn't see very clearly, but there was definitely a man with no hat striding across the moor from west to east, moving deeper into the moor. His dark hair—the only recognizable feature—ruffled in the wind. Instantly I thought of Alfred, and in my astonishment, I called out to him.

The man swiveled to look up at the tor where I stood, shielding his eyes from the sun. Whether he saw me or recognized what I was saying, I didn't know, but he lifted his hand and then turned and continued on his way.

I called out again, but he didn't stop. Perhaps he couldn't hear me at such a distance, but I thought it unlikely he hadn't seen me when he looked up at the tor. I was wearing a bright maize yellow gown, which should have stood out starkly against the gray, brown, and green landscape.

Whatever the reason, he moved away swiftly to the east. If it was Alfred, I wasn't about to let him get away.

Lifting my skirts, I dashed down the slope of the tor as fast as I dared. Every twenty or thirty feet, I continued to call out, until I was too short of breath to do so. At the base of the tor, the rocky ground gave way to deer grass and heath, and I was able to stretch out my stride, almost running in my haste. The earth was soft beneath my feet, squelching with each step, but I paid it little heed. I had gained on the man slightly, and I was intent on catching him.

So oblivious was I to everything else around me that I didn't hear the person behind me until their arm snagged me about the waist, wrenching me to a stop and driving the air from my lungs. I gulped, trying to inhale as I sagged back against the man who had grabbed me. I thrashed weakly, attempting to free myself from his grasp, but he held on tenaciously.

"Have you lost your mind?! That's Mistor Marsh you were

about to blunder headlong into," Rory scolded, and then proceeded to ring a peal over my head for my foolish recklessness while I struggled to regain my breath and my faculties.

When finally I could speak, I lifted a hand to point in the direction I'd been moving. "But the man. He's getting away."

Rory glared down at me as if I were talking gibberish. "What man? What are you talking about?"

I turned to look, lifting up onto my toes in my eagerness, but he'd vanished. "What? Where did he go?" I continued to scan the horizon, wondering if somehow I'd gotten turned around. "He was just there! Didn't you see him?" I demanded, not understanding how he could have disappeared in such a vast expanse of nothingness. There were no valleys or hills for him to hide behind in that immediate direction. No large rocks or tall vegetation to duck behind.

When I glanced back at Rory, it was to find him watching me with a strange light in his eyes. His anger mellowed into something more guarded, more wary.

"I'm telling you, I saw a dark-haired man striding across the moor in that direction. I thought maybe somehow it was your brother, and . . . and I didn't want him to disappear again." I broke off, scowling up at him in frustration. "You don't believe me."

He shook his head. "It's not that. It's only . . . I don't think it was really a man."

I narrowed my eyes. "I see." My words were clipped. "I'm hallucinating, then, is that it?"

"I . . . I think you were being pixie-led."

"I beg your pardon?"

"That's what the locals call it. They believe pixies inhabit these lands, and sometimes they like to make mischief—playing tricks on travelers out on the moor, leading them into trouble."

I frowned, not knowing what to say to that. I felt vaguely insulted. My mind was perfectly clear, as were my eyes. I knew what I'd seen. And yet, I'd grown up with tales of pixies and sprites, bogies and selkies, and the fae. Just because I'd never encountered them didn't necessarily mean they didn't exist.

I turned to look back across the marsh toward where I'd seen the man. How had he vanished so quickly? If he was real, then where was he?

Rory's feet shuffled backward, gurgling the boggy ground beneath our feet. "I don't know if I believe that. But . . . Dartmoor is different. The usual rules don't apply here. Maybe it's the light, or the peaty soil." He shrugged. "Who knows? But strange things do happen here."

I understood what he was trying to say. This mysterious place did feel different. The moors were almost a place out of time, somehow older than the rest of Britain, than the rest of the earth. If I stood still, and the wind stopped blowing long enough, I just might hear it humming beneath me, sharing its secrets.

Or maybe that was the pixies.

"Well, thank you," I told him, recognizing how close I'd come to literally stepping into a quagmire. "Had you not been here to stop me . . ."

I didn't finish the thought because the consequences were too dire. But also because I couldn't help but wonder why he *had* been here. Was he following me? Was he the one I'd sensed at Miss Galloway's cottage?

The look in Rory's eyes said he knew what I was thinking, but he didn't address it. He merely tipped his head in acknowledgment and offered me his arm to lead me out of the bog.

"If you should ever feel you're being pixie-led again, they say if you turn your coat inside out, that'll break the spell."

I couldn't tell if he was mocking me or in earnest. What I did know was that, despite his saving me from, at the very least, some troubling difficulties, I didn't trust him. That, if nothing else, was quite clear.

"Good to know."

CHAPTER TWENTY

Upon our return to the manor, Rory and I found ourselves ushered into the drawing room. I expected to find Lady Langstone imperiously awaiting our attendance, but she wasn't alone. Across from her sat Gage, listening attentively to a lovely young woman with soft red curls, while beside her hovered a man sporting gray at his temples.

I halted just inside the door, acutely embarrassed by my appearance. Had I known we had company, I would have insisted on changing out of my mud-splattered frock and kid boots, and repairing my windblown hair. Rory seemed similarly discomfited, rooted to the spot beside me.

Lady Langstone was, of course, the first to notice our arrival, narrowing her eyes in disapproval. I fought a blush and forced my feet forward to meet our visitors. Gage had risen to greet us, a question in his eyes as he took in my disheveled state, but I shook my head, conveying I would explain later.

"Lady Juliana, may I present my wife," he swiveled to announce, performing all the necessary introductions.

So this was the Duke of Bedford's daughter, the young woman Lord Tavistock wanted Alfred to marry. Gage had said she was soft-spoken and gentle, and I could see that was true. Her voice was so quiet I had to lean closer to hear her. However, whatever affection, or lack thereof, Alfred felt for her, it was evident she held some sort of fondness for him, for her eyes were rimmed with red from recent tears.

The other man was her brother, and had obviously been pressed into accompanying her on this errand. He spoke only when required, and didn't seem at all concerned with the whereabouts of his sister's near intended.

Apparently, Lady Juliana had heard about Alfred being missing, and the bloody coat we found, and had come to ask for answers.

"It's just so terrible," she repeated, sniffing into her handkerchief.

"Ah, don't cry, Lady Juliana," Rory murmured gently. "There's still hope yet."

"Is there?"

"Of course there is," he exclaimed with far more conviction than I'd yet seen him exhibit. For certain, this was for Lady Juliana's benefit, but I also couldn't help but notice the way he flushed under her regard as she gave him a grateful smile. Alfred might not have been interested in her, but I would have wagered a tidy sum that Rory wasn't averse to the idea of marrying her. If his brother was presumed dead, would he get his wish?

"Lady Juliana was just telling us about the last time she saw Lord Langstone, a month ago," Gage explained as we all sat. "She said he seemed distracted."

She nodded. "It wasn't like him. He was normally quite attentive. I . . . I asked him whether something was troubling him, and he insisted it was merely concern for Lord Tavistock, since he's been so ill. But . . . I wasn't so sure."

Astute girl.

"Did he seem himself otherwise, in manner, appearance . . . ?"

She tilted her head, gazing up at the ceiling. "I did notice he seemed a bit tired and, well, pale." She smiled in remembrance. "He kept yawning, and then apologizing, though it was obvious he couldn't help it. Mother suggested later he might have been suffering from some sort of illness himself, but, of course, it would have been impolite for him to speak of it."

Gage's eyes met mine over her head. Was this confirmation that Alfred had been suffering from some sort of complaint weeks before he disappeared? We needed to speak with his odious valet about the matter. Unless Gage had already done so and not told me. After all, he'd questioned some of the members of the staff.

"In any case, he didn't visit with us long. He'd hoped to speak with my father." A tinge of pink colored her cheeks, letting us know what she'd believed that conversation would be about. "But Father had already left for London. Though he did spend a quarter hour with my father's steward. He said his grandfather had some questions about the mine partnership."

"Mine partnership?" Gage repeated. "Between the duke and Lord Tavistock?"

"Yes." She glanced uncertainly at her brother, who was looking at his pocket watch for the second time since my arrival. "I assumed you were aware. It was announced in the newspapers and everything."

"It was," her brother confirmed. "Some men near Gunnislake uncovered a copper vein, and the duke and Lord Tavistock bought up the land to open a mine."

Was this, then, what that newspaper article Alfred dropped in the garden had been about? But why had such a partnership concerned him? Unless he recognized it meant there was no backing out of marrying Lady Juliana. Was their union supposed to seal the deal, so to speak?

"Juliana, we really must leave soon or we'll be late," her brother reminded her, already half rising to his feet. It was evident he expected compliance now and not in five minutes.

"Yes . . . of course." She lowered her face to hide how flustered she'd become as she gathered up her reticule. I recognized the move because I often employed it myself to cover some social blunder I'd made. Except she'd done nothing wrong but inconvenience her brother.

"Must you leave so soon?" I demurred, feeling a pulse of empathy for the girl. There was also the investigation to consider. I'd barely had time to even begin to develop an impression of her, and it sounded as if she might know more about Alfred and his possible whereabouts than she realized.

She glanced up, her eyes lighting with something akin to gratitude. How rarely was this girl's presence sought after or missed that she should so appreciate my eagerness to talk to her? It left me feeling rotten that all my motivations hadn't been so altruistic.

"I'm afraid so," she replied, glancing at her brother again, who was tapping his leg in impatience. "We're traveling to London today. Father wants us all there for the king's coronation, and there's much to do to prepare."

I suspected this was somewhat of an exaggeration. The coronation was scheduled for early September, and it was not yet August. Though as Lady Juliana was the daughter of a duke, I'm sure there were many arrangements to make—gowns to be ordered, soirees to plan, endless rounds of calls to make.

There was nothing we could do to make them stay, so we thanked them for coming and promised Lady Juliana we would keep her apprised of our progress in our search for Alfred. Lady Langstone soon followed them from the drawing room, but not before offering me a parting quip.

"A word of advice. Perhaps in Scotland, society is accustomed to such slovenliness, but here in England we prefer that our ladies make their appearances looking a bit less like heathens."

I scowled at her back as she swept from the room in all her understated elegance. Insult aside, she was cognizant I'd grown up on the English side of the Borders. Though, I realized many in the south viewed the wilder counties of the far north as essentially foreign soil.

Rory mumbled some excuse and ducked out after her, leaving me alone with Gage—a state I'd been endeavoring all morning to achieve. But I found, as I turned to face him, that suddenly I felt unaccountably tongue-tied. Perhaps it was Lady Juliana's reserved, apologetic behavior, or maybe it was Gage's perfectly groomed appearance, a glaring contrast to my rumpled, unkempt state, but I was starkly reminded of the person I'd been only a short year ago when I'd first met him. A frightened, lost, downtrodden woman feigning bravado and in desperate need of a reason to push beyond my pain and fear. If not for Gage, if not for our first inquiry together, I might still be hiding away in the Highlands.

Whether Gage could sense this, I didn't know. He'd often teased me about being able to read my expressions like an open book. Whatever the case, he flashed me one of his smugly knowing looks, ever aware of his potent effect on me and every other female in near proximity. It was an expression certain to annoy me, and this time was no different.

His eyes lit with a gleam that told me how much he enjoyed riling me, and he leaned close to murmur, "Don't you know I'm the only one allowed to render your appearance to such a state?"

My body flushed at the implication, and my breathing quickened even as I continued to scowl.

"Whatever the cause, I hope it wasn't as pleasant as I would have made it," he added with a wicked grin.

Had we been in our bedchamber, I'd no doubt how our exchange would have ended. But since we were standing in the middle of the drawing room with the door open, Gage kept his hands to himself, though not his gaze. I wasn't sure that didn't make our exchange all the more titillating because of it.

I inhaled a deep breath. Two could play at this game. "I've been looking for you."

His pupils widened. "Have you?"

I nodded, stepping nearer to smooth his already straight collar. "I was sorry to see you'd already risen from our bed before I woke." I flicked my gaze up at him through my lashes.

He inhaled a swift intake of breath and pressed a hand against the small of my back, drawing me ever closer. "Yes, well, that was my mistake." The gust of his breath and the brush of his lips against the tender skin behind my ear nearly made me forget myself.

But I hadn't forgotten the words we hadn't said to each other. The words that would be harder to say the longer they went unsaid.

I pushed against his chest, reluctantly urging him to stop nuzzling the side of my neck. Evidently he'd forgotten where we stood. Or perhaps he didn't care if we shocked his aunt or the staff.

"I'm sorry I lost my temper yesterday," I told him, growing serious again. "I should have recognized what talk of a curse would mean to you, to your mother's memory." I smiled sheepishly. "I think sometimes I become so determined to find the truth that I become blinded to the affect that truth might have on others."

Gage exhaled a long, slow breath, and lifted a hand to brush a stray tendril of hair back from my face. "But you weren't wrong. It is something we should explore." I could see how much it cost him to admit such a thing. He looked as if he would rather do anything else. And so he did. "But first, what did you think of Lady Juliana's revelation of the mine partnership?"

I shook my head at his blatant attempt to change the topic of conversation, but allowed him to do so. After all, the discussion of his mother and the curse was far too fraught to be conducted in such a public place. "I suspect, the same as you, that the partnership was the subject of that newspaper article Alfred dropped. The gardener did say he recognized the words *Tavistock* and *Gunnislake*, didn't he? But I think your grandfather could tell us more."

"My thoughts precisely. What of Lady Juliana? Did you find her trustworthy?"

"You spent far more time with her than I did. But from the little I observed, yes. She seems a caring, agreeable girl. And as terrible a match for Alfred as you feared."

His mouth flattened in sympathy. "I worry the duke is only interested in seeing her married off to someone with the right lineage. She's but one of six daughters."

"Do you think the coronation was simply an excuse for the duke to remove her from the vicinity of Langstone Manor and whatever scandal might erupt now that he knows Alfred is missing?"

"It's probable." He sighed. "Though royal events do require a great deal of preparation."

I studied his exasperated expression, trying to decipher what he wasn't saying. Normally such a countenance meant only one thing. "I'm surprised your father hasn't remarked on the coronation."

He grimaced. "He has. He's been pestering me about it, insisting we return from 'rustication' in time to attend."

I frowned. Well, that explained Gage's reaction to his father's last letter. Lord Gage knew very well we weren't off on some lark.

"He said we're to be special guests of the king."

My eyes widened. "Even me?"

First the letter to Lord Tavistock praising me and now this. What was Lord Gage up to? Perhaps he was bent on reforming my image, for purely selfish reasons. But if I'd learned anything from my encounters with Gage's father, it was that there were always hidden barbs.

"Yes, well, William is a bit different from past monarchs," Gage replied, linking my arm through his to guide me out to the hall.

That was true. Much of society was all abuzz about the rights and privileges he'd recently bestowed upon the numerous illegitimate children he'd had with his longtime mistress, as well as the fact he included them in royal events.

"I suspect if he has any interest in your past at all, it's more out of curiosity than scorn," he added. "Hammett, just the man I wanted to see," he declared as the butler appeared before us. "Are you aware whether Grandfather is feeling well enough for visitors?"

The butler's expression was so sour, I wondered what on earth could have made him pucker so. "Aye, sir. Though . . ." He hesitated, looking at me. "Ye might want to retire to yer chamber first."

I stiffened, thinking at first he was disparaging my appearance.

"Yer maid requested she see ye." Hammett's mouth barely formed around the words. His eyes darted to Gage. "Mr. Gage, too, if he's available."

So this was what the old retainer found so distasteful. A servant beckoning her mistress to attend her. Such things weren't done. But, of course, Gage and I weren't normal employers, and Bree and Anderley weren't merely servants.

"Thank you, Hammett," Gage said before leading me toward the stairs.

We entered our bedchamber to find Bree puttering about the room. She never was one to sit idle.

"Bree, you wanted to see us?" I asked.

In answer, she dipped her head toward the connecting door. "This way."

I shared a look with Gage before we followed her.

Upon seeing Anderley waiting for us, I assumed at first she was leading us into the other room because he also needed to be included in the conversation. After all, her waiting in Gage's assigned chamber, particularly with his valet present, would have been highly improper. But when his eyes flicked to the side, bright with derisive humor, I realized he wasn't alone. Before the wardrobe stood a fastidious man of middling height with an intricately tied cravat. He sported an impossibly trim waist that made me suspect he was wearing a corset.

This was the man whom Anderley believed was responsible for playing pranks on us. I would never have guessed. And from the manner in which he stared down his nose at us all, I suspected he would sooner go to the gallows than admit his culpability.

"This is Lord Langstone's valet, Mr. Cooper," Bree explained, offering the man a smile of encouragement. "He has something he wishes to tell ye."

He cleared his throat. "Yes. I . . ." He rocked forward on his heels before trying again. "In light of recent developments, I thought it best I inform you of what I know." His eyes lifted to meet Gage's and then mine. It was clear he didn't wish to do so, but something had impelled him to trust us. I glanced at Bree. Or someone.

"You're speaking of Lord Langstone's coat," Gage inferred.

"Yes, sir."

He nodded. "Go on."

Cooper's eyes slid toward Anderley, rife with animosity. It was apparent he wished for the other valet to be sent away, and just as apparent Anderley was not about to be budged. "Lord Langstone confided in me that, for reasons of his own, he did not wish to marry Lady Juliana."

I couldn't decide whether to be irritated or amused at the valet's dissembling. From everything I'd learned about Alfred, it was doubtful he was the type to take his servant into his confidence. It was far more likely that Alfred had grumbled about the matter, either too foxed or too angry to care that his valet heard.

"However, Lord Tavistock and the Dowager Lady Langstone were eager for the match. *Very* eager," he stressed. "I believe they were exerting some pressure on him to comply, but he said he was determined not to. He . . . he said he had other plans."

None of this was news to us except the last.

"What plans?" Gage asked.

Cooper straightened even taller. "I don't know. He was quite secretive about them. But . . . I'm astute enough to comprehend they would not be welcomed by his lordship or her ladyship."

"You think they might have decided to stop those plans had they known about them?"

"Maybe."

I wasn't sure exactly what he was trying to imply, and I'm not sure he was either. But something about the situation must have worried him enough to bring it to our attention. I didn't know how shrewd Cooper truly was, and I certainly wasn't going to trust only his word on it. However, I did know that the body often sensed things that the mind could not necessarily explain. If his intuition had been strong enough to impel him to overlook his dislike for Anderley and Gage and share his suspicions, then I was inclined to listen.

"But that's not all." He cleared his throat again more forcefully. "Lord Langstone was blackmailing someone. Perhaps they're the person who did him harm."

CHAPTER TWENTY-ONE

"I don't know who," Cooper hastened to say before Gage could ask. "But I believe it was someone in this house. He instructed me that if something untoward should happen to him, I was to retrieve some items he'd hidden underneath a loose floorboard in his chamber and destroy them. When I heard about the state of his frock coat, and that no other trace of him had been found, I decided I should follow his orders. But when I went to retrieve the items, they were already gone."

Gage and I stared at each other through much of this recitation, already acquainted with this hiding place.

"Do you know what items he'd hidden?" Gage asked, and then before the valet could reply added sternly, "It's important that you be honest with us. In order to help Lord Langstone, we need to know what he was concealing."

But Cooper shook his head sharply. "I don't know. He never told me."

"Did you ever peek?"

The valet drew himself up in affront. "Of course not."

Gage glared at him in challenge, but I pressed a hand to his arm, letting him know I believed the other man was being truthful. Cooper didn't know.

But I wondered if I did.

I frowned, recalling the sight of the dowager kneeling before her fireplace, frantically burning those letters from Lord Gage. I'd not yet had time to do much investigating into the matter, but I'd not forgotten. But if they were the items Alfred had used for blackmail, why hadn't she burned them as soon as she found them? She must have reclaimed them at least several days before, since the letters had already been missing from the hiding spot when Gage and I searched Alfred's room. Or had she wanted to keep them, but grown fearful when Alfred's bloody coat was found that Gage and I might discover them in the course of our inquiry?

"Do either of you know what it was he might have hidden?" Gage asked, turning first to Anderley and then to Bree.

Both shook their heads, though Bree's appeared less than definitive. Once Gage looked away, her gaze met mine, telling me she had something she wished to share with me. If she'd uncovered the same thing I had, I could understand why she didn't want to admit to it in front of Gage.

"Perhaps Mrs. Webley knows," Cooper suggested.

Gage frowned. "The dowager's maid?"

"Yes. She's been a servant here for longer than many of us." He paused, but I could tell he had more to say. "And she has a decided talent at uncovering things the other servants wish she hadn't."

I couldn't decide whether he admired this about her or he was purely intrigued.

"We'll speak with her," Gage said.

Cooper bowed. "Then, if there's nothing more . . ."

"There is."

Gage's words halted his steps, though the tiny crease between his brows told me he wanted to disobey.

"Had Lord Langstone been ill recently? We understand he was suffering from a stomach ailment in the days before his disappearance, but what about in the weeks and months prior to that?"

The valet's eyes were wide with mild surprise. "Yes, actually. Numerous times. Enough that I'd suggested he might wish to see a physician about it."

If he'd offered such advice, then clearly he'd not believed his sickness to have been caused by overindulgence, and I was given to understand that a good gentleman's valet knows the difference.

Gage tipped his head in consideration. "Did he accept your advice?"

"Not that I'm aware of, sir."

He nodded. "Thank you. You may go."

Cooper bowed again stiffly and hurried from the room.

"I have to say, McEvoy," Anderley remarked once the door closed behind him, "I'm impressed. Never thought you'd convince the fussy toad to talk."

Bree's eyes sparkled with mischief. "Yes, well, that's because ye dinna ken what I promised to tell him aboot *you* in return."

Anderley's eyes narrowed in suspicion.

"My valet's odd grooming habits aside . . ." Gage began.

I smothered a giggle behind my hand as Anderley turned to him in affront.

"What odd habits?"

His eyes glinted with teasing. "I'm sure Mrs. Gage doesn't want me to explain how you sometimes rinse your hair with ale."

A tinge of pink crested Anderley's cheeks. "Well, maybe I should share the method with Miss McEvoy. It's quite effective."

"Oh, aye," Bree agreed. "Does make your locks wondrously shiny."

"Why, thank you," he replied, turning back to Gage. "Though, I've heard the smell of hops on a woman can be quite tantalizing. Perhaps you wouldn't wish Mrs. Gage to attract so much attention."

At this, I could no longer contain my mirth and laughed out loud. The others joined me, possibly driven to such hilarity by our present frustrations.

When our laughter faded, I found myself perched on the edge of the bed, swiping tears from my eyes. Anderley stood with his arms crossed, looking at ease despite being the cause of such glee.

"What do we make of Cooper's assertions about Langstone having made other plans to avoid marrying Lady Juliana, and the possibility he was blackmailing someone?" Gage asked, recalling us to the matter at hand. He leaned against the bedpost beside me, lifting his eyes to the ceiling overhead. "Do we believe him?"

"Well, we've heard from several people that claim Alfred didn't wish to marry Lady Juliana," I pointed out. "But what plans could he have made to counter that?"

Gage's brow furrowed. "Grandfather has been ill. Perhaps he hoped he would die before Alfred was forced to propose."

"Yes, but I gather that's the reason for all the extra pressure they were exertin' on him to wed in the first place," Bree said.

I tapped my fingers against the mattress. "And what of the mine partnership your grandfather formed with the Duke of Bedford? Does that in some way force Alfred's hand? Is that what so upset him about it?"

"For that matter, why is he so against marrying her?" Anderley scoffed. "He must know he would be expected to wed sometime. He *is* the heir."

"Aye," Bree chimed in. "And Lady Juliana is a duke's daughter, and from all accounts, attractive and pleasant. He could do far worse."

"Is this the general opinion belowstairs?" I asked, for it sounded as if they'd shared these views before.

Anderley glanced toward Bree before shrugging. "More or less."

"I'm thinkin' there's another girl." Bree arched her eyebrows in emphasis. "Someone he'd rather tie the knot wi'."

Miss Galloway's face appeared before my eyes. Bree might not be far off. Though there was a great deal more information to be gathered before such a suspicion could be deemed as more than rampant speculation.

Had Rory debated the same thing? Was that the real reason why he didn't like Miss Galloway?

"Continue to keep your eyes and ears open." Gage scowled at the wall across from him. "I still think some of the staff know more than they're saying." He glanced at Bree. "And find out, if you can, whether any of the servants saw someone slip something into Lord Langstone's food or drink. If he was being poisoned, he was most likely ingesting it."

Bree nodded and turned to me. "Ye have need of me, m'lady?"

I knew this was her polite way of telling me I looked a dreadful mess.

"Yes. I'll be there in a moment."

While she moved through the connecting door, I looked to Gage to confirm he still wished to speak with his grandfather. I could see the questions about my disheveled state forming in his eyes—questions I didn't particularly wish to answer at the moment. Not when they would result in a scolding for my carelessness. So I hurried across the room after Bree before he could voice them. "If you can give me a quarter of an hour, I'll join you."

With the door shut firmly between us and the men, I swiveled to allow Bree to begin unfastening the buttons down the back of my dress. "Now, tell me what you know about the blackmail."

"I don't *ken* anything," she insisted. "But . . ."

I heard in her voice that she didn't want to admit whatever she knew.

"Tell me," I urged gently.

She inhaled swiftly. "I overheard some o' the maids talkin'. One o' 'em swears Lord Gage and the dowager used to . . . carry on wi' one another."

"Did she say why she thought that?"

Bree's hands stilled as she registered my lack of surprise. "She said she saw him take her hand in the drawin' room when they thought no one was lookin'. And that he used to send her letters." She resumed her movements. "You knew." She sounded relieved not to be the bearer of troubling news.

"I was told something in confidence that made me suspect the same thing," I admitted, pondering whether I was willing to take a risk. When Bree finished, rather than let her push my gown off my shoulders, I swiveled abruptly to face her. "May I assume you also think the item Lord Langstone was using for blackmail was those letters?"

"I did wonder." Her voice lowered and she glanced back at the door. "'Tis why I didna wish to say anythin' in front o' Mr. Gage."

"Then I need you to do something for me." I explained how I'd seen the dowager frantically burning papers, and about the singed corner of one letter I'd managed to save. Retrieving it from between the pages of the book where I'd hidden it, I passed it to her.

She gasped. "It's true, then?"

"It's probable," I replied sadly.

Her face blanched in misgiving. "Does Mr. Gage know?"

Unwilling to betray my husband's knowledge of the matter, I brushed her question aside. "You leave that to me. What I need *you* to do is show that around belowstairs. Make certain the maid who claims she witnessed their . . . affaire de coeur sees it. I also want Mrs. Webley to know you have it."

Her eyes lit with comprehension. "You want to try to flush her or her mistress out. See what they'll reveal."

"Precisely."

"I'll do my best," she declared, tucking the scrap of paper into her pocket. Her determined gaze then fell on my hair. "Now let's tend to this bird nest."

"I didn't tell you about the mine partnership because I didn't think it mattered," Lord Tavistock snapped back at Gage.

The viscount appeared a bit haler today. A welcome ruddy

tinge had entered his cheeks, and his breathing sounded less labored. But that also meant his words held more bite.

"It's public knowledge. Appeared in most of the local newspapers and probably a few in London."

"Newspapers that were published while we were in Ireland," Gage retorted to his implied criticism that he hadn't been keeping abreast of the latest news.

"That's hardly my fault."

"No, but it is your fault you never mentioned the mines." Gage narrowed his eyes. "In fact, I believe you deliberately neglected to tell us because you knew Alfred had been upset about it. He didn't wish to marry Lady Juliana, and he felt trapped into the union by this deal you'd made with the Duke of Bedford."

The manner in which the viscount looked as if he were chewing on something unpleasant told me Gage had hit the nail on the head. "Alfred has always been a stubborn and recalcitrant boy."

Gage snorted. "I wonder who he inherited those traits from."

His grandfather's scowl turned blacker. "He needed to be made to see reason. He's nearly thirty-six. It's high time he wed an appropriate girl and produced an heir."

"An appropriate girl?" I interjected, latching on to what I deemed the most important words in that sentence.

The viscount's silver eyes flicked to meet mine. "Yes. One of suitable family and lineage. I'm not ignorant to the sorts of women he courted while in London and at his friends' debauch gatherings."

Yes, but was that all he meant? I couldn't tell whether he was aware of Miss Galloway or any attachment that might have formed between Alfred and her. If one even existed.

"What did you threaten would happen if Alfred didn't accede to your demands?" Gage persisted.

His grandfather glared back at him, at first refusing to answer. Then he arched his chin like an obstinate child. "I told him I would strip everything I could from his inheritance. All he would be left with were those things that were entailed—Langstone Manor and its attached lands."

"The estate isn't self-sustaining," Gage replied, grasping the implications before I did. "Without the mines and other tracts of land, in short order, he would be crippled with debt."

"Only if he refused to wed Lady Juliana."

I watched as fury transformed my husband's face. "Is that why you really asked us here? You suspected Alfred had gone into hiding, and you needed us to find him so you could bring him to heel?" He flung his hand toward the window. "You never truly feared foul play. You simply needed a way to convince us to investigate."

"At first, yes. I thought maybe he was ducking me and his responsibility," he grudgingly admitted, shouting back. "But after a week, when he couldn't be found, I began to worry I'd been wrong. That something *had* happened to him. I never lied about that."

"Maybe. But you certainly summoned us with that letter under false pretenses." Gage moved closer to the bed, looming over his grandfather. "What else have you neglected to tell us? What other means were you using to persuade Alfred?"

I knew to what he was referring, but Lord Tavistock shook his head. "Isn't that enough? Power and money always did motivate Alfred more than anything."

"What about fear for his life?"

The viscount's eyes widened in shock and then his face suffused with red. "Are you accusing me of harming my own grandson?"

"Someone was. Someone has, if that bloody coat is any indication."

The old man blanched. "I am not responsible for that. Nor would I *ever* condone such an action."

Gage's eyes weighed and assessed him. "Maybe. But regardless, you've gotten your alliance. With Alfred out of the way, Rory will be a much more tractable heir, won't he? And I wager he'll be happy to wed Lady Juliana."

"You think he's dead?" he wheezed between coughs.

"I suspect we'll know soon enough."

"Do you really think he's dead?" I asked as we strode down the corridor away from the viscount's chamber.

Gage's arm was tight beneath mine, still holding in the anger and disillusionment he must have been feeling about his grandfather's actions. "I don't know. But the longer this search stretches on with no answers, the more I think we have to face the very real possibility that he has perished, either by natural or unnatural means."

At the end of the corridor, he glanced to the left and then the right before guiding me through a doorway two doors down and shutting it behind us. It was the library I'd failed to locate on numerous occasions.

"Is anything in this house designed in a traditional manner?" I groused.

It was no wonder I'd missed it. Tucked off a corridor among rooms I'd assumed were more bedchambers, it didn't appear anything like a normal library other than the shelves filled with books. Had I not known better, I would have called it a men's reading parlor, for it was filled with heavy leather furniture and stark tables bearing lamps. I suspected it *had* once been but another bedchamber until it was converted to this use.

Ignoring my comment, Gage crossed to the window, pushing aside the drapes to allow more light into the shadowed room. "Let's review the facts, shall we. We've searched for miles in every direction, spoken to all the people who live on the neighboring lands and in the village, interviewed Alfred's friends, and yet we haven't been able to locate him. Barring the possibility that someone is either a brilliant liar or that Alfred has fashioned himself some unknown bolt-hole—both options that are unlikely, but not impossible—I think we have to face the truth. Alfred truly has vanished." He exhaled as if making this pronouncement was almost a relief. "He's not in Plymouth." He ticked off on his fingers. "He's not in London. Father was almost certain of that."

"Then where is he, Gage? I know we all keep saying he vanished, but that's impossible. Unless you believe the pixies led him away, and I know you don't."

He planted his hands on his hips, shaking his head. "I honestly don't know. Unless a bog actually did swallow him up." He frowned. "Or someone buried him in a place where freshly turned soil wouldn't give us pause."

I considered this suggestion, but he rushed on before I could respond.

"Everyone in this family has purposefully led us astray, making this inquiry far more complicated than it needed to be. But I think it's time I faced a truth I haven't wanted to accept." He exhaled forcibly. "That Alfred has likely been murdered."

I'd considered murder to be a very real prospect almost since the beginning, but it was apparent Gage had not. After all, Alfred was his cousin. No matter their tussles in the past, he still cared about him. And it was obvious he found this shift in his approach to the inquiry to be troubling.

I wrapped my arms around his middle and rested my head against his chest, offering him what comfort I could. He continued to stare out the window, lost in disquieting thoughts, but he lifted his arms to embrace me back. We stood that way for some time with nothing but the clock ticking on the mantel to disturb the silence around us. From this vantage, I could see out into the front walled garden. Even in bright sunlight it still looked hopelessly forlorn.

"You know, I used to wish something awful would happen to Alfred," he murmured. "He was just so dreadful to me, to Mother. I wished he would go away and never return."

I looked up at his face, at the evidence of his tightly restrained emotion in the lines at the corner of his eyes and the brackets around his mouth. "You were just a boy," I reminded him.

"I know." His eyes dipped to meet mine. "But now I'm a man. And I owe it to him to find him."

"Then we shall," I replied, infusing as much confidence as I could into my voice. "Even if we have to dredge every bog between here and Okehampton."

His lips curled into a tight smile. "Well, let's hope it doesn't come to that." His gaze fastened on something on my right temple, and he lifted a finger to wipe it away. Lowering his hand, we stared down at a speck of mud. "Care to explain now what happened to you this morning? And who's been talking to you about pixies?"

"Rory." I briefly explained what happened that morning, including his cousin's part in saving me from an ignoble fate. As expected, my husband was not amused by my carelessness.

"Kiera," he began sternly.

"I know. I know. My only defense is that I genuinely believed the man I'd seen could be Alfred. But I shouldn't have lost my head."

"If it *had* been Alfred, and you were able to catch up to him, what did you think you would do? Insist he return home with you? I don't like to think it, but if Alfred is alive and he's gone to such lengths to remain hidden, he could be dangerous."

"I'll be more careful," I assured him. "In any case, Rory claims there was no man, and he was close enough he should have seen him as well. Though I didn't appreciate his trying to tell me I'd been pixie-led."

"No. That doesn't sound like him." His voice trailed away as he turned toward the window again.

I waited for him to say more, but when he didn't I redirected him to the more urgent matter at hand. "How do you wish to proceed?"

"Well, I think you should visit Miss Galloway again." He shifted so that he could see me more fully. "Provided you can avoid running into any more bogs."

"What if it's the same one?" I replied tartly.

He arched a single eyebrow at my pitiable jest. "I believe I'll try to speak with the Duke of Bedford's steward at Endsleigh House about these Swing letters. I would have liked to speak with the duke himself, but now that we know he's in London, I suppose that's not possible. And I shall pay Mr. Glanville another visit. I'm curious if he knows anything about the blackmail, or if he can direct me to any of Alfred's acquaintances further afield."

"He was certainly forthcoming the last time we spoke," I remarked, feeling slightly guilty for not sharing my suspicions about the blackmail. But I didn't want to raise the matter until I knew. Until I was sure. There was also the matter of the gold button I'd found in Miss Galloway's cottage, but I wanted to give her the chance to inform me of it herself, and Gage might not allow that if he were aware.

"Yes, well, let's hope he doesn't decide to share too much without your presence to rein him in."

"My presence reined him in?" I asked dubiously, recalling all the shocking things he'd said and done.

Gage nodded. "You do not want to see him when there are no ladies present."

"So long as you don't share his brandy, or any of his companions," I added pointedly, "I suspect you shall survive."

He pulled me close. "Have no fear there. Just listening to him will be unenjoyable enough."

CHAPTER TWENTY-TWO

The weather the next morning was not quite as auspicious as the day before, but Gage seemed certain I shouldn't encounter any sudden shifts in the next few hours. Given his protective inclinations, I trusted he was correct. Thin clouds wisped across the sky, blocking much of the sunlight, but the air was warm and dry, urging me to tuck my shawl into my shoulder satchel with my sketchbook and charcoals.

I rapped on Miss Galloway's door, and was met almost immediately by her relieved expression.

"I'm so glad you called," she exclaimed, gesturing me inside. "I read your note. Have you any news on the search?"

"I'm afraid not." I placed my bag on the floor and settled onto the bench before her table as she set a kettle over the fire. "There's still no sign of Lord Langstone or any more of his possessions. Not even the missing button from his bloody coat."

The last felt a bit heavy-handed, for I hadn't intended to even mention the button. But then I realized she might not be aware the button she possessed belonged to Alfred.

Her eyes flared wide. "Oh, a button?" She crossed to the cabinet and began rummaging through the drawers. "Was it gold? I found one outside my cottage about a week ago. Now, where did I put it?" Her hands rifled through the drawer in which I'd found the button, and then moved on to the one above it.

"Yes," I replied, trying to keep the wary confusion from my voice. "Gold with a series of ornate swirls."

"I believe I have it, then." She grunted in frustration. "Or I did." She returned to the original drawer, pulling all of the contents out of it and setting them beside her where she knelt on the floor. "I'm *sure* I put it in here."

I moved forward to study the items she'd removed, but there was no sign of the button.

She frowned down into the empty drawer. "I don't understand. I know I put it in this cabinet. Where could it—" Her voice broke off abruptly as her eyes flitted first toward the herb shelves and then toward the door.

"Do you normally leave your door unlocked?" I asked.

"Yes. So few people venture out this way, and it's not as if I have much to steal." Her tone tightened as she stared down into the empty drawer again.

"Maybe you mislaid it," I suggested, though I knew very well she had not. Not unless she'd moved it since the day before when I'd found it.

Of course, it was possible she was lying. Perhaps she'd slipped the button into her pocket or discarded it in the hours since I was last here. But then, why had she mentioned it at all?

"Maybe," she murmured, replacing all the items in the drawer.

There was another distinct possibility. Someone had taken it. Someone who'd known where it was. Perhaps someone who'd watched me remove it.

An image of Rory in his mud-splattered trousers standing beside me in the bog appeared before my eyes. Would he have done such a thing?

I resumed my seat at the table and Miss Galloway stiffly joined me. "Well, at least you know what became of the button." She frowned, clearly bothered by the missing object. "Even if we don't know where it is now." She inhaled a deep breath, settling herself. "Have they given up looking?"

"Most of the farmers and laborers have returned to their work, but my husband and I are still searching."

She nodded, her brow heavy with worry.

Impulsively, I reached out to touch her hand. "We won't stop looking until we know what happened to him. Whatever that might be."

Her pupils dilated, telling me she understood the implication I was trying to convey. "Let's hope it doesn't come to that," she murmured.

The harried look on her face, the telltale brightness in her eyes, and the discovery of the button outside her cottage all seemed to indicate more than a simple acquaintance, so I decided to venture a delicate question. "Miss Galloway—"

"Please, call me Lorna."

I flashed her a brief smile. "Lorna, forgive me if I'm treading where I shouldn't, but . . . are you and Lord Langstone . . . is there something between you? Something other than friendship?"

Her eyes lowered as she reached up to toy with an oblong piece of what appeared to be amber with some sort of leaf or feather trapped inside hanging from her necklace. I didn't know if she was aware, but the fact that she hadn't immediately denied it already gave me my answer.

"It's not so easy to define," she began tentatively. Her gaze darted up to gauge my reaction, and then back to the scarred surface of the table. "I didn't like him at first. I thought he was just another pompous, self-absorbed lordling out for his own amusement." Her brow furrowed. "But after I got to know him better, I realized that wasn't quite right. He was still a self-centered, vainglorious clunch," she jested with a small smile. "But there was more to him than that. Much more."

It was apparent she didn't quite comprehend it herself, but there was a softness that came over her features when she spoke of him that made one thing perfectly clear.

"You genuinely do care for him," I remarked, trying to keep any trace of my disbelief from my voice.

I must not have succeeded, for she laughed. "Don't sound so surprised. He's not a monster. Even if he behaved like one toward your husband in the past."

I flushed. "It's only . . . after all the things I've heard about him, I find it hard to believe . . . well, that someone like you . . ." I broke off, struggling to explain, and feeling I was only making it worse. "He just doesn't seem very likable."

But she seemed to understand what I meant, and fortunately she didn't take offense. "It's true what they say. My mother was Lord Sherracombe's *chère-amie*, and I am his natural daughter. But she chose to live here, just as I have. He wasn't hiding us away. My mother was too ashamed to live in town, even though they loved each other until the day she died. She could have wed a wealthy squire or a minor baronet, but instead she chose to follow her heart, and it had fallen in love with a married man." She sat taller, showing me she was unashamed of her mother's decision. "My father's marriage was an arranged one. The contracts were drawn up before he was even out of short pants. And it was not happy. So he and his wife amicably agreed to find their contentment elsewhere. No one was hurt in the arrangement. Lord and Lady Sherracombe never had children. His title will pass to a nephew."

She claimed no one had been hurt, but I could see the faint lines around her eyes that indicated otherwise.

"What of you?" I murmured.

She stared at me, as if surprised I'd given her that much consideration.

A shrill whistle broke the silence, and she rose from her seat to fetch the kettle.

"I cannot complain," she said. "There are many whose lives are far less ideal than mine. At least I had a father and mother who loved me, and a warm home to grow up in. One that is now mine." She crossed to the cabinet, rising up onto her toes to lift down a delicate teapot painted with yellow roses and two cups. "I'm grateful for what I have, and I'll not begrudge the rest."

I studied her profile in admiration as she spooned tea leaves into the pot and poured the boiling water over them. Hers was an example I could follow. For I'd struggled for some time to reconcile myself to the events of my first marriage, and to accept the knowledge that had been forced on me and turn it to good. Only recently had I truly begun to come to terms with it, and yet this woman had so humbly reconciled herself to a past that had not been of her making, determined to make the best of the present. Perhaps the events of her life had been less tormented than my marriage to Sir Anthony, but it didn't make her acceptance any less commendable.

It saddened me to think of how she was shunned and belittled purely because of the circumstances of her birth. I knew such was typical treatment of all by-blows, particularly those living in the countryside, and not Lorna specifically. It was society's way of discouraging such behavior, even if men of a higher rank were given leniency for keeping mistresses and their children in London. But it still galled me to see her derided thusly.

"As for Alfred, I'm not sure he's made himself very likable to most." She sat across from me again as we waited for the tea to steep. "He's certainly handsome and charming. Though, he hasn't the reputation your husband does. But those traits are superficial, aren't they? One can be handsome and charming and still an utter wretch."

I smiled, having met several such men. "True."

"And Alfred undoubtedly has a terrible habit of trying to dodge his troubles rather than face them."

"You know about his grandfather pressuring him to wed Lady Juliana?"

She tipped her head. "Among other things." She frowned at her hands folded before her. "But that's just part of who he is. Believe it or not, beneath all that bluster and past debauchery is a decent man he's rarely been forced to show."

"Until you?" I guessed.

"Well, I doubt I'm the first and only. But yes. I won't tolerate nonsense." She frowned. "I never intended to like him. I certainly never intended to welcome his company or the possibility of . . . something more. My parents were devoted to each other, but I also saw the way it tore my mother apart when my father had to leave us and return to his life, to his wife." She shook her head. "I never wanted that for myself. I'm still not sure I do." Her gaze strayed toward the window. "And now there may no longer be a choice to make."

It was evident whatever had happened between them, Alfred had made no promises to her. Which made his refusal to wed Lady Juliana all the more confusing. I would have thought Alfred was the type of man who would've been content to wed the duke's daughter and still visit Lorna here in her cottage as long as she continued to welcome him.

However, it might explain something else that had puzzled me.

"Did Alfred's brother Rory know about the two of you?" I asked. "Is that why he's taken such a decided disliking to you?"

Her mouth pressed into a thin line as she picked up the teapot to pour. "Mr. Trevelyan has never liked me. I suspect for the obvious reason—my being born on the other side of the blanket. But his aversion only increased after I sent him away with a sharp refusal."

"He made advances toward you?" I gasped, seeing now how that made perfect sense.

"Not very subtle ones either."

"Did Alfred know?"

"At the time, I don't know. But since then, yes."

She didn't share who had told him or how he reacted, and her firm answer did not invite questions on the matter, so I decided not to ask. Not when there were other topics to discuss.

My eyes lifted to the bouquet of herb bennet over the door. At some point since my first visit, it had been replaced. A fresh bundle of the flowers now graced the wall. "Did Alfred suspect he was being poisoned or did you?"

Lorna's hands stilled, and she followed my gaze toward the bouquet. "He did." She handed me my cup of tea, holding on to it a moment longer than necessary to make me look her in the eye. "And knowing what I did about Mrs. Gage's poisoning, and that of Alice Trevelyan before her, I had to agree."

My skin prickled, sensing the importance of what she was trying to impart. Lorna didn't say anything further, but I could sense that she was urging me to make the connection myself.

"You think they're related?"

She shrugged, lifting her own cup. "Three poisonings in one family? Don't you think that's suspicious?"

"I do." I frowned. "Though . . . Mrs. Gage's maid was proven responsible for hers."

She sipped her tea. "Yes, but did someone give her the idea?"

I wanted to ask her about her mother's possible role in that incident, but I struggled to find a tactful way to do so. Fortunately, Lorna knew what I was thinking.

"Perhaps someone has implied otherwise," she remarked coolly, "but my mother had nothing to do with it. I know because I remember that maid calling here and asking my mother for such a concoction, but when she couldn't give my mother a satisfactory answer for why she needed it, my mother refused."

Relief flooded through my veins. There was always the possibility Lorna was lying, but I didn't think so. What reason had she to do so? If I hadn't held her responsible for her birth, I certainly wouldn't hold her responsible for her mother's actions when Lorna had been but a child.

"Thank you for telling me that," I said. "I didn't want to think it, but it was mentioned."

"Of course it was. By Mr. Trevelyan, I wager."

I didn't confirm this. I didn't need to.

"So if Alfred believed he was being poisoned, did he know by whom?" I asked, curious to hear what his opinion had been.

"He didn't know. But you have to ask yourself, who was alive for all three deaths?"

I stared at her in astonishment as my stomach dipped, threatening to bring up my tea. "You think it was Lord Tavistock? But he's been ill for months."

"Yes, but he has servants willing to do his bidding. And he's desperate to have his heir wed to the Duke of Bedford's daughter."

"Because of the mine partnership."

She arched her eyebrows meaningfully. "Is that all?"

"I don't know," I replied, scrambling to reconsider everything I thought I knew. "Do you?"

"No. But it's difficult not to wonder."

I nodded. How on earth I was going to suggest such a thing to Gage? That his grandfather might be in some way responsible for his mother's death? It was horrifying.

Something rubbed along my leg and I glanced down to find the orange tabby begging for my attention.

Lorna leaned forward to see beyond the table. "Is that Sherry? If you don't like cats, just shoo him away." She smiled. "My father brought him to me. He thought I could use the companionship. And occasionally a good mouser."

I ran my fingers over his soft fur. "I didn't see him the first time I visited." I laughed. "So he startled me terribly yesterday when I stepped in to leave you a note. I heard a sound in the bedroom and thought maybe you were in need of assistance. When I opened the door, he shot past my legs."

But rather than joining me in laughing, Lorna stiffened. "Oh, did I shut him into the bedroom?" she remarked lightly. "It happens from time to time. The little devil is always underfoot, it seems."

"Yes, cats are like that, aren't they?"

I studied her face, trying to decipher what had unsettled her. She must have known I'd entered her cottage, for she'd gotten my message. Was she upset I'd done so? Particularly now that it appeared I wasn't the only one who'd come inside her home without her present.

I opened my mouth to apologize, but she cut me off before I could speak.

"Did you bring your sketchbook?" She gestured toward the satchel at my feet.

"I did."

"Then, if you've finished your tea, I'll take you to some of my favorite vantages." She rose to her feet. "I need to gather some fresh watercress anyway."

I gave Sherry one last scratch behind the ears and allowed Lorna to lead me from the cottage, though my mind was still puzzling over her uneasy reaction and her unwillingness to talk about it, as well as that missing button.

Several pleasant hours later, though the sky looked no different to me, Lorna suggested I should return to Langstone. She insisted the weather would soon turn, and I wouldn't wish to be caught out in it. Trusting her better knowledge of our surroundings, I obeyed, sticking to familiar paths I'd already trod lest I stumble into a bog again.

The bright colors of a butterfly caught my eye as I was fording the River Walkham, and I paused to pull my sketchbook from my satchel. I had one last page on which to capture the image of the insect. Though I didn't have my paints with me, in the margins I noted the vibrant hues and the approximate mixture of pigments I would need to recreate them later.

So absorbed was I in the task that the shift Lorna had warned me about began to happen. One moment the blue sky was streaked with wispy white clouds, and the next a dark gray ceiling slid into place over them. Tendrils of hair lifted from my temples in the blustery wind, and I realized I needed to hurry if I was going to escape getting soaked.

I scrambled up the bank of the river, stuffing my charcoal case and sketchbook back into my satchel as I went. My book tumbled to the heath, but before I could bend to pick it up, another hand grabbed it for me.

I gasped and whirled around. "Rory! You startled me."

He gazed down at the drawing the book had fallen open to. It was a rendering of one of the views from Great Mis Tor, though I hadn't been able to resist including Lorna in the foreground, staring pensively out at the landscape before her. "My apologies," he murmured as he passed it back to me.

He didn't sound very apologetic.

He fell in step with me as I resumed my hastened trek back toward Langstone Manor. Studying him out of the corner of my eye, I couldn't help but note this was the second time he'd snuck up on me unawares. I'd speculated he might be following me, and now I really had to wonder if it was true. But why? Because of Lorna?

"Miss Galloway warned me, but I'm still amazed by how swiftly the weather changed," I observed, curious how he would respond.

"Yes. Even the most experienced can be fooled."

"Does that include you? I had no idea you were so fond of the moor." In fact, I would have wagered he was more like his brother, rarely venturing this far out into the heath.

"I don't know that I would say I'm fond of it." His eyes slid sideways to meet mine. "But those of us who are more conversant with its hazards have an obligation to look after those who are not. After all, we wouldn't want something unfortunate to happen."

I nearly tripped over a rock, and by the time I recovered my footing he was already several paces ahead. Had I just been warned? Or was he rather clumsily trying to say he was concerned for my safety?

Either way, the swelling wind wasn't the only thing that made the hairs on the back of my neck stand on end.

CHAPTER TWENTY-THREE

We returned to the manor just as the first drops of rain began to splutter from the sky. However, Rory didn't follow me inside; instead he peeled off to circle the house toward the stables. I didn't wait to see where exactly he was going, but scurried inside to keep dry.

With the storms rolling in, effectively trapping me inside, and Gage still gone in the carriage, I set about amusing myself for the remainder of the day as I waited for him to return. I explored the remaining rooms in the manor, and then sat with Lord Tavistock, sketching while he dozed. I'd not forgotten the portrait he'd commissioned me to paint, and so diligently worked on a number of drawings of Gage in different poses. Not that drawing my attractive husband was any hardship.

Several hours later I'd filled the front of the new sketchbook I'd retrieved from my room with various images of him, but I was no closer to puzzling out Lord Tavistock. Lorna's suspicions continued to circle around in my head. Could the viscount be responsible? Was it really possible he'd helped poison three people—his sister, his daughter, and his grandson? I didn't want to believe it, but the particulars were too troubling to be ignored. And Lorna was right, he was the only person connected to all three incidences, even indirectly.

However, I was not looking forward to raising that specter with Gage.

He returned to the manor just in time to dress for dinner, saving me from an awkward meal alone with his relatives. Unfortunately, Rory had elected not to join us, leaving us in Lady Langstone's chilly company. What she did with her time, I didn't know, for I rarely saw her during the day. I suspected she avoided us as much as we avoided her. But she almost always appeared at dinner elegantly attired and armed with more sly insults.

As such, Gage was not in the most amenable mood when we retired to our chamber. It didn't help that Mr. Glanville had given him poor directions to the home of a mutual acquaintance of his and Alfred's. Not only had the coachman wasted precious time searching in the driving rain, but the carriage had also become mired in the acquaintance's muddy lane and had to be pushed out.

"What of Endsleigh House?" I asked as I rubbed a hand consolingly up and down his arm. "Was the steward able to tell you anything about the Swing letters?"

The furrows in his brow deepened. "The puffed-up peacock kept me waiting for nearly an hour. And when he did finally deign to see me, he denied their having received any. Whether that's true or not, I don't know. But as supercilious as the man behaved, I doubt he would have admitted it if they had." He exhaled heavily, sinking deeper into the cushions of the fainting couch. "Regardless, I think we need to set aside the Swing letters as the reason for Alfred's disappearance. There's been little indication of violence otherwise, and as has already been pointed out, it's quite precipitous to jump from written threats to deadly assault or outright murder."

I turned to the side, curling my legs up under the skirts of my bright rose evening gown with white lace trim before reaching over to cradle my warm teacup between my hands. The turn in the weather had brought cooler temperatures, making the stone manor's rooms even colder than usual. "I agree. That doesn't preclude the possibility they were used as an excuse for carrying out their own agenda. But I don't think they're the real motive."

He pulled at the ends of his cravat, loosening it so that it dangled around his neck. "I hope your visit with Miss Galloway was more fruitful. What is it?" he asked, reacting to my sound of disgust.

"This tea." I set the cup aside with a cringe. "Either the milk is curdled or Cooper is playing another prank on us."

"Do you want me to ring for another pot?"

I waved it away. "No. I've had enough today as it is. I don't know if my visit was fruitful, but Miss Galloway did give me some interesting prospects to consider."

"Oh?"

I'd been running this conversation over and over in my head all afternoon, but I still needed to take a bracing breath before I dived in. "First of all, she admitted she and Alfred were more than friendly, though she didn't delve into specifics. But I wouldn't be surprised if they were lovers. She also knew about Lady Juliana, and how Alfred didn't wish to marry her."

Gage's eyebrows arched in surprise. "Had he made promises to her?"

"None that she mentioned. From the manner in which she spoke, I don't think she even expected them."

"And no one would accuse Alfred of being too honorable to keep a mistress a short distance away from his wife after he wed," Gage remarked wryly.

I shifted closer. "Perhaps more interesting, you were right about the herb bennet. She did suspect Alfred was being poisoned. And more importantly, he did, too."

Gage's expression darkened. "But who would do such a thing? And why?"

He'd neatly provided me with an opening, and yet my words felt clumsy on my lips. "Have you noticed there's something of a pattern here?"

He stared at me blankly. I couldn't tell whether he wasn't following or he simply refused to react.

"Of poisonings in your family."

His eyebrows twitched with irritation. "Because of my mother?"

"And your great-aunt Alice."

"There is no proof that Alice was the girl from that legend or that she was poisoned," he insisted.

"Yes, but if she was, you must admit there's something troubling going on here. And it all seems to center around that curse."

He sighed in aggravation. "Kiera, there is no curse."

"But you said we should consider the possibility—"

"I said we should explore the ramifications. Not seriously give credence to the possibility there *is* such a curse."

I pressed a hand to his leg, imploring him to listen. "Well, then what if someone else believed in it? What if someone was certain enough to help it along?"

"What are you saying?" he bit out.

"I'm saying that curse or no curse, there is a disturbing pattern of poisonings." I paused. "And your grandfather is the only person who was alive to witness all of them."

His eyes turned to icy chips. "You must be jesting."

"I don't want to believe it, Sebastian." My voice was tight with distress. "But it has to be considered."

"It's utterly ridiculous!"

"Then convince me of it."

"First of all, *Annie* poisoned my mother, not my grandfather."

"But who gave her the idea?"

He glowered. "Second of all, he was not the only person alive for all three. Hammett was here, though he was a young boy at the time Alice died. Or do you suspect he was Grandfather's accomplice?"

"Maybe."

He scoffed in derision. "You actually think my grandfather is malicious enough to poison all of them simply because they defied the family's wishes? That's mad."

"I know," I replied solemnly, having expected such a vehement response. I couldn't even blame him for it. I would have done the same. But the way he glared at me, like I was the most loathsome person he'd ever seen, was almost too difficult to bear. It made my heart shrivel inside my chest. "Can't we speak with him about it?"

"And accuse him of committing *three* murders?"

"No. We'll merely ask about Alice and the curse, that's all."

He shook his head. "No."

"Why?"

"Why what?"

"Why won't you ask him?"

"What kind of question is that?" He shifted forward, ready to leap to his feet. "The man is deathly ill. I'm not going to send him to his grave with this nonsense."

I studied him, unable to ignore his alarmed movements. "Is that really the reason? Or are you more afraid of hearing his answers?"

The frantic glimmer in his eyes told me I was not far from the truth. But rather than face it, rather than face me, he stormed from the room, slamming the door.

I stared at the cold wooden door and wrapped my arms around myself. Had I just destroyed my marriage? And for what? A suspicion I couldn't prove? To punish a man who already wasn't long for this world?

Perhaps I *was* a loathsome person. I was certainly a fool.

Though I lay awake for hours, Gage never returned. I considered going to him and apologizing, but the one time I worked up the nerve to do so I found the connecting door locked. I wasn't about to pound on it and beg, so I lay back down, clutching my stomach. It churned with pain and anxiety, making my head spin. I curled into a ball under the sheets in my cold bed, eventually falling into a fitful slumber.

For the first time since our wedding, I slept alone.

That is, until sometime during the wee hours of the morning when I vaulted out of bed, barely reaching the chamber pot before I was violently ill. When I'd finished emptying myself of everything I'd ever possibly eaten, I crumpled to the cold floor, moaning in pain and exhaustion. My insides felt like they were being shredded with broken glass. I'd presumed my agony over hurting Gage had caused my nausea, but I didn't think love alone could cause such forceful sickness.

Moments later, I was back up on my knees. I thought someone said my name, but the sound of my retching blocked most everything else. Then I felt a warm, solid presence at my back, helping to hold me up.

"I'm here, darling," Gage crooned, smoothing my stray tendrils of hair back from my face. "Let me help."

When I collapsed to the floor again, he brought me a cool washcloth to bathe my face. Then he sat and held my hand as I begged God to make it stop, before scrabbling back up to my knees.

How many times this process was repeated, I don't know. I lost count. But at some point, the roiling subsided and Gage carried me back to bed. He climbed in next to me, though I must have looked and smelled like something my cat, Earl Grey, would have left as a present to proudly display his hunting prowess.

When I blinked open my eyes again it was to find morning had come. And from the look of the light filtering through the open windows, it was well advanced. I turned my head on the pillow to find Gage seated on the fainting couch with a book in his lap. When he saw me looking at him, he quickly crossed the room to perch on the mattress next to me.

"You're awake," he sighed in relief, reaching for my hand. "Can I get you anything?"

"Water," I croaked.

He poured me a glass, and then helped me to sit and drink it. The water was cool and refreshing, and I would have gulped it, but he forced me to take sips. When I'd had my fill, I lay back down, panting as I tried to gather my breath to speak. Gage's eyes scanned me fretfully.

"I think I'm recovering now," I assured him. "I'm tired, and thirsty, but it doesn't hurt anymore. At least, not like before."

"That's good. The physician told me that would be a welcome sign."

"Physician?" I tried to push to a seated position, but he pressed me back down.

"Slowly. I'll prop you up a bit more if you like."

I waited impatiently while he added another pillow behind mine. "When did a physician examine me?"

"Yesterday."

I stared at him wide-eyed. "How long have I been asleep?"

He glanced at the clock on the mantel. "About twenty-eight hours."

I couldn't fathom it. I'd slept an entire day, completely unaware time was passing?

"Did the physician know why I was so ill?"

Gage reached for my hand again, rubbing his thumb against mine as if he recognized I would need his support. "Poison."

Whether my mind had sustained all the shock it could for one morning or somewhere inside me I'd already figured this out, I wasn't as surprised as it seemed I should be. "From the tea?" I quickly deduced, realizing now why it had tasted wrong.

"More than likely. No one else has fallen ill."

"Do we know who—"

He shook his head before I could finish the question. "No one will admit to it, and all of the kitchen staff, as well as the maid who delivered the tea, swear they had no idea how it was poisoned."

"Do you believe them?"

He sighed. "I don't know. But the fact of the matter is, *someone* slipped the poison in. So someone is lying." He squeezed my hand tighter, his eyes stricken. "Thank heavens you didn't drink any more of it than you did. The physician said much more and . . . and it would have killed you."

I wondered if the poison was still coursing through me, for that seemed the only explanation for the numbness I felt upon hearing I'd almost died. Then I saw Gage's eyes dip ever so briefly to my abdomen. My body went cold. "What of a possible child?"

His eyes stared into mine, stricken with uncertainty. "The physician said it's too early to know, but . . . if you are with child, and the child has been affected, then . . ."

I stared at him mutely. Neither of us seemed to be able to say the words to finish that thought.

"But the doctor assured me you would recover fully," he assured me.

I turned aside, not sure how I felt. If there was, or had been, a child growing inside me, I hadn't yet known it, hadn't yet come to terms with what that meant. And yet, there was a sharp twinge in the depths of my heart that told me I wasn't unaffected. But instead I returned to a safer topic. "Do we know what the poison was?"

"Not for sure. There are several possible candidates. But . . . I'm ready to admit now that you were right. There may be some connection between all the poisonings. There's certainly one between yours and Alfred's."

I lifted my hand to touch his face, feeling my heart twist at the raw tone of his voice. "I'm sorry."

He shook his head, removing my hand from his face to clasp it between his. "*I'm* sorry. I shouldn't have stormed out like I did. Or, at least, I shouldn't have stayed away."

"Well, I might have handled matters better myself. Especially as another thought occurred to me."

He arched his eyebrows in question.

"Maybe your grandfather isn't doing the poisoning. Maybe he's being poisoned, too. After all, your mother's illness masked what her maid was doing for years."

I watched as the implications of such a possibility played across his face. "Then that would mean Rory has the strongest motive to be our poisoner. With Grandfather and Alfred both out of the way, he'll not only become the heir, but the viscount."

I grimaced in sympathy, not liking the possibility any more than he did.

His eyes glinted with determination as he rose to his feet. "You're right. I need to speak with Grandfather."

"I'm coming with you."

Gage scowled down at me. "No, you're not. You are not rising from this bed."

"Of course I am. I may be a trifle weak, but I'm sure I can manage to walk fifty feet. After I've eaten something and bathed, that is," I remarked, lifting my soiled nightdress away from my skin.

His expression was adamant, but I was not about to let him do this alone.

"Sebastian, let me do this for you," I pleaded earnestly. "I promise. The moment I feel faint or too overwhelmed, I'll let you carry me back to my bed, scolding me the entire way."

He glared at me a moment longer before relenting with a heavy sigh. "Agreed. The *moment* you feel too unwell, you'll tell me?"

"I will," I agreed, resolved that would not happen.

Fortunately, before Gage could challenge me further, Bree entered the room.

"Yer awake, m'lady," she exclaimed, setting her stack of linens aside and hurrying forward. She pressed a hand to my brow and reached for the glass of water, urging me to drink.

Gage nodded to me and slipped out of the room. I trusted he would wait for me as promised. However, convincing Bree of the necessity of my rising from bed would be another matter. So I chose to omit my intentions until I had to.

"Are ye hungry? Shall I send for some toast?"

I wasn't sure why she asked, for she'd already bustled over to tug the bellpull. "Yes, please." I pushed my covers down and slowly sat up, pausing when my head began to spin. "And send for hot water. I'm sure I'll feel even better after a bath."

"Aye," she agreed. But when I tried to swing my legs over the side of the bed, she shooed me back in place. "No need to rush. It'll take time for 'em to prepare it."

I sighed, resigned to being coddled.

"Ye gave us all a right scare," Bree said, folding the blanket back over me.

I was touched by the concern etched across her brow. "Well, had I any say in the matter, I wouldn't have caused it."

Bree smiled tightly.

"So tell me what I've missed while lying abed? Any thawing from Mrs. Webley?"

Her eyes lit with eagerness. "Nay, but she did show a great deal o' interest in that scorched scrap o' paper I let fall from my pocket."

"Did she?"

"Aye. She recognized it. O' that, I'm sure."

"Well, then, I wouldn't be surprised if I receive a visit from the Dowager Lady Langstone in short order. But don't let her enter until I've finished my bath."

CHAPTER TWENTY-FOUR

Like clockwork, almost to the second Bree inserted the last hairpin, a knock sounded on the door. My maid looked up to meet my eyes in the reflection of the looking glass and I held up a hand, forestalling her. It simply wouldn't do to let Lady Langstone, if it was indeed her, think I was overeager to speak with her. Let her wait.

I turned my head, examining the simple coiled chignon Bree had fastened at the back of my head, forgoing the hot tongues and side curls that were fashionable as of late. In truth, I preferred this smoother arrangement, but as Gage's wife it wouldn't do for me to completely ignore what was stylish.

When enough time had passed, I nodded to Bree. I examined my reflection one last time and then swiveled on the bench to face whomever entered.

I bit back a smile of wry triumph when the dowager strolled into the chamber. Coolly composed as ever, she glanced first at the bed, where no doubt she expected me to still be lying, and then

to where I was seated before my dressing table. I used my prerog-
ative as an invalid recovering from being poisoned to remain
seated. In truth, my legs might have shaken if I stood for long.

I nodded to Bree, who hovered near the door, and she departed to give us some privacy, though I knew she wouldn't go far.

"I wished to offer my apologies that you suffered harm while
under our roof, but I see you're making a swift recovery." Her eyes
glinted with cynicism. "To hear Sebastian talk, you were practically at death's door."

I refused to acknowledge such a remark with a response—not
when it was clear she wished to rile me. "Lady Langstone, what
can I do for you?"

She pressed her lips together tightly, considering me. It was
clear she was unhappy I hadn't taken the bait, and just as clear she
didn't want to say what I'd already guessed she was here for.

"I believe you have something of mine."

"Do I?"

"Yes. You instructed your maid to be certain my maid knew
she had it."

I flashed her an arch smile, giving her credit for recognizing
such a ploy.

She held her hand out. "I would like it back."

"Now why would I do that?" I asked, tilting my head.

Her gaze sharpened. "Because I don't think you want your
husband to know about it."

"And if he already does?"

This finally succeeded in unsettling her, for she stiffened. I
decided to press my advantage.

"Just as your son Alfred did, or he would not have been blackmailing you."

Her eyelids lowered to half-mast as she glared down at me.
"And is that what you are attempting to do now? Extort something from me? I should have expected as much from the butcher's
wife," she sneered, harkening back to one of the cruel epithets the

newspapers had called me once the scandal of my involvement with my late anatomist husband's work had broken.

But she would have to do better than that if she wished to upset me. "Actually, I'm more curious whether you had him killed because of it."

If not for the horrifying nature of our discussion, I would have enjoyed Lady Langstone's stunned expression.

"You cannot be serious?" she gasped before lifting her chin in righteous indignation. "I've never been so insulted in all my life."

"And yet I know he was blackmailing you."

"That may be," she begrudgingly admitted. "But I would hardly kill him over the matter. Especially when all he wanted in return was for me to try to persuade Lord Tavistock that Lady Juliana would not be the best bride for him."

I arched a single eyebrow skeptically.

"It's true."

"Do you have proof?"

"My word should be proof enough," she sniffed, but then some of her umbrage faded. "Do you truly think he's dead? I thought . . . you and Sebastian had hopes otherwise."

"I don't know," I said, finding it difficult not to soften under the signs of her obvious distress. "But the longer he's missing, the greater chance we have to face that possibility."

She looked away, swallowing hard as she worried her hands before her. I gave her a moment to compose herself, hoping my kindness would encourage her to confess what she knew. But I should have known better.

"Well, I had nothing to do with . . . with whatever has happened to him. And neither had that letter." She held out her hand as if she fully expected me to comply with the implied demand.

"You keep referring to the letter in the singular, as if I didn't witness you burning a whole stack of them."

She scowled. "I don't know what you're talking about. Those

papers you so rudely barged into my chambers to see burning were merely old bills."

I sighed and rolled my eyes, annoyed with her ridiculous pretense. "Regardless, I'm not returning it. Why are you indulging in an assignation with Gage's father anyway? I would have thought he was unworthy of your charms."

If she could have stamped her foot and not looked like a petulant child, I suspected she would have. "There was . . . *is* no assignation. There never was. That letter was from a long time ago." She crossed her arms over her chest. "I can't be faulted with the fact that the man developed an unhealthy attraction to me while his wife lay ill. One I *certainly* never welcomed. I always said he was a toad-eating scoundrel."

"Then why did you keep his letters?"

She stewed for a second before huffing. "If you're not going to be reasonable, then we have nothing to discuss."

If she thought I would call after her and try to persuade her from leaving, she was sadly mistaken. Her words and actions had already given me ample information to ponder. As did her flustered retreat.

Apparently Lord Tavistock had been kept apprised of my situation, for his first reaction upon seeing Gage escorting me into his chamber was to admonish his grandson for allowing me out of bed. "She should be tucked up resting," he scolded. "Not traipsing about the manor."

Gage pulled a chair closer to the bed and then helped me to sit. "She has a mind of her own, Grandfather."

"Well, whose fault is that?"

"God," I retorted despite being winded and a bit light-headed from the walk. I appreciated the evident affection that underlay his reproving words, but that didn't mean I was going to condone them. "I am well enough. And tired of lying in that bed."

The viscount grunted in disapproval and then turned to Gage. "Why are you here plaguing me, anyway? Have you found Alfred?"

"I'm afraid not." He pressed a steadying hand on my shoulder. "But we do have some questions for you that might help us locate him."

His grandfather sat back with his hands folded before him. "Then ask."

Gage glanced down at me, as if uncertain how to start. "This may sound unrelated, but can you tell us how your illness began?"

The viscount frowned. "With a slight cough and some wheeziness. As it always does."

"No stomach complaints?"

"No." His shrewd eyes flicked back and forth between us. "You're wondering if it was set off by poison. Like your mother."

"We thought it might be possible," Gage replied carefully. "Particularly given the fact it looks like Alfred was also being poisoned."

All the blood seemed to drain from the old man's face, and I sat forward in concern. "By whom?" he gasped.

Gage shook his head. "We don't know. But one can't help but notice a pattern."

His grandfather turned his head to the side, staring at the open window. The fact that he hadn't refuted this suggestion spoke volumes.

"Can we add Alice to that list?"

The viscount jerked his head back around to stare at him. "My sister?"

Gage nodded.

For a moment, I didn't know what his grandfather would say. He sat so still, so motionless, but then he exhaled as he sank deeper into the pillows behind him. "Yes."

My husband's hand tightened on my shoulder, and I knew he was restraining himself.

"The legend they tell about Stephen's Grave is true. I'm not sure why the family was so intent on denying that fact." He nodded toward the window. "She met that madman at the crossroads where they erected a stone. She was there to tell him she didn't care for him, and then he poisoned her and himself. I was away at school at the time. Learned about it in a terse letter from my father. It was never to be discussed. Not even among the family."

My breath caught at the long-buried hurt creeping along the edges of his voice. To be informed of his sister's death by letter and then never allowed to ask questions about it? It was heartless. Perhaps his parents had found it too painful, but I suspected it had more to do with shame.

"Is that the origin of our family's supposed curse?" Gage asked.

"A curse? Yes, I suppose it is, though I've always thought of it as more of a family motto." He shook his head. "No, that's much older." He studied each of us in turn again. "You think someone is out for vengeance against our family?"

It was more likely someone within the family was enacting their own agenda, but Gage did not say this. Not when it would point to his grandfather as an obvious suspect.

"We don't know. But it has to be considered."

The viscount's gaze strayed toward the window again, as if seeing something in the distance, or perhaps the past. "Yes, I suppose it does."

I was still contemplating his enigmatic reply several hours later while Gage and I enjoyed a quiet dinner in our rooms. Exhausted from my illness and the afternoon's exertions, I'd been too weary to descend to the dining room and fend off Lady Langstone's barbs. Gage, Lord Tavistock, and Bree—who still scowled at me for not listening to her earlier—had all been right. I should have stayed in bed. But how could I do so when I was certain we were so close to the key to figuring all of this out?

In any case, I was hesitant to eat any of the prepared dishes or beverages at the manor until we understood who had tried to poison me. So we requested a cold supper and an unopened bottle of wine—items we could examine and deduce with some confidence whether they had been tampered with.

A knock sounded on the bedchamber door while I nibbled on a piece of apple Gage had sliced with his own knife for dessert. Gage and I shared a look of mutual confusion and then he called out for them to enter. I nearly choked when Lady Langstone tentatively opened the door.

She was dressed for dinner in a gown of aubergine silk with garnets glistening at her throat and wrist. "I apologize for interrupting your evening," she murmured far more politely than I was accustomed to.

I scrutinized her in suspicion, pondering if she was here to discuss Lord Gage's letters again. This time with her goal being to hurt her nephew.

"What can we do for you?" he asked, unaware of my trepidation.

She clasped her hands tightly before her. "I merely wondered if either of you have seen Roland today."

"I haven't." Gage's eyes flicked toward me. "And I assume Kiera hasn't."

I nodded in confirmation even as a trickle of unease slid down my spine. "I haven't seen Rory since we returned from the moor two days ago, just before that storm began in earnest."

"I see." She fidgeted. "What of you, Sebastian? Did you see him yesterday?"

He frowned as if the same disquieting sensation was also settling over him. "No, I can't say I did. I was too concerned for my wife." He glanced up at his aunt. "I take it you haven't seen him since then either?"

"No. Not since the incident Lady Darby mentioned. I happened to be looking out the window when they came striding in from the moor."

"But Rory didn't enter the house with me," I recounted, thinking back. "He turned to go around the side of the manor. Where to, I don't know. It had begun to rain and I was concerned with staying dry."

Lady Langstone nodded. "Yes, I saw that." Her eyes flickered with something I thought might be fear. "And I saw him return a few moments later and go back out through the gate onto the moor."

"With a storm bearing down?" Gage said incredulously.

"Yes."

He set the knife and apple aside and rose to his feet, taking command of the situation. "Have you questioned the staff yet?"

"No," she replied. "I . . . I didn't want to unduly alarm them."

"Well, go do so now. Given the fact that Alfred is still missing, if Rory hasn't been seen in over forty-eight hours, I think we need to assume he may also be in trouble. I'll speak with Grandfather."

I pushed to my feet, shock and concern driving away much of my weariness. "And I'll search the study. Perhaps he made note of an appointment or some other affair that would explain his absence."

My husband's eyes scoured my face, as if to ascertain whether I was capable of the task given my evident exhaustion moments ago, but he didn't protest. "Send a servant if you find anything of importance."

The same neatly arranged piles covered Lord Tavistock's desk as before, so I set to work sorting through them. Everything seemed in order. Letters, bills, contracts, purchase agreements, crop-yield reports, repair estimates—all the things you would expect to find on such an estate. I paid particular attention to the letters at the top of the stack made up of miscellaneous correspondence, but nothing of note caught my eye. No new Swing letters. No complaints of any kind. If Rory or the viscount had kept an appointment book or agenda, I couldn't find it.

I was about to give up and return to our chamber when the bottom right drawer in the desk yielded something of interest. It was my sketchbook. The one I'd used the last page of to capture the image of that butterfly two days prior. The one Rory had handed back to me when I dropped it.

I stared down at it in bewilderment. I hadn't even known it was missing.

Why was it in this desk? And who had taken it? Thus far we assumed Rory had disappeared immediately after escorting me back to the manor, but perhaps we were wrong. If Rory had been the one to take my book, then he would have had to enter my room sometime after I returned, but before Gage and I retired for the night.

Of course, there was always the possibility someone else had nabbed it and stashed it here to keep suspicion away from them. But once again, why? I flipped through the pages, trying to comprehend what the culprit had hoped to find, and wondering if they'd found it. No pages were marked or missing.

Nevertheless, I still felt vaguely violated. As if someone had tried to use my art for nefarious means. If only I knew what they were.

When I returned to my bedchamber, I found Gage pacing back and forth.

"I was just about to come looking for you," he said, lowering his hand from his hair where he'd been raking his fingers through it in agitation. "Did you find anything?"

"Just my sketchbook," I replied, passing it to him.

"Your sketchbook?"

"I'm as perplexed as you are." I reached up to smooth down his hair. "How did your grandfather react?"

He sank down on the edge of the bed with a heavy sigh. "Not well. The truth is, I've never seen him like this. He seemed to shrink in on himself before my very eyes."

I sat beside him, taking his hand.

"This could kill him," he whispered, as if saying the words too loud would make them come true.

"We'll find them," I told him, not able to bear the stricken look in his eyes. "And . . . and if they aren't able to tell us themselves, we'll find out what happened to them."

"Will we?"

I infused all the determination I could into my voice. "Yes."

He offered me a weak smile of gratitude, but I could tell he didn't believe me. Not yet.

"So tell me the obvious, who is next in line to inherit after Rory? Your grandfather had three children, correct? One son and two daughters?"

He inhaled, furrowing his brow in concentration. "Let's see, it would have to be Grandfather's younger brother. Or one of his sons or grandsons. But the last I heard they still lived in America."

I worried my lip. "I'm assuming this information is at least fifteen years old."

"Yes."

"Then perhaps at least one of them has returned to England."

"It's possible," he admitted, though he sounded doubtful.

"Are you certain his brother had sons?"

He shook his head in frustration. "I don't know. To be honest, I never paid much attention."

"So what happens if none of them are alive or exist to inherit? Does it go back another generation?"

"That's normally the law."

I racked my brain, trying to think of any alternative possibilities. "You mentioned a cousin Edmund, your aunt Harriet's son. That they live in a cottage near here."

Gage shook his head. "I know what you're thinking, and the answer is no. I don't believe Edmund is capable of killing his cousins on the *chance* that if he requests a special dispensation from the Crown he might inherit."

I grimaced in apology. "I meant no offense. I'm just trying to understand why someone would harm both Alfred and Rory."

He wrapped his arm around me and pulled me close. "I know." Then he sighed again. "I'll speak to Grandfather tomorrow, and if he doesn't know the whereabouts of his brother and any of his descendants, then I suppose I shall have to write Father asking another favor."

"Is he keeping tally?"

His voice was wry. "He's always keeping tally."

CHAPTER TWENTY-FIVE

Gage and I made the same rounds we had before, visiting all the adjoining landowners and searching the moor closest to the manor. Lady Langstone had already spoken to the house staff, and Hammett handled questioning the gardeners and stable workers. No one admitted to seeing Rory. No one knew where he might have gone.

It was eerily similar to Alfred's disappearance. The only difference was that Lady Langstone had witnessed Rory striding back out onto the moor, while a gardener had been the last to see Alfred do the same. Beyond that, there was no trace of him. Not even a bloody coat.

Or had we simply not found it yet?

While Gage rode on to speak with some of the farmers who worked the land southwest of Langstone Manor, I spurred my horse to Lorna's cottage. If possible, she seemed even more distressed to hear of Rory's disappearance, but perhaps it was the cumulative effect. After all, if she'd been holding out hope that

Alfred would return, the disappearance of his brother must make that hope seem even more forlorn.

When I returned to the manor, I climbed the stairs toward our chamber, planning to change out of my riding attire and wait for Gage to return. But the shrill sound of a raised voice made me stumble to a stop.

"This is your fault! Your sole purpose in being summoned here was to find Alfred, and you couldn't even do it!"

Despite the strident tone, I recognized the voice as belonging to the Dowager Lady Langstone. Ascending two more stairs, I could see around the bend in the staircase to the landing above where she stood berating Gage. I'd never seen her in such a frenzied state, and the way her arms flailed about, gesturing dramatically, I believed for a moment she might actually strike him.

"And now . . . and now Roland is missing, too! Some sort of inquiry agent you are," she scoffed. "The great Stephen Gage's son, foiled by a simple disappearance." She reared closer. "Or don't you want to find them? After all, with your cousins gone you stand to inherit more of Tavistock's estate, even if you'll never achieve the title."

Gage held up his hands in a staying gesture. "Aunt Vanessa, I'm doing all I can—"

"Are you?" she shrieked. "It doesn't seem that way to me." She stabbed her finger behind her. "You should be out there scouring every inch of the moor. You should be demanding answers. You should be . . ." Her voice broke on a sob, and she quickly inhaled, turning her head to the side.

Gage reached a hand out to comfort her, but she shrugged it away.

"Is this your attempt at revenge?" she sniffed, masking her fear with fury. "For what happened to your mother. After all, I know how softhearted you were when it came to her. Always ready to defend her over the tiniest slight, even if it meant violence. If only she'd deserved such loyalty," she sneered under her breath.

"Leave my mother out of this," Gage snapped, his aunt having finally succeeded in riling him.

"Why should I? She's part of all of this. Even if, like always, she's not here to get her dress dirty."

"She's dead."

She shook her head as if in disbelief. "You still can't see it. And you're purported to be so clever. Yet your mother pulled the wool over your eyes and you've never removed it."

I was startled to hear Lady Langstone voice the same doubts I'd harbored about Emma Gage. The same misgivings about her failure to protect her son, though my view was tinted with outrage on his behalf while hers was tinged with scorn. The realization was not a welcome one.

"Well, fifteen years hasn't changed the fact that Emma got exactly what she deserved."

I knew Gage. I knew how honorable he was. He'd never raised a hand to me, and I believed he never would.

But my first husband had. So even at this distance, I could tell the moment the idea gripped Gage. The moment his hand clenched, seeking to take out his fury on the person who'd caused it. I flinched, bending my knees and bracing for what was to come.

Except it never happened. His body fairly vibrated with the desire to do it, but he never lifted his hand. He simply glared at her as if by a look alone he could turn her to ashes.

Unfortunately, his aunt didn't recognize how close she'd come to being struck. "Such a waste. She could have wed a duke if she wanted to be such a convalescent. She would never have had to lift a finger."

"You speak as if she had a choice."

She shook her head in contempt before pointing at his chest. "Find my sons! Or else I'll be forced to take my own revenge. Perhaps on your dear little wife."

Gage stepped forward to tower over her. "Did you . . . ?"

"Don't be such a fool," she retorted, not backing down. "I

didn't poison your wife. But don't imagine I won't harm her." She tilted her head. "Do you honestly think the family approves of your marriage to her?"

He stiffened.

"Your father isn't the only one who can make their discontentment known." With this parting comment, she turned on her heel to march away.

I watched Gage. Watched the agony and disillusionment flicker across his features. Should I go to him or give him a moment to compose himself? Before I could decide, the decision was made for me.

"M'lady?"

I gasped in surprise, whirling to see who had snuck up on me.

"I beg yer pardon, m'lady." Hammett's expression was carefully neutral. "I thought ye heard me climbing the stairs."

"No, I was just . . ." I stumbled to form a response, but I could think of no plausible explanation as to why I was standing halfway up the staircase seemingly staring into space. So I opted for the truth, guessing the butler had already deduced it anyway. "I was eavesdropping," I replied with a sheepish grin.

The old retainer's eyes lit with humor. "Yes, well, if the dowager was part o' the conversation, I'm sure yer ears are blistered." My distress must have been evident, for his amusement fled. "Badgering Master Sebastian again, was she?" He sighed. "She never could mind her opinion with the boy."

I glanced toward Gage, worried he would hear us talking about him, only to find he was no longer there. I frowned. "Why do you think that is? Gage was hardly a worthy target for such vehemence."

"Well, I suspect it's something to do with the fact that Emma was never around the manor enough for her to sharpen her tongue on her, so she took it out on the nearest thing. And also the fact that Sebastian was so much more intelligent and better behaved than her boys. He bested 'em at everything." He turned to gaze down the staircase, his eyes narrowing. "In a perfect world, the dowager would've been a more fitting mother for Master Sebastian. She so protective and anxious for him to achieve, and he so determined and eager to please." He shrugged. "But then, would Sebastian have turned out that way if he hadn't had a mother who was continuously ill and scorned by her family for her choices, and also dogged at avoidin' confrontation and unpleasantness?"

That was an interesting observation. For better or for worse, Emma had to some extent been responsible for the good, noble man Gage had become. Given his less-than-devoted relatives and belittling father, it was somewhat amazing that he had grown to be the confident, self-assured man he was today, and I suspected much of that was due to Emma's influence.

"I'll say one thing for Lady Langstone," Hammett remarked. "She does an admirable job actin' as his lordship's hostess and lady of the manor, and she receives little credit for it. Most of the servants see her haughty, exacting nature, which certainly doesn't endear her to anyone. But they fail to recognize the underlying care she has for 'em."

I didn't think Hammett was asking me to feel sympathetic toward her ladyship. After all, his previous actions had demonstrated how little he liked her himself. But he did seem to be reminding me there was usually more to a person than one first assumed. That every action, good or bad, could be motivated by something opposite.

I couldn't help but wonder if while making this point he was really thinking of something, or someone, different.

"You said you recall Lord Tavistock's older sister Alice?" Given his talkative mood, I hoped this time he might share more about her.

He searched my face, as if weighing something in the balance before he spoke. "Aye. She was lovely. And headstrong. Though, remember I was only a stable boy back then. I only ever saw her from a distance, but she had a reputation."

"Do you remember when she died?"

He drew himself up even taller. "I do. And I suppose you'd like to know if the official story is the truth." He shook his head. "But that's not for me to reveal. Though . . ." He nodded as if making a decision. "I do think you and Master Sebastian should know it. Tell his lordship I said if he doesn't tell ye all, then I will."

My brow furrowed in mild frustration, wishing the butler would simply share what he knew, but I didn't press. It was clear Hammett believed this was a tale best told by Lord Tavistock, and would not be budged unless the viscount refused. "I need to speak with Gage, then," I remarked, turning to look in the direction where he had once stood.

"M'lady, if I may," Hammett murmured tentatively. "If Lady Langstone was indeed harassing him, I should look in one of two places for him."

Seeing the concern in the old retainer's eyes, I quickly deduced the first. "His mother's grave."

"Aye. Or the woodworking shed. 'Tis where he always disappeared to after his lordship began teaching him."

His own personal sanctuary.

Nodding my thanks, I set off toward the shed first, following Hammett's directions. I had to admit, beyond locating my husband to be certain he was well, I was curious to see this place where he and his grandfather had always related best to each other. I remembered him telling me the woodworking shed was the only place they hadn't fought. I imagined it was something like my art studio in the conservatory at my childhood home, or the tower room I utilized at my brother-in-law's estate in the Highlands, where I'd escaped to whenever my emotions or my memories became too much to bear.

Following a path that led out of an ivy-covered door in the wall surrounding the front courtyard, I walked about a quarter of a mile into the woodland part of the Langstone property, which extended away from the moor. I hadn't paused to change, so I still carried the train of my riding habit looped over my arm, trying to keep the fabric from tripping me up. The land was pitted with stones and riddled with tiny streams, all sheltered under the branches of tall oak, birch, and hazel trees. Mosses and lichens grew on some of the barks and rocks, making them slippery underfoot. A dormouse scurried out from beneath a fern I trod near, almost tripping me.

I'd begun to wonder whether I'd taken a wrong turn when suddenly the trees parted to reveal a squat stone building—the gamekeeper's cottage. And next to it stood an even smaller structure, this one made of wood. The door was propped open to let in what sunlight penetrated through the branches above, and I knew I'd come to the right place.

I approached slowly, certain to make an ample amount of noise. The last thing I wanted to do was startle him while he was wielding a saw or driving nails in with a hammer. When at last I reached the door and peered in, it was to find him bent over a long piece of wood, running a plane over it again and again. He had discarded his frock coat, waistcoat, and cravat, and the force required to push the cutting blade over the wood made the muscles in his back and shoulders bunch and stretch. I stood watching his almost elegant, rippling movements, and my breath grew short as I waited for him to acknowledge me. Surely it wasn't wrong to ogle one's own husband.

"Hammett told you where to find me, didn't he," he grunted as he pushed on the tool once again.

I swallowed. "Yes."

He looked up at the wall before him, panting from the exertion. "You overheard part of my conversation with Aunt Vanessa."

It wasn't a question, but I answered him anyway. "Yes. I didn't know whether to speak up or go away, so I . . . eavesdropped."

He resumed his task. "It doesn't matter."

But I could tell it did. Though I didn't think he was truly angry with me for listening in on their conversation. It was more to do with the things his aunt had said, specifically about his mother.

"You know she was only out to wound you however she could," I said. "I'm fairly certain she would have said just about anything to make you hurt as much, if not more, than she's hurting."

It didn't matter what the truth was, I realized now. Emma was long dead, and completely unable to defend herself. It did no good questioning her motives, especially when doing so did more harm than good. What mattered were Gage's loving memories of her, the ones he so jealously guarded as if someone might steal them away. Except doing so also locked away the pain with them. He needed to share them, to let them breathe again. I didn't know how to convince him to do that, but I had to try.

"Your mother was a good woman. I know this. Even without ever having met her."

His movements stopped, as he stood hunched over listening to me.

"She is part of you. One of the best parts. It's simply not possible that she wasn't a wonderful woman. Yes, I'm sure she had her flaws. But so do we all. To suppose she was perfect only does a disservice to the complicated, caring woman she was."

"So you think my aunt was right?" he challenged.

I sighed. "Sebastian, how could I know? But does it really matter? Does it truly change who she was? Does it change how much she evidently loved you?"

"I . . ." He paused and spluttered, almost as if he were choking on his own thoughts. Then he shook his head. "I can't talk about this."

"You can't . . . or you don't wish to?" I replied gently.

He finally turned to look at me for the first time since I'd entered the shed, and there was a brittleness in his eyes I'd never seen before. I worried if I pressed too hard, he might shatter.

"Why haven't you visited her grave?"

He stared at me, refusing to answer.

I tilted my head. "Or have you, and you just didn't want me to know?" As fiercely as he protected everything else about her, I wouldn't have been surprised.

He looked away. "I haven't." But he wouldn't elaborate or answer my original question.

Eventually I had to concede. "I see."

His head snapped up. This comment for some reason ignited his smoldering temper. "No, you don't."

"Then help me understand," I pleaded. "You told me not to let you retreat. You said I needed to force you to provide answers."

He stood tall, turning full toward me almost in challenge. "But I didn't promise to give them."

I exhaled, acknowledging his point. He was right. He hadn't promised, and I couldn't force him. Not really.

My eyes dipped to the hollow of his throat, visible above his white lawn shirt now damp with his sweat. I didn't want him to see the hurt his refusal caused me. If he wouldn't speak to me of his mother, then I would just have to resort to discussing the inquiry. "Hammett knows the truth about Alice's death, and he told me to tell your grandfather that if he doesn't reveal it to us, Hammett will."

He stared at me blankly. "The truth?"

I turned to the side. "I'm going to speak with Lord Tavistock now. Do you wish to join me?"

When Gage didn't answer, I took that as dissent and began to leave.

But he grabbed my arm, halting me. "Wait."

I glanced over my shoulder at him.

"Yes, I'll come. Just give me a moment." However, he made no move to gather his discarded clothes, just stood gazing down at me.

I arched my eyebrows, waiting for him to speak.

For a moment, he seemed about to confide in me. The words

seemed poised on his lips. But instead he pulled me into his arms and kissed me.

At first, I didn't resist. As fascinating as I'd found the play of his muscles under his shirt moments ago, it wouldn't have been difficult to forget my disappointment and let him direct this where he wished. But deep inside, I knew by doing so not only would I be losing, but perhaps more importantly, so would Gage.

So after a feverish minute, I pushed against his chest, breaking our embrace. "You can't always make everything better with kisses," I whispered, peering up into his eyes. "I'm not going to let you hide behind physical distraction." I stepped back. "I'll wait for you outside."

I whirled away so I wouldn't have to witness the shocked confusion mixed with frustration that radiated across his face. Though I knew I'd done the right thing, it still made a knot form in the pit of my stomach. A knot I suspected was only going to grow tauter with our next conversation.

CHAPTER TWENTY-SIX

I'd not visited Lord Tavistock since Gage delivered the brutal news about Rory the evening before, so the sight of him left me in shock. Gage said he'd seemed to shrink in on himself, and a truer description could not have been made. The proud, stalwart man appeared to have collapsed into the mattress, all but being swallowed by the blankets and pillows surrounding him. His gleaming silver eyes were tarnished with pain, and perhaps dulled by the medication his valet had been dosing him with upon our arrival.

Seeing him in such a state, I hesitated to relay Hammett's message. But then I reminded myself the best, and possibly only way we might help the viscount recover was to find his grandsons. If forcing him to address disturbing facts enabled us to do that, then any discomfort they caused was worth it.

I'd hoped he might rage against his upstart butler for forcing his hand. Anything that might show a spark of life in him. But he merely sighed, his lips curling upward at the corners in reluctant amusement. "Hammett never did abide by the normal boundaries of master and servant." He waved a hand limply. "Come sit. I'll tell you."

He stared up at the bed curtains as if peering into the past. "Everything I told you the other day is true. I was away at school when it happened, and my parents did forbid us to speak of it." He sighed again. "But it wasn't for the reason I led you to believe, though I didn't learn the truth until many years later. From Hammett, of all people." He glanced at us. "Servants know everything. Don't forget that."

Gage and I shared a look.

"My sister Alice was often willful and stubborn. And when she decided she wanted something, she wouldn't rest until she got it. Usually that meant a new dress, or embossed stationary, or some other inconsequential thing." He frowned. "But for some reason, she fixed her heart on John Stephen. No one knows why. The man wasn't rumored to be particularly attractive or accomplished, and he certainly wasn't wealthy or titled. But whatever the reason, when my father ordered her to sever the attachment, she did the exact opposite. She agreed to run away with him."

His face contorted as he began to cough, his body crumpling up under the force of it. I slid forward in alarm, ready to summon his valet to dose him with more medicine. But then the racking coughs began to subside. Seeing my posture, he urged me to sit back. However, he didn't reject Gage's offer to help him drink a bit of water. I noted how little he swallowed, and my concern grew.

"My father was not a stupid man. And he knew his children well enough. He was aware of the possibility that Alice would disobey him. So he instructed the cook, under a strict veil of secrecy, to leave a bowl of poisoned apples out in the kitchen, and order the staff not to touch them."

I pressed a hand to my mouth, already guessing what had happened.

"If Alice listened, if she broke Stephen's heart, there would be no cause for concern. But if she snuck out to meet him, and if she stopped in the kitchen to grab what food she could find for the journey, knowing the man she loved owned little . . . well, then, as Father saw it, she would have her just punishment."

"That's . . ." Gage seemed incapable of coming up with a word horrible enough to describe such an action.

"Yes." The viscount inhaled a rattling breath. "As I'm sure you've guessed, she took the apples, and she ate one. I can only assume that when Stephen realized what happened, he also ate of the apple, killing himself rather than going on without her."

"That poor man," I murmured, shaking my head. Buried at a crossroad for his suicide, his name smeared for a murder he hadn't committed.

But Gage was focused on something more immediate. "So Mother wasn't the first poison victim in our family?"

His grandfather's eyes were stricken. "No." He hesitated and then added, "And Alice might not have been the first one either."

This startled both of us.

"Who?" I demanded.

"My great-uncle."

"The man who supposedly walked out on the moors, fell over some rocks and bashed his head?" Gage asked. "I always thought drink was to blame for that."

"That was the official story, yes. But our old nanny used to always warn us we'd best listen to our parents or we might die from a bash to the head as well."

My eyes widened.

Lord Tavistock coughed into his fist. "I assumed it was an idle threat until I grew older. Then I began to wonder. After all, my great-uncle was the original heir, and there were whispers he'd been indulging in . . . immoral acts."

What exactly that meant, I didn't know, and it was clear he wasn't about to elaborate with a lady present.

Gage leaned forward, bracing his elbows on his knees. "Is that the origin of the curse? Is that when it all began?"

"As far as I know," the viscount admitted with reluctance.

The viscount's great-uncle, Alice, and Emma. That was a suspicious string of deaths. And now Alfred and Rory were missing. We knew Alice's and Emma's deaths had been spurred along by human aid. I presumed the great-uncle's death had also, perhaps by his parents or the younger brother who would inherit.

But what of Alfred? Who had poisoned him?

And what about Rory? What had he done that constituted defying the family?

Then I remembered something. Several days before when I'd come to sit with Lord Tavistock, I'd interrupted an argument between him and Rory. I'd thought nothing of it at the time, deciding it was likely some estate matter they disagreed on, but now I had to wonder.

"You and Rory had a disagreement a few days before he went missing," I remarked, watching him carefully.

Gage sat tall, alarm radiating through him, but his grandfather never reacted.

"Can you tell us what it was about?" I asked.

If he was offended, he didn't show it. "He wanted me to write to Lord Sherracombe and ask him to forbid his natural daughter, a Miss Galloway, to sell her herbal remedies in the village."

I reached out a hand to clasp Gage's arm.

The viscount coughed. "I take it you're familiar with her."

"He truly does believe she poisoned Alfred," I told Gage.

"Yes, I gathered as much." Lord Tavistock frowned at Gage. "He also seemed convinced her mother supplied your mother's maid with the poison she used on her."

"Miss Galloway said that's not true."

"Well, even if so, it seems rather harsh to saddle the girl with her mother's crime."

Gage turned his hand over, reaching for my hand, which I gave to him. "And Rory was angry you wouldn't do as he asked?"

"I told him I preferred to wait until you finished your investigation before I took any action. He called me a fool, and told me it would be on my head if more deaths followed." His bleary eyes fastened on me. "To tell you the truth, when I first heard you'd been poisoned, I worried he might have been right."

I was grateful for Gage's hand in mine, for I needed his support as I reeled with shock at such a suggestion.

"You're sure the poison was in the tea you drank here?" he clarified.

"I . . . yes. At least, I think so. It tasted wrong. I only had the one sip."

But what if I was wrong? What if the poor taste of my evening tea could be attributed to curdled milk or another factor? After all, I *had* taken tea with Lorna earlier in the day. The same day I asked her about the button.

And now Rory was missing.

The possibility that it might have been Lorna who poisoned me left me feeling as cold as ice.

The dream began like all the times before. A sense of uneasiness slowly crept over me, prickling my skin all the way up to my scalp. Part of me wanted to open my eyes to see what was there, while the other part of me urged them to remain closed. But eventually, curiosity outweighed fear, and I peeled open my eyelids.

There, at the end of the bed, stood a man, his face cloaked in shadow. I supposed it could have been a woman, but somehow the presence felt masculine. Whether he could see me watching him, I didn't know, but his gaze bored down on me. Normally he held me pinned thusly for a few seconds and then suddenly disappeared into the darkness swirling around him. But this time his feet shifted.

That tiny movement roused me more than any of the other times before, and I sensed a change in Gage's breathing at my side. I was awake, not dreaming. Which meant . . .

Before I could finish the thought, the figure lifted something over his head and swung downward. Gage pushed me out of the way as he rolled in the opposite direction. The object struck the mattress with a jarring impact, narrowly missing us. It was heavy, and from the rending tear it made in the bedcoverings, also sharp.

Gage allowed his momentum to carry him out of bed. His feet hit the floor and he ran around the bedpost, knocking our assailant back as he raised the object for another swing. In the darkness, I could see little but shadows, but I could hear the impact of fists hitting flesh. Who was winning, I couldn't tell, as they crashed about, knocking into the walls and furniture.

I dodged past the men, racing toward the dressing table where my reticule was stored. It was impossible to know which shadow to aim at with my pistol, if, that is, they even separated for me to take a clean shot. But perhaps if I fired it into the floor or ceiling it would startle both men long enough for me to distinguish.

Before I could pull my reticule from the drawer, a sharp yelp pierced the air. I glanced over my shoulder, to see one shape disentangle itself from the other and limp toward the connecting door to the other bedchamber. A moment later, the other man, who from the grace of his movements I could tell was Gage, pushed himself up to follow him.

I cursed as my fingers caught in my reticule strings and I struggled to open the bag and extract my pistol. With it finally in hand, I picked my way across the floor, stepping through the puddle of water spilled out of the washstand they'd knocked over. Peering through the connecting door, I saw Gage hastily donning a pair of shoes.

"He's darted through an entrance into the secret passages I didn't even know was there," he retorted. Anger rippled through him as he rose to his feet and crossed the room to his dresser.

"And you're going after him?" Alarm made my voice rise in pitch.

"Yes." I heard the click of metal, and I realized Gage had lifted his pistols to check if they were loaded. "But this time I won't be unarmed."

He strode across the room toward the wall panel near the wardrobe, which I now realized stood open. Before he darted inside, he turned back. "You have your pistol?"

"Yes," I replied, lifting the gun in illustration.

"Good. Close this behind me, and shoot anybody who comes through it who's not me."

My eyes blinked wide, and before I could form a response he was gone.

I inched closer to the opening. The scent of must and damp issued from its interior, much like I imagined a crypt smelled. Shaking my head at the macabre thought, I pushed the panel shut as instructed and then crossed to the bellpull. Should Gage not return in short order, I would need Anderley's help.

Fortunately, it didn't come to that. Only moments after I'd managed to light a few candles to counter the darkness, I heard a snick and swiveled to see the wall panel opening. I raised my pistol, aiming it at the ever-widening slit, but lowered it at the sight of my husband's golden head.

I hurried forward, anxious to determine if he was harmed.

"Only a few cuts and bruises," he replied, feeling his cheekbone.

"What of your bullet wound?" I asked, reaching for his right arm. The wound he'd received in Ireland had been only a graze, and the skin had mended well, but I suspected it was still sore.

"Well enough." He pulled away, apparently having endured enough of my wifely concern.

"Did you catch him?" I asked, knowing full well he must not have, given the fact he'd returned emptyhanded.

His voice was tight with frustration. "No. Either he darted out of the passage through another door I'm not aware of, or that blow to his leg I dealt him wasn't severe enough to slow him down as I'd hoped."

"This one *was* a surprise, then?" I nodded at the opening that still stood ajar.

He pushed it shut. "Yes, or you can be certain I would have blocked it off as well." He shook his head. "I thought I knew all the entrances and passages. How many more are there?"

At that moment, there was a rap on the door and Anderley peeked his head through the opening. "You wished to see me?"

Gage glanced at me.

"I sent for him," I explained. "I thought it prudent to have help . . . should it be needed."

"Yes. Good thinking. Come in," he told his valet.

I crossed my arms over my chest, feeling awkward standing there in my nightdress in front of Anderley. Sensing my discomfort, he crossed to the wardrobe while Gage explained the night's events and pulled out a second dressing gown, this one made from midnight blue silk. I smiled in gratitude as he passed it to me. I swiftly wrapped it around myself, being enveloped in Gage's scent.

"What did he attack you with?" Anderley asked.

"Let's go see, shall we?" Gage replied, picking up a candle and leading us into the other room.

All told, for as much commotion as they'd made, there was little damage. Anderley righted the washstand and tossed a towel over the puddle while Gage bent over to pick up the wooden handle protruding from underneath the bed where it must have been kicked. He lifted it high for us all to see the weapon was an ax.

"Well, that could have easily disemboweled you," Anderley remarked almost offhandedly as he stared up at the sharp edge.

I scowled at him. As if we needed the reminder.

"Who do you think was so intent on killing you?"

Gage's eyes were hard with fury. "I don't know. But maybe we should speak with Alfred's valet, Mr. Cooper. I realize it's quite precipitous to escalate from a few harmless pranks to murder, but he would be as good a place to start as any." He turned to Anderley. "Perhaps you'd like to rouse him?"

Anderley's teeth flashed. "With pleasure."

After his valet left, Gage picked up his burgundy dressing gown where it was flung over the corner of the bed. He pulled it around his frame, knotting it with a sharp tug.

My eyes fastened on the long rip in the counterpane where the ax had struck between our vulnerable bodies. "I suppose this would be a good time to tell you this isn't the first time I've woken to find someone standing over us while we slept."

Gage whirled around to stare at me. "What?!"

I shoved my hands into the pockets of his blue dressing gown, which hung around me like a sack. "I thought I was dreaming. The figure would just stand there and then disappear. He never made any other movement. Until tonight." The excuse sounded pitiful, but it was all I had to offer.

"When did this start?"

I looked up into his angry gaze. "Our first night here. The night the windows were opened."

"And you said nothing?"

"I was going to, but then the windows seemed to be explained away, and I couldn't imagine how someone could have snuck in here without us knowing after you blocked the entrance to the secret passage. When it kept happening without any change, without my ever seeming to really be awake, I decided it was just a dream. And I didn't need to burden you with that."

He scowled. "Well, you should have told me anyway."

I conceded he was right. Had I known it would come to this, I certainly would have.

He glanced at the clock still ticking away on the mantel. "Let's see what Mr. Cooper has to say. And whether he enters with a limp."

CHAPTER TWENTY-SEVEN

"I had nothing to do with it," Cooper protested anxiously as Gage and Anderley stood over him.

I would have felt apprehensive too if confronted with their livid countenances and tightened fists. Both men were fit and well muscled, and their eyes said their intent was deadly serious.

"I went to my room immediately after dinner to read and then fell asleep. I haven't visited your chamber, except the other day when I told you about Alfred and his blackmail."

Gage narrowed his eyes, nudging his left leg. When the man didn't flinch, just cowered in alarm, this seemed to satisfy him that Cooper wasn't the man with whom he'd tussled. "What of all those petty little pranks you pulled when we first arrived? As we understand it, those would be typical of your modus operandi."

"I . . . I don't know what pranks you're referring to, but if you mean the misplacement of your trunks, that was Moffat's doing."

Gage straightened. "You mean Mr. Trevelyan's valet?"

I had no idea who this Moffat was, but Gage appeared at least familiar with him.

Cooper nodded briskly. "*He* was the one who suggested we put them in the attics, and, well . . . none of us objected."

Gage arched a single eyebrow. Apparently, our arrival had not been welcomed by most. "Do you think he's capable of poisoning Mrs. Gage's tea or attacking me with an ax?" he demanded.

The unctuous man swallowed. "I wouldn't put it past him."

I frowned, suspecting Alfred's valet would say just about anything to save his own skin. The look in my husband's eye told me he was thinking the same thing. Nevertheless, with Alfred and Rory missing, and Cooper seemingly out of contention, Moffat was our best suspect.

"Let's question him," Gage instructed Anderley.

But Moffat was nowhere to be found. Gage had spoken to him two evenings prior about Rory, and some of the staff had seen him throughout the day before. However, following dinner, no one could recall his whereabouts. This did not make matters look good for him.

It was perplexing. The meddlesome pranks aside, why would Rory's valet attempt to kill Gage or poison me? Had he been directed to do so by Rory, or was he acting on his own? And if Rory *was* behind the attack and poisoning, did that mean he wasn't actually missing? Then where was he? And why was he hiding?

The only sliver of hope for Moffat came when one of the maids suggested he might have gone into the village. She claimed he seemed extremely distraught about his missing employer, and that perhaps he'd gone in search of forgetfulness in the form of a bottle. To this end, Gage sent Anderley to Peter Tavy and the other villages nearby to ask after the man.

Gage and I were about to set off across the moors on another search when I spied the figure of Lorna Galloway striding rapidly toward us. We spurred our horses in her direction, slowing them to greet her.

Her face was tight with distress. "There's something I need to show you."

My stomach dipped, thinking she must have stumbled across a body.

"You found one of them?" Gage asked urgently.

But Lorna wouldn't answer him. "Just, please. Will you come with me? You need to see for yourselves."

Gage and I shared a look of confusion coupled with dread, but we agreed. I helped Lorna to mount behind me, and we set off toward her cottage as she instructed.

When we reached the structure, she slipped from Eyebright's back and gestured for us to follow. "Please, it's inside."

Given my recent poisoning and the doubts our conversation with Lord Tavistock had raised the evening before, I was hesitant to enter. Had I been alone, I think I might have refused. But knowing Gage would be beside me, I complied.

He pressed a hand to my back, ushering me forward as Lorna opened the door. I searched her face for any sign of duplicity, but I could see no deviousness, only dismay. And I soon understood why.

Seated at the table was an attractive man with dark hair and eyes. The structure of his face and the shape of his eyes left me in no doubt who he was. Gage's cursing only confirmed it.

"Fiend seize it! Is this your idea of some appalling jest?! We've been scouring the entire bloody moor for your moldering corpse. Your family is worried sick."

"Are they?"

Gage stiffened and then charged forward, pulling Alfred to his feet by his collar. "You rotten bastard! Grandfather is practically at death's door because of you and your brother. Or was that your plan?"

"No, that wasn't the plan. But I hardly think Grandfather, or my mother, or my brother are brokenhearted by my absence."

Gage shoved him, releasing his lapels in disgust.

I looked toward Lorna, who stood rigidly by the door, crossing her arms over her middle. "He's been here the whole time, hasn't he?"

Her eyes shifted to meet mine and she nodded, at least having the grace to appear abashed. "There's a trapdoor in the floor of the bedchamber."

So he'd likely listened to every conversation we'd ever had without my even knowing it. I turned to glare at him in accusation. "It was *you* I heard in the bedchamber that day, not the cat. And *you* on the moor."

He finished tugging his coat back into place, eyeing both Gage and me with wary displeasure. "Yes. Both of those were near things."

I narrowed my eyes. "So Rory *did* see you that day?" I glanced around. "Where is he?"

Alfred's expression tightened. "I don't know." His eyes flicked toward Lorna. "That was what convinced me to show myself to you. In truth, I thought I might be hiding from him. But now that he's missing . . . that seems questionable."

Gage huffed, his face still flushed with anger. "What on earth are you talking about?"

But my head was clearer than his. "The poison," I guessed.

Alfred nodded. "Someone kept dosing me with poison, and each time they increased the dosage, for the stomach pains were growing worse."

Having experienced my own bout with poison, likely the same one, I could empathize.

He sank back down on the bench, staring at the herb bennet above the door. "That last time, just before I vanished, I realized they were intent on killing me. And eventually, they were going to succeed. I . . . I couldn't help but think of your mother," he told Gage. His gaze dropped to Lorna. "So I came here, and we decided I should hide for a time. At least until the poison had completely left my system and I could formulate a plan to uncover the culprit." He glanced over his shoulder at Gage. "But then you arrived and I decided it would be best to stay put. You're an experienced inquiry agent. You and your father are purported to be the best. I figured if anyone would be able to expose the truth, it would be you."

As far as compliments went, it was a fairly weak one, but from the look on Gage's face, I suspected it was the only one he'd ever received from his cousin. "That's all well and good, but why did you bloody your own frock coat and leave it out near Cocks Hill? You had to know that would set everyone into a frenzy."

He dropped his gaze somewhat shamefacedly. "That was a miscalculation on my part. When you and your wife showed up here with Rory, I worried Rory had convinced you I was off somewhere merrily enjoying myself. Lorna assured me otherwise, but I wouldn't listen. So I smeared the coat with pig's blood and planted it for you or someone else to find, hoping that would convince you to keep investigating."

"But you didn't realize you'd dropped a button," I guessed, drawing his gaze. "And when you or Lorna found it, you tucked it into the drawer." Gage scowled at me in confusion, but I ignored him, arching a single eyebrow at Alfred in contempt. "You must have panicked when you realized I was hunting through the cabinet for paper. I assume you removed the button then without telling Lorna. Hence her confusion the next day when she was looking for it."

Alfred's mouth turned downward. "Yes, Lorna has already berated me for that foolish move as well."

"Maybe next time you'll listen to her," I couldn't resist remarking.

"So this wasn't about Grandfather's pressuring you to wed Lady Juliana?" Gage interjected. His tone conveyed doubt.

Alfred tapped the table before him and looked up at Lorna, his eyes sharp with anguish. "I would be lying if I didn't say that was a consideration. But no." He sighed. "Hiding here would not make that problem go away."

I was already heavily predisposed not to like Alfred, and this meeting had not altered that. But I also believed he was being truthful. He'd not tried to make himself sound better or more noble than he was, and I suspected this was Lorna's influence at work. However, the question of Rory's whereabouts was another matter, and Gage seemed to feel the same way.

"Assuming all of this is true, why should I believe you didn't decide to take things into your own hands and kill Rory before he could kill you?"

Alfred's expression turned bitter. "I suppose you can't. Except that I didn't. Had I known for certain he was the one poisoning me, I would have enjoyed nothing more than making that clod suffer. But I *don't* know who is trying to kill me. Given that fact, harming Rory would be pointless."

Gage turned to meet my gaze, silently asking my opinion. But Alfred must have viewed this as disbelief.

"I didn't have to come forward and tell you all of this," he snapped. "I only did so because whoever it is must have turned their sights on Rory."

The petulant tone of his voice more than his words convinced me he was being honest. I nodded and Gage stepped toward his cousin.

"If I'm to believe you, there's one thing I need to check." He bumped his left thigh with his knee.

"What the bloody hell was that for?" Alfred groused, but he didn't flinch in pain.

Rather than answer, Gage gestured toward the opposite side of the room. "I need to see you walk."

Alfred's face contorted with rage. "I'm not some dashed hound to do tricks at your bidding."

"This isn't a jest," Gage retorted. "Do it."

"Just do it, Alfred," Lorna murmured.

Alfred huffed an aggrieved sigh, but with Lorna's urging finally complied. There was no noticeable limp.

"Thank you," Gage replied, ignoring his cousin's venomous gaze, so like the dowager's. There was no doubt where Alfred had learned it from. "My wife and I were attacked last night in bed."

Lorna gasped.

"I was able to land a serious blow to the assailant's leg, but he got away."

At this explanation, much of the malice drained from Alfred's face. "So either the culprit has moved on to other members of the family, or you're getting too close to the truth?"

"It certainly seems that way." Gage crossed to the door. "Either way, you're returning to the manor with us."

His cousin opened his mouth to protest, but Gage would hear none of it.

"You can eat unprepared food like Kiera and I, and lock your doors until the culprit is caught. But I'm not going to be the one to explain to Grandfather and your mother where you've been."

"You should go," Lorna agreed, though her brow furrowed with worry. "At least with Mr. and Mrs. Gage now aware of what is happening, you won't be alone."

Alfred moved forward to take her hands, his eyes soft with concern. "But what of you?" he leaned close to murmur. "I don't like your being out here in this cottage by yourself."

"I'll be fine," she assured him. "They're not after me, remember."

"Yes, but . . ." He began to lower his hand, but she held to it tightly. "What if they knew?"

She shook her head.

I glanced at Gage, wondering if he'd witnessed the same thing I had. But he'd politely averted his gaze, staring out the open door toward the sun-dappled moor. His stance was rigid, his gaze conflicted, and I could only imagine what a tumult his emotions were at the moment.

I turned to watch Alfred and Lorna again as he urged her to take caution. His voice was thick with affection even if the words he spoke were not particularly tender. If this entire affair was, in fact, about the inheritance, then it appeared whoever was behind it truly did have cause for concern. But only if Alfred proved to be honorable. That remained to be seen.

The dowager saw us first upon our return to the manor. From the manner in which she hurried down the rear staircase, I suspected she'd been gazing out her bedchamber window again and seen us enter through the garden gate. She stopped short four steps from the bottom, staring down at Alfred with wide, hopeful eyes. I thought he might go to her, but he scarcely spared her a glance as he moved deeper into the house.

"Yes, Mother, I'm alive. You may rejoice now," he drawled acerbically.

Sharp pain radiated across her features before being squashed in the face of my and Gage's observant gazes. She lifted her skirts and whirled about, marching back up the stairs.

Gage and I hastened to overtake Alfred as he strode toward the entry hall, where we mounted the main staircase, which was situated nearer to Lord Tavistock's chamber. It was almost as if now that he was here he was determined to have all of these awkward encounters over and done with. I wondered if he was also set on leaving as much damage in his wake as possible.

Gage tried to stop Alfred from entering their grandfather's chamber ahead of us, undoubtedly concerned what such a shock would do to him in his weakened state. But Alfred wouldn't listen. He charged through the door with barely a knock and threw his arms opened wide.

"Here I am. Alive. Shall we kill the fatted calf?"

However, even Alfred wasn't immune to the sight of his

grandfather's shrunken form sunken into the mattress before him, his face gaunt with illness. His words died away as his face paled.

Lord Tavistock stared up at him in mute shock. I'm not sure what he believed he was seeing, but the sight of Gage and me entering the room after Alfred made some of the alarm fade from his expression. He tried to speak, but a cough overtook him—possibly brought on by surprise—and he crumpled forward, trying to restrain it.

When his coughing subsided, Gage stepped forward and began to explain. Such was Alfred's astonishment that he all but had to be prodded to deliver each aspect of his confession. I don't know how I expected Lord Tavistock to react, but apparently after the surprise of Alfred's appearance nothing else could unnerve him.

He turned to Gage, some of the steely resolve returning to his eyes. "You intend to get to the bottom of this?"

"I do."

He nodded and then resumed his scrutiny of Alfred. "Then it's more important than ever that you should wed Lady Juliana, and quickly. There's more than yourself to think of. There's the future of the viscountcy and all the people who depend on it."

Alfred scowled. "Do you think I'm not aware of that? You've been hammering it into my skull since the day my father died."

"Yes, well, we always had Rory to fall back on should you fail to do your duty. That might no longer be true."

Alfred clenched and unclenched his hands. "I'm not going to wed Lady Juliana simply to beget an heir, your partnership with the Duke of Bedford be damned."

I wondered if Alfred would admit he might have already accomplished that responsibility. So long as he wed Lorna. But he remained silent about her.

Lord Tavistock lifted his head up from his pillows by his own will for the first time in days. "You will. You must. All of Langstone is relying on it. I'll not let you throw it all away with your stubbornness, not while I still have breath in this body." He collapsed back, a cough rattling up from his chest.

I waited for Alfred to snap something back about how he wouldn't have long to wait. The thought burned in his eyes. And given the fact that he'd not held back from making his previous cutting remarks, I didn't anticipate him having any qualms about throwing his grandfather's encroaching death in his face. But he kept the words bottled inside, though his body shook and he had to press his lips together not to speak. Then he turned on his heel and charged from the room in much the same manner as he'd entered it.

Gage watched his cousin leave and then turned back to his grandfather. The old man lay with his eyes closed, his face tight with what I suspected was a mixture of pain and frustration. From the line that had formed between my husband's eyebrows, I could tell he wanted to say something, but he backed away from the bed instead.

"I need to find out if Anderley has returned." When I didn't immediately follow, he paused. "Are you coming?"

"I'll be along in a moment," I said over my shoulder.

Gage's footsteps crossed the room and then receded down the hall.

Lord Tavistock blinked open his eyes as I moved closer to the bed, pouring some more water into his cup. "I know that face. My Edith used to wear the same expression when she had something on her mind she was determined to say whether I would hear it or not." His voice was rough from all his coughing.

I refused to be rushed or bullied, setting the ewer back down and turning to him with the cup.

"I don't want any of that," he groused.

I met his hard gaze with a stern one of my own. "You *will* drink it, as much as you can. Or I'll pour it over your head."

He glowered at me a moment longer before relenting. I helped him to sit up and then coaxed him to take as many sips as he could bear even as he flinched at each swallow. When he'd managed all he could handle, I helped him sit back again.

"Out with it," he snapped between panting breaths. "Now that you've tortured me, you can tell me what you stayed behind to say."

"I only wondered why you're so intent on seeing your grandson unhappy."

"Happiness has nothing to do with it. The boy needs to wed. And he needs to do it soon."

"But does it have to be to Lady Juliana? What if there were someone else? Someone he genuinely cares for."

"If you're referring to Sherracombe's natural daughter, then it's out of the question."

I wasn't surprised he knew about Lorna. If not Rory, then someone else had likely been happy to apprise him of Alfred's visits to her.

He sniffed. "I'll not see my heir wed to a bastard."

"That's it, then. You're determined for things to end with enmity between you? I know we dance around the truth, but I can tell you're well aware that you're dying."

He grunted, turning his head away from me.

"You lie there, hell-bent on making your grandsons toe the mark when you could do so much more good by speaking to them like the grown men they are and healing the rifts that are already between you."

He looked up at me wearily. "You don't understand. It's not my choice. You've already discovered how things end for those who defy the family. You know what it did to Emma."

I tilted my head, confused by this remark. "So you're trying to save Alfred by making him do the family's bidding?"

"Yes."

"But *who* is the family?" I asked, trying to make him realize his logic was faulty.

He stared up at me in irritation, clearly not following my reasoning.

"Are Gage and I doomed as well because the family does not approve of our match?" My chest clenched, even as I waited for the answer I hoped he would make.

"Of course not."

I exhaled. "Why?"

"What do you mean, why? Because I approve of you."

I felt a pulse of affection for this old man, even hearing his words issued in a tone that said I was a fool to think otherwise. I wished Gage could have heard it, too. It might have blunted the sting of his aunt's earlier comment.

Something of the point I was trying to make seemed to seep into his understanding, for his scowl softened.

"Then why can't you approve of Alfred's choice in a bride as well?"

He stared up at me. His mouth was still set in that thin line, but his eyes said he was considering what I said.

"Change the family's wishes," I pleaded softly. "Give Alfred your blessing, too. Before it's too late."

CHAPTER TWENTY-EIGHT

I entered the room assigned to Gage through the connecting door to find him and Anderley standing over a man with a great crop of fiery hair, much the same way they'd loomed over Cooper. The sight of them standing shoulder to shoulder, working in accord to interrogate a suspect, always made me wonder just how many times in the past they'd done this.

Not that the man before them seemed to require much coercion. I suspected the maid had been right, for Moffat looked as if he'd spent the night dead drunk on a bench. His face was unshaven, his hair stood on end, and the ashen hue of his skin made me want to urge Gage and Anderley to back up a step lest they be soiled if he should cast up his accounts.

"I'm sorry, I'm sorry," he stammered, rocking back and forth. "I didn't want to do it. I knew I shouldn't have done it. But I did. I did."

He was all but sobbing, and I looked to Gage for an answer to what exactly he was confessing to. However, Gage and Anderley appeared perplexed themselves. Perhaps the man was still half-sprung.

"You admit to committing the pranks?"

"Yes."

"Were they your idea?"

He sniffed and began to shake his head, but then abruptly stopped, pressing his hand to it. "Mr. Trevelyan told me to make trouble. That he needed you to leave."

Gage frowned.

"But then two days later, he told me to stop," Moffat continued. "That we shouldn't hinder your investigation."

So Rory had been behind the pranks? Why? Had he not trusted us?

But clearly there was more. Otherwise, why the maudlin tears?

"What about the rest?" Gage pressed.

"He . . . he . . ." Moffat swallowed, either fighting nerves or nausea. Possibly both. "He told me to sprinkle some sort of herb he gave me in a jar into Lady Darby's evening tea."

I withheld a gasp.

"Said it would just make her feel a little queasy." He began to snivel again in earnest. "Except I got startled, and I dumped in too much. And then a maid almost caught me." He looked up to plead with Gage and caught sight of me standing in the doorway. His eyes widened, and his already pale face lost all color. "I'm sorry, so sorry," he repeated again and again.

I stayed where I was, worried if I moved any closer he might keel over in his chair. So Rory had been behind my poisoning as well? Was he also responsible for Alfred's? His valet claimed Rory only intended to make me queasy. Was that true? But to what end? He'd seen me leaving Lorna's cottage earlier that day. Had he hoped the blame would fall on her and shatter whatever trust I held in her?

Except based on everything we knew, Rory had gone missing

immediately following that. He wouldn't have had time to tell his valet to put the herbs in my tea.

Clearly pondering the same question, Gage snapped his finger, surprising Moffat enough to make him stop apologizing. "When did Mr. Trevelyan instruct you to poison my wife?"

"Earlier that day, just after midday." The man was so cowed, there was little chance he was lying.

"You told us you hadn't seen him," Gage argued.

"I . . . I hadn't. I was out on an errand. I found a note from him and the jar when I returned."

Gage's voice was sharp with anger. "Had he asked you to sprinkle herbs or poison on anyone else's food or drink?"

"No! Just . . . just Lady Darby's."

My, wasn't I lucky.

Gage narrowed his eyes, scrutinizing the ruddy man. Then he jostled his left leg as he had with Cooper and Alfred. Moffat recoiled further, but he didn't wince.

"What of last night? When did you leave for the tavern?"

Moffat's Adam's apple worked up and down. "A-after dinner."

"So you didn't try to disembowel me with an ax in the middle of the night?"

The valet's eyes bulged. "N-no! No, sir. You can ask the publican. I-I was there all night."

Considering the state he was in, I had no trouble believing that. Or his earnest promise to inform us immediately if he saw or heard from Rory again. Then Anderley helped him to his feet as Gage sent him on his way.

"What do you think?" Gage asked, pulling me close to his side.

"Honestly?" I shook my head. "I don't know what to think. Is Rory behind all of this or just another victim? Was he intent on hurting me or protecting me, in admittedly his own flawed way?" I leaned back to look up into his face. "But what do you think? He's *your* cousin. You know him better than I do."

His eyes were troubled. "Maybe when we were boys. But fifteen years is a long time. None of us are exactly the same people we once were."

The manner in which he spoke made me wonder if he was talking about more than Rory.

"Including Alfred?" I guessed.

His gaze flicked down to meet mine. "Yes. Though, he's still capable of being the same unmitigated jackass he always was." He sighed. "The truth is, I never thought I'd see him treat a woman with as much esteem as he showed Miss Galloway. He seems to truly care for her."

"I thought he was going to wish your grandfather to the devil there at the end."

"Yes. There's that, too. He's never shown such restraint in the past." His expression communicated he was confounded, and perhaps maybe even a little uneasy about witnessing this new side to his cousin.

"It troubles you?" I prodded cautiously. Having been so abruptly denied answers to my queries about his mother, I was sensitive to the possibility of it happening again.

He seemed to reflect on my question. "Yes, I suppose you could say that."

I waited, hoping he would say more.

"Alfred was always so horrible. I can't remember a time when he wasn't acting as my tormentor. Even my good memories of us playing together always end with him making some snide remark or shoving me out of a tree. And now I'm confronted with a man who's different, but also the same. I'm hesitant to believe he's actually changing. And I'm not sure I want him to." He huffed a breath. "Which troubles me. Shouldn't I *want* him to be better?"

"In a perfect world, yes. But Alfred treated you terribly in the past. You knew how to categorize him, and now you don't. It's understandable that you would find his *possible* transformation— let's not get ahead of ourselves—difficult because of the past you can't forget. A past you've never forgiven him for."

His voice hardened. "Because he's never apologized. He's never asked for my forgiveness."

I stepped away, recognizing it might be best for me to retreat, lest he shut me out again. "True. I can't blame you for your dislike and mistrust. Based on what you've told me, I'm none too fond of him either. But continuing to stoke all that anger is hurting no one but yourself. Alfred certainly isn't bothered by it."

"My mother—"

"Your mother is gone," I gently interrupted him before he could begin a tirade. "She's past caring about your loathsome cousin or his mother. And if she could speak to you now, I'm certain she would tell you the same thing."

His eyes gleamed with all the conflicting emotions about his family he'd been carrying inside him for so long.

"Just think about it," I murmured, pressing a kiss to his lips before I slipped from the room.

I wanted to stay, to hold his hand through the maelstrom swirling inside him. But I was beginning to apprehend that with Gage sometimes retreat was the better virtue. For if I wasn't there to argue with, then he had only himself to rage against.

I decided to take a walk in the garden to clear my head and focus on the conundrum at hand. After all, Rory was still missing, either by misfortune or by choice, and someone seemed intent on harming the members of Gage's family, be it by poison or ax. As the person most on the outside, I suspected I might have the best chance of unraveling the truth.

I rounded the corner to descend the stairs and spied Alfred seated on a bench placed before the window at the end of the corridor. His gaze was directed outside, so I could have slipped by without saying anything, but he seemed so pensive, so agitated, I realized I couldn't. Not even knowing I risked receiving one of his scathing snubs.

He glanced up as I approached, and I couldn't help but think of the conversations he must have overheard between Lorna and me while hiding beneath her cottage. He knew I didn't like him. I'd said so. However, he didn't seem the least bothered by this fact. But given the way he treated others, he must have been accustomed to people's animosity.

If ever given the chance, I'd fully intended to ring a peal over him for the dreadful way he'd treated Gage when they were younger. But since meeting him, I decided he would probably enjoy it, so I kept a civil tongue.

"You don't have to be polite," he told me before turning back to the window. His forehead furrowed. "Your family may be different, but the Trevelyans have never found such niceties to be necessary."

"Then perhaps that's your trouble," I replied, perching on the opposite end of the bench. "After all, kindness and courtesy go a long way. And oftentimes family members need it to fall back on more than anyone."

"But then our family gatherings would be so mundane. Much better to dance a quadrille trying to avoid all the hidden daggers."

I studied his handsome face, intrigued by the similarities to Gage. When he drawled sarcastically like that, they sounded much the same. And yet, they were so very different. Though Alfred seemed to have been wounded by someone much the same way he in turn mistreated his cousin. But who had hurt Alfred? His mother? His father before his death?

He turned to meet my gaze, his mouth curling into a sneer I suspected preceded a vicious set down. But the insult never came. Instead, a curious light entered his eyes and the scorn slowly drained away to something more thoughtful, something harder to define. I waited patiently for him to speak, wondering what, if anything, he would tell me if I allowed him to take the lead.

In truth, I didn't expect him to reveal anything significant. So I was genuinely surprised when he posed a question.

"What do you think? Should I yield to Grandfather's pressure and wed Lady Juliana?"

My astonishment must have been evident, for he smiled in reluctant amusement.

"What of Miss Galloway?" I asked before he changed his mind about asking me.

His humor fled. "We . . . we could still be friends."

I arched my eyebrows, letting him know I realized *friends* was merely a euphemism for *lovers*. "Is that fair to Miss Galloway?" I paused before adding, "Is it fair to your unborn child?"

This time it was Alfred's turn to be startled. "I'd heard you were unnervingly observant. Lorna said you would notice." He glanced out the window toward the garden below and the moors beyond, agitation thrumming through him once again. "No, it wouldn't be fair."

"You genuinely care for her, don't you?"

"I like myself better when I'm with her." He frowned. "No, it's more than that. She makes me want to be better because she deserves better. Does that make sense?"

"It does."

"I'm trying to do the honorable thing, for perhaps the first time." His shoulders drooped. "But maybe it's not so honorable after all."

A large portion of society would, indeed, agree with his grandfather. That Lorna Galloway was perfectly acceptable as a mistress, but definitely not viscountess material. That Alfred owed it to his family to wed the daughter of a noble house, especially now that his brother was missing and his grandfather was so ill. But I didn't happen to be among their number.

"Well, you should appreciate that I don't hold much respect for society's opinion on such things. And neither does Gage."

"Yes, but wedding an anatomist's widow is a bit different than marrying another lord's by-blow."

I glared at him incredulously. "Even when that widow was

forced to participate in her anatomist husband's dissections, and accused of macabre solicitation, cannibalism, and more in the penny press?"

This seemed to give him pause. "Yes, well, I'd forgotten about that."

My skepticism did not wane.

His gaze skimmed over my features. "You're much different than I thought you would be."

I didn't know whether to view this as a compliment or an expression of disappointment, so I returned to the subject at hand. "I suppose your grandfather will argue that Miss Galloway should be treated like Philinda Warne?"

His face crumpled into resentment. "The vicar's daughter? Yes, I suppose so. Though the chit lied about my seducing her."

"I'm well aware of your reputation."

"Yes, and it's well deserved. I know I'm a rogue. But I'm not so bad as to get the rector's daughter with child." He scoffed. "Give me some credit." He nodded his head in the direction the village must lie. "She was also dangling after the innkeeper. And she married him. I imagine he was in on the scheme to inveigle money out of my grandfather."

A notion suddenly occurred to me. "Does he pay something to them every month?"

"No. Gave them a tidy sum upon the child's birth. He might give them a bit more from time to time." His lip curled. "If they make him feel guilty enough. But nothing regular."

"But anything they hope to get in the future will go away once you're the viscount and hold the purse strings."

His expression darkened as he realized what I was suggesting. "If they had anything to do with my poisoning, they would need a conspirator among the staff."

"What did Rory think of the matter? Did he believe Mrs. Warne's story?"

"I imagine he believed whatever Grandfather told him to."

"So he would have been more sympathetic to them." I tilted my head. "Unless he discovered what they were doing."

Even so, such a theory seemed far-fetched at best, though technically possible, regardless of who was telling the truth. Both Alfred's and Mrs. Warne's outrage seemed genuine, so I didn't know whom to believe. Except Alfred had no reason to lie. He readily admitted he was a scoundrel, and that he'd gotten Lorna with child. Why would he deny fathering Mrs. Warne's baby, but not refute the other accusations?

"What do you think happened to Rory?" I asked, curious if he'd formed any other opinions on the matter since we'd returned to Langstone. I considered telling him what Gage and I had learned from Rory's valet, Moffat, but decided it would be best to keep that information to ourselves for the moment.

"I haven't the foggiest. As I said earlier, I was almost convinced he was the one behind my being poisoned, but I can't see how his going missing fits into that scenario. He was never one for theatrics. He would be more likely to bide his time, or claim that given the amount of time that had passed the bloody coat must indicate my death."

And he might have, at that. Except Gage and I had been here to examine the coat and raise doubts that the blood on the fabric was enough to clearly indicate death. But I agreed on one point. Rory did appear to be a very patient, methodical man.

Alfred, on the other hand, was not. I only hoped that whatever occurred in the next few days, he would not do something rash. Life-changing decisions should not be rushed. And neither should his bid for his grandfather's goodwill.

CHAPTER TWENTY-NINE

The morning of Gage's thirty-fourth birthday dawned grim and dreary, but I was not going to let that keep me from making his day as enjoyable as possible. I would be glad I ensured it began in such an agreeable way, for I would have no control over everything that came later.

We still lay in bed, wrapped in each other's arms pleasantly dozing, when someone rapped on the bedchamber door. I yawned and lifted the sheets to be certain I was sufficiently covered while Gage pulled his dressing gown over his broad shoulders. After our disagreeable visitor the night before, we'd elected to lock all the doors and place chairs under the handles. This meant the hearth was still cold, for the maid could not enter to tend it, but that was a small price to pay for peace of mind. It simply meant we had to rely on each other for heat.

He removed the chair and unlocked the door to admit Bree, who hovered uncertainly near the door, glancing back and forth between us. Such timidity was not normal for her, and I sat up straighter, puzzled by her reaction. A closer look at her face made my heart begin to beat faster.

"What is it? What's happened?"

"'Tis Lord Tavistock." She turned to Gage. "He's taken a turn for the worse."

Gage turned on his heel and strode toward the connecting door while I scrabbled for my dressing gown.

"Anderley's waitin' for ye," she called after him.

I hurried over to the dressing table. "Help me dress. Something simple," I ordered her.

Ten minutes later, we reached the corridor outside his grandfather's bedchamber only to find Alfred and the dowager badgering a footman to let them enter.

"I'm sorry. Mr. Hammett gave me strict instructions that no one was to enter until the physician finished his examination. Not even family."

"This is an outrage," Lady Langstone protested. "Since when does a butler issue orders that supersede the wishes of the family?"

"Be calm, Mother," Alfred drawled, leaning back against the wall opposite the door. "I'm sure Hammett's only following Grandfather's instructions or the physician's request. After all, who wants a woman pacing back and forth, flapping her arms while you're trying to do an examination?"

I felt quite certain this was meant to be directed at his mother and not women in general. In either case, the insult hit its mark.

"I do no such thing," she snapped. "But I *would* make certain this physician is doing a thorough job."

I suspected she must have already been up for hours. What else explained her perfectly turned-out appearance and elaborate hairstyle at such an unsocial hour? Alfred, on the other hand, looked as if he might never have been to bed. At the least, the dark circles under his eyes and wrinkled clothing spoke of a restless night and hasty dressing.

He was opening his mouth to make another quip when the

bedchamber door opened. We all swung about to hear what the brawny man dressed in a rough coat had to say. However, Lady Langstone seemed intent on slipping past, until Hammett closed the door firmly, standing in its way.

The physician didn't look much like one expected a medical man to appear, even a country one, nor did he sound like one. But I had no doubt he must have been competent. Lord Tavistock was not the sort of man to suffer fools gladly, and even without a great deal of medical knowledge he would have recognized slapdash practicing.

"Lord Tavistock's illness has worsened," the physician pronounced in a gruff voice with little inflection. "The ague has settled into his lung tissue, inflaming them and making it difficult for him to breathe. He needs rest and little excitement." His gaze swung toward Alfred. "Which I understand there's been a great deal of in the past few weeks."

"Will he recover?" Gage asked anxiously.

"If he were a younger man, perhaps. But at his age, it's not expected."

Gage nodded, his mask of indifference carefully in place, but when I offered him my hand, he gripped it tightly.

"May we see him?" Lady Langstone intoned in a manner that wasn't really a question but a demand.

The physician shared a glance with Hammett. "Only if he wishes to see you. And only if you do not rile him. As I said, he needs peace and quiet." He nodded to us all. "I'll stop by again this evening. Send for me if I'm needed before then."

Before the physician had even turned the corner, following the footman who was to show him out, Lady Langstone stood toe to toe with Hammett.

"I will see him."

Hammett drew himself up to his full height and dignity. "I'm sorry, my lady, but he's already said he doesn't wish to see you. Not just now," he added, softening the sting he must have seen his words had caused her. His eyes shifted over her shoulder. "He's asking for his grandsons, Lord Langstone and Mr. Gage."

Gage's hold on my hand tightened and then released as he stepped forward. He and Alfred shared a look filled with mutual apprehension.

"I want to see him," Lady Langstone repeated. Her voice was so brittle I thought it might crack.

Hammett shook his head. "I'm sorry, my lady."

She huffed and spun about to stride off down the corridor. I watched her go. Didn't the others realize she was masking her hurt at the viscount's refusal to see her with anger? I turned back to find Hammett studying me as he shuffled to the side to usher Gage and Alfred into the bedchamber. The look in his eyes made me recall our previous conversation and the things he'd said about her. Before I could reconsider, I set off down the corridor after her, lifting my pomona green skirts in my haste to catch her up.

She was about to turn another corner, headed toward I knew not where, when I called her name. Her steps halted abruptly as she glared over her shoulder at me.

"What is this?" she sniffed, arching her chin upward. "Come to gloat?"

But all of her venomous disdain could not hide the gleam of tears in her eyes.

"No, my lady," I replied gently. "I merely wanted to know if there's anything I can do for you."

Her eyes widened in surprise. "For me?" she snarled.

"Yes. After all, Lord Tavistock is your family, too. You've lived with him for over thirty-five years, and served as his hostess since Lady Tavistock died. This must be difficult for you as well."

She stared at me in shock and then almost in horror as her bottom lip began to quiver. "I-I can't . . ." she choked and spun away, continuing to walk in the same direction she'd been headed. But now her steps were more of a stagger.

I followed her uncertainly, not wanting to leave her alone, but unsure of my welcome. When she pushed through a door, leaving it open as she went inside, I decided she wanted me to join her.

I'd not yet explored this room, for it had been locked, and now I understood why. It was a tiny stone chapel adorned with stained glass windows and an altar arranged with gold holy objects. A handful of wooden pews lined the floor, their surfaces polished to a sheen that was evident even in the dim light. I smelled the lemon wax.

Lady Langstone sat on one of the benches, her head bowed. But from the manner in which her shoulders shook I realized she wasn't praying. Or, at least, not only praying. I slid into the pew next to her, offering up my own silent prayer for Lord Tavistock, Rory, and the entire family as I waited for her to speak.

She sniffed and then dabbed at her eyes as she inhaled a quivering breath. "I've been a good hostess for him, you know. And a good mother. I've seen to everything with nary a word of complaint. And what thanks do I receive? A son who sneers at me and a father-in-law who won't even . . ." She hiccupped on a sob. "Who won't even see me on his deathbed." Her voice constricted with tears again as she broke off.

I moved closer, silently offering her what comfort she would take.

"I've given them everything," she murmured breathlessly. "I could have remarried, you know. Even to this day, I still receive offers. Instead, I chose to devote myself to my sons and the Tavistock estate. Fool, I've been." She snapped open her handkerchief and then folded it again and again, as if she could straighten her tangle of emotions like she could the piece of cloth.

"I can't blame you for feeling hurt and angry," I replied. "I would be, too. But perhaps Lord Tavistock will ask to see you later."

She scoffed.

"Perhaps he merely felt an urgency to speak to his grandsons first."

She shook her head. "Lord Tavistock has never been fond of me. He approved of my marriage to his son well enough because I came from a good family and I comported myself perfectly. My parents made certain of that," she added almost under her breath. "But he has never liked me. Not with anything that comes close to the affection he showed his own daughters, particularly Emma." She spat Gage's mother's name as if she'd just bitten into something sour.

"Why did you dislike her so?" I had to ask, not understanding this extreme animosity to her sister-in-law.

"Because she always did as she very well pleased, regardless of anyone else's feelings, and yet no one else seemed to see that. Or if they did, they never reproved her for it." She gestured toward the door. "Even her own son, who suffered the most because of it, still believes she was this blameless, perfect woman ruled by elements out of her control. Her poisoning at the hands of her maid only underlined that image."

"Well *that* was certainly out of her control."

"Was it?" she challenged. "She brought that incompetent girl with her from Plymouth and kept her on rather than let her go. She could have given her a good reference. One that would have helped her easily find a position elsewhere. But she didn't, because it suited her to be coddled and thought generous. When she first moved back here, her illness was never terrible enough to prevent her from doing the things she wanted to—attending dinner parties and local soirees, or traveling on shopping excursions to Plymouth and Exeter. It wasn't until later, I suppose when her maid had begun dosing her with poison, that it truly afflicted her in any way. Unless she was deluding herself as well, she would have noted the change."

I had no idea if any of this was true or simply the vitriol of a spiteful, resentful woman, but it said much about the state of affairs here at Langstone when Gage was growing up.

"You were jealous of the others' blind devotion to her," I remarked lightly, coming to the crux of the matter.

"Of course I was. She insisted on marrying Stephen Gage, despite her family's wishes. Got herself with child just to insure it would happen. Only to realize after she moved to Plymouth what life would really be like as the wife of an officer of the Royal Navy while the country was at war. This was before Gage made his fortune. She lasted all of three years before she came crawling home, blaming her illness when the truth was she simply couldn't stand it anymore. I suppose she also recognized what that life would mean for her son—shipped off to sea at a tender age," she begrudgingly admitted. "But that was only a secondary consideration." She scowled, clenching her hands in her skirts. "She did all this and more, and yet Lord Tavistock still adored her." She sounded as if she just couldn't fathom such a thing. Such unconditional love.

I felt a pulse of sympathy for her. "I take it your parents were not like that."

She stared blankly ahead. "One did as one was told, to perfection. And if you were lucky, they told you they were pleased."

I wanted to ask her about her marriage to Emma's brother, whether he had loved her, but I didn't dare. There were certain things an acquaintance didn't encroach upon, and that was one. However, there was one thing I was willing to risk broaching.

"But I suppose Emma Gage got her just deserts when her husband attempted to initiate a relationship with you? You must have relished informing her of his infidelity."

Lady Langstone's mouth pressed into a thin line and I wondered if she would actually tell me the truth or continue to choke it down like bitter medicine. Then she exhaled, almost in resignation. "No. I never told her. Because . . ." She turned to look at me as if facing her own execution. "Stephen Gage wasn't the only one who wrote letters."

"But I thought you despised him?"

"I did." She frowned. "Or it was more I despised the fact that Emma had married someone of such a lower rank and little fortune and not been ostracized for it. But Stephen Gage was a very attractive man and extremely charming, even to one such as me." She stared down at her lap where she fiddled with her handkerchief. "And I was lonely. It was after my husband died, and I felt so very . . . unwanted at times here. At first, I was shocked by his flirtation. But then I began to flirt back, and I enjoyed it." She blushed either in remembrance or shame. "I knew it was wrong, but . . ." She shrugged.

But she felt isolated and unloved, and here was her chance to perhaps take some of that affection Emma received with so little effort, and perhaps even less appreciation.

"We began to exchange letters. Webley acted as our go-between when Gage was here. And she mailed my letters and collected the ones he sent to an abandoned cottage at the edge of the estate after he'd gone back to sea."

"How long did this go on?"

"The better part of seven months. And then . . . and then he returned to Langstone on his next leave."

"Is that when you met in the emerald chamber?" I ventured to ask.

She blinked at me in surprise. Perhaps I shouldn't have revealed I knew as much. I could see a dozen questions forming in her mind, but she didn't ask them. Perhaps because she didn't wish to know.

"Yes. He convinced me we should meet. Before that we hadn't . . . I hadn't . . ." She cleared her throat. "He said he wanted more than words from me, so I agreed to meet him." She paused. "I suppose you already know about the secret passage?"

I nodded.

Her voice dropped practically to a whisper, perhaps because we sat in the chapel. It must have felt rather like a confession. "Well, he entered that way, finding me waiting for him, as requested, though I had half a mind not to come." She clasped her hands together, the knuckles turning white. "I should have listened to my conscience, for when he arrived, he threw the entire affair in my face." Her cheeks burned with remembered indignation. "It had all been a ruse, retribution for my treatment of his wife."

Shock radiated through me, for I'd not foreseen such an explanation for Lord Gage's actions. In my defense, Lord Gage had never given me any reason to think well of him. So imagining him as a philandering husband had fit my already negatively formed opinion of him. But apparently I was wrong. Apparently he *had* loved his wife, though I was sure guilt over his continual absence might have also played some part.

Nevertheless, to enact his revenge in such a cruel, protracted way, and on a woman who was so vulnerable? It was difficult to fathom such malice. Lady Langstone had certainly deserved a stern set down, but not that.

She must have sensed my uneasiness, for she met my gaze solemnly. "You should understand just what sort of man your father-in-law is. If you have his loyalty, then you have nothing to fear. But otherwise . . ."

She didn't need to finish that sentence, for I already felt the chill of the possibilities.

We turned to stare at the altar, perhaps both reeling from the implications of our conversation.

"There's one more thing that confuses me," I murmured.

"His letters?" she guessed. "Why did I keep them?"

"Yes."

"For leverage. He told me he would be keeping mine to ensure I remained civil to his wife, and so that if I ever showed anyone his letters he would have a counter."

"And then Alfred found them," I surmised.

"Yes." Her gaze turned wary. "Are you going to tell Lord Gage about them?"

"I'm not going to tell him anything," I admitted with full honesty.

She exhaled in relief, and then straightened again. "What about Sebastian?"

I considered what, if anything, I should reveal to her that Gage already knew. It seemed unnecessarily unkind to tell her he already suspected the affair. I fully expected she assumed my claim during our last conversation had been a bluff. However, I did think Gage should know the truth about what he'd seen all those years ago. He needed to know his father had not been conducting an affaire de coeur with his aunt under his mother's very nose. But perhaps, in this case, a bit of deceit was in order.

"Are you going to quit treating him like he's the scourge of the earth?" I countered. "After all, he's done nothing to offend you except draw breath."

"You're right," she admitted. I was surprised to hear genuine remorse in her voice. "I can treat him better. I will."

I met her gaze, letting her know I would hold her to that. "Then Gage never need know," I replied, crossing my fingers behind my back.

CHAPTER THIRTY

Somehow it seemed appropriate that today of all days Gage should finally decide to visit his mother's grave. Even though I knew it had been his grandfather's worsening illness and whatever words he'd imparted to him this morning that drove him here, and not the fact it was his birthday. But whatever the rightness, my breath constricted and my heart clenched at the sight of him kneeling before the ornate grave marker topped with a cross.

Upon leaving the dowager in the chapel, I'd returned to our bedchamber, thinking to find Gage there. However, Anderley told me Gage had changed into his riding boots, though he'd not said where he intended to go. Given the distressing events of the morning, as well as the fact that he wouldn't need his riding boots to visit the woodworking shed, I had a fairly good idea where I would find him.

The leaden skies of early morning had lightened somewhat, but not enough to make the heavily shadowed churchyard appear any cheerier. And not enough to clearly illuminate Gage's expression, though I imagined it well enough from his slumped posture and bowed head. The air was ripe with the scents of moss and damp earth, and thick with the lingering sense of time lost. I waited a dozen feet away under the heavy branches of a yew tree, worrying the train of my charcoal gray riding habit between my fingers. My eyes stung as I struggled to suppress my answering emotions. It didn't matter that my own mother was buried hundreds of miles away. She was still with me, at least in my memories.

When finally Gage lifted his head, I decided this meant he was ready for me to approach, though he never looked at me. Stepping up next to him, I turned to face his mother's grave and the stark letters of her name carved in granite. He clutched his hat between both of his hands, spinning the brim round and round between his fingers.

There were no flowers planted before her grave, but then there were few in the entire graveyard. The overshadowing trees didn't allow enough sunlight through their branches for them to grow. However, the grave had evidently been carefully maintained, and I supposed he had Lord Tavistock to thank for that.

"When Mother died," he began softly, "I was so *furious*. Furious with Father. Furious with them all." He heaved a sigh. "But later, I realized I was mostly furious with myself."

"Oh, Gage," I murmured, my heart breaking to hear the pain, the self-recrimination in his voice. "Why?"

"Because I didn't do more to protect her, to shield her. And this was before I ever knew she'd been poisoned."

"But darling, you were so young. Just eighteen upon her death. You take too much on yourself."

"I know that now," he admitted. "But at the time, I was just so *angry*, so overwhelmed by it all. All I could do was lash out."

"You were grieving, with no one to help you through it. Your father was away at sea—not that he would have been very consoling *had* he been there. But at least you wouldn't have been on your own." I studied his face, and reflected on all the things that had been mentioned in passing during the last few weeks, all the things I hadn't understood. "Is that what happened at her funeral? You lashed out?"

He nodded. "I . . . I didn't behave in a very becoming manner."

"Well, I imagine not. It was your mother's funeral, after all." I found it difficult to imagine the amount of composure such a thing would take. Having been only eight years old, I'd been deemed too young to attend my mother's funeral, as had my ten-year-old brother. But we'd snuck away from our governess to visit her grave just a few days later and stood immobile before it for hours, unable to fully contemplate or accept our loss. If our father hadn't found us and taken us away, I'm not sure we would've ever torn ourselves from the spot.

"Yes, but . . ." He faltered as if he didn't know how to put his recollections into words or if he even wanted to.

"Tell me," I coaxed him, hoping this time he would trust me.

He closed his eyes and exhaled a ragged breath. "The entire event was one long torment. I was already struggling to maintain my composure. I'd traveled by coach for days from Cambridge in order to escort my mother's casket. I'd barely slept since her death."

His face tightened in remembered pain, and I couldn't help but wonder why his cousins, who would've also been up at university, had not ridden with him. What a lonely final vigil.

"And then . . . I heard Alfred and Rory whispering with one another, jesting about how perhaps she should've been buried in a plot in a Royal Navy graveyard. And then . . . and then they made some rather crude insinuations."

"That's horrid!" I gasped. The insensitivity, the cruelty.

"I . . . I swung around in the middle of the rector speaking words over her grave and told them to shut their mouths." He shifted his feet. "Though I used rather more vulgar language than that. Then Rory tried to justify his comments by saying they were only thinking of my father. How he was unlikely to be buried in the family plot next to his wife."

"Oh my," I replied, guessing how this stray comment would

have ignited Gage's smoldering temper already made raw from grief and lack of sleep.

He grimaced. "Yes. In the end, I had to be escorted from the graveyard before I pummeled my cousins before my mother's open grave."

"Oh, Sebastian." I threaded my arm through his, pressing my body to his side to offer him what comfort I could. "No wonder you never wanted to come back."

"I visited her grave alone the next morning and then left for good."

"Until now."

His expression was bleak. "Yes."

We stood silently side by side, sharing our warmth as we gazed down at the cold grave. The only sound to break the hush of the churchyard was a small bird of some kind, tweeting from the upper branches of one of the trees.

"Tell me about her," I murmured, feeling the weight of her memory pulling Gage into the grave with her. Perhaps if he shared them, perhaps if he released some of them into the sunlight, the load might be lighter. When he didn't respond, I decided he might be at a loss for where to begin. "What were some of her favorite things? Her favorite food, for instance? Or color? What made her smile?"

"She . . . she loved strawberries," he began tentatively, gaining strength and momentum as he talked. "With cream. She . . . she used to say she could eat them at every meal. Her favorite color was violet. And that was her favorite flower, too. Father never realized that. He always brought her grander bouquets. But she loved the shy violets that grew in the tiny garden behind our cottage the most." His brow furrowed momentarily at his mention of the cottage, but then he pressed on. "She loved to receive the post. I think because it brought letters from Father and friends both far and near. But when days would go by without even a short note she would grow sad. So sometimes I would write her a letter and post it, just so she would have something to open. That always made her smile." He paused. "Or when she was really sad, I would do this silly dance for her. She claimed I began doing it the moment I could walk."

I smiled at the image of Gage dancing just to make his mother happy and at the pink cresting his cheeks at such an admission. Arching up onto my toes, I pressed a kiss to the underside of his jaw. There was a light dusting of stubble there from the hasty shaving he'd performed earlier that morning.

He glanced down at me in surprise. "What was that for?"

"Nothing. Everything. For reminding me how much I love you."

His lips pressed together and his eyes grew suspiciously bright. Wrapping his arm around my waist, he pulled me to his side and tucked my head against his chest, jostling my bonnet. I heard the telltale sniff of someone fighting tears, but I didn't speak. If he didn't wish to be seen openly weeping in a graveyard, I couldn't blame him. So I held him just as tightly and waited for his grip to loosen.

In the end, it was a light rain that staved off Gage's brimming emotions and propelled us out of the graveyard. In our haste to leave the manor, neither of us had grabbed an umbrella. Not that they would have proved very useful on horseback anyway. Resigned to a little dampness, we paused for a moment beneath the covering of the lych-gate.

"If I may be so bold," I said, "what did your grandfather wish to speak with you and Alfred about?"

Gage turned to stare at the horses tethered outside the gate. "He told Alfred to quit dodging his responsibilities and find the courage to decide what he really wanted." He paused, furrowing his brow.

I leaned in to catch his eye. "And you?"

"He asked for my forgiveness." He sounded uncertain and still slightly shocked. "He said he hadn't made my mother live at Windy Cross Cottage, that it was her choice to reside there. And after he learned she'd died from being poisoned by her maid, he tore it down because he was ashamed not of her, but of himself. That if he'd made her live at the manor, perhaps she wouldn't have been made ill so often in our drafty, damp cottage. That someone would have realized what her maid was doing."

"It sounds like he blames himself for her death," I murmured, just as surprised by his confession, though I'd suspected something of the sort.

He nodded numbly. "I think he does. He also apologized for not stepping in more often to halt my cousins' teasing and Aunt Vanessa's spiteful gossip. He said he thought it would make me stronger, that it would better prepare me for society's slights and insults. Except they never came. Father proved to have even higher-ranking friends than himself, and I was accepted based on them and on my own merits. It never mattered that Father held no rank. And then he was given a barony, so the point was moot."

All of this should have made Gage feel relieved, but instead he still seemed troubled. "I would have thought your grandfather's apology would please you, or at least reassure you, but it doesn't," I prodded, hoping he would explain.

"No. It does. It's only . . ." He reached out a hand to touch the rough wood of the arch holding up the lych-gate, running his gloved fingers over a set of initials carved there. "I believed hearing those words was what I wanted, more than anything. To prove my family wrong, for my sake, and for my mother's. To show them I'm as worthy a descendent as any of them. Worthier, even. And yet . . ."

"It rings hollow?"

He nodded. "What does any of that matter? *I* know I'm worthy. *You* know it. Those I count closest to me do also. I'm glad Grandfather and I reconciled. But . . . now he's dying. Why couldn't it have happened sooner? Would he have confessed all of this if I'd come home sooner?"

"Darling, you can't punish yourself like that." I urged him to face me. "There's no way to know whether coming home would have made any difference. It's just as likely it could have made relations between you even worse." I pressed a hand to his chest over his heart. "You know as well as I do that life doesn't always turn out like one would wish. You have to embrace the good when it comes and let go of the bad. And your reconciling with your grandfather, no matter how late it came, is good."

He inhaled a shaky breath. "You're right."

He might say he agreed with me, but it would be a long time before he truly believed it.

I tucked my arm through his again and pulled him toward where the horses were tethered. "The important thing now is that you should spend as much time with your grandfather as you still can. Let me worry about coordinating the continued search for Rory."

"You're not planning on searching the moors in this weather, are you?" he protested.

Our eyes lifted to the sky where the latest cloud bank had slid past, allowing a sliver of sunlight to pierce through before the next one smothered it again. Normally I wouldn't have been overly concerned with such weather. Rain was more often than not a daily occurrence in Britain. But the wary manner in which Gage watched the skies, like they were a portent to something worse, gave me pause. Perhaps the fast-moving clouds were even more indicative of the capricious shifts to come.

"Not unless it clears. And not alone. If I do set out from the manor, I'll be certain to take a few servants with me."

"Speak to Hammett. He'll know which men would be best."

"Is that Anderley?" I asked in surprise, as our horses cantered into the courtyard upon our return to Langstone Manor.

The valet stood next to the stables, chatting with one of the groomsmen. But as soon as he caught sight of us, he swiftly moved forward. Gage's expression turned stony, anticipating poor news about his grandfather. As we brought our horses' heads around, he vaulted from his steed's back.

"What news?"

"We've uncovered some information you should know straight-away. Miss McEvoy's waiting for us in your chambers."

I could see relief tremble through my husband as he exhaled. This was about the investigation, not his grandfather.

I scrambled to dismount, allowing Gage to assist me, and then led the men through the manor and up the stairs to our rooms. Bree stood inside my bedchamber next to the young maid who tended the fires. The same one who was infatuated with Anderley. Her skin flushed a fiery red the moment the valet entered the room behind Gage and me.

"Tell them what you told us," he coaxed her. He smiled encouragingly when she seemed to falter. "Go ahead. I assure you, they don't bite." But the smirk he displayed next plainly said he might.

Bree rolled her eyes. "Give the lass some time. Yer flashin' yer charms aboot 'll only make her stammer more."

The maid swallowed, glancing at each of us nervously. "I . . . I just finished sweepin' out the hearth in Mr. Trevelyan's room when I saw Lord Langstone hurry past. He looked like he was goin' out, so I . . . I decided I'd best sweep his, too." She worried her fingers. "I hadn't done so in a while, with him bein' missin' and all." Her eyes communicated she was worried she would get in trouble for this dereliction.

I nodded. "Go on."

"But when I got to his room, I . . . I found this lyin' on the ashes in his hearth." She pulled pieces of paper from the pocket in her apron. "I normally would never 've taken 'em," she hastened to say, flicking her eyes toward Anderley. "But . . . but Mr. Anderley told me I should tell him if I saw anything strange, and I thought this might be what he meant."

"Indeed, it is," Anderley confirmed.

I took the paper from her grasp as she beamed shyly at the valet, and turned to allow Gage to read over my shoulder. The paper had been torn in only four pieces, so I was easily able to fit it back together to tell that it was a letter. One hastily jotted off.

Alfred,

I know where your brother is. Meet me at my cottage as quickly as you may.

Lorna

I looked up at Gage, seeing the same dawning worry in his eyes. There was no indication whether Rory was alive or dead, but if he were dead, why would she have phrased it so? In that case, she would've come to the manor to share what she'd uncovered. Which meant Rory was likely alive.

"You don't think Alfred would do anything hasty, do you?" I asked Gage.

He shook his head. "I don't know. But it would be best if we didn't give him the chance to." He turned to the maid. "How long ago did you see Lord Langstone leave?"

Her eyes widened in alarm. "I . . . I don't know."

"She came to me about half an hour ago," Anderley interjected. "Straight after finding the note?"

She nodded in confirmation.

"How long did that take?" he asked her.

She flushed again. "Not long."

"So maybe three-quarters of an hour," Anderley deduced.

Gage's expression turned grim. "Too long." He moved toward the window, staring out at the swirling cloud-strewn sky. "Gather as many men as can be spared," he told Anderley. "Then have the groomsmen saddle horses."

Anderley nodded and hastened out the door.

"I'm coming with you," I said when Gage swiveled to face me. I wasn't about to be left behind, not when Lorna was somehow mixed up in all of this.

He glowered at me for a moment, but did not protest. "Dress for rain and wind," he replied as he strode toward the connecting door. "It's not going to be a comfortable ride."

CHAPTER THIRTY-ONE

Gage was right. No sooner had we set off across the moor toward Lorna Galloway's cottage than the rain began to fall in earnest. That wouldn't have been so bad had the wind also not decided to kick up a fuss. Our range of vision swiftly deteriorated as the rain blurred the landscape, making it all too easy to become disoriented. Out of necessity, we were forced to slow the horses to a steady walk, bowing our heads against the periodic gusts that flung icy raindrops into our faces.

By the time Lorna's cottage came into view, my cloak was thoroughly soaked and my cheeks stung with cold. We must have looked a sorry, bedraggled sight, and Lorna's wide eyes as she emerged from her cottage with a shawl draped around her shoulders only confirmed it.

"Where's Alfred?" Gage demanded to know as we drew our horses to a stop before her porch.

She blinked, glancing at me. "I . . . I don't know."

"What do you mean?"

"I haven't seen him since he left with you yesterday." Her skin appeared extremely pale in the dim light. "Why? Has something happened to him?"

But Gage was not so easily swayed. "We found your letter."

"What letter?"

"The one you sent him today, telling him to meet you here. That you know where Rory is."

Her mouth gaped slightly as she looked to me and each of the other men in turn. "I . . . I never sent him a letter. I've been here all day."

"Is Alfred inside?"

"No!" Her voice grew agitated. "He's not. But he could have been." She glared at me and Gage. "You said he would be safe. You said nothing would happen to him while you were there to keep watch."

Gage's voice softened with concern. "He truly isn't here?"

"No." She shook her head, clutching her shawl tighter as she turned to stare out at the rain drumming down on her roof. I could almost hear her anxious thoughts, for this was not the sort of weather to be caught out on the moors.

"Well, we know he took a horse and set off in this direction." Gage glanced around him. Even if Alfred *was* hiding inside, he couldn't very well conceal a horse.

"Then where is he? I haven't seen or spoken to a soul all day. Until you. And I haven't heard the sound of a rider." Her voice rippled with panic.

"I think the more important question is, who actually wrote that note luring him here?" I grunted, guiding my horse around, so that I could use the edge of the porch to dismount. "For if they elected to do so by falsely impersonating Miss Galloway, then I doubt their intentions were noble." That was the gentlest way I could think of to phrase the fact that Alfred was in serious trouble.

Lorna's eyes were stricken with alarm. So much so that she didn't even balk at my offer of support as I draped an arm around her waist.

"If someone were going to . . . surprise one of your visitors coming from Langstone, where would they lie in wait?" Gage asked. "Near the river."

She inhaled a deep breath, lowering her shoulders and smoothing the fear from her features. "You mean if they wished to ambush someone?" she replied, recovering her usual cool insouciance and insistence on calling a spade a spade. "Yes. I suppose the river would be best. Though I don't know which path he took—the drier one that loops to the north or the boggier trail you used."

"We'll search both." Gage's eyes flicked to mine. "You'll stay here with Miss Galloway?"

He was asking more than that simple question, but all I did was nod.

"Keep a sharp eye out," he added before ordering Anderley to take two of the men to search the path on which we'd come for any signs of a struggle while he took the other servant and rode north to the shallow river crossing there.

As we watched them canter away, I was grateful for the solid weight of my pistol pressed against my side inside the pocket of my deep sapphire blue redingote lest we should encounter any trouble. Then Lorna and I turned as one to enter her cottage and escape the cold and damp.

She bustled forward to set a kettle of water over the fire while I tried my best to shake the damp from my outer garments. Though Gage's unspoken urging had been clear, I didn't expect to find Alfred inside the cottage. Lorna's reaction had been too genuine, and far more pronounced than her almost taciturn answers to our questions during our first visit when she'd known all the while Alfred was hidden under her trapdoor. Even so, I glanced around for signs of his presence.

I thought my searching had been unobtrusive, but Lorna turned to face me with a resigned expression. "I suppose you need to see beneath the cottage."

My lips curled into a humorless smile. "I'm sorry. But yes."

It was always difficult to tell a person you genuinely liked, whom you wanted to believe, that you didn't entirely trust them. But such was the lot of an inquiry agent. However, perhaps more distressing than people's usual annoyance or outrage was Lorna's easy acceptance of the matter. It was clear she was used to others' mistrust, and that made me squirm with remorse.

I looked around the bedroom and peered underneath the cottage in the small space revealed by the trapdoor, though I didn't go down inside. That seemed excessive. In any case, Alfred would've had to squeeze up into the joists located below where we were standing and lift his feet for me not to see him.

Lorna closed the trapdoor and spread her rug back over it before joining me back in the main room, where the water in the kettle had begun to boil. She busied herself with the tea things, moving to and fro and fretting over small details. It was so unlike her that I knew she was mulling over something troubling.

"What is it?" I finally asked.

She looked up at me blankly.

"What's put that furious furrow between your eyebrows?" I reiterated, letting her know I wasn't fooled.

She glanced down, her mouth working as if she didn't know how to voice the thoughts inside her. Or perhaps she sensed what significance she would give them by actually putting them into words. "Do . . . do you think Alfred might have gone missing on his own?"

I considered her words. "You mean, that *he* forged that note and left it for someone to find?"

She nodded, her eyes stark with dread.

The suggestion had some merit. After all, he'd only ripped it into quarters—tears that were easily mended—and thrown it into a cold hearth. He might have even known the maid who handled such tasks was nearby and likely to visit his rooms soon. But more pertinent was the implication.

"So that he could avoid all the difficulties, avoid his . . ." my gaze dropped to her abdomen ". . . responsibilities."

She lifted a hand to timidly touch her still-flat stomach. If she was surprised I knew, she didn't show it. But then again, she'd told Alfred I would figure it out. "Yes. I . . . I don't want to think it. Not after everything. But . . ."

"But this *is* Alfred." The man didn't exactly have the most dependable history.

She sighed. "Yes."

I deliberated over the last time he'd "vanished," the spontaneity of it, and about my conversation with him the previous day. He didn't tend to plan for things. He did them when he thought of them. And the looming decision he had to make, whether to give in to his grandfather's wishes and wed Lady Julianna or defy him and choose Lorna, definitely troubled him. Troubled him enough that he might decide avoidance was a better option. But I highly doubted he would pause to forge a letter from Lorna—one he must know would swiftly be proven false—and then tear it up, hoping it would be brought to our attention.

I glanced at the rain-splattered window as another gust of wind flung the icy pellets at it. "No, I don't believe this time Alfred vanished by choice."

Lorna nodded, and although her shoulders lowered I could still see a glimmer of uncertainty in her eyes.

We both sat straighter at the sound of a horse's hooves striking the earth. Rising to our feet, I followed Lorna toward the door, taking my redingote and the pistol tucked in its pocket with me. However, we discovered it was only Gage hunched inside his sodden greatcoat. He reined in just short of the porch, and Lorna opened the door wider.

"There are signs of a scuffle just to the north, near a large outcropping of exposed granite," he shouted. "Do you know the place?"

Lorna nodded.

"If I were planning an ambush, that wouldn't be a bad place to choose. There are horse tracks leading from that spot in several directions, so we're going to split up and follow them. You're certain you would have heard someone ride by your cottage?"

"Yes," she confirmed. "I suppose a pounding downpour might drown out the sound, but while the rain has been steady, it hasn't been falling that hard. Nor has the wind been gusting continuously enough."

"Then we can rule out this trail." His gaze flicked to meet mine. "Are you going to remain here with Miss Galloway?"

I knew what he wanted my answer to be, though I appreciated the fact he was allowing me to make the decision. At least ostensibly. Fortunately, this time I was in complete agreement. "Yes, I think that would be best."

"Stay together, and stay inside the cottage." He glanced toward where my horse stood, tethered to the porch. "If, for whatever reason, you should you have to depart, leave us a note."

If the situation weren't so serious, and water weren't dripping from the brim of his hat, emphasizing how miserable he must feel, I might have found the tense mixture of both insistence and restraint he exhibited amusing. If our past inquiries had taught us anything, trouble had a way of finding us, no matter how much care and caution we took. Gage had learned he couldn't swaddle me in cotton padding, and I had accepted that the nature of our exploits often placed him in dangerous circumstances.

Instead, I simply offered him a word of loving caution. "Be careful. We don't know exactly what we're dealing with."

His pale blue eyes stared into mine for a long moment of silent affection and solidarity. "We will."

We watched him ride away, though this time it wasn't long before the rainy mist that had descended swallowed him up. A shiver trembled through my frame. One I wanted to attribute to the chill wind and not a yawning sense of foreboding.

To ease her anxieties, Lorna pottered around the cottage doing small tasks, cleaning things that didn't need cleaning, while I paced fretfully about the small space and tried to stay out of her way. Our tea sat cold and untouched on the table. I couldn't stomach the idea of even that panacea, though I wasn't certain why my nerves were so raw. Alfred was the one in imminent danger, and I knew Gage was highly capable and vigilant. But I couldn't shake the sense that something was very wrong.

Lorna seemed to feel it, too, for she would glance up at me from time to time as if she had something to say and then resume whatever chore she'd begun. Finally the silence became too much for her. She threw down the cloth in her hand and planted her fists on her hips.

"Who could have done this?" she demanded.

"I don't know," I admitted with a frown of genuine frustration. "But I keep returning to the question of whether Rory is truly another victim or the villain of this whole piece."

She sank down on a stool. "What do you mean? You don't believe he's missing?"

I shrugged. "He could be. Or he could be hiding like Alfred did before. But if so, the question is where? And why? It's not as if he's here, and we've searched the usual other places. As for why . . ." I sighed, turning to stare out at the rain-soaked moor, at least the small portion I could see that wasn't shrouded in mist. "I can only think of two options. Either he felt he was in danger like Alfred, or . . ."

"Or he suspected the truth about Alfred's 'disappearance,' and vanished himself in an attempt to draw his brother out," she finished for me.

I nodded grimly. Neither scenario was good.

"If the latter is true, then . . ." She gasped. "Then forging that note from me could have been his final ploy to lure Alfred somewhere secluded and . . . and finish him off."

"Yes."

Her shock turned to outrage. "Ooh, I knew there was a reason I never liked him."

I held up my hands. "Hold on. We don't know yet that that scenario is true."

"Yes, well, the more I think about it, the more I believe it." She picked up her cloth and began wiping the surface of a table again. "He was lurking around my cottage during the days before he 'vanished.' Alfred had to remain inside much of the time, lest he be found out. Said he saw Rory following *you* about the one day."

"I must admit, his actions have been suspicious. I suppose you could say I wouldn't be surprised to learn he's behind it all. But until we have proof . . ."

She scoffed. "I don't know how much more you could need."

Worry tightened her voice, and I knew she was speaking more from fear than anything else. However, she did have a point. If not Rory, then who else could it be?

I resumed my pacing, watching an hour tick by on the clock and then another. Gage and the other men could be gone until nightfall, and I was beginning to feel I might go mad before then. Meanwhile, Lorna continued to clean and shuffle items about the cottage, finding it as impossible as I did to sit still. Having tired of dusting and organizing her already perfectly ordered shelves of herbs and tinctures, she turned to the cabinet near the door and tugged open the top drawer. Then she unceremoniously dumped the contents on the table behind her and began sorting through what appeared to be mostly a stack of correspondence.

I cast a disinterested glance over the papers as I pivoted, but then something caught my eye as Lorna lifted the top page to crumple it into a ball. I reached out to grab her arm, preventing her from hurling it toward where the cat lay curled up on the rug before the hearth. Her eyes widened in surprise as I took the paper from her hand.

"What is this?" I asked as I unfolded the paper and smoothed it out.

"A letter I received yesterday."

My back stiffened as I read over the contents. "And it didn't alarm you?"

She shrugged. "No more than the others I've gotten."

"You've received more than one?"

Her mouth twisted wryly. "One gets delivered to my door every few weeks or so to remind me they know I'm a witch, an abomination. And warn me that someday I'll get what's coming to me."

"What?! Someone actually writes such things to you?"

"Oh, yes." She sighed. "And worse."

I glanced down at the stack of papers. "Where are the others?"

"I usually burn them as soon as they arrive." She frowned down at the letter. "But I kept this one for some reason."

Whatever the cause, I was glad she had. "Are they usually addressed this way?"

She stepped closer to peer over my shoulder at the offending missive. "Well, no," she replied uncertainly. "I suppose I didn't pay much heed to the contents, simply wanting it out of sight."

I grimaced in commiseration. "Take a closer look now and see if anything leaps out at you."

Vixen,

You and yours will get what's coming to you. A short, swift drop.

Lorna inhaled sharply, grasping the same implication I had. An implication that would not have been so clear the day before. "You and *yours*."

"Precisely. What did you think they meant by 'a short, swift drop'?"

"I . . . I suppose hanging or some other witch trial. I tried not to give it much consideration."

I couldn't blame her. Not if her receipt of these letters was a common occurrence. Not when there was nothing she could do about them. I would want to ignore them, too.

"And what do you make of the fact they addressed you as 'Vixen'?" I asked, curious if she would come to the same sneaking conclusion I had.

She began to shake her head and then stopped. "Wait. Are they referring to that witch Vixana?"

"I've heard the legend and I wondered . . ." I let my words die away as I saw the light of comprehension in Lorna's face. "What is it?"

"Rory has been very vocal in calling me a witch."

"Yes? I've heard him say so. But—"

"And he's accused me more than once of being the descendant of Vixana."

I turned to face her. "You think Rory wrote this?"

She scowled. "Who else?"

I had to admit, I could think of no one. And Rory had a history of using notes to carry out his mischief, given the fact he'd instructed his valet to poison my tea with a note. Then I recalled something else Bree had mentioned in her retelling of the legend. "Isn't there a tor named after her?"

"Yes. Vixen Tor. It lies a few miles south of here." Her eyes widened. "And there's rumored to be a small cave below it, though I've never visited to see if that's true. Do you think . . . ?"

I understood what she was asking even without her saying the words. "I think that if there is a cave there, that might be an excellent spot to hide. So long as one isn't afraid Vixana's spirit haunts it."

"Rory would believe himself immune to such things."

I suspected she might be right about that.

"We need to go there," she insisted, grabbing her boots from beside the door and sitting down on one of the benches to remove her slippers.

"Hold on." I glanced at the window, where outside the rain fell and the mist swirled unabated. "I understand your urgency, but in this weather? I've been told over and over how dangerous the moor can be even with fair skies." I gestured toward the door. "These conditions are far from favorable."

"Yes, but you forget I've lived out on these moors all my life. I've traveled to Merrivale many times, even if I've never gone beyond to Vixen Tor. All we have to do is follow the river. We can't get lost if we do that."

I deliberated over what she'd said, not doubting what she claimed, but still hesitant to go. Was this a risk worth taking? Particularly when we didn't know what sort of threat we faced at the other end, and with Gage and Anderley miles away. Alfred could already be dead.

And if he wasn't and I didn't try to go to his aid? Could I live with that? Could Gage?

"Please." Lorna sat up. Her eyes pleaded with me. "We can't just let Rory kill him."

I inhaled, still torn about what to do.

Her eyes hardened. "I'm going whether you will or not. And short of tying me up, you won't stop me from taking your horse."

She'd called my bluff. I wasn't very well going to tackle her. I could aim my pistol at her, but I suspected she knew I wouldn't pull the trigger. And I certainly wasn't going to let her go alone. "Very well," I relented. "Give me a sheet of foolscap and a pencil to write my husband a message. And pack us some food and water. We may have need of it."

Minutes later, we both mounted my horse and set off down the trail to follow the River Walkham southward. Before descending the hill, I glanced behind us to see the cottage swallowed up by the haze of mist and falling rain. I could only hope it wasn't the last human habitation we would ever see, and that we weren't riding into a trap.

CHAPTER THIRTY-TWO

There was one thing I could say for our journey. I now intimately understood what Gage and so many others had been trying to convey about the treacherous nature of the moors. Traveling through the swirling, eddying mist over such boggy, rocky terrain disoriented and terrified me. Not only could I not see beyond a few feet in front of me, but I also started to doubt if anything outside of myself was even real. It was like wandering through the fog of your dreams—or, more accurately, nightmares—uncertain where reality ended and illusion began. If not for Lorna's solid presence at my back, I was quite sure I would have panicked.

It was no wonder so many people had died on the moors, swallowed up eternally by the mist. If not for the river and Lorna's keen sense of direction, we could have roamed forever until either bog, or dehydration, or mysterious beast claimed us. It was also clear where the idea of being pixie-led had derived from, for if I'd been a slightly less logical person I could well have believed there was some supernatural force at work.

I had to blink my eyes several times when the few buildings that populated the village of Merrivale emerged out of the mist, just to be certain I wasn't hallucinating. Much as I wanted to knock on one of those doors and demand sanctuary, we pressed on. At some point, the rain had slackened, but that only made the mist intensify. And now we had to contend with the falling darkness. Though we couldn't see the sun, we could still sense its setting, taking what little light it had afforded us with it.

We clung to the course of the ever-meandering river like a limpet until about a mile south of the village. Then the most dangerous part of our trek began. At the river's junction with a trickling spring we struck out to the southwest along a little-used trail. Here and there, there were signs of recent usage, which was both encouraging and alarming. As such, we didn't dare light the lantern Lorna had enough foresight to bring out of fear that if Rory *was* at Vixen Tor, he might see us coming. Fortunately, the horse was a hearty soul and kept to the trail almost by instinct, avoiding the blanket bog that edged the path to the north. In this way, we inched our way onward, peering intently into the dim fog for any sign of the towering Vixen Tor.

Making the matter all the more difficult was the fact that Vixen Tor was not situated as many of the other tors at the top of a stark hill. It was nestled on the upward slopes of a woodland area studded with trees and bracken. So there was no telltale rise in elevation, especially as we were approaching it crossways. In fact, we might have blundered right up to it if not for the sharp thuds emanating from the mist before us.

I pulled Eyebright to a stop so that we could listen more carefully. The mare tossed her head, not liking the sound, and I reached forward to run my hand over her neck, to soothe her.

"What do you think it is?" I whispered to Lorna over my shoulder.

"It sounds like . . . stone hitting stone."

I paused to listen. "I think you're right. But what does it mean?" Was Rory building something?

"I don't know."

We sat listening for a moment longer before I spoke again.

"The ground here looks less boggy, yes? Perhaps it's time we approach on foot."

"I think you're right."

She slid off Eyebright's back and I followed suit, gripping her reins to draw her off the path toward the right where I spied a stand of trees peeking out of the mist. Leading her to the farthest rowan tree, I tethered her to a branch and rubbed her flank before rejoining Lorna on the path.

We slowly edged our way toward the sound, straining to see anything ahead of us. At first there was nothing but trees and the occasional rock. Somewhere off to the left, I could hear the jangle of a horse's harness. Then the craggy stones turned into boulders, growing in size, until suddenly the massive tor loomed up before us. We turned sharply to the right, drawing closer to the granite outcropping. From this position, I could tell the sound was coming from the other side of the tor.

"Let's see if we can climb up onto the rocks to get a better view from above without being seen," I suggested.

She nodded, following my example as I reached between my legs and drew the now-sodden hem of my skirts through my legs and tucked them into the belt of my redingote at the front. Then I carefully began to pick my way up onto the tor toward the direction of the thuds.

The climb was not as difficult as I'd anticipated, what with all the ice-shattered grooves and ridges to place my hands and feet into, but it was by no means easy. At one point, a wrong step sent a cascade of tiny pebbles down the face of the tor. I dropped down against the rock, fearing discovery. But the sounds on the opposite side of the tor never abated, I supposed drowning out the softer noise of the shingle.

I began to climb again, slower this time, but even so, I gained the summit within a minute. The stone there was worn smooth from the wind and elements. I crawled across it before lying down to peer over the edge.

At first, the mist seemed too thick, but then the wind shifted, billowing some of the smoky haze away from the figure who stood before the gleam of a lantern. My breath caught and Lorna smothered a gasp with her hand as she crept up beside me.

"Isn't that . . . ?" She couldn't seem to form his name.

"That's Mr. Hammett," I whispered, still reeling from the revelation. "Lord Tavistock's majordomo."

She turned to look at me, her eyes still wide with shock. "But why?"

"I can answer that. Or we can stop him from doing what I think he's doing."

We peered over the rock face again to see Hammett stacking another stone on the pile before him.

"If that's the cave we've heard mention of . . ." I leaned closer to her ear to murmur ". . . and he's attempting to close it off, then there must be something inside worth hiding. Something, or rather someone, he doesn't want found." The butler was about seventy, and while hale and hearty, I couldn't imagine him eagerly undertaking such backbreaking labor without very good reason.

"Alfred," she gulped.

"And perhaps Rory. We won't know until we can get down there." We wouldn't know if they were alive or dead either, but I wasn't about to mention that.

Her eyes flashed with fear, but I could hear resolve ringing in her voice as she turned to ask, "What should we do?"

I glanced behind me and then below once again. "How do you feel about channeling your supposed ancestress?"

She blinked and then smiled with vicious glee. "Tell me what to do."

Pressing my back against the cool outcropping, I leaned to the right to peer around it at the man who'd fooled us all. I'd believed him a steady bulwark of the family, a sympathetic figure to Gage, but if I was correct, his duplicity stretched back much further than the past few weeks. The thought of his high-handed, self-righteous deception made me want to slap his face and more.

Instead, I tamped down my anger and turned to hurl the pebble I had chosen up toward the top of the tor. I hoped my aim was true, but not too true, lest it strike Lorna where she lay in wait. Then I transferred my pistol to my right hand and pressed close to the rock, waiting to see how Hammett would react. I only hoped he would prove himself a proper Dartmoor man about superstitions so I wouldn't have to use it.

A hair-raising shriek pierced the air, making me jump even though I'd been expecting it.

"How dare you use this place for your own purposes," Lorna screeched, glaring down at Hammett from above.

Hammett startled, dropping the rock he hefted. He howled in pain and stumbled back a step.

"You have no right to meddle in *my* domain, or with *my* people. Begone from here!"

"I *knew* ye were in league with the devil. An eye-biter to tempt our young." He fairly spat the words, though he trembled with evident terror. "I warned 'em not to have anything to do with ye. That naught good could come of it."

The sound that issued from Lorna's throat, a sort of hiss-shriek, made my heart rise into my throat. Had I not known any better, I would have been tempted to believe her act.

"I said begone! Or that first stone won't be the last to strike you," she shrieked. "I'll hurl this entire tor down on you if I must."

Hammett shuffled backward. "Keep 'em. There's naught you can do now. For either o' 'em. The Trevelyans' honor is restored."

My stomach dipped. Were they dead? Both Alfred *and* Rory?

I wanted to charge around the rock and discover for myself, but I forced myself to remain still. Revealing myself would not help. It was safer to let Hammett believe what he would and escape rather than have to confront him now. There was no telling

how he would react. Or whether he would do something to precipitate Alfred's and Rory's demises sooner if they were *not* in fact
dead.

I felt Lorna's answering scream in the pit of my stomach, and
I instinctively shrank away from all the fury and distress it contained. It was far too genuine.

Hammett recoiled and turned to hobble off toward his horse,
whose harness we'd heard jangling. His body moved in an awkward shamble, his shoulders hunched in discomfort. The foot he'd
dropped the rock on visibly pained him, but the other leg also
appeared to do so. I realized then the other leg must have been
injured during his scuffle with Gage in the middle of the night.
He had been our intruder.

Once Hammett moved out of sight, I dared to skirt around the
rock and pick my way around the face of the tor to the place where
Hammett had been at work. At first, I didn't understand what
he'd been endeavoring to conceal. The tor was riddled with cracks
and crevices. But then I saw it. Just below the base of one of the
outcroppings was a hole. If I hadn't known something was there,
I would have assumed it was merely another ice-shattered fissure
in the granite. However, when I placed my hands inside, I could
pull back the stones below it.

Working quickly, I wrenched as many rocks from their places
as I could. I started at the sound of a horse's whinny somewhere
in the distance, but when I turned about I could see nothing but
the swirling mist. It must have been Hammett, setting back off
across the moor. I resumed my frantic work, and moments later
Lorna arrived to help.

We scrambled to remove the stones, panting from the exertion. All the while we called out to both Alfred and Rory, praying
one of them would answer. Regrettably, the lower in the pile we
progressed, the heavier the rocks became, until neither of us could
budge them, even working in concert.

I sat back, gasping for breath. "They're too big." I touched her arm when she continued to strain. "Lorna, stop. You'll only hurt yourself. They're simply too big."

She leaned against the side of the outcropping. "We can't stop. Alfred could be in there."

"Then let's see if he is." I stood to examine the opening we'd created. "I think I can squeeze through here. But I'll need the lantern to see. Do you think—"

Before I could even finish the question, she hurried off into the mist, presumably to draw our horse and the lantern she carried closer. I pried at some of the other stones, but while a few shifted, they were too unwieldy to dislodge. That Hammett had managed such physically demanding labor, and at his age, amazed me. Clearly I'd underestimated him in more ways than one. Or had he purposely been misleading us all with his shambling walk and creaky voice?

I heard the clack of the horse's hooves before I saw the light of the lantern Lorna had lit. She held it before her as they emerged from the fog, its light refracting the water droplets to form a sort of fuzzy halo around them. We lifted the lantern up to the small entrance to the cavity under the tor, but the light couldn't penetrate deep enough to illuminate anything.

Reaching up to remove my hat, I glanced up at Lorna and paused. "Perhaps you should be the one to climb inside. The space might only be large enough to fit one of us, and if the men require medical attention, you might be more skilled at giving it to them."

Her eyes were stricken. "I only know how to use herbs. I don't know how to stitch up wounds and . . . and such." She swallowed, gazing up at me hopefully. "Surely you would know better than I."

A strange feeling gripped me, for this was the first time I found myself wishing my late husband had actually taught me more about practicing medicine. Chiefly, the skills that pertained to his work as a surgeon rather than an anatomist.

I passed her my hat, breathing deeply to settle the nerves roiling around in my stomach. "I'll do my best. But remember, my first husband more often diagnosed ailments after the fact rather than treating and saving people's lives before it was too late." I could only pray the former skills would not be called upon.

I stared into the darkness of the tiny crevice, refusing to let myself contemplate what other creatures might be dwelling inside. Then I squared my shoulders and crawled inside.

The gap was narrow and difficult to navigate, particularly in my skirts, but I wasn't about to remove any layers of clothing unless necessary. Not when my cheeks and nose already stung from the cool mist. The space smelled of dirt and stagnant air, making me suspect this was the only opening. Once inside, I reached my hand up to ask for the lantern. Together, Lorna and I were able to manipulate it through the opening without dousing the light.

"What do you see?" Her voice was shrill with desperation as I turned to survey my surroundings.

The cave sloped downward, opening up into a space about eight feet wide by four feet high. Not tall enough for me to stand up in, but at least high enough for me to sit or kneel comfortably. It was impossible to tell how deep the cave went, nor did I truly care. For immediately before me, at the base of the slope, lay the sight we were looking for.

"I see them," I replied, clambering forward, anxious to check for signs of life.

"What?! Are they alive?" Lorna gulped. "Tell me what's happening!"

"Give me a moment."

Alfred lay closer to the entrance, and as I drew near I could hear him breathing, pained though it sounded.

"Alfred is alive," I reported.

She sobbed in relief.

"I'm checking Rory now."

Of the two men, he definitely looked worse. His skin was ashen, his eyes were sunken in their sockets, and his lips were dry and cracked. When I passed a hand under his nose, I could scarcely feel his breath.

"And Rory is, too. But barely." I moved back toward the entrance. "Pass me the water." If he'd been down here since the evening after he was last seen five days prior, he could be close to death simply from lack of water.

I tried rousing Rory, but when it became apparent he wasn't going to wake, I parted his lips and dribbled a bit of water into his parched mouth, careful not to give him so much he might choke on it. Then I rubbed his throat, hoping I might stimulate his muscles to swallow. For a moment, it seemed futile, but then his throat worked as it should. So I poured a bit more into his mouth, repeating this process two more times.

I shifted over to Alfred. When I patted his face, he moaned.

"Alfred," I said. "Alfred, can you hear me?"

His eyes slit open to peer up at me. "Lady Darby?" he croaked.

"Yes. Here, drink." I lifted his head, helping him to sip the water. When he lay back, he sucked in a harsh breath, clutching his chest just below his shoulder.

I moved closer to him, urging his hand aside. "Let me see."

He reluctantly complied as I hefted the lantern to better see his injury. Peeling back his coat, I could see the blood-encrusted shirt beneath. It was now stuck to the wound, and loosening it would be difficult and painful, but necessary to prevent infection.

"I don't know whether to be happy to see you or not," he grunted as I prodded at the cloth. "But I suppose if you're offering me water and examining my injuries, you don't intend to dice me up."

I flicked my gaze up at him, realizing it was a jest. One made in poor taste, but a jest nonetheless. Rather than chide him, I elected to take that as a good sign.

"What's happening? Is he drinking?" Lorna called in to me.

"Who is that?" Alfred asked.

"Lorna," I replied, before raising my voice. "Yes. Alfred is awake."

"Oh, thank heavens," she gasped. "Alfred, are you well?"

"Yes," he responded hoarsely, and then had to gather breath to speak louder. "Yes! Just a few bumps and bruises."

This was a lie if ever I heard one, though I knew it was done with good intention.

"He shot you," I pointed out.

"Yes." He sucked in a harsh breath as I prodded a particularly tender spot. "But Lorna doesn't need to know that."

I snorted. "As if you can keep it a secret." I sat back, turning toward the cave entrance where Lorna peered down at us, unable to see us past the low-hanging barrier of the ceiling. "He has a bullet wound, and though I haven't examined him yet, I suspect Rory is suffering from much the same. Without proper medical supplies I can only do so much. One of us needs to go for help." I didn't complete my thought, though Lorna must have understood the implication. If we didn't get help soon, one or both of them would die.

She didn't respond immediately, and I remained silent, giving her time to absorb the information I'd just relayed.

"I should go." Her voice was firm with resolve. "I know the way far better than you. Surely someone in Merrivale will be able to assist us."

She was right. Much as the idea of remaining here with the two injured men frightened me, the thought of striking out across the mist-shrouded moor without Lorna to assist me was infinitely more perilous.

"Pass me down one of the saddlebags," I told her. "Did you bring any of your herbs?"

"No. I should have thought to do so," she fretted.

"You couldn't have known," I replied. "But bring back some garlic to pack the wounds with to ward off further infection."

"I'll grab some calendula as well."

I accepted the saddlebag from her, reaching past it to grip her hand before she could withdraw. "I'll do everything I can," I promised her, hoping it would be enough. "You just focus on staying safe and finding help."

"Thank you." Her voice shook with repressed emotion, but she smoothed it out as best she could as she called down to Alfred. "I'm going for help, Alfred." Then almost as an afterthought she added, "Don't die on me."

"Is she out there alone?" Alfred asked as I heard the sounds of her moving away.

"Yes."

He shoved my hand aside, as I reached again for his wound. "You can't let her go alone."

"We don't have any other choice," I replied. "She's certainly not going to let me leave you and Rory here alone."

"Well, make her."

I arched an eyebrow at his petulant tone. "I don't think you're in any position to make demands. Now lie still. This is not going to be pleasant."

There was one positive thing about his peevish behavior. It made it easier for me to do what I needed to. I trickled cold water over the wound to loosen the encrusted fabric and then peel it upward. He winced and gritted his teeth.

When I'd finished, he was breathing hard, and the sweat I'd already observed dotting his brow ran in rivulets down his face.

"Maybe I spoke too soon," he panted. "Maybe you do mean to finish me off."

"Hush," I retorted, prying carefully at the skin around the wound. It was red and inflamed, but the placement and the relatively minor loss of blood suggested the bullet hadn't hit any major organs or veins. If we could combat the infection and get him help soon, he should survive. So long as there weren't worse injuries.

"Where are your other injuries?" I asked, sweeping my gaze over his form.

"There are none."

I glared at him. "From the labored sound of your breathing, I know that's not true. Did he crack your ribs?"

"I don't know," he replied honestly.

I leaned closer, inspecting the stain on his shirt and skin just above his shirt collar where his cravat had been removed.

"Lady Darby, I hardly think this is the time," Alfred quipped weakly.

I looked up past his dry lips a few inches from mine to meet his eyes. "What is this?" I demanded to know, ignoring his attempt at levity. "What is smeared on your neck? It's not blood." I moved even nearer to smell. "I think it's a plant of some kind."

"I . . . I don't know. Hammett must have done it while I was unconscious."

I flicked a glance at Rory's neck, seeing the same stain. Then a speck of something on his coat sleeve caught my eye. I reached across to pick it up, bringing it closer to the light. It was a cluster of leaves. Rue, if I wasn't mistaken.

"Why would he rub rue into your skin?" I voiced out loud. "It's not a poison I know of."

"Perhaps because it's supposed to ward off spells," Alfred surprised me by replying. He attempted to shrug, which resulted in a grunt of pain. "Don't ask me how I know that."

I suspected Alfred knew a great deal more than he wished others to realize, but I didn't comment on that. "I suppose that makes sense given the fact he believes Lorna is a witch."

He blinked up at the rock ceiling. "He kept babbling something about saving us from our own sinful inclinations and restoring the family honor."

I didn't question him about it further, wanting to focus on what was most important here and now—keeping both men alive. I shifted across the cave again, settling next to Rory's side. "Has he woken? Has he spoken to you?" I asked Alfred while I searched him for injuries.

"For a short time." His voice grew rough. "Though I'm not

certain he was in his right mind. He kept trying to apologize. Said he swore Lorna was behind my disappearance. Then he saw me one day on the moor. Probably the same day you did. And he made the mistake of saying something to Hammett instead of you and Gage, thinking the butler might be an ally." He swallowed. "He was worried the two of you might not take him seriously, that you already knew he'd been hindering your investigation. I guess he initially hadn't wanted me found. He was angry, and wanted me to stew in whatever trouble I'd gotten myself into. But then he'd changed his mind, growing worried I might truly be in some sort of danger."

Alfred coughed, gritting his teeth in pain. I lifted a hand to halt his flow of words, but he pressed on, urgent to relay it all.

"He wanted to tell Grandfather what he'd seen, that I was alive and well, but Hammett insisted they needed proof. However, when he took it to him, Hammett attacked him instead."

"What proof?"

"He wasn't very coherent, but I gathered it was a drawing of Lorna. She was wearing a necklace with a piece of amber strung on a chain. The piece of amber I'd found one day on the moors when we were boys. He knew I always kept it in my pocket."

The sketch of Lorna at Great Mis Tor. That's why Rory had taken my sketchbook. He'd noticed the distinctive amber necklace when my book fell open to that image that second day we met on the moor. It was something that, as an outsider, I'd had no chance of discerning.

I frowned, unable to find the source of Rory's injury. "Did he tell you how he was attacked?"

"Shot. Just like me."

"Where?" Frustration tightened my voice, and I pressed my hand into the ground beside his arm in order to reach up by his head. It sunk into wet earth and I nearly recoiled. I must have made a sound, for Alfred's eyes snapped to mine in the darkness. I didn't spare time for an explanation, sliding my knee between the two men where they lay side by side in order to try to gain enough leverage to roll Rory onto his side. There I found the hole near the center of his back, and from the scent emanating from it, it had already begun to fester.

My heart rose into my throat. I laid him back as gently as I could and turned to meet Alfred's gaze. I could see the same horror and pain I was feeling glimmering in his eyes in the lantern light.

Placing my hand around his wrist, I felt for Rory's pulse. It was faint. I counted its beats, recalling something I'd overheard my late anatomist husband telling his assistant about the time he'd served as a surgeon during the Napoleonic Wars. He'd said that one of a field surgeon's most important skills was his ability to distinguish between those injuries which were survivable and those which were not. Not only could he save more lives by focusing his time and attention on those he could mend, but by staying his hand he also prevented further suffering for those who couldn't survive by not forcing them to endure an unnecessarily long and painful death when they could already be at peace.

No matter how much I wanted to balk at the truth, somewhere inside me I recognized reality. This wound was not survivable. Even had the best surgeon in all of England swooped in at that very moment to attend to him, the chances of his recovering from such a wound while in such an advanced state of dehydration were infinitesimal. If the bullet had damaged an organ, the odds could be even smaller than that. He would lie in bed, slowly waiting to die. Perhaps even praying for it.

It was far kinder not to do anything, but infinitely more difficult.

I could see the moment Alfred recognized the same thing I had, though from the way his mouth worked, he seemed to want to fight it.

"I'm sorry," I murmured, not knowing what else to say. After all, the men were brothers. Regardless of everything else, there was still that bond between them.

His throat worked as he swallowed, and then he nodded in acceptance. I glanced at Rory one last time, blinking through a sheen of tears. I hated that I'd allowed myself to think the worst of him when the truth was he'd been trying to protect me. Those letters he purportedly wrote telling his valet to poison me and threatening Lorna almost certainly had come from Hammett, not him. If only he'd trusted us with his suspicions and not Hammett. All of this could have turned out differently.

Tamping down my emotions, I returned to Alfred's side to try to clean his wound the best I could. If I couldn't save Rory, then I was going to do everything I could to save his brother.

Sometime later, I looked up as Rory suddenly inhaled a deeper breath than those before. I tensed, as did Alfred, who lifted his head, hoping against hope that he was not as far gone as we'd feared. But then Rory exhaled one last, long sigh, and I sensed the change in him. His supine body went completely slack, and as the moments ticked by his chest never rose again.

Cold crept over me, gripping my heart and making me want to curl into a tiny ball, but I forced myself to continue my ministrations on Alfred. I noticed then how he was holding Rory's hand, and I couldn't stop the tears I'd been fighting from overflowing my eyes and trailing down my cheeks.

I recovered Alfred's wound as best I could with a strip of fabric torn from my shift. Then I settled onto the cold earth beside him, leaning against the stone wall. When I reached for his other hand, he quickly gave it to me, I supposed as anxious as I was to feel another person's warmth. To know that yours wasn't the only heart still beating.

That was how Gage found us hours later.

CHAPTER THIRTY-THREE

I don't recall much about the ride back to Langstone Manor except how cold and numb I felt. But I supposed sitting with a corpse would do that to you.

Gage and the other men had returned to Lorna's cottage to find our note and then journeyed on to find us. They'd just stopped to ask after us at the inn in Merrivale when Lorna arrived. However, the mist had grown even thicker, further hindering their trek to Vixen Tor, which had taken three times longer than it had initially taken me and Lorna to reach it. Upon their arrival, they'd quickly cleared away the rest of the stones from the cave entrance to unearth us.

I'd climbed out first to stand torpidly by Lorna's side with a blanket clutched around my shoulders while they extracted Alfred and then Rory's body from the cavity. Unable to hang back a moment longer, Lorna had rushed forward to kneel beside Alfred. She'd not been able to return to her cottage for the herbs we needed, but fortunately someone in Merrivale had already possessed a stash of calendula lotion and yarrow powder. I packed the wound with the yarrow to slow his continued bleeding, while she rubbed the calendula lotion into the inflamed skin surrounding it to combat the infection.

Someone from the village had also produced a litter of sorts, which dragged behind Anderley's horse to transport Alfred to the inn at Merrivale. Most of us waited there for the Tavistock carriages to retrieve us and carry us the rest of the way to Langstone Manor. Rory's body was rolled up inside a blanket and carried on the shoulders of the men, to be loaded into the carriage.

Between coordinating the others, Gage plied me with tea, which I dutifully drank without really tasting it. The warmth should have revived me, but it did nothing to thaw the cold pit yawning inside me.

Apparently the entire household had been informed of what had happened, for when we returned to Langstone, despite our dawn arrival they were lined up waiting to be assigned tasks. The first footman stood in Hammett's customary place next to the housekeeper, so I assumed the duplicitous butler had been detained. A surgeon stood at the entrance to the drawing room, ready to attend to Alfred's injuries. But I barely had a chance to explain what I'd done to clean the wound and try to stave off infection before Gage and then Bree bustled me off to my bedchamber.

I allowed my maid to fuss over me, letting her comforting chatter wash over me as I soaked in a steaming bath. Whether it was the warm water, Bree's soothing fingers in my hair, or a combination of both, the chill that had gripped me since Rory breathed his last began to thaw, and with it, my emotions. Before I knew what was happening, I found myself shaking with sobs, my head resting on my knees as my tears mixed with the bubbles.

Gage appeared at my side and lifted me from the bath, wrapping me in a warm towel. He sat on the edge of the bed and cradled me, allowing me to weep into his collar. When my hiccupping sobs at last subsided to sniffles, I began to stammer an apology, but he wouldn't hear it.

"Hush," he murmured. "I understand exactly why you're crying. If anyone should be apologizing, it's me."

I reached up to fiddle with the buttons running down his shirtfront. "Yes, but I . . . I should be the one comforting you. After all, Rory was *your* cousin. And Hammett . . ." I whimpered. "Hammett . . ."

"Shhh. Yes. I know."

I heard the pain in his voice, even restrained as it was, and reached up to wrap my arms around his neck. Pressing my cheek to his, I whispered, "I'm so sorry, darling," trusting he would know what I meant. For surely he must realize now that Hammett had likely had some part to play in helping Annie to poison his mother.

He inhaled a ragged breath and held me even tighter.

When his grip began to loosen, I pulled back to look up into his face. "Has Hammett explained his actions?"

He brushed aside a strand of damp hair clinging to my forehead. "He hasn't returned yet."

I sat taller. "He hasn't?"

"We don't know whether he realized his contemptible actions had been discovered, or he stumbled into some sort of trouble out on the moors, but no one has seen him since yesterday morning."

I mulled over this information. "Is someone searching for him?"

"Not yet."

A sudden thought occurred to me. "What of Lorna? He might—"

"I insisted she remain here," he replied, halting my harried words. "On the chance that Hammett would come after her next. Particularly given her delicate state." His lips curled into a tight smile. "I'm not sure I could have torn her away from Alfred's side anyway."

"How is he?"

Gage's expression turned grim. "The surgeon removed a bullet from his chest. His condition is serious. But he thinks he'll survive so long as we can keep infection from setting in."

I exhaled the breath I'd been holding. "Lorna will make sure of that."

"I suspect she will." He pressed his lips to my forehead, almost speaking into my skin. "Regardless, if it hadn't been for you and Miss Galloway, and whatever made you believe he and Rory would be at Vixen Tor, Alfred would not have survived. And Hammett's treachery would have gone undetected."

I thought of the stone wall Hammett had been building, and how near to completing it he had been. Had Lorna and I arrived but half an hour later, we might never have found them.

Gage shook his head. "What I can't understand is why he attacked Rory. It's clear he was obsessed with the curse, intent on carrying out what he believed to be the family's will. But Rory *was* doing his duty. He would have made an excellent viscount and cheerfully wed Lady Juliana. So why did Hammett shoot him?"

"I think I know the answer to that." I explained what Alfred had revealed to me in the cave. "Rory was already too delirious to reveal everything to his brother, but I suspect Hammett tried to convince him to remain quiet about Alfred's survival so that he could find him and kill him. That he tried to bribe him with the promised inheritance of the viscountcy. But Rory balked at this suggestion, so Hammett realized he would also have to die. I also suspect it was Hammett who left the note instructing Moffat to poison me, not Rory. Nothing else makes sense."

His brow furrowed. "He fooled us all," he murmured in horrified wonder. "I never would have believed he was capable of such things. I honestly believed he cared for me. He was always there—a silent bulwark of support against my family when I needed him. But all along, he was silently colluding with Annie to poison my mother."

"We can't know that," I argued half-heartedly. "Not for certain. Not unless he admits it."

His stare told me he knew very well I agreed with him. That my objection was only made in attempt to shield him from further hurt. "Are you going to try to argue he wasn't the one who tried to murder us with an ax?"

"No," I relented. "He had an obvious limp. It was him."

Gage absorbed this bit of information stalwartly, but the pain reflected in his eyes became a little more pronounced.

"What of your grandfather?" I asked. "Has he been informed?"

"I was trying to work up the nerve when Bree sent a maid to find me." His eyes strayed toward the door. "Actually, my aunt Vanessa asked to be the one to do it. She promised to do it gently." He sighed. "I hope I wasn't wrong to trust her with this."

I pressed a hand to his chest to assure him. "You weren't."

His eyes met mine, asking questions I knew it wasn't the time to answer. Instead I pressed a kiss to his cheek and rested my head on his shoulder.

I was glad to hear Lady Langstone had stepped up to do what she could. I wondered if anyone had recognized the amount of power Hammett had subtly wielded in the house. He'd restricted access to Lord Tavistock, especially since he fell ill, though I didn't believe he'd poisoned the viscount. Given what we knew about Hammett's motives, such a move made little sense. But he had controlled who and what information reached the viscount whenever possible. Lady Langstone, in particular, had been blocked from his presence, and I couldn't help but wonder if that was because he'd feared her perception. Unfortunately, her sour demeanor toward most everyone had made such an action seem justified. But now I could see it for the manipulative move it was. Just as his defense of her had clearly been a ploy to keep my trust by making me think he was fair and impartial.

"Will you go to him now that I'm recovered?"

"Are you?" he asked, forcing me to look him in the eye.

"Well enough," I responded honestly. "It will take some time for me to heal completely." I inhaled a shaky breath. "And I suspect the memory will always cause me some distress. But I promise I won't shatter." I sank limply against him. "I just want to rest."

He searched my eyes as if ascertaining my truthfulness, and then nodded. "I'll send Bree to sit with you."

I opened my mouth to protest, but he overruled me.

"I'm not leaving you alone. Not after your ordeal."

"I am fine, really . . ."

He cupped my jaw gently with his hand. "Kiera, please. Just humor me."

I sighed in surrender. "Wake me if there's news."

In the end, I was only allowed to sleep for three-quarters of an hour. Then Bree woke me with a shake.

"My apologies, m'lady. Lord Langstone is asking for you."

I pushed myself upright, trying to clear the sleep from my mind. Bree handed me a cup of coffee to sip as she coiled and pinned my hair. Even so, my thoughts still seemed a bit bleary when I descended the stairs a short time later.

I found Alfred lying in a bed that had hastily been assembled in the drawing room. Lorna stood at his side, clutching his hand while Gage and the dowager lined up along the opposite side of the bed. At first, I feared the surgeon had been wrong. That Alfred's injuries had been even more severe than he realized. And the man in the clerical collar who stood at the end of the bed didn't ease my dread.

But then I noticed the gentle smile on Lorna's face, and the glimmer in Alfred's eye, despite the pain he must have been feeling.

"You needed me?" I asked in confusion.

"Yes," Alfred answered feebly, beckoning me closer. He looked up at Lorna. "We wanted you here to witness our marriage."

My eyes widened in shock. "Of course," I stammered, before adding more sincerely, "That's wonderful." I didn't understand how such a thing was possible so quickly, but I wasn't about to dispute it. I suspected there was a special license involved, but that meant Alfred must have obtained it from the bishop weeks ago.

My gaze swung toward Lady Langstone, curious how she'd accepted this development. Her eyes were rimmed in red and her complexion pale, but she seemed reconciled to the match. Perhaps the loss of her other son had softened her and made her more willing to concede to Alfred's wishes. Or perhaps her reasons were far more practical. After all, we all knew Lord Tavistock wasn't long for the world. If the worst should happen, and Alfred succumbed to his injuries, the title and estate would then go to Lord Tavistock's younger brother or some other distant relative. However, if Alfred wed Lorna, making the child she carried legitimate, then if the baby was a boy he would be next in line to inherit after his father. And if it was a girl, at least they would have almost nine months to prepare for that eventuality.

Interestingly enough, the dowager's silent acceptance of Alfred's marriage was not the most surprising discovery. It was the sight of her arm looped through Gage's as she leaned on him for support, and possibly even a bit of comfort. One glance at Gage told me how bewildered he was by this development, though he gave no indication he was averse to it. He was too good a man to deny a woman in need of his assistance whatever aid he could render, even his hitherto-acrimonious aunt. Neither was he opposed to Alfred and Lorna's marrying. He looked on with approval, standing tall at his cousin's side, even though just a short twenty-four hours before, the prospect of being asked to stand up with Alfred at his wedding would have seemed laughable to him.

"Grandfather has given us his blessing," Alfred explained, his voice hoarse with fatigue and exertion. "And given the circumstances . . ." he squeezed Lorna's hand ". . . I decided it was best not to wait. Lest she change her mind."

Lorna shook her head fondly, though I could see the lines of worry radiating from the corners of her eyes. It would be some days before we knew if he would suffer further complications, before we knew for certain if he would survive. Until then, she would not rest easy.

I moved to Lorna's side, taking the small bouquet of flowers a maid handed me that someone had plucked from the garden. By necessity, the ceremony was swift, but for all that, extremely touching. I found myself dabbing at the corner of my eyes with my handkerchief even though I thought I'd cried myself dry just hours before. They would not have an easy time of it, for some would find it difficult to accept Lorna as the new viscountess, but I had hopes their affection was strong enough to outlast it.

Once the deed was done, we all issued our congratulations to the happy couple and slipped from the room to allow Alfred to rest while Lorna sat by his side.

The first footman was waiting for us when we emerged, and the look on his face told us he did not have happy news. "Mr. Hammett has been found."

Gage stepped forward determinedly, his eyes hardening with resolve. "Where?"

"Not far from Vixen Tor. Some men from Merrivale found him. Said it looked as if his horse had spooked and bumbled into the bog just north of there. They found the steed struggling to free itself from the muck. Mr. Hammett lay several feet away, his head bloodied from striking a rock."

"He's dead, then?" Gage clarified, being the first to find the words to speak.

"Yes, sir."

I turned to look up at Gage, finding it impossible not to think of Lord Tavistock's great-uncle who'd supposedly died in a similar manner, perhaps beginning the curse. It was somewhat ironic, and downright eerie, that Hammett, the perpetrator of so much pain and sorrow, should die in the same way.

"Good," the dowager sniffed, her eyes narrowed in spite. "It's better than he deserved, but at least it's a neat end to his wickedness."

For once, I couldn't have agreed with her more.

Later that evening as the light began to wane, Gage and I perched in our chairs next to his grandfather's bed. What stubborn will had remained in his old and ailing body had since drained away in the face of the news of his longtime majordomo's treachery. Whatever astonishment and anger the rest of us felt about Hammett's cold duplicity, it was clear the viscount endured it tenfold. He'd trusted the butler, had viewed him almost as a friend. Or as close to one as a nobleman and his servant could be. To then learn Hammett had murdered one grandson, attempted to kill two others, and likely helped orchestrate the death of his daughter, all in the name of a family curse, was devastating.

His form had shriveled almost into nothing, leaving a gaunt, sticklike figure to lie in the bed looking up at us. My heart ached for the viscount and all the pain it was evident he felt, both physically and emotionally. And it ached for Gage, who was losing his grandfather after only just reconciling with him. I supposed if one blessing had come out of this entire sordid tragedy, it was that. But my heart also ached for myself. I'd grown fond of the cantankerous viscount, and I was sorry to lose him so soon after meeting him.

We hadn't planned to push the viscount for any answers he could supply about his butler's actions, but Lord Tavistock seemed to want to discuss it, to try to understand what had happened, and why no one had realized it sooner.

"My father groomed him, you know," he said. "Starting from a very young age, when he was but a stable boy."

I recalled Hammett admitting as much to me.

"When I was younger, I wondered at that interest. Wondered if maybe he was perhaps my father's by-blow or the product of another illicit relationship in the family. But then later I decided it didn't matter. Hammett was good at his position, indispensable even. So I never asked, I never pushed either my father or Hammett for the truth." He heaved a sigh, his eyes staring off into the twilight. "Perhaps I should have."

Gage gently shook his head. "I don't think knowing whether Hammett was your bastard brother or not would have made a difference. In fact, it might have only made you even blinder to the possibility he could commit such horrible acts." He paused. "But it does give us some insight into why he was so recklessly determined to enforce what he saw as the family's will. Why he became obsessed with enforcing the 'curse.'"

Whether or not Hammett had been the natural son of the previous viscount, after being in his position for so many years he must have felt part of the family, while knowing he was not truly one of them. To see those who had the full privilege of being a Trevelyan then squander it must have infuriated him, and so he had fallen back on what he'd witnessed the previous viscount do to his own daughter with those poisoned apples.

"Yes, well, my illness certainly didn't help matters." The viscount coughed. "Had I not been bedridden, had I not been so weak, I might have realized what he was doing."

"You can't know that," Gage protested. "Perhaps your illness precipitated matters, forcing him to act more quickly than he might have otherwise. If Alfred inherited the viscountcy, as well as the ability to do as he wished, he could wed Lorna Galloway or dismiss Hammett from his position. But you cannot blame yourself for that. All of the culpability falls squarely on Hammett himself."

"I wish I could believe that, Sebastian." His eyes glinted with remorse. "But I know the truth. And I shall have to take that guilt, that knowledge that I've been a blind fool to my grave."

Gage gazed back at his grandfather, his face a mask of pain and uncertainty. He was struggling with what to do, what to say to ease some of his grandfather's agony. When he finally spoke, his grandfather had already closed his eyes, though I knew not whether he slept or merely rested them. "Well, I do not blame you," he murmured.

Such was the power of his simple statement that I felt an answering swell of emotion just to hear it, just to see the peace it gave my husband to utter it. And when I glanced at Lord Tavistock, I spied the tears glistening at the corners of his eyes.

CHAPTER THIRTY-FOUR

Two days later, the family laid Rory to rest in St. Peter's Churchyard, not far from the site of Gage's mother's grave. And sadly, Lord Tavistock joined him a week later. The pain and shock had simply been too much, and he'd succumbed to his illness and his advanced age.

The entire family—in fact, the entire household and surrounding communities—mourned his passing greatly. But it was not as distressing as it could have been had the viscount not made strides toward reconciliation with all his family members as best he could with such limited time left. Gage and the Dowager Lady Langstone had each spent an hour or more alone in his company during the days before he passed. And even Alfred had been well enough to be helped up to his grandfather's bedchamber two days before the viscount died.

The effects of these reconciliations were felt all through the house as Gage, his aunt, and his cousin each became more civil with one another than I suspected they'd been their entire lives. I still doubted they would ever be close, just as I questioned whether

Gage and Alfred would ever consider one another as friends, but at least their sharp tongues had been blunted and their cold glares had thawed.

So when it came time for me and Gage to set off for London about a week after his grandfather's funeral, we departed with some sadness. I was sorry to say goodbye to Lorna, who I'd begun to consider a friend, and even Alfred, whose irreverent sense of humor reminded me of a marquess I was unaccountably fond of.

There was also the matter of those hours we'd spent alone with Rory's body in the cave below Vixen Tor. That incident had forged a sort of bond between us. One I wasn't sure would ever fade.

Perhaps most surprising, I was even reluctant to say goodbye to the dowager, for she had proven to be more intelligent, more thoughtful than her previously frosty demeanor revealed.

As we turned from the manor's long lane onto the road that would carry us east, I settled back against the plush cushions of the Tavistock carriage Alfred had allowed us to borrow for our journey and sighed. Gage glanced over from the window he'd been staring pensively out of and reached for my hand. His thumb brushed against my skin.

"It's many miles to Exeter if you wish to take a nap," he told me as the carriage jolted over a rut in the road. Anderley and Bree had gone ahead of us to secure rooms for the night in another carriage laden down with some of Gage's mother's belongings he'd never claimed.

"Not yet," I replied, anxious to relay something I'd not yet revealed. Something I'd felt I owed his Aunt Vanessa my silence on until we'd left the manor. "I was pleased to see your cousin and your aunt embrace you so warmly before we departed."

"Yes." He inhaled past a tightness in his chest. "I'm not sure I would have ever believed such a thing could be possible, but I'm glad, too."

I squeezed his hand, smiling in empathy. "Perhaps they'll call on us the next time they're in London. I would like to see Lorna again. And I intend to introduce your aunt to the Duke of Norwich."

Gage coughed, choking on his own astonishment. "Marsdale's father?"

"Yes. She's already accustomed to impertinent sons. And as Marsdale has led me to understand, the duke is quite lonely. If he's even half the doctrinaire his son claims, he and your aunt should fare well together. So long as he's kind," I added at the end. After so many years of unhappiness, even partially of her own making, the dowager deserved some contentment.

His brow lowered, and I knew his thoughts had turned to the very subject I wished to broach.

I reached for his hand, threading my fingers through his. "Darling, your father was not having an affaire de coeur with your aunt."

A flicker of hope sparked in his eyes. "How do you know that?"

"Because I spoke to her about it, though you can never tell her I revealed such a thing to you."

He scowled and opened his mouth to argue, but I hurried on before he could speak.

"She said your father indulged in a flirtation with her and wrote her letters, making her believe such a thing. But when she finally agreed to meet with him, in the emerald chamber that night you followed your father, he threw the entire liaison in her face. He'd only feigned interest in her to avenge her treatment of your mother, and to prove her a hypocrite."

Gage's face was slack with shock. "You're certain?"

I arched my eyebrows. "Why would she lie about such a humiliating experience?"

He continued to search my face, and then exhaled in acceptance. "You're right. She wouldn't. I just never could have imagined that was the truth." He grimaced. "How cruel. Unnecessarily so. Why didn't Father simply defend Mother like he should have? Or move us somewhere different."

"Perhaps your mother wouldn't go."

His mouth flattened in displeasure, but he nodded in agreement.

"Whatever faults we can lay at his door, I don't think failure to love your mother is one of them," I said softly, resting my head against the side of his shoulder. It felt strange to defend his father after all the awful things he'd done, but in this case I knew it was right.

He didn't speak for a long time, and rather than pry, I closed my eyes and let my thoughts drift. That morning and several before it had not begun in the most pleasant of manners, and I still felt somewhat drawn. However, the rustle of a paper brought my eyes open.

"What's that?"

Gage stiffened, and I wondered if he'd presumed I was asleep. "Something Alfred gave me. He said Grandfather made him promise to give it to me after he passed." He stared down at the letter almost as if it were a wild animal that might bite him.

"Are you going to open it?"

He didn't reply, and I began to wonder if he was afraid to.

"Would you like *me* to open it?"

"No. It's just . . ." He shook his head. "I thought we'd said everything we'd needed to say . . ." His voice trailed away.

"And you're worried this will reveal something that will change that, something you don't wish to know."

He smiled grimly. "Yes."

When he still didn't move to break the seal, I gently prodded him. "There's only one way to find out."

His finger slid beneath the folded paper and paused for a second before tugging upward, breaking the seal. I sat upright, affording him the privacy to read his correspondence without my interfering unless he wished me to. But I couldn't stop myself from observing his reactions.

At first his expression was stony, braced for unpleasant news. But it quickly transformed into disbelief and then amazement. Although the further he read, the darker his countenance became, until I wished I'd never suggested he read the note. It might have been better if he'd simply ripped it up.

"Grandfather has left me three of his mines," Gage suddenly declared without preamble. "As well as any artwork of your choosing." His eyes glimmered at me with affection. "He says that you would value and appreciate it more than any Trevelyan, heathens that we are."

"That's generous," I stammered, touched beyond measure that he'd thought of me, and slightly overawed by the prospect of selecting from Langstone Manor's impressive collection of artwork.

"He also says he wants you to honor your agreement to paint a portrait of me to be hung in the gallery alongside my mother." His eyebrows arched in question.

I cleared my throat. "I may have failed to mention that. But in my defense, I thought it was something your grandfather should tell you." My eyes flicked down toward the letter. "I suppose this is his way of doing so," I remarked wryly.

Gage's mouth curled in an attempt at a smile.

I waved my hand. "Does all this mean we'll be returning?" But when Gage failed to respond or elaborate, I began to reconsider. "Or am I presuming too much?"

After all, there was no guarantee Alfred would honor his grandfather's wishes in regard to my preferences in the artwork, and I hadn't the slightest notion how time-consuming or profitable the mines Gage had been given were.

"It *is* generous. And I don't believe my cousin or aunt will begrudge us any of it. Not when Grandfather still left the bulk of his estate to Alfred," he replied.

"Then what has brought that thunderous expression to your face?"

He lowered the letter to meet my bemused gaze. "He also says he wrote to the king and asked him to consider granting me a title for my services to the nobility and the Crown."

I blinked wide eyes. "Well, that hardly seems something to become angry over."

He held up his hand to forestall me. "There's more. He also says he wrote to Father to ask if he would do the same, or at least consider doing so."

This must have been what that letter Rory had referred to had been about, the one from Lord Gage he'd seen on his grandfather's nightstand. As far as I knew, Lord Tavistock had never explained it. "And?"

His pale eyes gleamed with fresh hurt. "Father told him to mind his own business. That he had no concept of what he was speaking of."

I gasped in outrage.

"Grandfather thought I should know. He thought it was important that I be aware of . . . of . . ."

"Of what a cad your father is," I declared furiously. "Of all the nasty, dirty, despicable . . ."

Gage reached out to clasp my arm. "Don't get worked up, Kiera. I appreciate your indignation on my behalf, but it's doubtful the king would ever give me a title of my own, even if I had earned it. Which I'm not sure I have. Not when I'll eventually inherit Father's."

"Yes, but your father could at least lend his support!"

"Perhaps." He sighed. "But you know him. Are you honestly surprised by this information?"

"Yes. I understood he was eager for you to rise in rank. I thought that was his main objection to our marriage. Or is he keen for that to happen so long as it doesn't take you completely out from under his thumb or overshadow him?" I sneered.

"I'm sure that's part of it," he murmured wearily.

I looped my arm through his, my temper abating at the sight of his evident distress. "I'm sorry, Sebastian. That's rotten."

He frowned. "Yes, well, I've suffered worse insults when it comes to my father. I'm simply glad my inheritance from my mother allows me the freedom to ignore him when I choose."

"Perhaps you should choose to do so more often," I retorted.

He nodded, his gaze straying toward the window. "Perhaps."

I sank my head against his shoulder, wishing there was some way I could ease this hurt. But short of miraculously transforming his father into a better man, there was little I could do.

"Kiera, perhaps you *should* lie down."

I glowered up at him. "Why do you keep insisting that? I'm not some fragile doll. I recovered from my ordeal in that cave weeks ago. Unless . . ." I gazed up into his soft, expectant eyes and felt my cheeks grow warm at the implication that he knew, or at least he suspected. I recognized I needed to say something, but my tongue stuck against the roof of my mouth, making speech impossible. Coherent speech, in any case.

"Kiera," he murmured, cupping my face between his hands. "I had no intention of forcing the issue, but you do realize I'm an observant person."

I swallowed and nodded.

"Then, unless you're suffering from some sort of ailment or lingering effects of the poison, I can only assume your recent illness in the morning and uncharacteristic lethargy is from something else. Perhaps something happier?"

I swallowed again, feeling tears begin to well in my eyes, though I didn't know why. "I . . . I think," I whispered. "But I don't know. Not for certain. I haven't . . ."

He smothered the rest of my words with his lips, kissing me once, twice, three times, as his face broke into a wide grin that fairly made my heart burst from the joy it contained. I was glad I'd been forced to tell him, no matter my conflicting emotions over the discovery, for it had all but erased the pain of his father's disloyalty from his eyes.

"But this is wonderful!" He stroked his thumbs over my

cheeks, wiping the tears from my face. "Kiera, love, why are you crying?"

"I don't know," I blubbered. "But Alana used to do the same thing when she was with child."

He laughed, lifting me unceremoniously up from the seat and onto his lap in order to hold me closer. I started to object, and then subsided, nestling into his shoulder. After all, in his arms was exactly where I wanted to be, propriety be dashed.

I wished I could say that the months that followed in London were as peaceful and uneventful as any expectant mother might wish, but that was not to be. Both our public and private lives would be shaken by turmoil, and before the end of the year we would face our most fraught inquiry yet. Gage and I had both worked hard to lay our shadows to rest. If only they would stay buried.

Ready to find
your next great read?

Let us help.

Visit prh.com/nextread

Penguin
Random
House